BOOK TWO | TAPACHE'S

ECH⊙ES OF TIME

JAMES MURDO

CRANTHORPE
—MILLNER—

James Murdo was born and raised in London, where he still lives. He graduated from university with a Master's degree in Physics, which added fuel to his early love of science fiction.

Echoes of Time is the second book in the Tapache's Promise Trilogy, set in the Sci-Fi Wanderer Universe, alongside many of James' other books.

AVAILABLE BOOKS
By James Murdo

All set in the Wanderer Universe.

Tapache's Promise Trilogy:
Echoes of Gravity (Book 1)
Echoes of Time (Book 2)

Standalones:
Siouca Remembers
Long Paradise
Fractured Carapace

Wanderers Series:
Gil's World (Book 1)
Searching the Void (Book 2)
Infinite Eyes (Book 3)

www.jamesmurdo.com

Echoes of Time
(Tapache's Promise, Book 2)

By
James Murdo

To Nicky and Pete, for your enthusiastic support

Chapter 1

Dangerous Mission, Commander

Paran waited for the transport ship to land. His body was still; only his eyes moved as they scanned the darkness ahead. The outskirts of Lortein, the largest city on the underside of Ringscape after Upper-Fadin, were just about visible through the thick atmosphere. A great, taut tether speared out of the city and into the night sky, fading to nothingness. A sky-factory, unobservable from this distance away, would be attached at the tether's other end. Bright flashes of colour sparkled like stars around the tether: drones.

A gentle wind buffeted Paran's combat suit, and he glanced at the information displayed in his peripheral vision, detailing the wind's vector properties. The transport ship continued its descent, its expansive bloom fragment manoeuvring it lower down, emitting flashes of multihued light far more brilliant than those produced by the drones in the distance.

Considering the scale of the transport ship, its bloom was vastly oversized, typical of military vessels, but the rest of the ship's frame was simple, segmented into easily discernible sections. Its bow was pointed, with grooves that ran off and twisted around the rest of the ship, fluidly shifting positions to control the airflow. A band ringed the ship, a little way back from the bow, signifying the end of the first compartment: the pilot-cabin, semi-reflective from the outside, fully transparent from the inside. The carrier compartment swelled out behind the pilot-cabin, complete with a flattened base for landing. Behind the carrier compartment were the bloom unit attachment mechanisms.

Seven others were stood in a line behind Paran. They talked quietly amongst themselves, though Paran's suit amplified their conversations. Mostly, they were speaking about him. They had been waiting for some time. The ship was on schedule, but Paran had taken them to wait early.

"Have you ever met the Commander before?"

"Not before this, no. Have you?"

"No. That's everyone I've asked then. That means none of us have."

"He's a lot bigger than I thought."

"Why d'you think he chose us for this mission?"

"Because the Members gave him the authority—"

"No, I mean, why 'us' specifically?"

"Because we're dependable. You realise this hasn't ever

been attempted before, right?"

"Of course it has! The Breaker's ancient, it must have been."

"No one's done it successfully then."

"Obviously."

"We'll be the first to trap the Breaker. If the Commander's leading us, he must know something. He's never failed."

"I agree."

"Me too."

Another voice chimed in. "I've met him before, once."

"When?"

There was some hesitation from the new voice. "Well, not 'met' exactly. I've seen him."

"When did you see the Commander?"

"During the early Podenwinth Battles. Well before Varenheim."

"You were there?"

"Yes."

"Which one?"

"The Battle of Ualbrict."

More hesitation. Another new voice joined that particular conversation. "I heard the real records were destroyed."

"They can't take my eyes."

"That's why he's called the *Butcher of Ualbrict*."

"Exactly."

"They can't be true, the stories about him—"

"They are."

"Surely some were embellished?"

Paran winced.

"The Commander led the charge. Same as at Borminth, Lotwith, and then Bauhict. If anyone's leading us against those sordid Vaesians, you want it to be him."

"Those Ualbrict Vaesians had Nesch tech."

"That's why they held out for so long."

"Nonsense, there's no such thing."

"How d'you know?"

"Do you think the Nesch control all the lattice ships now?"

"Who cares?"

"They're the most dangerous—"

"That's not true. They just—"

Paran flexed a fist. The chatter was extinguished. His focus remained on the ship ahead. As it came in to land, the bloom unit arced upwards and extended away from the ground in a wide spread, whipping Ringscape's dusty, brown surface into a frenzy.

A few paces in front of Paran, Mericadal flashed into existence. A holo-type label indicated the image was being internally projected by Paran's suit helmet directly into his eyes. A private communication channel between them opened, the seven waiting behind oblivious to their conversation. Mericadal's appearance was neat, cultivated as always. In reality, he was smaller and slimmer than Paran, by some way, though the holo scaled him to the same height. Mericadal smiled, transforming his face handsomely, and glanced at the descending ship, as though physically seeing it, watching it land.

"Commander Paran." Mericadal's image flickered. The signal was weak this far away from the main infrastructure of the influx network. "How long do you expect this little jaunt to last?"

"I don't know, Mericadal."

Mericadal's facial muscles twitched in annoyance, but his smile held. "Days? Weeks?" He threw his hands up exaggeratedly. "You do answer to me. You know that, don't you?"

"But no one else does, do they?"

Mericadal laughed. "Your candour is a delight, as always."

"I'm glad to be of service."

Mericadal nodded and pursed his lips, appearing almost pensive. "You've always been my favourite."

"Do you torture all your favourites, Mericadal?"

"Do you still hold that against me? You've done far worse than I since then, Commander Paran."

"All in your name, Mericadal."

"All in the name of the Administration, Commander Paran."

"You're concerned that having a name would make

you a target."

Mericadal looked Paran up and down. "You're exactly as Tapache intended for you to be."

"It annoys you when I use your name, doesn't it, Mericadal?"

"I'm being practical. You know who I am, as does everyone else who matters."

"I know exactly who you are, Mericadal."

Mericadal's smile vanished. "You're a valuable asset, Commander Paran. Don't forget what I can do. What I still could do." The image of Mericadal flickered again. "If you betray me, I will kill her."

Paran did not reply, returning his gaze to the sparkling bloom of the transport ship.

"No one has ever seen the Breaker and lived, let alone been able to trap it," Mericadal said. "It's going to be very dangerous. What if I have second thoughts about allowing you to go?"

"Then you will stop me."

Mericadal began pacing, taking only a few short strides before doubling back. "I could, couldn't I? But then, if I did, I suspect you would be angry with me. You can be..." Mericadal squinted, his lips having already formed the first part of the word he was about to say. "... obstinate."

Paran shrugged. Immediately, the chatter from the seven behind him, which had delicately resumed, was stifled. "The Breaker can't be aimlessly wandering; there must be a reason. It's just an animal, a creature, like all of us. It's not a machine-lect."

"And you want to find its home, brave Commander Paran, Butcher of Ualbrict, *the Commander*?"

Paran's jaw tightened. "Only then will we know how barren Barrenscape really is."

"You have no fear?"

"The Breaker appears to steer clear of the higher technologies given to us by Tapache – more and more over time. This combat suit you have given me—"

"Lent you."

"This combat suit you have lent me is likely of a high enough level to be included in that. It's the others who should be worried." Paran gestured behind him. Again, their nascent chatter dulled. "They're unprotected."

"You think it's all down to your casket-ship, don't you, Commander Paran? You think there's a special bond, between you and the Breaker, and that's why it avoids some of the higher technologies." Mericadal sneered.

"The Breaker wasn't able to penetrate the casket-ship that brought me through the Haze Rings. Since then, its behaviour has been altered. Encountering the triamond casket-ship may have caused it to reconsider its destructive behaviour." Paran stared Mericadal directly in the eyes. "Don't think I don't know that this is what you need, Mericadal. A victory over the Breaker would solidify your rule. You might even use it to finally come out of the shadows, under the guise of this triumph. You can't stay hidden forever; you know that. You should have revealed yourself long ago. The Roranians deserve to know who actually rules them."

"You forget your place, Commander Paran."

"And you fear yours."

"I control the Members."

"But they will expect to see progress somewhere, Mericadal. Memories of the wars with the Vaesians will fade, but you continue to expend significant resources keeping the Vaesians cowed. The Members will grow restless."

Mericadal's eyebrows pushed together and raised in the middle, condescendingly. "The Members will do as I say, Commander Paran." He clasped his hands together. "No one else speaks to me the way you do. Not even Commander Miren. If they did…" He bit his bottom lip furiously. "Well, in any case, you are valuable to me. You know this. This mission is dangerous, and that's why I let you choose your team, but I'd be a fool to let you face the Breaker without a contingency in place. You have another guest coming with you."

"Don't tell me *you're* coming, in person?"

"What makes you say that?"

"You've become a little braver, Mericadal. Sometimes you're not just a holo. Sometimes you're really there." Paran chuckled. "Not now though."

Mericadal's face spasmed as a glimmer of annoyance resurfaced. "I wasn't aware you'd noticed."

"You should be careful," Paran mused.

"Is that a warning?"

"Caution, Mericadal, that's all. Now, tell me, who is this guest?"

"Oh, don't worry. She won't be with you down on Barrenscape itself; she has her own ship. She'll be observing from above." Mericadal pointed into the distance. Something was approaching, only just visible in the gloom. It had a spherical hull, like those of the drones that defended the sky-factories, though it was larger and had no bloom unit attached.

"A drone?"

"She's called Influxa." Mericadal laughed, as though he had just said something humorous. "Think of her as an extension of the influx network, a proxy in its absence. She's equipped with a conventional drone to relay information to me periodically, and she also has a passenger cabin to whisk you away from danger, if needed, as well as some offensive capabilities."

Paran squinted. "No bloom?"

"New propulsion unit. She's a prototype, a select series. You should be flattered."

"What makes her fly?"

"We've made some progress with heavy-graviton drives, partly derived from our gravity emulators. Lasts far longer than anything else we've come up with. We think they'll have certain benefits over bloom fragments."

"And what is she exactly?"

"She's here to help, Commander Paran. Consider this a test for her."

Paran sucked his teeth. "I didn't know the influx network could move."

"The Administration is working on many things, Commander Paran. Why would you know? You're just a soldier."

A new voice chimed through Paran's communication channel with Mericadal, despite no formal request for access having been made. "The Administration does not have the capabilities for remote access to the influx network. You may consider me an extension or a separate component, both are accurate."

The voice was emotionless, soft, just like an influx. Mericadal's eyes lit up with delight upon witnessing Paran's confusion.

"I am Influxa, and I will be observing your mission, Commander Paran."

Mericadal took a step closer to Paran. "She can hear everything you say and see everything you do."

Influxa's spherical ship settled in the air above the transport ship. Confused chatter rang out from the seven behind.

"What do I tell them?" Paran asked, motioning to his

team.

"Whatever you like," Mericadal said. "Although maybe not that Influxa's only here to protect you. I don't think they'd appreciate that."

"Fine."

"Then we are set, Commander Paran." Mericadal smiled. "Just one thing. Don't be too long in Barrenscape. We may have need of you back in Ringscape soon. Some of the further cities are becoming restless."

With that, Mericadal's image vanished, and Paran walked towards the landed ship. The seven followed.

Chapter 2

Barrenscape's Trap, Commander

Paran and the seven soldiers were sat along two parallel benches that took up most of the dimly lit, windowless carrier compartment. A holo in the centre depicted their transport ship as a flashing blue sphere, speeding towards a simplified representation of Barrenscape. Ancillary information rotated around the blue sphere, including speed of travel, negligible haze winds, time till daylight, gravitational readings and other environmental data.

Now and then, the grey divider at the front of the compartment would ripple up and one of the pilots would check on them, as dictated by protocol. Other than that, there was little distraction; conversation was intermittent. Paran had closed his eyes and set his helmet faceplate to opaque.

"I wouldn't have given up command of my own troops for anyone other than the Commander," a deep voice rumbled. "It is the highest honour to serve alongside him."

A grunt of acknowledgement came in response.

"What do you think about this Influxa?"

"We'll see."

"Seems like the Administration's figured out how to make the influx network extend beyond the settlements."

"Finally."

"Commander," a nearby voice said.

Paran opened his eyes and silently flickered his gaze over a sequence of holo controls. The name of the soldier – Unriel – was displayed; his background and general history mapped directly onto Paran's field of vision. Once he had finished processing this information, Paran straightened up, his faceplate shimmering to transparent. He glanced to the left.

"Unriel."

"Commander."

Unriel's voice was higher-pitched than his base-level data indicated was usual. The other six soldiers cast interested looks their way, although Unriel spoke too low for them to hear.

"I wanted to thank you for picking me for this mission. To know that you've investigated our records... for my personal chance at redemption..."

"You sufficed," Paran responded.

"I won't let you down. Thank you for intervening and

seeing potential in me."

"Your thanks won't help us when the Breaker comes knocking."

Unriel shifted uncomfortably. Paran set his faceplate back to opaque, then adjusted the suit's auditory controls to filter out background conversation. A chemical diffusion sent him into a light sleep.

"Commander. Commander."

The suit amplified the noise, irritating Paran. One of the pilots was in front of him. The seven soldiers were quiet.

"We're nearly there," the pilot informed him.

Paran cleared his throat, his faceplate still opaque. "Where is the Breaker?"

The pilot stood to the side, revealing the compartment's central holo. An indicator showed the Breaker's expected position, well outside the targeted landing zone.

"There'll be more than enough time to set up and test the proximity sensors and the trap equipment."

Paran closed his eyes. "Wake me once we're down."

*

The transport ship disappeared into the thick atmosphere, back in the direction of Ringscape. Paran peered up, squinting for automatic magnification in the dim light.

Influxa's ship circled above, too high for the other seven soldiers to resolve, but not him.

Swirls of fine yellow debris brushed against his suit. Paran felt the impacts as though they were brushing against his skin. The seven were busy making their preparations around him, setting up their equipment as fast as they could. Their suits appeared flimsy in comparison to his.

Unriel and Jabayan were installing the sensor poles, placing them in a wide circular perimeter. They lifted each upright, resting them on the ground, allowing automated stabilisers to pierce a short way down and fan out. As soon as each was activated, a blue light was triggered.

Nalict was directing two of the others – Lotolen and Dorera – in preparing the bait: a wide, circular platform upon which a whole raft of equipment was located. They were talking via what they believed was a secure, three-way channel.

"The bait's going to project senseless signal noise," Nalict was telling the others. "Omnidirectional."

"Has it been tested before?" Lotolen asked.

"A few times. In all the tests, as soon as the noise was projected, the Breaker came to investigate."

"To investigate?" Dorera asked.

"It's just a phrase, fool. It'll come for us, that's what I mean." Nalict rushed over to Dorera, smacking her hands away from the equipment to show her the correct setup.

"Do it like this."

"What does the Breaker do when it arrives?" Lotolen asked.

"It'll destroy the source of the noise," Nalict replied. "But this time, we're setting a trap for the Breaker, alongside the bait."

"And the trap's beneath us?"

Nalict looked over to check Dorera's work, then lifted a small device off the platform and tapped its interface, before setting it back down. A raft of holo controls appeared in the air in front of her, alongside images of various components that quickly aggregated into a dome shape. Nalict ran a diagnostic test, verifying that all the components were functioning as expected.

"The hemispherical skimmer components we sunk are in place, right below us." She searched for the information. "They've managed to tunnel down to about twice our height, that's almost a record. And they're positioned perfectly beneath the bait." She moved her hands against the holo controls and a simulation began to play. A hazy form – the Breaker – wandered onto the platform to investigate the senseless signal noise. Half of the hemispherical components slid up from below the ground, arcing around the trap and interlocking, forming a spherical prison. The simulated Breaker was caught. "Dual layered, pure triamond coating."

"Only triamond can break triamond."

"Exactly."

Eight sub-cutters waited, motionless, next to the bait platform being worked on by Nalict, Lotolen and Dorera. The sub-cutters were identical: dull-coloured and box-shaped, rising to two-thirds a typical Roranian's height and just over an arm-span wide. The sub-cutter surfaces were lined with grills and small conical drills, almost like miniature sky-factories.

Morbayen and Cestial were setting up defences, in case the trap for the Breaker did not work. They placed portable pulse-spheres between the sensor pole positions and calibrated each one through a raft of holo controls.

"Will those work?" Loloren asked Nalict, gesturing to the pulse-spheres.

Nalict shrugged. "Not my area of expertise, but gravity pulses have been demonstrated to confuse the Breaker before. Stands to reason they might repel it too."

"Maybe it reminds the Breaker of Ringscape," Dorera said, humorously. "And the flips at the edges. That's probably why it came here."

Nalict sighed. "There's no proof the Breaker was ever on Ringscape, idiot."

Paran stopped eavesdropping and accessed the data from the sensor poles Unriel and Jabayan were placing. They were able to scan a wide area around them, but so far, the Breaker was outside their area of detection. Paran accessed his suit's own sensors and began a similar scan of the surroundings.

"The sensory data you are collecting from the surface matches my own." The voice came through to his suit, despite no communication channel having been requested. "Both from your combat suit and from the ground-based sensors. Might I ask why you are not using your suit's sensors to their full capabilities?"

"Influxa," Paran muttered. "So, you are listening in."

"I am monitoring you so that I can be of assistance."

"I'm just checking my personal sensors, that's all. Tell me, Influxa, what are you?"

"Commander Paran, my records indicate you know full well what the influx network is. You have higher-level access to Administration systems."

"Fine. Who were you?"

"That is unimportant. I'm Influxa now."

"It's not unimportant." Paran shook his head. "Setup's nearly complete."

"Indeed, it is. I suggest you start attempting to track the Breaker by—"

"We're going straight to capture today, no tracking. The latter leaves more time for mistakes to happen," Paran interrupted.

"That's not the plan."

"It's my plan."

"It's too soon. Your equipment can shield you for many—"

"I'll judge that for myself."

"That is inadvisable. It's unclear why you've come to this conclusion, Commander Paran. You need to gather evidence about the Breaker. It may be able to destroy the trap and the defences, or otherwise render them inoperable. You need—"

"Tell that to Mericadal."

"I sense that you're being sarcastic."

"Tracking the Breaker tells us nothing. I want it to come here. I want to find out what it is."

"The trap needs to be configured to the Breaker's movements, and the pulse-spheres need an extended period for proper calibration."

"The Breaker just needs to get onto the trap, that's all. We don't even know what it looks like, and I don't want to waste time. We both know the pulse-spheres are probably useless. The sooner we try this, the better."

"Many movement patterns concerning the Breaker have been established, over long timespans. You need to ascertain whether it's undergoing an erratic period. If that's the case, there is a possibility it will search around the trap instead of being directly attracted to it, and you'll be exposed—"

"Erratic periods have extremely remote probabilities."

"Even so—"

Paran checked his own vitals – he was becoming agitated and Influxa would know that. He clenched his jaw. "Influxa, if the data is important, you go get it. Take what you can and then return to update the trap's systems. Otherwise, we're running this mission to my specifications. You do not have the authority to circumvent me."

"My instructions are primarily to ensure your survival, and secondarily to assist with the mission. Your survival is not currently at stake, therefore, if you refuse to acquire data about the Breaker's current movements, I will need to do this myself and update the trap's systems. I will require approximately one day to complete this task. If you do not agree to hold fire on the trap until then, I must inform Mericadal."

"You have one day," Paran snapped.

"Will you refrain from initiating the trap until I return?"

"Yes. We will not start the sub-cutter tunnelling process until tomorrow, so you have at least that long." He squinted up, watching Influxa speed off and disappear into the distance. Paran tried to reach her. "Influxa?" There was no response. "Influxa, are you there? Answer me." Again, no response. He smiled, and resumed scanning the area with his own suit's sensors, increasing their range to maximum. He located the site that had been promised. Encrypting a message, he relayed a series of instructions – he was going to need help dealing with Influxa. Once sent, he deleted the message from his suit's memory cache and set his faceplate to transparent. He walked over to Morbayen. "Let Cestial finish the defences, you can move on to the sub-cutters."

Chapter 3

Fadin's Sprawl, Top Official

Mericadal glanced around the ship. It rattled loudly. Warning chimes sounded all around, barely audible above the growing haze winds. Flashing lights vied for his attention. His eyes widened, his smile expanding. He tapped the ship's controls, pushing the vessel higher. Outside, the white nothingness was becoming brighter; the Haze Rings were extremely close. The transparent window in front of him darkened, automatically.

"Come on!" he shouted, smashing his fists onto the controls. It was no use; they ignored him, and the ship began to descend under the guidance of automated safety systems.

Before long, Ringscape came back into view, the rattling diminishing. Upper-Fadin loomed close as they journeyed back past the sky-factories. A cluster of drones accompanied the ship, protecting it within an aerial cocoon. The main shipyard was below, filled with mostly stationary vessels. Daytime was almost in full force. Mericadal's ship dropped further, landing on top of one of the two large towers at the mouth of the shipyard. The ship powered down. Mericadal pressed the controls for the front cabin to open and exited.

Member Vodal waited, standing beside one of the many thermal cannons, their dark red and black colourings contrasting against the rooftop's faintly yellow surface. Light winds ruffled Member Vodal's hair, which he continually patted down. The drones circled a safe distance above them. Member Vodal dipped his head, also taking the opportunity to uncrumple his sleeves.

"Trade terms have been agreed between Halfad and Lomintern, and their industries are expected to grow well above average once routes are established. Population at Lomintern will surpass fifty thousand within a standardised year."

"Just one year? Are you sure?" Mericadal strode across the roof, towards the open entrance of the tower.

"My apologies. A little closer to two." Member Vodal swallowed nervously and cleared his throat, reaching up to pat down some stray hairs again. "Population—"

"All is as we expected then?" Mericadal interrupted.

Member Vodal nodded and hung back, allowing Mericadal to walk through the entrance first. He rushed in behind. "Yes. And the Fendari representative is here. It awaits your meeting."

"I pushed myself further than usual out there," Mericadal said. The entrance mechanism rippled closed behind them as they climbed down a winding sequence of steps.

Member Vodal sounded confused about how to respond. "You certainly did…"

"I was inspired by our Commander Paran," Mericadal said. "We need to push ourselves, you understand?"

"I…"

"Paran's filling himself with raw excitement, emotion, *danger*. I need to do the same. Being inside a ship; taking the risks of approaching the Haze Rings; knowing that if I make a single mistake, that'll be it for me… well, until the safety systems kick in." Mericadal shook his head excitedly. "Do you understand what I mean, Member Vodal?"

"Yes, I do."

Mericadal arrived at the bottom of the steps and stopped, facing the darkness of the room ahead, clenching his fists. Member Vodal was forced to come to an awkward standstill behind.

"No, you don't understand, Member Vodal. Why do you always say you do, when you don't?"

"I…"

"Do you even remember what Tapache sent us here to do?"

"Tapache?" Member Vodal repeated. "I… that was

24

quite some time ago, I need to… I wasn't even alive, then. We can't seriously continue to—"

"No one understands anymore, except Commander Paran. That's why he's so effective." Mericadal walked into the main part of the room. The surrounding walls shimmered to full transparency. A wide, unfiltered view of Fadin shone through. More gleaming towers than ever before jutted into the sky: Fadin's sprawl. A platform rose from the centre of the white floor, forming a neat, wide bench. Mericadal sat upon it, swinging his legs up and swivelling to lie horizontal. The platform contorted beneath him, rising comfortably beneath both his neck and the bend of his knees.

"There have been some…" Member Vodal looked to the side, his eyes flicking across and surveying Fadin's features. He made an awkward rasping sound as he cleared his throat again. "… concerns… about the Commander… Commander Paran."

"And we have made provisions for those concerns, Member Vodal. Commander Paran knows the power we hold over him. Do you have something caught in your throat?"

Member Vodal spluttered his response. "I was… just clearing it."

Mericadal stared at the pristine ceiling, high above. "Commander Paran is effective. And even if he did want to leave us, where would he go? The Vaesians? Those pathetic Silvereds?" Mericadal snickered. "His name is known by all Roranians. He cannot just vanish."

Member Vodal nodded. "Yes, you are right. He would be known wherever he went."

"And if he can solve the riddle of the Breaker, well, that would be significant." Mericadal pointed lazily away.

The message was understood. Member Vodal said nothing more and walked off, exiting down the spiral staircase to the level below. Immediately, an obscuring haze spread over Mericadal. A spherical ball of yellow light appeared in the simulated darkness.

"What do you need?" the influx asked.

"Follow Member Vodal. Use Conceal. I want to see what Conceal sees."

"The Conceal drone prototype has been activated."

From Mericadal's perspective, both the ball of light that represented the influx, and the darkness, dissipated, replaced by his own image, from above. The Conceal prototype had been stationed overhead, and he saw himself from its viewpoint. The view changed as Conceal sped through the room and down the staircase, slowing just as it reached Member Vodal, keeping a precise, close distance between them.

The entrance mechanism at the base of the stairway closed behind Member Vodal a little later than usual, allowing the invisible Conceal to follow undetected. Member Vodal glanced behind, raising an eyebrow at the empty space.

"Member Vodal, what level would you like to go to?" the electro-boost platform operator asked.

"Three," Member Vodal said, gesturing for the two heavily armed guards to move aside. He stepped onto the platform and began to descend.

"Nice to see you again, Member Vodal."

Member Vodal did not reply, clearing his throat with a staccato cough as the electro-boost platform took him down. Conceal followed, hovering above Member Vodal, unnoticed. They descended twenty levels until the platform came to a stop. Member Vodal stepped off. Mericadal watched him go about his business for a little longer.

"Member Vodal is broadly sticking to his schedule, as expected." The influx's voice came through to Mericadal.

"Keep Conceal following him," Mericadal said.

"Including when Member Vodal leaves this building?" the influx queried. "The Conceal drone prototype has not been tested externally, and it is currently the only prototype drone we have that is capable of complete concealment in the visual spectrum. Its data will be required to upgrade the Influxa prototype's capabilities. Furthermore, its fuel compartment is smaller and will only last for one day, assuming vigorous movement is not required. Any damage to the—"

"Member Vodal lives close to the shipyard," Mericadal

replied. "If he strays further, tell Conceal not to follow. Consider this its first real test. Tell Conceal to record everything at maximum detail for my perusal tomorrow. In the meantime, if its connection to the network is in any way compromised, tell it to return immediately."

"It has been done."

"Good. End the simulation."

With the haze gone, Mericadal scanned the empty room. Fadin remained visible before him, displayed through the transparent, circular window that spanned the circumference of the room. The sky was dotted with drones zipping about.

"Show me the ten year plan for Fadin. Replace any conflicting imagery," he instructed the still-listening influx. Immediately, the image of Fadin changed. Higher, thicker towers dominated the city; no patches of visible sky remained; skimmers flew between buildings. Mericadal watched for some time, breathing heavily. "Change the spiral staircase over there. I want an electro-boost platform instead."

Words rang out around him. "For this one level only?"

"Yes." He paused. "Prepare a report on influx traffic for me. No, first, show me the Emox Room." A simulation haze began to re-engulf him. "I want visual stats, separated by individual."

Chapter 4

Breaker's Call, Commander

Paran and the seven soldiers were ready. The eight sub-cutters had finished digging into the ground and lay in wait not far beneath the surface, each of them containing one of the Roranians in their cramped compartments. The ground matter that had been tunnelled through appeared undisturbed, all evidence of their presence concealed. The sub-cutters were arranged in a circular perimeter, just within the boundary of the pulse-sphere defences above.

The sub-cutter compartments were fitted with the bare essentials: thermal cooling units, waste containment and a few other necessities, miniaturised and adapted to operate as quietly as possible. Each compartment was just large enough that a typically-sized Roranian could sit on the small bulge that rippled up from the floor in basic comfort. Simple holos were projected into each, displaying data from the sub-cutters' military-grade sensors as well as the more detailed information from the sensor poles on the surface, and the interfaces for short-distance communications with the other sub-cutters.

Paran sat still in his compartment, his faceplate set to transparent, scanning over the images and data projected internally by his suit. Slow music rolled about inside, alongside the sweet smells of soothing relaxants, produced by his suit to keep him calm. Paran's jaw clenched tightly despite them, the tension in his face only increasing as he flicked through more images of Jabayan's past.

Not long before the Administration had declared their short war with the Vaesians, Jabayan had been the leader of a small group tasked with infiltrating one of the Vaesian cities – Cosobrit – in preparation. The mission had been simple: sow fear and dissent, to make it easier for incoming soldiers; crush the Vaesians before the Administration soldiers arrived, if possible. Make them more likely to yield before the fighting started.

A dependable soldier, Jabayan had approached his mission with unexpected fervour. Images of deceased Vaesian children flashed one after the other, their mangled bodies twisted beyond the limits of the high levels of agility their species possessed. They had been alive before the contortions, their screams muzzled by tight masks. Only their dark eyes remained visible. Subsequent evaluations of Jabayan had revealed a previously unlocked, staggeringly high predisposition towards extreme violence, given the right triggers, and a lack of empathy.

These evaluations had been heavily suppressed; few had access. Jabayan had received many accolades, and had been hailed as a hero for preventing the loss of Roranian life. This current mission, to capture the Breaker alongside the famed Commander, was one such reward that had followed many before.

Paran skipped to another member of his team: Lotolen. Like Jabayan and all the others, she had been heavily involved in the war effort. However, the holos were currently displaying moments from a more obscure time in her past. Her activities *after* the main part of the war, when she had been tasked with infiltrating the Veilers – a secretive group of Vaesians who had held obscure beliefs about the Source's hidden secrets. After determining their beliefs to be nonsense, she had set about dismantling them with as much zeal as Jabayan had shown in Cosobrit. The Administration had wanted to destroy any other groups that might compete for power, no matter how small or inconsequential. The Administration's power had to be absolute. Even once the Administration had deemed her work complete, the Veilers terrified and incapable of functioning as before, she had continued. As far as was known, the Veilers were extinct. Like Jabayan, she had received numerous accolades.

The current image froze: a dead Veiler, all three legs missing. A warning flashed at the centre of the image. The sensor poles on the surface had identified an incoming entity. A moment later, the incomer had been identified. Influxa. A direct communication channel was requested. Paran cancelled the music.

"Commander Paran, I am uploading the data I gathered."

"Thank you, Influxa. I notice you requested the communication channel this time, instead of forcing your way through. That's polite of you."

"Even I cannot penetrate your suit's highest security settings, which you have now initiated. I do not believe Mericadal would have agreed to this. You also ordered the sub-cutter digging before the agreed timeframe. Why have you done these things?"

"In case the Breaker comes early."

"That does not make—"

"How was your excursion?"

"The Breaker appears to have either failed to notice your presence on Barrenscape, or it does not care. It is exhibiting its Type One pattern – non-erratic. I predict that if you do not initiate the trap early, you have between three and four more days before it comes here."

"Good to know."

"Commander Paran, I would like to know, when will you initiate the trap? Your actions suggest an expedited—"

"Soon."

"Once you are finished looking through your team's

histories, again?" Some silence passed. "I can tell by your facial expression that you are surprised."

"How did you know?" Paran asked.

"While I cannot examine your suit's current operations, I can still access those of the sub-cutter—"

"The holos I'm viewing are generated internally by my suit."

"But your faceplate was set to transparent, and your eye movements were almost identical to past movements – patterns recorded when previously looking over your team's histories."

Paran swore. Immediately, his helmet faceplate shimmered opaque. He checked over his most recent viewings, cross-referencing them for times the faceplate had been transparent. Satisfied, he ended the search and cancelled the images.

"Paran, why do you continually examine these same pieces of information? You have examined your team's histories many more times than is necessary, and the team is already selected. The exercise is redundant."

"I need to be sure."

"Sure of what?"

"That I am not making a mistake."

"The only request denied to you was having Commander Miren on your team. Another commander would have been redundant, and would have confused the hierarchical chain of authority. The team you have are highly competent, and mistakes are unlikely—"

"I'm not referring to that type of mistake."

"Then what are you referring to?"

An internal warning from the suit chimed. The threshold that Paran had set had been breached again. He upped the amount of chemical relaxant being pumped into the suit. His anxiety calmed and the warnings vanished.

"Influxa… when they came for you, when they split you in half and turned you into whatever you are now, did they really take everything from you? Everything that makes you Roranian?"

"That is an obvious change of topic, Commander Paran. Are you no longer willing to discuss your team?"

"Just tell me, Influxa."

"Commander Paran, as we have discussed before, you have the required seniority within the Administration to understand the construction and maintenance of the influx network."

Paran smiled. "You have a little more personality than a typical influx. What do you remember?"

"My prior self, as a unified Roranian, was requisitioned for the network because of crimes against the Administration."

"What was your name?"

The response was not immediate. Paran checked. The channel was still open; Influxa was simply taking her time to respond. Finally, the answer came.

"My name is Influxa."

"What was your name when you were *unified?*"

"That is irrelevant. I am Influxa."

"I pity you, Influxa. I pity what was done to you. You were the wrong type of criminal."

"There is no wrong type of criminal, by definition, Commander Paran."

"You were a criminal of no use to the Administration."

"I am of use now—" Influxa stopped communicating abruptly, then resumed. "Commander Paran, I have just received a single message from the Administration."

"How?"

"It is certified. Weak but high-level encryption. From another prototype on Barrenscape, one such as myself, sent by Mericadal. It will be here soon. I have been tasked with scouting down the other side of Barrenscape, before returning to liaise with it. Mericadal is testing our ability to work together. It will guard you in my stead."

"It seems like Mericadal's testing an autonomous part of the influx network," Paran said. "Maybe you should give autonomy a thought."

"Autonomy is not the correct term, Commander Paran. And this situation is only temporary."

"Go."

The communication channel closed. Paran watched the telemetry that displayed Influxa's departure. As soon as the strange influx network proxy was out of range, he sent the signal to activate the bait for the trap. Immediately, on the surface, omnidirectional signal noise was projected. He had initiated the call for the Breaker.

Chapter 5

Aspersive Exchange, Top Official

Member Vodal strode over to the electro-boost platform operator on floor three. He glanced out of the window, the day's light nearly gone.

"Floor sixteen."

"Yes, Member Vodal." The two guards standing in front of the platform moved aside. "Goodbye, Member Vodal."

Upon reaching floor sixteen, Member Vodal strode forwards, ignoring the greetings of the new operator. He waited for the entrance mechanism to ripple up and stepped into the small anteroom beyond. The entrance mechanism resealed behind him. An official waited patiently behind a counter.

"I assume there's space," Member Vodal said, clearing his throat.

"Yes, Member Vodal. The Emox Room is at half capacity."

"Wake me up after my usual time limit."

"Yes, Member Vodal."

The entrance mechanism on the other side of the anteroom rippled up and Member Vodal entered the Emox Room, fingers fidgeting excitedly. There were twenty compartments, with a generous degree of space between them, circularly positioned around the room's centre. Half were indeed in use. Member Vodal picked an empty compartment directly ahead. He was about to enter when the entrance to the next compartment along rippled up.

"Member Slautina," Member Vodal said, curtly.

Member Slautina smiled widely in his direction, her eyes unfocused and her gaze distant. One hand rested on her slender hips, the other steadied her against the compartment entrance. Her well-formed, if somewhat over-attended-to features, were both disarming and unsettling at the same time.

"Member Vodal." Her voice was breezy. "I'm surprised to find you here."

"Surprised?" He raised an eyebrow, the hint of a smile forming on his lips.

"I was under the impression you didn't frequent the Emox Room."

"And why is that?" He took a step closer, looking past her shoulder, into the empty compartment behind.

She wagged a finger and shook her head. "Oh, some

say you consider yourself... above the rest of us."

"Do they?"

"They say that you prefer to focus on other things."

Member Vodal chuckled dryly and cleared his throat. "And where did you hear that?"

Member Slautina shrugged. "Rumour, that's all."

"Rumour? Member Slautina..."

"Others talk about you, Member Vodal. And they don't say nice things."

Member Vodal stood firm, the remnants of his smile evaporating. "I don't consider myself above any of the other Members. And besides, I'm here now, in the Emox Room, aren't I?"

"Quite so," she said, conversationally, as though she had not noticed the shift in his tone. Her eyes focused upon him, her gaze less distant. "How could anyone resist?"

"Exactly."

"Although..." She brought a finger to her lips, frowning exaggeratedly, in a manner that made her appear almost foolish. "I haven't seen you here in a long, long time. I was starting to think you were something... special." She bit her lip and whispered conspiratorially, "As special as Mericadal, perhaps."

Member Vodal clenched his jaw, his narrow cheekbones prominent. "What exactly are you saying, Member Slautina? You know he doesn't like it when we use his name."

"No, he doesn't…" Her eyes lit up. "Rumour has it, he doesn't come here because he underwent the process himself, once." She giggled, childishly. "Split himself into an emox and an influx, then recombined. What do you say to that?"

"Member Slautina, you're…" Member Vodal's face tightened some more. "… relaxed. I understand the emoxes have that effect. But I must remind you: whatever you tell me, I will report to him. And we both know how much he despises rumours about himself… almost as much as he despises us using his name." There was a brittle stillness to Member Vodal's voice.

"I'm only making conversation."

Member Vodal cleared his throat, smiling thinly. "Perhaps you should focus on your work for us, for the Administration. Theoretical research is coming under increasing scrutiny. The Second State Hypothesis won't solve itself. Neither will the Power Dissipation Enigma, the Information Loss Conundrum, nor any other problems we still face."

"Ah, yes. Results. Wasn't the Second State Hypothesis once *your* assigned area of oversight, amongst the many others you have… temporarily overseen during your years of service?"

"I wasn't a full Member for most of that."

"Past performance is a useful indicator of future

progress."

Member Vodal's face became flooded with colour. "Member Slautina, are you insinuating that I am in some way incompetent?"

"Of course not, Vodal."

"Member Vodal."

"If you say so." Without another word, she left the room.

Member Vodal exhaled in irritation, still shaking as the emox compartment closed behind him. A resting platform lay waiting, similar to the platform on Mericadal's floor at the top of the building, although a little smaller. Member Vodal settled onto it and closed his eyes, loudly clearing his throat one final time. Whirring machinery rose from the floor beside him. One eye flicked open, watching as the thin, white tubes slithered across his arms and legs, wrapping themselves around him, fastening him into place. His palms were forced open as minuscule needles were painlessly inserted into his flesh, chemical mixtures pumping into his body. As they infiltrated his cells, his eyes rolled upwards, and a few breaths later, his eyelids closed, forcing him to embrace oblivion.

*

Member Slautina left the Emox Room, the innocent smile across her face gone. She said nothing to anyone, other than the electro-boost platform operator, whom she greeted by simply stating the floor she wished to travel to: 'the top'.

Upon reaching the tower's penultimate level, the electro-boost platform stopped. The operator cleared his throat. "There's been an alteration." He gestured to another, far larger electro-boost platform, in the space where there had previously been a spiral staircase. "You can reach the top by single-level electro-boost now."

Member Slautina nodded and walked across to the new electro-boost platform. As it rose, she discovered Mericadal, reclining horizontally in the middle of the room, enveloped in a dense simulation haze. He raised a finger, beckoning her towards him.

"What do you think?" he asked.

"I'm sure you saw." She nodded at the simulation haze. "I did as instructed. I came at him from many angles; he did not understand my motives."

"I'm not asking what happened, I'm asking what you think, Member Slautina. As you are singly aware, I may be looking for another primary Member. I have concerns about Member Vodal, for he has neither the capacity nor the loyalty. What are your instincts telling you?"

Member Slautina took a deep breath. "Member Vodal did not want to prolong the... small-talk. He acted well, with respect to discretion and loyalty."

"Yet he does not use his full emox allowance. Does he

not feel that is reward enough for his work? Perhaps he does have ambitions above his current status..." Mericadal pursed his lips, deep in thought. "What of his competence? Your thoughts?"

Member Slautina gulped, bowing her head guiltily. "His past failures still haunt him, as do his insecurities regarding his own abilities. That much was obvious. I think you are correct in believing that he may be of limited assistance to you."

Mericadal sucked his teeth. "Thank you for your candour, Member Slautina. I trust you to keep this between us."

She turned and began to leave.

"Oh, and Member Slautina," Mericadal said, smirking. "I know you are playing your own game too. Just remember: everything has its limits. Make sure your game is aligned with mine."

Chapter 6

In the Flesh, Commander

The communication channel requests were persistent. Paran's team were terrified, as expected. Paran declined each request, although he did listen to the conversations they had with each other.

"Why isn't the Commander responding?"

"What's he doing?"

"The Breaker is coming!"

"My control over my sub-cutter is gone, I'm stuck!"

"Me too!"

"Wait, mine's taking me back to the surface—"

"Mine too—"

"They all are!"

Aside from Paran's, the other sub-cutters burrowed back to the surface. He sent some more commands to each machine, including inoperability orders. There would be no escape.

"The entrance of my sub-cutter is opening!"

"Mine too! I can't stop it!"

"I don't believe it… mine's received an inoperability order!"

"Same—"

"What're they…?"

"They'll render our sub-cutters useless!"

"Inoperability orders!"

"Is this a test?"

"What's—"

"Why's the Commander silent?"

"There's no—"

"I can't access any information from the sensor poles."

"That's because of the inoperability orders!"

"Those shouldn't affect the sensor poles!"

"But the Breaker—"

"Can someone get through to the Commander?"

"I'm trying!"

"This is suicide!"

"I'm being pushed out! The sub-cutter's forcing me out!"

The walls of the team's sub-cutters were indeed shifting inwards, reducing the space inside and forcing each team member out, onto the unprotected surface of Barrenscape. It was dark now; no light glimmered from the Haze Rings. The only brightness came from the blue flashes of the sensor poles. The bewilderment and terrified screams of Paran's soldiers continued, their conversations becoming increasingly panicked. The team huddled together, outside, near the bait. Exposed.

"The trap isn't initiated; it's not functioning yet, only the bait. Quick, let's destroy it. Otherwise, we're dead. We need to stop the noise."

"But the Commander—"

"Obviously something is wrong."

"We can't destroy the bait, we have no weapons. They're all in our sub-cutter compartments."

"Plus the bait's triamond-reinforced, same as the influx network hubs."

"But the Breaker will be on its way—"

"Someone get through to the Commander!"

"I'm shut out of everything. This suit's got nothing."

"Same, it's useless!"

"I can't even see if the defences are functioning anymore—"

"Even if they are, we have no way of accessing them."

"We're completely shut out!"

"Is there any way we can get back into the sub-cutters?"

"Don't be—"

"There's smoke coming from them!"

Paran sent further commands to his own sub-cutter. Coordinates. It pushed silently under the surface of Barrenscape, away from the commotion. The seven were none the wiser.

"Maybe it's that Influxa?"

"What for?"

"Wait – did you see that?"

"Shh!"

"What?"

"Listen. There's something out there…"

"Where—"

"In the darkness…"

"Is it coming this way?"

Paran instructed his sub-cutter to move away as fast as it could. The engine was not designed for extended use at such speeds, but that did not matter. He had to get as far away as he could. It would still take a while to reach the meeting point, but the sub-cutter would be of no use after that.

"Run!"

"What the—"

"Please—"

"Comman—"

Multiple screams ripped through the communication channels. Paran was too far away by now for a visual, or almost any other type of sensor detection from his sub-cutter or his suit – the thick atmosphere and depth of the sub-cutter put a stop to that. The channels were audio-only, and the signals far from perfect.

First, Unriel's communications were severed. The sudden, rapid breathing of the remaining six was loud.

They were running. Paran reduced the volume of his music.

"No, please—" Dorera's final words were cut off by an unpleasant crunching noise.

Five left.

Cestial screamed, briefly begging as Dorera had done, but to no avail. A similar crunching sound put an end to his life. The remaining four were all wheezing, fleeing as fast as they could.

. The clamour of the wheezing changed. Nalict shrieked. "No, don't. The trap wasn't for you. I'm sorry! If you let—"

Silence.

"Nalict," Jabayan whispered. "Are you there?"

"I... I... please forgive..." Nothing. Nalict's channel was severed.

Three left. Lotolen, Moryaben and Jabayan.

"Where are... you?" Jabayan asked. His position was far, the signal quality extremely low.

"I... the... Commander must have... known..." came the response from Lotolen. "No... traitor..." Lotolen's channel was cut.

Two left.

Morbayen's breathing was heavy and consistent. His channel was the clearest, indicating that he had run in the same direction as Paran's sub-cutter.

"Can anyone hear me?" he whispered.

An omnidirectional communication channel request came through to Paran. From Morbayen. Paran dismissed it. Morbayen requested again. Paran increased the volume of his music a little, reflexively tapping his finger against his suited leg. A moment later, Morbayen's channel requests ended.

One left.

Paran knitted his eyebrows. If the Breaker had been on Morbayen's trail, then it was possibly headed towards Paran's sub-cutter. His expression relaxed as Jabayan's distorted screams came through the final communication channel. The Breaker had doubled back, away from the position of Paran's sub-cutter. Jabayan's screams lasted the longest.

The sub-cutter continued to speed under the surface, towards the target location. Paran steadied his breathing and further increased the volume of his music. A short while later, he instructed the sub-cutter to release a short-distance, encrypted signal. In response, a communication channel of unidentifiable origin was requested, straight to the sub-cutter. He patched it through to his suit. Simple instructions.

Paran raised the sub-cutter's internal holo controls and manually took over. A soft chiming from his suit indicated his breathing rate had crept up. He changed the music and brought it back down.

Once he had followed the directional instructions to

their end, Paran scanned the ground above as far as was possible, both with the sub-cutter's sensors and those of his suit. No Breaker, fortunately, but nothing else either. He brought the sub-cutter to the surface and opened the entrance, then sent a fast-acting inoperability order. As soon as his feet touched Barrenscape's surface, the sub-cutter entrance sealed behind him. The vehicle slunk back into the ground with a brief scraping noise, reburying itself.

Paran paused the music playing inside his suit, maximising external sounds. Faint whirrings came from the sub-cutter, followed by silence. The inoperability order had been enacted; the sub-cutter was destroyed. Now, only the sounds of Barrenscape's winds dragging across its surface were audible, whipping the ubiquitous yellow debris into small eddies. His faceplate shimmered to transparency and slid to the side, then his entire helmet folded into the back of his suit. He inhaled sharply.

"The Butcher of Ualbrict, in the flesh," a gruff voice said.

Paran turned rapidly. No one was there. Pursing his lips, he began to scan the area more closely, just as a thick, sweet smell began to fill the air.

Chapter 7

Official Concerns, Top Official

Member Vodal leaned forwards and swung his legs over the resting platform. Taking a moment to right himself, he exited the Emox Room, dismissing the anteroom official's polite attempt at conversation, and waited for the two guards to step away from the electro-boost platform.

"Ground level," Member Vodal said, walking forwards.

"Goodbye, Member Vodal," the operator said.

"Wait," Member Vodal yelled, shuffling to move off the platform as it sped up. "I said ground!"

Mericadal watched through Conceal's sensors, chuckling to himself at Member Vodal's confusion. Member Vodal reached the next level up, then the next, and so on. He shouted and cursed at every electro-boost operator he shot past.

Upon arriving at the penultimate level from the top, Member Vodal's indignant shouts had attenuated to non-vocal panic. He cleared his throat constantly. The statistics floating beside the holo representation of him highlighted his stress: his heart raced; perspiration was exacerbated; hormones relating to anxiety flooded his body. He was scared.

The waiting guards chaperoned him to the new electro-boost platform. Neither they, nor the floor's operator, said anything, though each wore a hint of a smile. The guards stood back from Member Vodal, and the electro-boost platform rose. A moment later, Member Vodal was in the room with Mericadal, at the top of the tower.

Mericadal was still engulfed in the simulation haze, viewing the room through Conceal's sensors. He waved for the trembling Member Vodal to come closer. "Something the matter, Member Vodal?"

"No, Mericadal..." Member Vodal stuttered. "I apologise, I didn't mean to say your name... I... I think there's been a mistake, an issue with the electro-boost platform." He laughed, slightly louder than was typical, then comically attempted to quieten his voice, before clearing his throat.

"No," Mericadal replied. "There's no problem with the electro-boost platform. And please stop clearing your throat, Member Vodal. It's insufferable."

"I'm sorry, I didn't realise I was..." Member Vodal's eyebrows furrowed. He repeated Mericadal's words pensively. "There's no problem with the..." He looked about, eyeing the empty room, searching aimlessly.

"There's no problem with the electro-boost platform."

"Really?"

"Yes."

"There's no…"

"No problem with any of them, in fact. I've just checked. They're all working fine, Member Vodal."

"The operators were no help, I tried to stop the platform…" Member Vodal uttered weakly.

"Why would you do that? I wanted you here." Mericadal paused, allowing Member Vodal's tremulous breathing to fill the silence. "Did you know, the operators are actually allotted time in the Emox Room too?"

"Oh really?" Member Vodal managed, his voice barely a whisper, failing to look the slightest surprised.

Mericadal nodded. "And the guards too, some of them. I personally ensure it. It's not just Members who have access. Of course, I never let you or any of the other Members realise this. The operators and the guards never visit the Emox Room during official hours. That would give it all away, wouldn't it?" Mericadal cancelled the simulation and sat up.

"Give it all away?" Member Vodal's eyes bulged.

"*This.*" Mericadal gestured around them. "What I'm trying to relate to you, Member Vodal, is that the operators, the officials and the guards are all very discrete and very loyal, to me, because I reward them. They're always watching you. They speak to me and they tell me things."

"Good." Member Vodal straightened up, looking almost reasonable. "They're loyal. That's important."

Mericadal pushed himself to his feet and patted down a single crease in his well-fitted regwear. He ran a hand through his hair, tidying it. He was a little shorter than Member Vodal, and stood comfortably, shifting his weight slightly onto one leg. "I'm not going to lie to you, Member Vodal. This won't be pleasant for you. I have concerns about your competence. That's why you're here."

"You have concerns…" Member Vodal swallowed audibly. "I can improve, I assure you—"

Mericadal held his hand up to silence Member Vodal. "No, I don't believe you can."

"Why not?" The colour drained from Member Vodal's face.

"I also have concerns about your loyalty."

"My loyalty?" Member Vodal exclaimed with incredulity. His head shook vigorously. "I've never been disloyal, never!"

"Not yet, but in the future, perhaps. Believe me, I've seen it all before. The fact that you ration your own time with the emoxes does little to assuage me of that feeling. If I can't control you, I can't trust you."

"I ration my… but I ration my time with the emoxes

because they alter my mind. I want to be more effective for you! I want to keep my senses—"

"I need someone competent, who I can trust now, immediately. I'll admit, it's a tall order, but I do not have time to wait, Member Vodal. The Administration is in danger of becoming stagnant. We came here for a reason, don't forget that. Tapache gave us a mission that you've utterly forgotten. And there's also the matter of my own circumstances. You see, if I'm to personally reveal myself, which I intend to do, I need someone dependable and capable as my chief advisor."

Member Vodal appeared lost. "You're going to reveal yourself to everyone? Then… I could help, I really could. Just give me the—"

"Member Vodal," Mericadal whispered soothingly. "You must be aware that you have overachieved?"

"So… I'm to be moved to another department?"

"Not exactly."

"I… I should step down? Is that what you're suggesting?" Member Vodal's eyes were wide. Desperate. "I don't mind, given… given the circumstances."

Mericadal frowned. "No, no, that wouldn't do. With what you know, you could become a liability in the future. We both know that."

"But…" Mericadal shook his head. "I don't understand."

"Oh, I think you do. You've helped me remove other

Members before. This can't have come as a complete surprise."

Member Vodal began to whimper. Tears rolled down his cheeks. "No, no! I can help, I know I can! I *want* to help, I *want*—"

Mericadal's eyes narrowed and his face contorted with rage, becoming ugly. "I want you gone!"

A change wafted through Member Vodal. His quivering diminished; his tears stopped flowing. He stood tall, looking down upon Mericadal, a smile of contempt drawn across his face. He cleared his throat, loudly.

"You're paranoid, Mericadal, and an old fool." He edged forwards, confident. "You're so *arrogant*, Mericadal. You've even stopped positioning guards around you. Mericadal—"

"Don't make this personal, Member Vodal."

"I'll kill you before you kill me!"

Member Vodal lunged, but before reaching Mericadal, he was knocked violently to the side, sliding across the room and slamming explosively against the curved window. He lay crumpled on the floor, damaged, one eyelid fluttering open, shocked. An object materialised out of thin air. A spherical drone.

Mericadal strolled over to Member Vodal. He took a step back, then aimed a vicious kick at Member Vodal's head. Again and again. Blood poured from Member Vodal's mouth. Finished, Mericadal knelt and whispered into Member Vodal's ear.

"Not bad for an old fool."

Member Vodal wheezed in response, breathing heavily. Mericadal slapped him roughly, spattering yet more blood across the floor.

"That was the prototype I've had following you for a while. You understand its implications, don't you? An invisible army, answering only to me." His tone became relaxed. "There are a few things to sort out, unfortunately. Range isn't so great; bloom fragments interfere with the concealment mechanism so we can't use them together. But don't worry, we're working on it. Soon, the Administration will be unstoppable. Our sky-factories will become great warships, the like of which have not been seen for millennia. We'll spread across Ringscape in its entirety; we'll rule it all. We'll finally complete Tapache's mission."

Member Vodal tried to speak, but only succeeded in coughing painfully, his face scrunching in pain.

"Need to clear your throat, Member Vodal?" Mericadal lowered an ear to Member Vodal's mouth. "Something insightful to say?"

"You're insane," Member Vodal gurgled, his voice only just audible. "Meric... Mericadal..."

"Best you don't try to speak, *Member* Vodal. It'll take you quite a while to heal. But when you do, you can use my name all you like. Soon, everyone will know it. Not that it'll change anything for you." He laughed, pushing himself up to his feet. "It's ironic that you limited your contact with the emox network, Member Vodal. You're about to become a part of it."

Everything went black.

Chapter 8

Expected Liaisons, Commander

Paran waited for the hidden observer to reveal themselves, not bothering to check his suit's sensors. He did not have to wait long. In the direction he was already facing, a Silvered Vaesian flashed into being, engulfed in a sweet-smelling blue cloud. It stood about a head taller than Paran and appeared to be floating on empty air. The Silvered's mouth opened, exposing a dense wad of something being chewed. Wispy blue tendrils streamed towards him.

"Commander Paran, Destroyer of Vaesian Cities, I now welcome you as traitor to the Administration."

The Silvered was topless, its silver hairs ruffling in the wind, and as Paran looked down, he realised its three legs were firmly planted on a hard metallic surface, which had also rippled into visibility. The surface was a ramp, descending to a finger's width above the ground, and led up to the front cabin of a ship. Once fully revealed, it was obvious the ship was of Roranian design. An antiquated, skeletal propulsion unit was fastened underneath by a series of rods. The propulsion unit glowed orange.

"Nice trick," Paran replied.

"Trick." The Silvered guffawed and a puff of blue escaped. "Is that what you call saving your life?"

"What's your name?"

"I am Topinr."

"How can you be sure *this* isn't a trick, Topinr? That I am who I say I am?"

"Oh, I'm sure." Topinr gestured to the ship. "I was able to track you with this old thing, using the permissions you sent. I saw what you did. You have already lived up to your reputation." Topinr waited for a response from Paran that did not come. "Settling grievances?"

"Something like that."

"Even if you're not the Commander Paran who's been communicating with Osr over the years, you're no longer a friend to the Administration."

"I never was."

"Don't lie." A prominence of cloud billowed out towards Paran, as though emphasising Topinr's words.

"So, what now?" Paran asked.

"Are you nervous?" Topinr's tensirs at the ends of both arms rippled strongly.

Paran eyed them with suspicion. "Should I be?"

"Are you concerned we'll renege on the agreement?"

"I did my part."

60

Topinr's tensirs stopped rippling. "Fear not, Commander. We will honour it." The Silvered looked up and across the horizon. "We'll fly along Barrenscape for the next few days. Then, when the haze winds are quiet, we'll cross to Ringscape and I'll leave you near the Alpuri, as agreed. After that, you're on your own."

"Where, exactly?"

"What do you know of the Alpuri?"

"Not much."

"Not much." Topinr guffawed. "You didn't think to find out?"

"I couldn't find a Prietman with the capacity to hold a conversation," Paran answered irritably.

Topinr's guffaw continued. "Difficult creatures. They take a long time to say nothing, and they never reveal what they know." Topinir met Paran's gaze. "Like the Administration, we only know of one Alpuri city, so that's where we're going."

"Are we invisible already?"

Topinr guffawed even louder. "You overestimate my capabilities, Commander, do you—"

"My name is Paran."

"Concealing myself and this ship, then flying it… that took a while. Concealing you too is going to take me a little longer. It's not as simple as you might think." Topinr's middle leg replanted to the side, and the other two legs rearranged themselves so that Topinr's body faced up the ramp. "Come inside. The Breaker won't wait for us to continue our pleasant conversation." Topinr walked up the ramp. "The sooner we get started, the sooner I can conceal us."

Paran followed Topinr into the cramped pilot-cabin, which was filled with the same blue haze that streamed from Topinr's mouth. Paran's helmet automatically sealed over his head, using visual augmentation to scrape away most of the haze, leaving only pale blue impressions. Internal scents took over, expunging the sweet smell. Topinr sat on the far seat as Paran took the second space, closer to the entrance. A bank of controls lay before Topinr, adapted for Vaesian tensir use. The ship rumbled.

"What's that?" Paran asked, pointing to a small, silver cube that was attached to the far side of the console, beside Topinr. His suit did not recognise it.

"Vaesian storage unit. Never seen one before?"

"No. What's it for?"

"Storage, obviously."

"What's that one for?"

"It reconfigures control sequences for Vaesian use, that's all."

"I thought you didn't have access to that sort of technology."

Topinr guffawed. "Think what you like, Commander."

Paran quietened. He looked about some more, then relaxed back, moving his hand in the air before him, eyeing the faint blue turbulence in its wake. "Do all Silvereds have your abilities?"

"Which ones?"

"Concealment."

"Perhaps."

"You don't know?"

"We're still learning."

The ship's rumbling increased. Topinr's tensirs froze. Finally, the rumbling became more or less consistent, with occasional, heavier jolts. Topinr resumed manipulating the controls.

"What is this?" Paran gestured to the blue trails.

"Muvaeyt." Topinr's mouth opened, exposing the dark blue wad inside.

"You had better hope the Administration doesn't discover it. I saw it in Sunsprit too; I know you Silvereds with abilities use it."

"What's your point?"

"They'll be able to use it to find you. All of you."

Topinr adjusted various controls. All three legs twitched gently, as though restless. "Let them try."

"You should be concerned."

Topinr guffawed. "Its chemical properties are altered by our concealment fields. The trails decompose to untraceable levels, unless you're very close."

"I can detect it."

"That's because we're not concealed yet," Topinr

answered, testily. "I'll get to that soon."

The ship began to rise and Barrenscape drifted away. "Still works," Topinr said, the words coinciding with a particularly sharp jolt.

"Are you sure this ship's airworthy?"

"At least this one has soft-gravity emulators. I've heard you lot don't like flying without them." They stopped rising and began moving laterally, although the rattling did not abate. Topinr sat back, holding a clump of muvaeyt ready to chew. "Tell me about this Influxa and why I had to transmit falsified communications. What is it exactly?"

"A surprise for me too."

"I doubt that."

"It's true, otherwise I would have warned you about her."

"Her? I thought it was an automated drone."

"In either case, you don't need to worry about Influxa."

No further explanation came from Paran. Topinr grabbed another clump of muvaeyt, chewing it loudly.

"No matter, I'll inform Osr upon my return." A few moments passed. Topinr reached for yet another clump. "This is going to be… tougher than I thought. I'm having trouble including you in the concealment field. That suit you're wearing… it's from your Great Ship, isn't it?"

"Is that a problem?"

"Artefacts from the Great Ships are often tougher to

conceal."

"How long will it take?"

"I don't know."

"I'll leave you to it then."

Topinr guffawed. "No, speak to me. That'll help me concentrate on you and that suit."

"Speak to you?"

"Tell me about yourself."

"You already know all you need to."

"Come on, Commander. What changed? Why defect from the Administration now?"

Paran shifted uncomfortably, staring at the empty skies outside the ship.

Topinr persisted. "Go on, tell me, Butcher of Ualbrict."

Paran rocked his head back, allowing the suit's helmet to collapse away. Immediately, his vision was obscured by thick blue. "Don't call me that."

Topinr continued, unabashed. "Why defect now?"

"Everything's changed."

"Keep talking."

"Mericadal's power over me is gone."

"Mericadal?"

"Yes."

"Who's that? I'm just a simple Vaesian. I don't know much about Administration politics."

"No one does." Paran paused. "Mericadal controls the

Administration; he sits above all the Members. But even if you lived in Fadin, it's unlikely you'd know of him. Extremely unlikely. There are rumours, but no one takes them seriously."

"Sounds a bit strange."

"He learned caution a long time ago."

"You're not much of a talker, are you, Paran? Go on. Tell me about this Mericadal. Where and why did he learn this special ability to be cautious?" Topinr guffawed loudly.

Paran closed his eyes. "We used to fight amongst ourselves. Long before I came to Ringscape, before I ever entered the Source, the Roranians down here had already been through several iterations of rule, by various groups. You probably know that. Anyway, Mericadal was there through all of them, always sitting behind the violence, learning, hiding, surviving. Never the warrior. And now, he sits at the top." Paran slowed. "But soon, Diyan will be successful, and it won't—"

A chime sounded. Paran allowed his suit helmet to reseal. Topinr had leaned far over the controls, almost engulfing them, three legs splayed out for stability. Paran accessed what he could of the ship's sensory data, and by the time Topinr spoke, he already knew the problem.

"Influxa. She's coming," Topinr said. "I thought you said we didn't have to worry about her."

Paran swore. "She's smarter than I thought. She must

have realised the scouting order was a lie. Are we concealed?"

"No. She's coming straight for us."

Paran swore again.

Chapter 9

Rumours and Observations, Incarcerated

The primary observer waved her hand through the holo images, flicking between them. Many Incarcerateds were still eating, squeezing out the last morsels from their food packets. A few had already finished and were going about their evening routines: pacing about the limited floor space of their cells; drumming their fists and legs aimlessly against the walls with no real resolve; staring blankly at nothing in particular.

The secondary observer was seated beside her. He yawned loudly, then stood up and bent over, touching the floor with his hands, straightening his legs. His long brown hair fell over his face. He flicked it back as he straightened up again.

"Did you hear about the new Incarcerated?" he asked.

"There are many new Incarcerateds, Morial. Which one specifically?" the primary observer asked.

The secondary observer paced around the domed

observation room, which was only slightly larger than the Incarcerateds' cells. It consisted of two manoeuvrable seats with arced control banks affixed at their sides; undisguised holo projectors dotted about the walls; an ancient, temperamental food dispenser next to the entrance, and an even smaller side-room for washing.

"Apparently," Morial began, "the new Incarcerated claimed he was a *Member*. He was shouting it... well, whispering it really. He was in a terrible state—"

"You and your rumours," the primary observer said, irritably. "I don't even know who the current Members *are*. Who did you last vote for in Potensein?"

"I'm just telling you—"

"It's always 'this Incarcerated said this' or 'this Incarcerated said that' with you. You shouldn't believe everything they say. In fact, you shouldn't believe *anything* they say."

"Oh, come on—"

"You never hear any of these things directly, it's always from someone else. You're being taken for a fool."

"I don't just believe what they say, Oberend," Morial argued.

"You do!"

"Fine, but what's your issue? What's the harm in discussing it?"

The primary observer – Oberend – sighed. "Go on then, Morial. What did this *Member* supposedly say?

Well... ex-Member now I suppose."

"He said that he was only taken for incarceration because the top official in the Administration—"

"Stop right there," Oberend said. "Top official?"

"Yes."

"And who is that?"

"The one in absolute control. You know the rumours—"

"Yes, I've heard the rumours." She snorted. "Really, Morial? The Members *are* the top. They're elected by us; no one's higher up than them. I don't remember voting for some *top official*. Do you? And even if there was a top official, why would you care? It's not like we really tell the Members what to do anyway."

"I'm just telling you what I heard."

"But no one knows about this top official?"

"Some must do, but only some. The... the top, highest level positions, and those directly interacting with the top official, they would need to know."

"But how does anyone else know to follow the top official's orders? They can't stay insulated from the rest of the Administration. They'd need to be able to get about."

"The top official has Member-level access."

"Ah, of course!" Oberend said, mockingly. "With a status set to urgent, full authority."

"Must be. And if you're not in the know, who's going to question anyway?"

"Morial, I sense you've thought about this for too long already…"

"So what if I have? This Incarcerated said that he knew too much. The top official wanted him gone."

Oberend sighed again. "What do you mean by *too much*?"

"He said there's some other network, besides the influx network. It's not a network of information, but control. Control of the Members. This top official's got them all addicted to it. It's how he controls everything."

"*He*?"

"Yes."

"And what's this secret network called?"

"The emox network, or something like that. He said it's incredible… pure ecstasy—"

"You do love to embellish a story, don't you?" Oberend said. "At least there's something new about this version of the 'top official' rumour."

"I'm not embellishing anything!"

"Tell me," Oberend chuckled, "did this new Incarcerated say anything else about this *top official*?"

"He said that he's scary, really scary. And that he models himself on the first Roranians, from the Great Ship."

"Let's see what I remember from those studies of the first Roranians at the learning centres… does he have his own little annexe?" Oberend cooed.

"In a way. He's always changing things, as though rearranging an annexe. And he pushes himself, undertaking risky challenges—"

"Let me guess why: to mimic the competitions the first Roranians used to take part in aboard our Great Ship?"

"Yes—"

"Morial, this sounds utterly ridiculous, even for you. This apparent 'ex-Member' didn't even give you a name for this 'top official'."

"Apparently, he was too scared to say."

Oberend laughed. "Extremely convenient."

Morial huffed. "Well, *this* facility is a secret. Who's to say the Administration doesn't have more? And what's wrong with discussing what I've heard? It's not as though there's anything else to do…"

Oberend emitted a protracted yawn. "You're not wrong about that. The night shift arrives soon though; then we can leave."

"Yeah… and embark on the long crykel ride home."

Oberend tutted, turning away from Morial and shifting to a different position. Her seat responded to the movement, flattening horizontally. "Prefer to sleep in the facility, would you?" Oberend asked.

Morial slumped back into his seat with one foot hanging off the front, pressed against the floor. He pushed against the surface beneath him and spun around. "Of course not, even if I was allowed to. We're just so far from

72

anywhere here—"

"Would you rather we were in the middle of Potensein or Fadin, at risk of everyone finding out?" Oberend shook her head.

"We could use remote observation. The facility could be directly plugged into the main influx network, and moved closer... to either city, I don't care... but not too close, so that the power requirements would be minimal."

"Minimal?"

"Well, fairly low. That way we wouldn't have to physically be here," Morial argued. "It's the same reason there's a physical blockade around Sunsprit... you know... for the Silvereds. The power requirements are too high for anything remote. But, if this facility wasn't so far away..."

Oberend rolled her eyes. "We're not going to discuss this again. Every time I'm paired with you, you bring this up."

The conversation ended and Morial repositioned his body, the seat contorting horizontally flat, same as Oberend's, as Morial continued to spin around. He tapped the holo controls to his left, and a larger, rotating holo screen appeared above him: the live feed from one of the Incarcerated's cells. He waved the image away and a different one replaced it: another Incarcerated's cell. He waved to the next.

"I remember this one from the other day." Morial

expanded the image and stopped his spinning, directing the holo's orientation towards Oberend. "He used to shout and shout. Even more than the one I was just telling you about." He winced.

Oberend looked over. "Serves him right for helping the Vaesians during the war."

"I can't believe the Administration's still finding collaborators, even now."

"I'm glad. Round them all up and lock them in here, I say. Punish the traitors."

"What if they're angry when they come out?"

"Have you ever heard of someone returning to a facility?"

Morial brought a contemplative finger to his lips. "No…"

"That's because no one reoffends. When they leave, they're merged back into society, corrected. The system works." Oberend cancelled her own holo and watched Morial's as he flicked through yet more images.

"How are they released?" Morial asked.

"What d'you mean?"

"You know what I mean."

Oberend sucked her teeth. "How would I know? It's nothing to do with us. What is it with you today?"

"I've heard…" Morial hesitated. "… I've heard that it's to do with the influx network. When they're released, they're taken to work for it, or something like that. Maybe

74

it also has something to do with this emox network."

"Oh, not this again—"

"Maybe they're trained to help maintain it?"

"Maybe," Oberend replied curtly. "Maybe not. I don't care."

Morial clenched his jaw and continued waving between the holo images. Suddenly, he stopped. The eyes of the Incarcerated being displayed were closed. She appeared perfectly still, in the same cross-legged pose as always.

"She's absolutely beautiful," Morial said.

"I'll give you that."

"She only ever moves to eat and wash." Both of the Incarcerated's hands rested on her knees, palms facing up. "Sometimes she opens her eyes and they flit about, but tracking shows the patterns are nonsense."

"What a life."

Morial tapped the holo controls to pull up some additional information. "She's been eating more, recently, though. What do you think that means?"

"That you have too much free time, and are showing a worrying fascination in this particularly attractive Incarcerated."

"I'm being serious. Who do you think she is?"

Oberend shrugged. "Lots of them have their information obscured. We're not important enough to know. Maybe your 'top official' can help us with that."

"Do you think she helped the Vaesians too?"

"Probably."

"They say she was caught with a device. Something she was trying to infiltrate the influx network with. Somehow, it damaged a load of the influxes; a large part of the network had to be cauterised." He began to whisper. "They say the device had... strange gravitational signatures on it. Possibly from straying too close to the edge. Have you heard of the 'flips'? They say—"

"*They, they, they.* Always *they* with you, Morial!"

Morial ignored the comment and navigated through more holo controls. Further information appeared around the central holo, both historical and current. Sleep cycle patterns; consumption and metabolic rates; electrodermal activity. Oberend leant across and pushed her finger through it.

"You've selected *deviation instances*," Morial said. "Why?"

Oberend said nothing, selecting another sub-option. She stopped once a fresh set of statistics was displayed.

"The Incarcerated's *shiver rate*," Morial said. "What's interesting about that?"

"One of the other secondaries I'm paired with showed me. Check the historicals."

"Who?"

"Doesn't matter who," Oberend said. "Just check the historicals."

Morial peered closer. "What does this actually mean?"

"Records of small muscle movements. Look at the historicals," she repeated.

Morial scanned the information. "She's cold? Seems... it's been like this for the better part of half a year now. Her shivering's increased, but it's still not particularly significant. Look, it shows the threshold is still way beyond—"

"But she's not cold," Oberend interrupted.

"Then what's the shivering for?" He squinted. "It's impossible to see anyway. Are you sure the information's correct?"

"It's almost like she's controlling it, isn't it?" Oberend pondered, with a faint smile.

"Her shivering?"

"Almost as though she knows we won't be able to see it and doesn't want to be detected. But look at the historical trend. Too consistent to be random, isn't it? Like she's doing it on purpose..."

Morial's hand started trembling. His gaze was firmly stuck upon the Incarcerated. He began breathing harder. "What are you implying?"

"Oh, I don't know." Oberend spoke barely above a whisper. "But... if you correlate her shiver rate with her muscle fibre diameter..."

Morial navigated the holo controls. His eyes widened. "There's a strong positive correlation."

"It's undeniable."

"The shivering is building her muscles?" he asked.

"And take a look at some of the other statistics too." Oberend began selecting them, displaying them to Morial, one after the other. "They're all just below warning thresholds, but they're all showing a sustained increase. It's like she's getting ready for something."

"But what?"

"You tell me."

"We need to inform someone... surely—" He stopped.

Oberend had begun laughing, loudly.

"What?"

Oberend sat up and slapped her knees. The lighting in the room had been subtly dimmed from a tiny holo she controlled beside her right hand. She brought it back up. "You're too easy."

"What's wrong with you?" Morial scowled, cancelling the image.

A high-pitched chime sounded in their small room and Morial flinched. The entrance mechanism rippled up. Oberend slid off her seat and stood to greet the expected replacements, only to find a single Roranian waiting.

"Oh, you're new," Oberend stated, her voice lighter and higher pitched than before.

Morial spun the chair around to look. The replacement was well-muscled, with a handsome, friendly face and short hair.

The newcomer nodded. "Torina's late. But I've worked at other Administration facilities before." He smiled. "They're all the same, right?"

Oberend blushed. "Torina's late again. She'll be in trouble."

"I won't tell if you don't." The replacement winked.

"You should really have a primary observer present before you can start," Oberend sighed, turning to Morial, who had also risen to his feet. "If something goes wrong..."

"Fortunately, I am quite capable."

"I'm sure you are."

Morial cleared his throat. "What's Torina's excuse this time?"

The replacement's attention shifted to him. Their eyes met. "Skimmer malfunction midway, I think. She was already out of Potensein. Something like that anyway."

Morial rolled his eyes and glanced at Oberend. "We were just discussing the problems with this facility being so remote. No replacement skimmers ready to—"

"That's why we're advised to take crykels to work," Oberend interrupted, dismissively. "They're fully Roranian tech, simple. No remnants of the old Tapache there. They integrate far better with the influx network." She hummed loudly to stifle a rising retort from Morial. "Well... I'm Oberend, and this," she gestured to her side, "is my secondary."

"I'm Morial."

The replacement smiled confidently. "Well, maybe we'll be on one of the next rotations together. Then I can properly introduce myself."

"I look forward to it," Oberend replied quickly.

There was an awkward pause.

"Well," Morial said. "We should be going then." He walked out of the room, waiting for Oberend, who dawdled, ensuring to brush past the replacement's thick shoulder. "It's all yours."

The replacement waited for them to disappear; for the sounds of their quarrelling to fade, before he strode into the main part of the room, pausing while the entrance mechanism rippled back down. He retrieved a vial from his pocket and spun it in his fingers. His countenance had changed, all joviality gone. Moving beside one of the seats, he tapped at the holo controls. When the image came up, his face registered brief surprise.

"Already looking at her, were you?" he muttered.

He expanded it so that the subject being displayed was the same size as himself and hovered in the air before him, sitting cross-legged, face up, eyes closed. A tear rolled down the replacement's cheek.

She opened her eyes. She mouthed a word. *Diyan*.

He mouthed one back. *Kera*.

Chapter 10

Concealed Trajectory, Commander

The ship hurtled through the growing haze winds over Barrenscape as fast as its propulsion unit would allow, trembling even more than before. Every so often, a loud crackle sounded and the cabin's lighting dimmed. Topinr's legs twitched, seeming to take turns tapping against the casing of the control panel as the Silvered grabbed clump after clump of muvaeyt, chewing furiously.

"I'm going to take us higher, Paran," Topinr said. "This Influxa is smaller and lighter than us, she'll be more susceptible to the haze winds."

"She'll catch us before we're high enough; any more of this turbulence and this ship's done for." Paran looked around them through his faceplate. The suit's sensors pinpointed various issues with the ship, overlaying most of the innards with warnings. "There's only one thing we can do, and you're not going to like it."

"No then."

"There's no other way. You've not been able to conceal us and we're running out of time."

"I know what you're about to suggest, Paran, and it's suicide." Thick blue wisps streamed from Topinr's mouth.

"Taking the ship any higher will be suicide."

"There's no way—"

Paran cut Topinr off. "Influxa is ordered to protect me, and she'll catch up. This ship has no offensive capabilities. She'll take me and destroy it. You'll be killed."

"But... you can't be serious?" Despite the situation, Topinr turned, fixating a pair of large, black eyes on Paran.

"I am. We need to head for the Breaker. It's the only thing I can think of. Maybe it will destroy Influxa."

"Or us!"

"Do you have a better idea?" Paran projected a holo between them – of the camp he had prepared with the seven deceased team members. "We should head for the Breaker's last known position, where I left the others. The sensor poles may still be there; they're more sensitive to its location than anything we have on this ship. With any luck, we'll pick up its position on the way."

"That's not luck."

"Call it what you want, then."

"Just what do you suggest we do when we find the Breaker?"

"We'll think of something. The trap's still there too; it's not been used." Paran cancelled the holo. "Topinr, I know you're brave, otherwise you wouldn't have been chosen to collect me in Barrenscape. This was always going to be risky—"

"Flattery... flattery, Paran."

Topinr's tensirs moved deftly across the ship's controls. A moment later, the ship dropped and turned in the air, quicker than the soft-gravity emulators could compensate for. They were forced to hold onto their seats, Topinr's legs again splayed out against the control bank's casing for extra stability. The ship shook violently, despite the lower altitude and calmer airflows.

"Ship's definitely damaged," Paran muttered. "And Influxa's halved the distance between us."

"The sensors are set to maximum, searching for the Breaker," Topinr replied. "Here, you take the controls. The crucial ones still react to Roranian touch." The Silvered pushed up from the seat. "I need to concentrate. I was almost there; I will be able to conceal us, I just need a little longer. I'd rather not visit the Breaker if we can help it."

They swapped seats. Paran's faceplate overlaid images onto the controls, informing him of their uses. Topinr was correct, many of the crucial controls did still allow for Roranian touch, although Paran's suited fingers were capable of tensir-mimicry anyway. While controlling the ship manually, Paran also initiated a process to pair his suit more directly with the ship, all the time keeping a strict eye on Influxa's position.

An alert informed Paran that the pairing was complete and he sat back, controlling their trajectory with simple eye movements and brief physical gestures. A communication channel request reached Paran – from Influxa. He swore and dismissed it. In response, Influxa began to close the distance more rapidly between them.

Paran's suit projected a holo of Influxa. "Topinr, we may have a problem, it looks like—"

"We're hidden!" the Silvered said, accompanied by a self-congratulatory guffaw. "It's done."

"Really?"

"You can't tell from the inside of the concealment field, but I can." Topinr leant over to look at the controls in front of Paran. "You're still directing the ship. How?"

"My suit." Paran studied the information available about Influxa. She was slowing down, presumably to investigate the position where they had disappeared.

"What did you do?"

"I connected them."

"You should have asked first."

"There was no time to check." The distance between them and Influxa continued to increase. Paran's faceplate slid to the side and he flashed Topinr a grin. "You did it." They hurtled away, and soon, Influxa was out of sensor range. "I'm going to resume our prior course."

Topinr began to rise. "Why don't you give me back—

Warning chimes sounded. The ship was in trouble – its propulsion unit was failing. A new rattling took hold.

Paran clenched his fists and swore. "Another change of plan, I'm afraid. We're going to have to land, very soon." Paran replaced the holo of Influxa with a blue-tinged sequence of ship schematics. The various issues were displayed in bright red.

Topinr studied it. "Any sign of the Breaker?"

"Fortunately not." Paran directed Topinr to the central part of the holo. "Your cargo manifest shows you have the tools we need to fix the propulsion unit and its supports. We can do it manually. It'll take half a day, if we're lucky, although more likely a full—"

"That's a long time for me to maintain the concealment field."

"We really don't have a choice," Paran said, as the ship descended rapidly.

Topinr grabbed another clump of muvaeyt.

*

The ship landed violently, but remained in one piece, its two inhabitants shaken but unharmed. They exited and inspected the propulsion unit from the outside. Most of the structural rods supporting the unit were dangerously warped, a few completely absent.

"The holo wasn't wrong," Topinr observed. "We're lucky it didn't fall off."

Paran pointed to the base of the ship. It was depressed a little into the ground of Barrenscape. "Is that hidden by your concealment field?"

A set of Topinr's tensirs wafted to the side. "I can only hide things within the field, I can't change the visuals of what's left. The betervope's stuck that way."

"Betervope?"

"This." Topinr kicked at the ground, creating a small yellow cloud. "Waste matter. This is betervope and the ground matter on Ringscape is retervope."

"It's just dirt, isn't it?" Paran asked distractedly, inspecting the propulsion unit again.

"Sort of, but not really. They look different, but betervope and retervope have the same properties. Tough to penetrate, physically or with signals." Topinr kicked at the ground again.

"We need to start the repairs as soon as possible," Paran said, as the ramp from the ship's cargo compartment began to descend. "Let's get started."

*

The daylight began to wane as the repair work progressed. They spoke infrequently. The occasional clanging sounds of their tools and the intermittent tapping of Topinr's legs against the rods provided the only accompanying noise to the blowing of Barrenscape's winds. So far, there had been no sign of Influxa.

"So... tell me about this... retrope..." Paran said distractedly, sifting through the propulsion unit's exposed innards.

"Retervope," Topinr corrected him, surrounded by thick blue clouds. The Silvered patted one of the structural rods suspiciously, then leaned around it to bring a tool up to an exposed crack. "Retervope's the surface matter on Ringscape, betervope's the surface matter on Barrenscape."

"You said that already."

"There's not much more to say. They're just leftovers, probably."

"Leftovers?"

Topinr's arms dropped as they waited for some quick-dry resin to harden. "There are stories that we tell our young."

"I'm listening."

The resin now dry, Topinr patted the rod again. It held. The Silvered moved on to the next. "Some say they're leftovers from an ancient war: weapons-debris. Don't ask me who was involved. Most stories say Barrenscape was first, then Ringscape."

"What sort of weapon creates so much debris?"

"Don't ask me."

"Did you have anything to do with it?"

"Me?"

"The Vaesians—" Paran cursed as a spark flashed from the propulsion unit. "It's fine," he mumbled. "It's fine."

Topinr tested another structural rod's strength. "There are many variants of the stories, but... I hope not. However, it's sometimes said that we used to be similar to the Administration. We were quire warlike." Topinr guffawed. "Can you imagine?"

"Is that so hard to believe?"

Topinr's guffaw died down. "As I said, the stories have many variants. All at least in some way contradictory."

"Don't you have actual records?"

"We've been in the Source a long time. It's impossible to know the exact truth."

"Any stories you... particularly like," Paran asked vaguely, still concentrating.

Topinr thought for a moment. "Some say we had machines to control the winds, once. Wouldn't that be nice? No more haze winds, unrestricted travel."

"And what happened to these machines?"

"They died long ago, of course." Topinr's guffaw returned.

"Perhaps the weather machines were once a part of your great, long-forgotten war, and they made this... retervope."

"Betervope's the stuff here, Paran, not retervope. And

perhaps. Some stories have it that way." There was a creaking sound as Topinr bent a support rod.

Distracted by the noise, Paran looked up from the propulsion unit. "You're strong," he observed.

"You can thank my cell-scales."

"Normal Vaesians can't do that."

"I'm not a normal Vaesian."

"Being Silvered allows you to do that?"

"Often, yes. The over-activation of our cell-scales means we're far stronger than ordinary Vaesians, especially when we're trained properly. We don't need suits like yours."

Paran stopped what he was doing and clasped the nearest rod, which was bent in the middle. He straightened it faster than Topinr had, before smugly returning to his work. "But they help."

"That was an easy one," Topinr insisted. "How long till you're done?"

"Not long to—" Another spark, brighter than before. Paran shouted something unintelligible. "We're... closer than when we started... ah! That wasn't so bad, actually—" He stopped as his faceplate slid across.

"What is it?" Topinr asked. "Influxa?"

Paran's eyes widened. "Unidirectional gravitational anomalies, and they're getting stronger."

"The Breaker's coming this way?"

"Erratically, but in this general direction, yes." Paran

created a small holo for Topinr. "It doesn't look like we have long."

"My concealment field is holding up."

"The Breaker has the ability to manipulate gravity, that's how it's supposed to see. Your concealment field doesn't mask gravity, does it?"

"No."

Paran changed the holo, expanding it to show the propulsion unit and surrounding structure. "It's going to be tight. Very tight." He exhaled, heavily. "At least you've repaired enough of the rods already. Nothing's going to fall off." The central unit expanded in the holo. "It's this that's the problem."

Topinr reached for a clump of muvaeyt. "What do you suggest?"

"We're nearly there." Paran cancelled the holo and his faceplate slid away. "Either we continue to work, or…" He looked around, despondently. "Well, that's our only option, to be honest. We can't hide anywhere, there's nowhere to go. The ship won't protect us against the Breaker…" He frowned. Topinr was grabbing yet more muvaeyt to chew. "You said the concealment field was holding?"

"It's possible I can create a projection of us – similar to a concealment field, but the reverse. Far more realistic than a holo."

"You told me you couldn't change visuals, and even if

you could, there's no reason to think that'd fool the Breaker."

"I can't, but with extreme quantities of muvaeyt, some have reported… look, if I *can* create a projection of us, as far as possible from our current position, that may distract the Breaker enough to change its course. It's worth trying."

"And here I was thinking you just liked the taste of that stuff."

"Sometimes, that is indeed the case." Topinr guffawed and rushed up the ramp to the cargo compartment, where the bulk of the muvaeyt was stored, and shouted back. "Paran, you continue with the repairs. Let me concentrate. Work as fast as you can."

"Understood."

"It has been…" The rest of Topinr's sentence was too quiet for Paran to hear.

"What was that?" Paran called out, his hands moving rapidly inside the central propulsion unit.

"Nothing, Paran," Topinr shouted. "Just be quick."

Chapter 11

Liberated Time, Liberation

Neither had said a word since leaving the main facility. Kera simply kept pace as Diyan directed them towards a vehicle, waiting innocuously in the distance. From afar, it appeared to be a skimmer, though once they reached it, certain differences became obvious – not least the delicately rippling base. The overall colouring was also not a homogenous grey, but a patchwork of different shades where new components had been welded against the old. Inside, the layout was typical of a skimmer: bare, mostly seating. Somebody waited inside, a Roranian of medium build, with a warm smile and long, scruffy hair. A single, central fold opened.

"Welcome back, Kera." The occupant's smile became an affectionate grin as he gestured for them both to enter.

Kera smiled back. "Good to see you again, Ilouden." Her voice was friendly, light.

"It's been too long."

"It has."

Kera settled opposite Ilouden. Diyan followed, sitting beside her. Once the central fold had closed, discrete holo controls appeared between Ilouden's hands and they moved off. There were no other vehicles nearby.

Kera looked around. "You've upgraded Osr's glazer."

"You figured it out. Diyan thought you would." Ilouden smirked. "Extended sensors; a few other pieces. Nothing to do with me though. I haven't been back to Sunsprit for some time, but the new controls are fairly straightforward to be honest."

"You've been away too?"

Ilouden chuckled, clearly surprised by Kera's lucidity. "In Fadin, for the last twenty years. Well, mostly Fadin. Doing my bit."

Kera continued to look about the glazer. "I'm sure you've been a great asset."

"I thought you might be a little... quieter, perhaps," Ilouden said, carefully.

"I've been quiet enough. It's good to be out."

"I'm glad to hear it. We all are."

Diyan nodded in agreement.

"And Osr?"

"Alive," Diyan said.

"Good." Kera's eyes sparkled. "How is he?"

"Ha! So you figured out that Vaesians cycle from female to male," Ilouden excalimed. "Diyan was right, again!"

Kera appeared bemused. "The majority were projected to cycle into males just after I was taken, and their cycles are long. I thought it was unlikely that they'd have cycled back already." She sat back in her seat, making herself comfortable. "So, how is Osr?"

"Seventy years older than when you last saw him, Kera," Ilouden said cheekily.

Diyan hummed in agreement. "And it shows. He's well... for the most part. But, sometimes, his memories fail. I don't know if he'll see the end of this cycle."

"Knowing Osr, he'll probably surprise us all. He'll have life in him yet," Kera said. "Is he still in Sunsprit?"

"Yes."

"It's the only place Silvereds are allowed anymore," Ilouden added, still focusing on the holo controls.

"There was a war..." Kera said. Both a statement and a question.

Diyan sucked in a heavy breath. "There was. And it was my—"

"It wasn't your fault, Diyan. It was inevitable, as soon as I attacked the influx network."

Diyan frowned. "I... I betrayed you, and it's taken me so long to find you. You should hate me, you should be angry for what I did, Kera..."

Kera took him by the hand. "You didn't betray me."

"I shouldn't have done it."

"I know why you did what you did."

"They took you."

"But they had Yena, and Paran too. You had no choice."

They stared into each other's eyes, unmoving. Even the air around them stilled.

A murmur from Ilouden shattered their focus. "I'm sorry. You both seem…" He looked up, apologetically. "I'm just glad to see you both together, again."

The glazer meandered slowly through the narrow channels leading to and from the main facility. A few crykels passed, the occupants barely paying them any attention, speeding to their destinations.

Ilouden looked back down. "I'll need to concentrate on this, just briefly…"

"Tell me about the war," Kera said, looking back at Diyan. "I didn't hear much inside the facility."

Diyan took a moment, his eyes growing dark. His jaw was clenched; his mouth flinched. Finally, he spoke. "It was brutal. The fighting was vicious, fierce, and… the Administration's ruthlessness surprised the Vaesians. It seems we Roranians have an unparalleled appetite for violence and… well, after some time, the Vaesians grew weary." He shifted his gaze. "Unveiling the special abilities hidden by the Silvereds and using them brazenly would have terrified the Administration, and pushed them to even greater extremes. It would have meant the

95

annihilation of one of us: our kind or theirs."

"The Vaesian Union capitulated?" Kera asked.

"For the greater part."

"But Osr disagreed, didn't he?"

Diyan nodded. "Osr only agreed not to fight. Sunsprit remains free. And while the Silvereds have kept their secrets, there are still rumours. But the Administration fears them more than ever before. Sunsprit has remained blockaded, officially due to that cell-scale outbreak they fabricated at the start of the war, but we all know that's not the reason. The city is surrounded by Administration military, on both the upperside and underside."

"The Administration can't be seen to have lost such a high-profile battle," Ilouden said.

"Especially one so close to Fadin."

"So, technically, the war's still ongoing." Ilouden motioned to the facility around them. "And now, Sunsprit's cut-off. Can't get in or out. In theory."

The glazer moved faster, having left the central hub of the facility. Large white walls lined their path, extending high up into the sky. Kera looked between them.

"There's something different about you both."

Ilouden's eyebrows raised in the middle. "What?"

"You're different…"

"Are we?"

Kera looked at Diyan. "What was in that vial you gave me?"

"Cell-scales," Diyan replied, puzzled. "How can you tell?"

Kera also appeared surprised, for the first time. "You've figured out how to use them on Roranians?"

"Not exactly," Diyan replied. "For us, they don't do anything except shield against tracking technologies."

"And they were in that vial?"

Diyan nodded. "Our lifespans, everything else, all unaffected. They don't draw power correctly from our bodies, so they stop working after a few days. Then, they break down, like they were never there. But in combination with the concealment fields that some Silvereds can project... well, you understand. They'll make it harder for the Administration to find us, if they even realise you're gone."

Kera looked amused, her eyes flickering over to the empty space beside Ilouden.

Diyan continued. "I scrambled all the facility's records from their control room. Less obvious than destroying them. It'll take the Administration a long time to figure anything out."

Quiet descended as the glazer picked up even more speed. The walls on either side of their route decreased in height, unveiling an empty expanse.

"You were being held in an Administration facility between Fadin and Potensein," Diyan explained.

"Potensein..." Kera mused. "Just a small settlement."

"Used to be. Now it's the second or third largest, after Fadin, depending on how you measure it." Diyan's tone became serious. "That facility can't be found on the main parts of the influx network. It's hidden. That's one of the reasons it took so long to find you. Gaining access was even harder."

"You had help, didn't you?"

Diyan nodded. "We did."

"From someone well placed within the Administration hierarchy. Someone with access…" She took little time to think. "Paran?"

"Yes."

"It was the least he could do," Ilouden muttered. "After betraying you."

"He never told anyone what he saw in Sunsprit," Diyan said, quickly. "None of those from the Anti-Vaesian Movement survived, and he never told the Administration about the Silvereds' abilities. If he had—"

"You never used to defend him," Ilouden said, darkly.

"He also let Osr live," Diyan said. "If he hadn't, the Vaesian Union would have fallen."

"Where are we going now?" Kera asked.

"A small settlement close to the edge," Diyan replied. "Jenrone."

"I've never heard of it."

"It's new."

"And then?"

"We visit the Alpuri, just the two of us."

"We've got trouble!" Ilouden blurted out. The holo between his hands expanded and filled the glazer. Their position was displayed, as were multiple other incoming vehicles: crykels and skimmers, in a triangular formation. "Diyan, I thought you said we'd have longer."

Diyan cursed. "I thought we would!"

"The facility observers must have realised and raised the—"

"No, it's not that." Diyan shook his head. "We're just unlucky, must be an irregular patrol. They probably haven't noticed us yet. The plan stays the same."

"Are you sure?"

"Yes. Are you ready?"

"Of course." Ilouden's hands fluttered rapidly across the holo controls. The glazer began to rumble. A sudden smell of muvaeyt thickening in the air.

"Come on, we don't have much time," Diyan said, rubbing his hands together nervously.

"One moment…"

"We're hidden." A Silvered with a deep voice appeared next to Ilouden, blue wisps streaming from his mouth.

"Perfect timing," Ilouden shouted, too entranced by the holo controls to look away.

He raised his hands, dragging the holo higher between them. Immediately, the glazer rose into the air. A moment later, the Administration patrol sped past beneath them, without giving any signs of alarm. Ilouden moved his arms to the side and the glazer swerved diagonally, over the thick white walls that lined their path. It arced back down to the ground, and they hurtled perpendicularly away from their previous direction of travel.

"Hespinr," Kera said, smiling widely.

Hespinr's hair was long, the silver colouring more pronounced. The yellow strip lining the bottom of his mouth had a new crack to the side, although it was mostly hidden by the blue wisps escaping as he spoke. "Welcome back, Kera."

"You've developed new abilities."

"I have." Hespinr's two sets of tensirs rippled excitedly. "Our scientists have made progress in understanding cell-scale abilities, as you've already been told."

"You can create a concealment field."

"It took a lot of practice."

"Pity you can't do the things some of the other Silvereds can do." Ilouden said, cheekily.

"Maybe I could practice on you." Hespinr guffawed as he put some more muvaeyt into his mouth. Immediately, thicker swirls of blue streamed into the air.

"And you've figured out how to make glazers fly," Kera mused. "I'm sure the Administration would like to know that for their skimmers."

"Only in short bursts," Diyan clarified. "The

Administration forgets that the Vaesians have been around for a lot longer, and they've been trying to reactivate Tapache's technologies too."

"Unfortunately, the Administration's also been working on other propulsion systems," Ilouden said. "There's direct competition."

"You'll be expected to debrief fully, Ilouden, once we're back in Sunsprit," Hespinr said.

"Likewise," Ilouden replied. "I want to hear what's been going on while I've been away."

Chapter 12

Legacy Companions, Top Official

Mericadal watched the Members in the Emox Room, observing them despite the privacy controls of the different compartments. Their bodies writhed in ecstasy. Embraced in the pure, unadulterated love of the emoxes. Mericadal focused on Member Slautina, relatively young and not long a Member, though she was now his most senior advisor.

"I want daily updates on Member Slautina – her output; her relationships and affiliations; her loyalty estimates, all of it," he directed the influx. "The same as I had for Member Vodal and the others."

"Yes, Mericadal."

Member Slautina's legs squirmed, her fingers curled. Glowing statistics overlaid the image, detailing her current status; highlighting her extreme satisfaction.

"She always uses her entire emox allowance… good. Increase it by five percent," Mericadal said.

"Should an explanation accompany the notification to Member Slautina?"

"She'll understand."

Three Members were in the central part of the room, two preparing to enter private compartments, one just having left. They were superficially discussing recent disruptions to Administration activities in Fadin: suspicious devices, of suspected Vaesian origin, had been found near important tether infrastructures.

Mericadal shifted, his attention dwindling. "Give me an update on the Triad Group's progress."

The influx displayed the Triad Group data to him.

"Good. Now, set Conceal to follow me. I'm not going far."

"Yes, Mericadal."

Mericadal cancelled the simulation and pushed himself up. He picked up a pack that had been left close by and ascended to the tower rooftop. Alone, aside from the noisy winds; thermal cannons; concealed influx terminals, for his own personal use; drones circling about in the skies, and a few other personal facilities. Mericadal smiled, pulling his facepiece up over his mouth and nose, ensuring the pack was tightly strapped across his back. He knelt down and placed a hand against the cold, flat roof surface, then propelled himself forwards, gasping as he leapt from the roof edge.

Air rushed against his body as he plummeted, a pair of

wings unfurling from the pack behind him. He arched his back, pulling up the front tips of the wings, levelling off his trajectory and re-ascending just before impact. Well-placed thermal vents aided his flight and he rose up, soaring high over the city. Still smiling to himself, he shifted direction, gliding over the hidden military shipyard.

*

Mericadal landed gracefully on his feet. He pulled down his facepiece as the wings receded.

"You're lucky," came a voice from behind him. "If Administration officials catch you gliding over the city, you'll be in trouble."

Mericadal turned around. Two young Roranians had just turned a corner and were strolling by, both barely past learning centre age. A girl and a boy.

Mericadal was unable to suppress his grin. "My mistake. I'll find somewhere more secluded next time."

"It's not like we've never done it, Emeni," the boy said to the girl, before glancing at Mericadal. "Nice wing-pack, by the way."

Emeni glared at her friend. "Not during the day. You're far more likely to get caught. And this place is about to get quite busy." She turned back to Mericadal. "You need to be more careful."

"I will be."

Mericadal watched them both walk off. He fixated on the entrance beside him. It was simple, unassuming. Just a typical Administration building façade. He waited for the entrance mechanism to ripple open, then stepped inside. An Administration official waited behind a counter, lazily tapping a small, obfuscated holo at chest height, glancing only briefly in his direction.

The official frowned, her eyes narrowing as she searched the holo. She stood up straight, head craned over. "You have full access... but..." The holo flashed red. Her eyes widened. "I'm sorry I can't find... your name doesn't seem to be attached. I can see you have full access, you must be a Member, but..."

Mericadal waited patiently as the panicked official flicked through screen after screen. Finally, he intervened. "Are you new?"

She half-nodded, her eyes continuing to search the holo. "I can't seem to find the associated details."

Mericadal leaned politely over and pointed to a section of the holo she had missed. "That means to let me through with no questions asked. It's often used when Members are in a hurry." He pushed himself back off the counter.

"You're in a hurry..." The words were caught in her throat.

"Just let me through and I'll sort myself out."

The gratitude in the official's demeanour was immediate. "Yes, Member. Right away."

Another entrance mechanism rippled up, and Mericadal stopped underneath it. "Make sure to undergo corrective training."

She nodded readily, barely able to meet his gaze. "I will. I'll schedule it for as soon as possible."

Mericadal smiled and she faltered again, taken aback by the change it caused in his appearance. He walked off, allowing the entrance mechanism to ripple closed.

He continued to access deeper layers of the facility, with more capable officials standing in wait. The last official held him up, only briefly, offering to store his wing-pack – which he declined – then raised the entrance mechanism for him. As he marched through, the official's surprise at the mechanism remaining open for a little too long, to accommodate Conceal, was audible.

Mericadal had entered a high-ceilinged room with clusters of Roranians dotted around. Some were talking quietly together, but most were engrossed in their work. Holos were expanded and dismissed, a few as tall as the room itself. Some physical screens were present too, depending on preference. Many other rooms stemmed off. Mericadal could see into one of them – there was a single plinth at its centre, with a grey, metal orb at the top. Two scientists observed it, tapping at small holo controls.

Mericadal cleared his throat. The nearby scientists looked up and one of them shuffled over to him, looking flustered. She held the fingers of one hand in the palm of the other, massaging them anxiously near her waist. "You're here, I wasn't expecting you."

"I know, Invira." He squeezed her shoulder deliberately.

She jolted, her hands separating. She gestured to the space they were in. "It's been over ten years since you came here. Do you want a detailed influx traffic report?" She hesitated, squinting her eyes. "Latency has been reduced by three percent, unauthorised access has been reduced to negligible levels and we've completely reorganised all of the legacy configurations..." She looked about. "I'll have all—"

"I didn't come for an audit."

"Something else?" Invira cocked her head. "Are there issues with Influxa? I met with Member Olana already and gave her an update for her own projects."

"You tell me," Mericadal countered. "Nothing is wrong as far as I know."

Invira shook her head, displaying relief, though she continued to fidget. "None of her drones have returned yet, so I assume all is well. Her decision-making processes should closely match allowed parameters for a long time, well over ninety-seven percent for a year or more." While Invira spoke, the curiosity of the surrounding scientists waned, and their focus returned to their work. "But, she is still classified as highly experimental, for many reasons. We'll need to analyse the results of this primary live testing."

"And you shall." Mericadal strolled further into the room.

Invira kept a half-step behind, though her short stature forced her to walk faster than Mericadal. They reached the end of the room and entered an offshoot passage to a smaller chamber. Upon reaching the chamber, an entrance mechanism rippled down behind them both, sealing them in. The chamber was spherical and empty.

"You've not been here for quite some time," Invira pointed out.

"You've reminded me of that already."

There was a faint hiss. The chamber vibrated and began to move, and a short while later, the walls became transparent. They were inside one of the city's great white domes. All around, hundreds of poles jutted vertically upward, each a few long strides apart, similar in scale to those that facilitated solitude gliding. Some were taller than others. A faint blue light pervaded everything. The chamber drifted forwards and upwards, nearing the top of the closest pole. Grey spheres were affixed along the pole's length, from the very top, all the way down to just above the bottom, where the base spread out and merged with the floor.

"You're certainly not starved of resources, are you?" Mericadal murmured.

"Not at all, we've been allocated everything we've

asked for. That's why the influx network has progressed to its current capacity," Invira replied quickly.

"You've come a long way since those neural conjoiner experiments, Invira. Before any of this existed. Who knew your fascination would turn out to be so important?"

Invira scrunched her face. "Those *failed* neural conjoiner experiments."

"Without which, none of this would have been possible." He glanced at her.

In the awkward silence, Invira began massaging her fingers again, her eyes searching about for something to latch on to. "Those neural conjoiner failures helped me develop the technologies to parse consciousness into streams—"

"Parsing without destruction."

"Preservation against our entropic tendencies."

"Yes," Mericadal whispered. "Very clever of you. Don't you think it all flowed so smoothly, as though Tapache had always intended it?"

"It's... possible." Invira scrunched her face again.

"The influxes and the unexpected emoxes were born." Mericadal chuckled. "And to think, we once discarded the emoxes, thinking them little more than waste."

"We wasted a great number of sleeping c-automs too," Invira said. "I do regret that."

Mericadal's sucked his teeth. "Regrettable, but also necessary. We needed to understand how to create the vessels capable of containing our parsed consciousnesses. Our crude attempts at reverse-engineering the c-autom repositories were crucial to that. You helped create the Administration, Invira. Without you…" He looked at an upcoming pole, which the chamber was drifting towards. Spheres were affixed along its length, the same as all the others. "Together, we ended the pointless fighting and wasteful vying for power. We created order." He sighed, deeply. "If only the parsing could have worked on the Vaesians, instead of us… but, the Administration and all it stands for is worth everything we've done, Invira."

Invira nodded, readily. "Without our past experiments, the Administration would probably have failed, like those before it."

"Perhaps Tapache knew exactly what we'd achieve." Mericadal looked animatedly at the chamber around them, his speech taking on a lighter tone. "Do you think this is what it felt like to be in a working skimmer – one that could actually fly?"

"This is a modified electro-boost platform, effectively," Invira said. "The levitative and propulsive abilities would fail outside the dome."

"I know that," Mericadal said. "But the freedom. Going wherever we wish. Any direction. No inertial effects, no concerns about the haze winds…"

"Yes… yes, I suppose it is a sufficient imitation in these circumstances. As a ship would be, too."

"The faster you improve the capabilities of the influx network, the sooner we'll be able to know for sure. The influxes can help us fix the skimmers. The influxes are the key to everything." Mericadal cleared his throat. "But I do note the progress you've made already. Lortein, Potensein and some of the other cities have access to the influx network in a manner almost comparable to Fadin. They have sky-factories; they have everything they want, for now." He patted the side of Invira's shoulder, ignoring yet another flinch. "Keep up the good work."

Chapter 13

Stubborn Companionship, Commander

Paran paused as his arms began to ache again, to the point where the suit actioned a relief and the soreness disappeared. A moment later, he felt fine. He continued working on the extirpation catalysts. Just a few more fixes were required before the ship would be operational. Some of the final repairs had taken a little longer than expected, but he had worked efficiently.

A while ago, he had altered various threshold limits of the suit's systems – increasing the levels of urgency required to bring matters to his attention – allowing him the peace to concentrate. He was no longer alerted to the swathe of potential *hazards*: suspicious valleys in the ground betervope; changing directions of the wind; mechanical creaks emanated by the ship. They were now simply monitored by the suit, only to be brought to his attention if his life was threatened. Auditory noise was also filtered, save for Topinr's voice, though so far, the

Silvered had left him to work undisturbed. The suit kept Paran's body cool and pumped soothing chemicals around its internal airflow.

Paran's helmet slid back and receded into the suit. "Topinr, we're nearly operational," he shouted. "Once the mechanical isolators have cooled, we're there. Just a slight calibration after that, nothing more." Paran walked around the base of the ship, surveying his handiwork with a grin. He glanced up the ramp at the cargo compartment. "Were you successful in creating that projection?"

There was no response.

"Topinr?" Paran frowned as his helmet resealed over his head. He delimited the threshold limits of the suit, returning them to normal, and searched for Topinr's position. The Silvered was not found. "Well done, Topinr, you've even fooled *my* sensors—"

He cut himself short, expanding the sensor range whilst conducting a chemical analysis of the air around them. The wafting clouds of muvaeyt were gone. The Breaker had already closed two-thirds of the distance between them. However, its path had deviated from all expected parameters. It was now strafing to the side... drawn towards something else.

"Topinr, you fool!" Paran looked up from the ship to the empty landscape, in the direction Topinr must have gone. He paused, setting his suit to the highest level of combat readiness, then ran swiftly. There was not much time.

*

Paran called into the empty landscape for Topinr, his faceplate transparent. He had already altered his suit's sensors to search for traces of muvaeyt, but as Topinr had informed him, its constituents decomposed quickly and could not be remotely detected.

"The Breaker's coming this way, Topinr, and I know you're near. You must be able to hear me!" An alert was projected into his vision. The gravitational anomaly most likely caused by the Breaker was not far off. Paran amplified his voice as loudly as the suit would allow. "Topinr!"

He continued to rush in the direction his suit had extrapolated would intersect Topinr's path, based on where the Breaker was being drawn to.

"Topinr!"

Finally, muvaeyt was detected. Paran turned around. Topinr stood there, a pack slung across his front, with part of its cover folded down, exposing an enormous muvaeyt clump.

"You should have fixed the ship and left, Paran," Topinr said.

"We can leave together." Paran gestured urgently for them to return back. Topinr did not move. "I'm not leaving you!"

"You are too stubborn, Paran."

"I don't care what you think, we're both going!"

"Even if it kills us both?"

"I'll kill you myself if you don't come with me!"

Topinr flexed his tensirs, then slowly obliged and began to move back in the direction they had come. "This is a mistake, Paran."

"Just hurry up."

They ran together. Paran turned to watch the Silvered's gait – Topinr's three legs pushed against the ground, one after the other, swinging his shoulders widely as he moved, his body more horizontal than vertical. His arms flailed loosely to the sides, alternately scraping the ground.

"What a strange sight we must make."

"You should have left me," Topinr said. "Instead, you're risking your life."

"Perhaps I still will, you're beginning to irritate me."

"I'm beginning to irritate you? What about those strange sounds you make? Why do Roranians always make—"

"We make strange sounds?" Paran interrupted.

"All the time."

"Have you heard yourselves? The constant guf—" Paran stopped and raised a hand to halt Topinr too. A warning had flashed across his vision. Another entity had been detected, separate to the gravitational anomaly of the

Breaker. Paran swiped angrily at the air. "Influxa's back, and she's coming straight for us."

Topinr's tensirs rippled. "How long?"

"Simultaneous with the Breaker, at our current position."

"Influxa intends to save you?"

"I assume so."

"Can we use her as a distraction?"

"Possibly…" Paran projected a simple holo scenario between them and altered various factors, muttering to himself.

Topinr watched, quietly chewing muvaeyt.

Paran gestured to Topinr to come closer. "Look, here's us, here's Influxa, and here's where the Breaker roughly is." It was a diminishing isosceles, with them at the extended vertex. The ship was also displayed. "If we make our way towards the Breaker now, and then…" He pointed to a specific section of the holo. "…here, you conceal us. Influxa will assume the Breaker's reached us. She'll have to change her trajectory and head straight for it. Then, when she reaches the Breaker, she'll realise we're not there, and she'll flee." He nodded, satisfied. "And when she flees, that'll draw the Breaker away, after her. We'll return to the ship and leave."

Topinr's tensirs fanned outwards, almost like a miniature bloom. "Okay then, Paran. We'll follow your plan." The Silvered pulled the cover tightly over his pack, which he shifted behind his back, and began to run off, back in the direction of the Breaker. "Come on then!"

Paran set off after Topinr. The suit's sensors continued to pick up gravitational disturbances ahead of them.

"We've not got long," Paran said, edging ahead of the Silvered.

"Then we'll know soon enough whether this plan of yours is going to work."

Again, Paran glanced at Topinr as they ran. "Is your speed a product of the cell-scales?"

"Maybe it's just me, Paran."

"I'm still faster."

"Take off that suit and then we'll see." Topinr accelerated to catch up with Paran, bringing them level.

"We'll do that another time. We need to hide. Are you ready?"

"Always." With surprising dexterity, Topinr reached back to open his pack with one arm, then delved inside with the other, retrieving a large clump of muvaeyt. "Although I've never tried creating a concealment field while running like this."

"You didn't think to mention that before?"

"I did think about it," Topinr replied, a guffaw escaping his widened lips as he scooped the blue substance into his mouth. Immediately, thicker trails streamed out.

"Now, Topinr!"

Topinr persisted in scooping yet more muvaeyt in as they slowed to a stop.

Paran checked his sensors. "Are we hidden?"

Topinr looked about. "Yes. How close is it? All I hear is wind."

"Very." Paran paused. "Influxa's taken the bait. She's adjusted her course, straight for the Breaker."

"Which is where, exactly?"

Paran directed a hand away from them. "If the Breaker continues to come this way, it'll probably be in your visual range just before Influxa intercepts it. Wait a moment."

"I'm waiting."

"Are you nervous?"

"Are you, Paran?"

Paran squinted into the distance, the suit magnifying faraway features. "There." He pointed. "Look there, you'll see it."

Topinr peered into the distance, middle leg planted forwards. "Where?"

"There!"

A light, yellow haze rising high into the air approached their direction. It soon became apparent that it was less of a gentle haze and more of a swirling vortex, a violent storm. Barrenscape's yellow debris sprayed out at the bottom, and curved up into the air at the top, like a circling fountain of water that scattered away as mist. It was as though the thick atmosphere had decided to viciously distort this particular column of itself.

"I thought it'd be different," Topinr said.

"You're not seeing the Breaker itself, there's too much debris around it."

"Maybe we need to get closer?" Topinr suggested.

"Be my guest, if you'd like to see what its gravity manipulations can do to you."

"I think the team you came to Barrenscape with already know that."

"And so will we if our plan doesn't work." Paran pointed away from the Breaker, into the air.

Topinr followed the line of his finger, waiting. A spherical object resolved into view. It shot through the sky and circled the Breaker's column of disrupted air in a wide loop, then sped off again, in the direction the Breaker had originally come from.

"The Breaker's stopped."

"Now what?" Topinr asked.

The Breaker vanished.

"It's gone," Paran replied.

"Excellent!" Topinr guffawed. "Your plan worked, Paran. Which way is it to the ship?" Topinr waited for an answer. "Paran?"

Paran swore loudly.

"What is it now?" Topinr asked.

"Influxa's changed course. She's headed towards our ship. I don't think she's detected it yet, but that's where they're going. I doubt it'll survive the Breaker's path."

"You're being humorous?"

"I'm not." Paran kicked at the ground.

"What now then? Should we make our way to your camp after all?"

Paran sighed. "I suppose that's all we can do... perhaps we can use the bait the team set up to draw in the Breaker—"

"Actually, that doesn't sound like a good idea, Paran."

"The bait is just a series of basic systems that project senseless signal noise. Not exactly sophisticated, but more powerful than I can generate with this suit. I might be able to alter them to broadcast a distress signal, in case anyone happens to fly nearby."

"Mightn't that draw the Breaker to us, Paran?"

"I've no clue, but we're out of options."

"Then lead the way." Topinr shoved a clump of muvaeyt into his mouth. "It can't get any worse than it is already, I suppose."

Chapter 14

Isolated Seclusion, Liberation

The glazer sped along with no other vehicles in sight – Roranian or Vaesian. Ilouden and Hespinr chatted amicably, with the former intermittently glancing at the control holo between his hands. For the most part, Diyan and Kera simply listened.

"Our scientists really believe the Source is undergoing some... whatever-you-want-to-call-it... a change of some kind?" Ilouden asked.

"The evidence is there," Hespinr replied. "Historical records show the daytime period used to be longer and more stable. Then, three thousand years ago, that was suddenly no longer the case. The units of time are minuscule, but important. The change is one way."

"But the scales... even if a million years passed, we'd barely notice it. Does it even matter?"

Hespinr guffawed. "The Modal Change Hypothesis does not rely on whether Ilouden notices it. It is based on observation. Even the Administration is working on it, we know that for a fact. They call it the Second State Hypothesis."

"The Tugs really need to start talking, or we're going to be in for a lifetime of boredom!" Ilouden sucked his teeth. "The daytime has become infinitesimally smaller over three thousand years, and that bothers us? There are far greater mysteries to unravel!"

His words elicited a wry smile from Kera.

"It is important," Hespinr argued, motioning to the landscape around them; to the featureless sky. "Do not forget where we live. This place is a mystery, but everything about it must be connected: the Haze Rings, Ringscape, Barrenscape, the probability wave of death, the winds, the daytime, the light—"

"Yes, yes. But there must be other areas of research that will illuminate the nature of the Source more quickly." Ilouden sniggered at his own joke.

"Ilouden, you're aware the daylight is a function of the Haze Rings," Hespinr said. "You also know, as does everyone else on Ringscape, that the Haze Rings are an unimaginably vast collection of hyperfine loops rotating extremely fast. They slice almost everything that tries to pass through. Destruction to nothingness. Those hyperfine loops are what keep us trapped here. So, don't you think that all of their properties should be examined, in great detail? It is of paramount importance that we understand the light they generate."

"When you put it like that, of course." Ilouden sighed excessively. "But I'd rather focus on the barrier itself, not the light, which is just a by-product."

"Just a by-product." Hespinr guffawed loudly. "We only know about the existence of the hyperfine loops, their ordering, the supermerge patterns, and all the rest of it, from the light they produce. The light is the key."

"You're certainly a lot more interested than you used to be," Ilouden argued.

"I've been learning a lot," Hespinr said.

"Really?"

"And anyway, my point, before you changed the discussion, was that the Modal Change Hypothesis tells us we're entering a new phase of operation for the Source."

"Meaning?"

"The Source is changing."

"Meaning?" Ilouden repeated, smiling cheekily. "Ah! We're nearly there." He gestured ahead. "Probably time to make yourself scarce, Hespinr."

*

No one greeted them upon their arrival in Jenrone. Instead, floating holo arrows appeared at the sides of the glazer, bobbing up and down in the air, lining their path. Ilouden's attention darted between the holo at his hands and the outside.

"And… we're done!" he said, cheerily. "We've been accepted onto the *skimmer trail*." Kera looked at Ilouden and frowned, so he elaborated. "Places like Jenrone are reached from the cities by designated skimmer trails; they've only minimal connections to the influx network for basic skimmer guidance." He craned his neck and gestured back along the trail. "This one actually goes all the way to Fadin, if you follow it long enough. The trails are controlled by the influxes, but with such tenuous connections, they're a little easier to fool." Ilouden looked at the controls again. "And more good news – we're the only ones here."

"There's nothing here at all," Hespinr said, his voice coming from the empty air beside Ilouden.

"Not quite. Give it a moment," Ilouden corrected. They waited. "Three buildings, coming up ahead." As the winding trail took them closer, the three buildings began to resolve in the thick atmosphere.

"I thought Jenrone was a settlement," Kera said.

"It is and it isn't," Diyan replied. "There's no permanent population, just some who come for temporary visits. More places like this are being created all the time."

"Why?" Hespinr asked.

"They're attractions," Ilouden said. "Obviously."

"What's attractive about this place?"

"Didn't you and Diyan make this plan together?" Ilouden quipped.

"Hespinr dealt with getting us through Sunsprit's barricade, which wasn't easy," Diyan answered. "And he's here to provide concealment wherever we need it. I selected Jenrone." He looked at Hespinr's empty seat. "What Ilouden means by attraction, is that places like Jenrone are far enough from an edge that you're safe and comfortable, if you're Roranian, but close enough that the odd flip reaches you about once a day. Apparently, people come and experience the flips for fun, like solitude gliding."

"That doesn't sound fun," the Silvered answered.

"I agree." Ilouden chuckled. "If visitors are impressed by single flips, I'd like to see them survive a day in Sunsprit!"

"Sunsprit will take you some time to become re-accustomed to as well," Hespinr cautioned.

"Nonsense."

"Don't forget how many Administration spies I've accompanied through my city. Many returned, also thinking they were prepared. None were."

"It's my city too, Hespinr," Ilouden said confidently. "The flips won't bother me."

"If you say so."

"We're isolated in Jenrone," Diyan continued, ignoring them. "That's its most important feature. No one's going

125

to come looking for us here aside from the ship picking us up in a few days. Ilouden's also helped us divert some of the Administration's attention in Fadin, as an extra precaution to keep them busy."

"What did you do?" Kera asked.

Ilouden smirked. "Nothing much, just placed a few imitation Vaesian items near key city infrastructures. Feeding the Administration's paranoia about sympathisers, the usual."

The holo arrows ended at an empty spot just a short distance away, set before the first of three buildings. Each looked the same – sturdy cuboids, single-levelled, no obvious windows or any physical openings aside from a single entrance. They were aligned in a neat row, with just enough space between for a typical skimmer.

The glazer stopped at the end-point. Diyan glanced at the seat beside Ilouden. "I'd stay concealed for now, Hespinr. We can't be too careful about any external sensors. I doubt there's anything, but let's not take any risks."

"Of course."

The glazer's central fold opened and Ilouden stepped out. A small, flat plinth rose to hip-height in front of him. "How exciting," Ilouden gasped. "A network proxy. Anyone else want to try?"

"Just get on with it, Ilouden," Hespinr growled. "You know you're the only one with an Administration alias."

Ilouden slapped his palm against the plinth's surface. It chimed, and when he removed his hand, a small, simple physical screen demanded certain inputs. The others exited the glazer as Ilouden entered the information.

"All done?" Diyan asked.

"It's telling us to wait," Ilouden said, raising his hand. "I believe there's a little trick about to happen." He dropped his hand. "Here we go!" A fist-sized, white holo sphere appeared above the plinth, which receded into the ground. The holo sphere flickered green, then sped to the entrance of the nearest building and vanished. "That's our allocated accommodation."

They walked to it. The entrance slid to the side and closed once they were inside. The room was simple and low-ceilinged. Its contents included a circular table with some chairs, some other battered furniture and a food dispenser. Non-interactive holos were projected into each of the room's corners, displaying images of the outside – the light was dimming, the day coming to an end. There were no partitions, aside from a small screened-off washing area.

Hespinr reappeared, amidst a cloud of blue that dissipated into the air. His shoulders were slumped, his legs a little more splayed than usual. He moved economically. "It'll do."

"Not a good place to jump," Ilouden said, eyeing the low ceiling. "Hespinr, are you okay?"

"I just need to sleep," came the reply. "Concealment fields aren't easy."

"Well, there you go," Ilouden said, motioning to some of the furniture. "Apparently, our civilisation used to call them flairfolds, or something like that. Yet more interesting but useless information that Tapache left for us about our past. They're teaching more and more of our history in the Administration's learning centres. Some in Fadin have even returned to using the old words."

"Flairfold or floor, I'll rest on it." Hespinr went to the nearest and grunted. The flairfold was far too small, they all were. His legs splayed further outwards and he sunk to the ground, straightening them once his top half was prone. His body visibly slackened.

Ilouden shook his head. "Never gets old seeing a tired Vaesian fall asleep, does it? They need it so much more than we do." He yawned loudly. "I didn't realise concealment fields were so tiring to generate."

"More so if they don't come naturally," Diyan said. "But, Hespinr insisted on coming. He'll be fine." Diyan pointed outside. "Did you set the glazer—"

"Yes, yes," Ilouden said, rolling his eyes. "I remember your instructions. It was easy to figure out, the automated navigational capabilities have basically been copied from the Administration's skimmers, just without the influx component. Bit riskier travel-wise, but I'm sure it'll make the journey just fine. Osr must have been very upset to have his glazer changed so much."

"He wasn't," Diyan replied. "He's too old to use it anymore. And there are plenty others with a use for it."

"Well, the glazer's set to leave in the morning anyway, for the next location it's required at. Anything queries it, it'll appear to need some repairs." Ilouden ambled over to the food dispenser.

Kera turned to Diyan as she gestured towards Ilouden. "He's become quite knowledgeable, hasn't he?"

"Ilouden's been in Fadin for a long time now, helping maintain our presence," Diyan said. "He's had to learn fast."

Ilouden strode back over, holding three food packets, stifling another yawn. He passed one to each of them and opened his own. "I have actually left Fadin, too, a few times. I just haven't been anywhere that wasn't under the rule of the Administration. Potensein, Horendein, a few others. Nowhere that far though."

"You must be excited to return to Sunsprit," Kera said.

"I am. When Diyan contacted me with the plan to help free you, I thought it was about time I returned." Ilouden looked at Diyan. "That's still also part of the plan, isn't it?"

Diyan nodded. "Once the ship comes here, we'll take it and drop you off just outside Sunsprit, and you'll be able to pass through a weak point in the barricade, concealed by Hespinr."

"It's a pity he can't conceal the entire ship. Then you

could take us all the way back."

"He'll do just fine. And trying to take the entire ship back past the blockade would be too risky."

"So then you'll continue on your way?" Ilouden lifted the food packet up, tipping the last morsels into his mouth.

"To the Alpuri, yes."

Kera's brow furrowed. "Doesn't Osr want me in Sunsprit, after all this time?"

"He does, very much," Diyan replied. "As do the rest of the council. But we'll go there after the Alpuri. It was Paran's condition of helping free you, he wouldn't budge."

Ilouden yawned again and looked at the two of them apologetically. "Unlike Hespinr, I'm actually going to use one of the flairfolds. I'll leave you both to... discuss things." He walked over to the flairfold adjacent to Hespinr and slumped down, face first. A low snore ensued.

Diyan moved over to the table, pulling a chair out for Kera and then himself. "Let's talk."

Chapter 15

Time of the Roranians, Top Official

Mericadal watched the sky-factory looming closer in the darkening skies, whirring grills moving endlessly across its surface. The capsule took them closer, along the tether.

One of the guards coughed politely. "We're nearly there."

Mericadal's gaze did not waver as the capsule was swallowed whole, its transparent walls surrounded by complete darkness, a pervasive rumbling taking hold. A dim yellow light appeared from above, running down the capsule's sides. They stopped.

"Difficult to tell, isn't it?" Mericadal said. "These hard-gravity emulators... it's as though we're still on Ringscape."

"Yes," the guard who had coughed replied.

A side of the capsule slid open and Mericadal stepped out. An official, who was waiting on the platform surrounding the capsule, took a step forward. A bank of subordinates stood back in a line.

"Welcome to Sky-Factory Seven."

Mericadal acknowledged him. "The new emulators are sufficient?"

"More than sufficient, they're a significant upgrade to the soft-gravity emulators." The official grinned. "You don't realise, until you realise, if you understand me." The grin evaporated as Mericadal's expression remained unchanged. "The trial period is almost over, then we'll submit our report... we think they'd be a useful addition to the Administration's ships."

"They're resource-heavy."

"They are, somewhat, yes..." The official wiped a bead of sweat from his forehead.

"But it's progress, isn't it?"

"Yes, that's true. I should introduce myself—"

"Captain Guran, where do we start..."

Captain Guran appeared startled. "Ah! Yes, of course. I'll show you around, personally."

"Good. I have greatly anticipated this visit. I look forward to seeing what you are about to show me."

They set off, leaving the silent bank of subordinates, with the guards from the capsule keeping a few paces behind. Mericadal allowed a little small talk. They visited the updated input tanks, the expanded repurposing and fabrication chambers, and many other improved areas of Sky-Factory Seven. Then, Captain Guran took Mericadal through to the crew compartments, showing him a selection of the cabins where the crew slept, ate, and spent their leisure time.

Mericadal rested a hand on one of the food dispensers. The crew were all engaged in their shifts, no one else was in the galley aside from the two guards. "We have plans for the sky-factories, Captain Guran. All of them."

"We can increase processing efficiency, reduce fabrication times…" Captain Guran trailed off upon noticing Mericadal's disinterest.

"Do you know anything about our Great Ship, Captain Guran?"

"Our Great Ship?"

"Yes."

"I… I learned like everyone else about how Tapache sent us; that the ship was destroyed—"

"Do you know anything about *life* aboard the Great Ship?"

"Life?"

"How they lived, what they did, how they prepared for Tapache's quest?"

"Some things, yes, but…"

Mericadal stared at the galley's pristine walls; the permanent seating benches; the fixed tables. "I used to think we were better than them. That we were different, matured. I disregarded all the stories my parents used to tell me." He clicked his tongue. "I used to think *they* were

133

unworthy." He gestured to the floor, "Down there, on Ringscape, we scrabble around in the dust, but we're really no closer to understanding the Source. Our minds have become closed. That's going to change."

Captain Guran's eyes darted about, following Mericadal's gaze across the galley, flicking briefly across his face and then to the food dispenser. "I've spoken to a survivor... from our Great Ship. It was a while ago now, but..."

Mericadal shook his head, a flash of irritation revealing itself. "Those who survived have mostly forgotten, believe me. I've spoken with most of them. Their memories are too long. They've placated themselves in complacency. It's up to us to remember again, to resolve it all." Mericadal paused. Captain Guran opened his mouth to speak, but Mericadal continued, seemingly oblivious. "Like I said, we have plans for the sky-factories. More upgrades, no need for any permanent features." He pointed at the tables and benches. "Furthermore, considerable resources will be expended. Removal of the tethers for instance—"

Captain Guran's eyes widened. "But the influx connections..."

Mericadal smiled. "You'll still have them."

"Is that possible, without physical conduits? The tethers are required, I believe—"

Mericadal tsked, dismissing Captain Guran's concern.

"Anything's possible. We're going to remove the tethers and we're going to unchain the sky-factories. We'll create our own Great Ships, and all that we've done, our internal quarrels, our battles against those decrepit Vaesians... it'll all be forgotten." He rested a hand on Captain Guran's shoulder. "You should be excited. This is what Tapache wanted for us."

Captain Guran swallowed. "I'm honoured to be entrusted with this plan."

"It's always been the plan, we just forgot." Mericadal took his hand off Captain Guran's shoulder. "We're long-lived, Roranians. It's a gift, but it's also our greatest undoing. We've had time to fester. Some even think..." He grimaced. "Some even believe that Tapache lied to us, about everything."

Captain Guran did his best to appear incredulous. "The fools," he hissed.

Mericadal waved Captain Guran's words away. "Here, in the Source, we operate as an extension of Tapache, as a protrusion of its will. I do admit, the idea of our compulsion to do Tapache's bidding has always struck me as suspicious. It's obvious the promises it made to us long ago introduced a compulsory element. We must do as Tapache directed, or else it will not honour its promises. Captain Guran, I can understand why some have come to view its intentions with mistrust, but..." He clenched his fist. "Tapache knew us, it still does – we must assume that, in as much as we can hope to understand the mind of a Wanderer craft-lect. The annexes, the competitions, the purpose. For each and every single Roranian, it devised incentives and encouragement. Now, I'm not confused about where that puts us within Tapache's plans, because that certainly doesn't mean we're special. Tapache sent many different species to the Source, we know that, but they didn't survive like us. They didn't thrive like us. We have a chance to win this contest, and don't think for one moment that a competition isn't exactly what this is. We cannot afford to squander our opportunity."

Captain Guran shuffled awkwardly. "Yes, we… must do what Tapache intended, because that is the only thing we *can* do for ourselves, and in as much as we can… we must do what we must because…" He trailed off weakly.

Mericadal cocked his head, looking genuinely confused. "Captain Guran, it's up to us to succeed. You and I, and the rest of the Roranians. We cannot fail." He exhaled, slowly. "Remember what is at stake. Remember the promises made, the chance Tapache has given our species. All else is irrelevant. It's rare that anything gets through the Haze Rings, and even rarer that anything gets through undamaged. The lattice wars outside do not impact us, they've occurred for uncountable millennia. All of them wonder what's going on inside the Source, and the answer is us. We're winning. This is the time of the Roranians."

Chapter 16

The Dig, Commander

They ran as fast as Topinr could manage. Every now and then, Paran projected a holo of their trajectory for Topinr to glance at.

An oddly shaped mound of betervope was suddenly brought to Paran's attention – ringed in blue. The type of danger posed was not identified, though avoidance was strongly advised. Paran barged Topinr out of the way and they fell to the ground together. Topinr rose to his feet in an aggressive stance, legs curved inwards, his body a central axis with both arms directed at Paran, tensirs rippling.

Paran raised his hands amicably. "You were about to hit that." He scraped his foot across the ground, revealing a small brown corner.

Topinr relaxed. "It's Vaesian technology," Topinr said. "The grooves across the surface..." He bent over to peer closer, wiping some debris away. One side of the brown corner continued, revealing a long edge about the length of a Vaesian arm, stopping at another corner.

"Topinr... I think..." Paran said.

"It's the top of a docking ring." Topinr stepped back and trawled his tensirs through the ground. An extended surface was revealed. Paran's suit projected a holo extrapolation – a docking ring floated ethereally between them.

"I can't scan it properly," Paran said. "But the suit's data archives agree. It is a Vaesian docking ring. And it's covered in the same ground matter as your cities in Ringscape. Retervope, not Barrenscape's betervope."

"Yes, it's..." Topinr paused. "I hadn't realised... I'm so used to seeing these in Ringscape, but you're right. It is retervope, not betervope."

"Why would that be?"

"I don't know."

Paran grunted. "Do you dump your old docking rings here?"

"No. Why would we, and how? We haven't had ships for so long." Topinr lowered himself, his body resembling a squashed tripod. He ran his tensirs along the docking ring's surface. "We use retervope coatings to block prying sensors – good dampening properties."

"I know," Paran said. "The Administration wants to do the same but believes it'd look weak to copy you."

"But betervope has the same properties, so I'm not

sure why… it doesn't make sense. And either way…" The Silvered glanced at Paran. "This shouldn't be here." He shifted, digging more of the docking ring structure out of the ground. "Why bother taking a docking ring here, and why cover it with retervope?"

"And why bother at all when the docking ring's buried anyway?" Paran asked.

"A not insignificant effort," Topinr mused.

"To bury something this large, this deep, can't have been easy. Those sub-cutters, the machines my team had to dig into the ground, they had quite some power behind them." Paran glanced anxiously around. "Unfortunately, we're not going to have the luxury of finding out, Topinr. I'm detecting Influxa and the Breaker on the periphery of my sensors. They're not coming directly towards us, but that could change at any moment. We need to go." He began to move off.

"Wait," Topinr said, still squatting. "What if this one's still operational?"

"What?"

"Our docking rings in Sunsprit and our other cities are just relics, but, they used to work. There's a chance…"

"Topinr, even if it is operational, what difference does that make? We don't have a ship and we're not trying to dock. Come on, let's go." He waved for Topinr to hurry up.

"Do you know how they work?"

"We don't have the time for a lesson on—"

"Paran," Topinr spoke quieter. Paran's suit increased the auditory volume. "What if there's... a structure beneath the surface, here. Somewhere we can hide from the Breaker."

Paran burst out laughing. His faceplate slid away. "A structure? Like what, a settlement? Come on, Topinr. We need to leave, we don't have the time."

Topinr continued to speak quietly, almost to himself, whilst staring at Paran. "Our ships would dock on top of these rings, and upon doing so, an aperture at the base would open. Crews would then disembark down, through the aperture. I've never seen it myself, but—"

Paran froze. "Down?"

"Yes."

"Beneath us?"

"Is there any other *down*?"

"You're saying there might be something buried beneath us, right here?"

"It's a possibility."

"It would have to be shallow, nothing goes deep."

"It could be somewhere to hide."

"But how would we access it? We'd need a ship. And I assume this docking ring needs a power source."

"Docking rings are passive. Simple; mechanical. The open ends are forced together, that's how it works."

"But... pushing the ends together... isn't that a glaring

hole in your defences?"

Topinr guffawed. "According to the stories, we used to set traps inside. If an enemy wanted to enter, it was up to them."

"Traps? And you think this is a better option than going to my camp?"

"They're just stories, Paran. Anyway, that's not the bad news."

"What is, then?"

"Well, there's no way we're going to be able to apply mechanical pressure and both enter the aperture."

"We don't have time. You don't actually think we're going to try and enter—"

"You're going to have to stay here, or rather, your suit is."

"Topinr, I've not agreed to anything."

"I believe your suit will have more than enough enhanced—"

Paran raised his arms wide in exasperation. "We'll be completely defenceless. This suit's the only thing we have."

"Either your suit stays out here and helps us enter, by keeping a constant force on the docking ring, or we take our chances out there, with your old camp. It's up to you. But, if I'm wrong and nothing happens, we could just move on. It won't take long to find out."

Paran swore. "What do we do then?"

"First, we need to excavate the docking ring as much as we can."

They dug away at the betervope from the top of the docking ring. Their work became harder once they were about an arm's length down and they were forced to stop. The docking ring appeared to be in perfect condition. Topinr showed Paran where to apply pressure.

"Here," Topinr said, placing one set of tensirs on one side of the docking ring, and his other set on the other side. His three legs splayed out. "I suggest you grip like this, and pull."

Paran checked the sensor data. Influxa and the Breaker were no closer radially, although the Breaker was still undoubtedly following the Administration's influx network proxy. "Okay. I'll exit the suit if an aperture opens. Once we're inside... or down, or wherever this docking ring leads, I'm setting the suit to leave on a tangential path to Influxa and the Breaker as fast as it can. That may give us some more time." He paused. "What if we're stuck down there?"

Topinr guffawed. "Then we're certainly no worse off, Paran."

"Fine." Paran moved into position and began pulling both ends closer. A moment later, beneath Paran, the betervope began to sink, causing the ground to depress.

"It worked," Topinr said softly, watching the hole form. He twisted his head to peer down.

"My sensors can't tell me anything about what's down there." Paran gave the command, and the suit rippled open at the back. He cautiously pulled himself out, holding onto the suit and swinging across to the side, ensuring he did not fall into the hole. He stood at the perimeter, beside Topinr, in his black regwear undersuit. "I haven't felt these winds since I first came here."

"Feeling a little more exposed now, Paran?" Topinr asked, staring down at the hole.

Paran pulled his regwear facepiece up over his mouth and nose, then crouched down. "Just remember, if anything goes wrong, you're the one who wanted us to do this. Ready?"

"Yes, I am. I'm very ready."

Chapter 17

Nested Concerns, Liberation

The room was dark – the lighting extinguished everywhere except where Kera and Diyan sat. Diyan's elbows were on the table. His body shifted about, his hand and facial movements giving life to his words. Ilouden's intermittent snoring was the only other sound.

"The Administration called you a Vaesian spy, at the start. They didn't name you directly, but they were talking about you. They said the attack on the influx network was proof that the Vaesians were plotting to seize the Roranian cities, to invade. They hinted the Silvereds were behind it all. Everything became muddled, rumours circulated, all justifications for what came next – their war against the Vaesians."

"And we... all the Roranians just let it happen?" Kera asked.

Diyan shrugged. "Some didn't know, many didn't understand. Same as with the fighting. Much of it was hidden from ordinary Roranians, and the records still are. And now... with the Administration controlling everything, the influx network, transport, manufacturing, the learning centres, it can create any history it wants. In many instances, it's made to seem like the Vaesians simply handed control of their cities over to the Administration, in recognition of the Administration's superiority. But really..." Diyan hung his head. "It's all because of what I did. If I hadn't betrayed you—"

"I told you already," Kera said, grabbing his hands, her countenance soft. "You didn't betray me, and the Administration planned the war long before you arrived. We were just the catalysts."

"At first, the Administration questioned me. I gave them nothing, I kept what you told me secret, after you'd seen whatever it was that you saw in the dummy node. They didn't seem to care anyway, they had you, after all. They didn't even ask about your augmentations – I'm not sure they knew anything about them. And I was just incidental, left to my own devices. An honest citizen of Fadin." He laughed bitterly.

"I never told them anything either."

"Even when they tortured you?" Diyan whispered. "I know. Paran told Osr. The Administration didn't know what to do with you. Over time, they began to see you as a closed mystery, and they forgot about you."

Kera's hands moved to the sides of Diyan's face,

pulling his head up. Tears rolled down his cheeks. "You did so well, Diyan. I knew you'd come for me. Everything happened as it needed to." She shook him.

Diyan clenched his jaw. "It took me seventy years."

"I mean it." She brought their heads together. "It couldn't have happened any other way."

"It took so long."

"And now, it's over, in the blink of an eye." She gently pulled her head back. "So, you were an honest citizen of Fadin, but you didn't stay?"

Diyan cleared his throat. "I left for Sunsprit. I managed to sneak in before the barricade tightened."

"Have all the other Vaesian cities really fallen?"

"Except two, but they're powerless anyway, as good as controlled by the Administration."

"Only Sunsprit remains free?"

"Only Sunsprit."

"How is it there?"

The hint of a smile appeared at the corner of Diyan's mouth. "Osr is in charge, still, for as long as his health holds."

"And the Tugs?"

"Hidden. The Administration knows nothing about them."

"Echoes?"

Diyan frowned. "Echoes?"

"Echoes of Gravity."

"Ah. Still there. Same as the Tugs." His frown deepened. "Is that important to you?"

"To everything." She stared intensely into his eyes. Diyan opened his mouth to speak, but Kera continued. "Did you tell Osr about what I said — from when I activated the dummy node?"

Diyan's eyebrows upturned in the middle. "You mean, that the Source is just one big machine? That there's something in here with us, hidden, and by the sounds of it, it doesn't want us here? And it's something so terrible it scared you beyond... beyond anything I've ever seen? That the probability wave of death doesn't actually kill machine-lects, but it stores them somewhere? That we need to destroy the Source?" He slowed down, taking deep breaths to control his shaking. "That there might be a way out?" He interlocked his fingers, thumbs pushing against each other. "I think about what you said all the time, Kera. All the time. But no, I didn't say anything. Not to Osr, not to the Administration, not to anyone. Ever. In the time that's passed, I've even doubted I heard you correctly."

"You didn't tell them anything?" Kera seemed relieved.

"Even if I'd wanted to, who would have believed me? No, once I was in Sunsprit, I focused on other things. Like finding where the Administration was keeping you and getting you out."

Kera took her time to respond. "And Paran really

helped?"

"He did. He established contact with us. With the Silvereds. I think... he felt the same as me, once things had... settled. Now, he hates the Administration, maybe even more than me. The things he told us, about what he had to do, and... and about the influx network, how it's possible—"

"I know," Kera interrupted. "I know all about the influx network."

"Why didn't you ever say anything?"

"What good would it have done? And I won't lie to you, Diyan – we needed it to decode the dummy node, remember. We needed the cognitive capabilities of thousands of influxes, all contributing their own parts of the analysis." Despite her words, her lip curled uncomfortably. "Nothing else would have worked." Ilouden shifted in his sleep, and a snore was distorted into a more high-pitched wheeze. Kera was unable to stifle a smile. Her face became serious again. "Have you seen Paran?"

Diyan folded his arms across his chest. "No. I've not spoken with him directly either. Not since they came for you, in Fadin. Neither of us tried to make contact with each other before I left for Sunsprit. But... we'll be meeting him, when we reach the Alpuri."

"Yena?"

An involuntary grimace flickered across Diyan's face.

"I ignored her attempts at contact. I was too ashamed. She left Fadin a long time ago too."

"Where to?" Kera's voice elevated slightly.

"To the Alpuri, Paran believes. That's why we're going there. We're all going to be reunited. That's what all this was for. I know there are things you aren't telling me, Kera, even now, but we need to be together. The four of us – you, me, Paran, and Yena."

Kera sniffed, her lips tightened. "Diyan, the dummy node did show me things, important things, and I do want to tell you…"

The building rattled around them and their bodies shook, accompanied by a yelp of surprise. Ilouden had awoken and was disconcertedly looking about. Hespinr had also awoken and watched him, guffawing loudly from the floor.

"Ah," Kera said. "I'd almost forgotten what a flip felt like."

"It's nothing like some of the ones in Sunsprit, the complete field reversals, but it's a reminder."

"Diyan," Kera reached forward to place a hand on his knee and spoke very quietly. "We can't go to the Alpuri, not yet. There's something we need to do first. We need to…" Her face contorted, as though she did not want to finish. She barely spoke above the slightest whisper. "We need to find the Breaker and bring it to Sunsprit."

"You can't be serious!"

"I—" Kera was on her feet just as a thunderous crash rocked the room, far more forcefully than the flip moments before. Rubble fell from the ceiling, landing between the table and the flairfolds. A large, dark figure dropped down from the night sky, easily a quarter taller than Hespinr and twice as wide. It had enormous, bulbous muscles that rippled across a pitch-black body. Light from the room's holos glistened across it as though it was water. It stood still, only its large head twisting around.

Before Diyan had time to rise from his chair, Kera was in front of the figure. Hespinr was also up, making his way over, but Kera raised her hand to stop him. Ilouden scrambled to his feet, eyes wide in shock. The figure focused on Kera, craning its neck over her, stopping when its face – smooth, with faint imprints of Roranian-like features – was just a hair's width from her own. Kera stared defiantly into the two empty recesses where eyes should have been.

Hespinr vanished, the faint smell of muvaeyt filling the air. Diyan and Ilouden crouched into low combative stances and edged closer.

"Who are you?" Kera asked.

The figure gave no response.

Without warning, Kera spun around and slammed the back of her elbow against its head. Despite its enormous size, it staggered backwards and crashed violently against the side of the room, dropping motionless to the floor with a heavy thud. Its body shimmered and its muscles spasmed, though it remained down. Hespinr appeared nearby, charging towards it.

"No, Hespinr, leave it! We need to go, now!" Kera commanded.

Hespinr stopped.

"What is it?" Ilouden shouted, following Kera's order and moving to the entrance. "Far too big to be a Fendari, but they're the only—"

"A Nesch," Kera stated, simply, gesturing for them to hurry.

"A Nesch! From where, the lattice?"

"Are you sure?" Hespinr asked as they filed out. "That's not what I expected."

"Yes, that's how it's chosen to appear. We're lucky, I think it's still learning." She exited last and the entrance sealed behind them.

Ilouden swore. "We're too late, the glazer's gone." He gestured hopelessly to the empty landscape.

"We haven't got any transport, our ship's not coming for days," Diyan said. "We'll have to barricade ourselves inside one of the other buildings."

"Barricade ourselves? That thing broke through the ceiling!" Ilouden replied, looking around. He pointed animatedly up ahead. "There, look!" A lone skimmer was coming towards them.

Chapter 18

Contained Abilities, Top Official

Mericadal dived forwards, somersaulting through the air and landing on the outstretched palm of a gloved hand. He straightened his arm and pushed off, spinning around to land comfortably on his feet, legs bent. Commander Miren rushed at him, jumping and propelling her body horizontally to drive both feet against his chest. He moved to the side, then drove his fist into her leg, just above the ankle. There was an audible crack from the broken bone. She landed, skidding on the floor. Her suit helmet receded as she screamed in pain.

Mericadal strolled over and extended a hand. His faceplate shimmered to transparency. "You fought well. Keep the suit on for the remainder of the day, it will numb the pain and reduce your recovery time."

Commander Miren clamped her mouth shut, scrunching her face tightly. A moment later, her expression relaxed. She took his hand and accepted the leverage as he pulled her to her feet. More crunching, but the look of pain was gone.

"Thank you. I've never felt… such power. To think, Commander Paran has had all this at his disposal, all this time. I could get used to this." She flexed one of her hands, smiling at it lopsidedly. "I could crush a Vaesian horde all by myself. This would have made my work a little easier, all that time ago… and more efficient." A holo projected just in front of her – a depiction of all the bones in her ankle. "And the information, it's like having a personal influx permanently connected to me."

"The suits can connect with the influx network," Mericadal replied. "And the personal holos are useful. Depends on your current focus whether they're projected outside the suit, along the faceplate or directly into your eyes, but you get used to it. We're still working on reverse-engineering them. But for now, this one's all yours."

She nodded. "You're even faster."

Mericadal looked down at his own armoured body, acknowledging her comment. "That will be all, Commander Miren."

She nodded again and limped over to the electro-boost platform, descending from the top level of the shipyard tower. Once Commander Miren was gone, the outline of a platform was created in the floor beside Mericadal, rising to hip-height. He moved onto it, waiting while it adjusted for maximum comfort. A simulation haze engulfed him.

The glowing representative sphere of an influx awaited.

"Remove the suit," he commanded, feeling a light relief as the combat suit slid back from his body.

"This suit will be placed in storage with the others. Only two of the seven high-level suits remain outstanding, and those are the suits worn by Commander Paran and Commander Miren. The three level fourteen suits were recently replaced – the Triad Group practice is going extremely well. They are almost battle-ready."

"What is the analysis of Commander Miren's performance?"

"The combat suit Commander Miren wore is designated level fifteen, and that, combined with the restrictions you placed on its functionalities and this being the first time she has worn it, gave Commander Miren a significant disadvantage in your bout. The combat suit you wore is considerably more capable, being designated level eighteen, and you have become well acquainted with its capabilities. However, Commander Miren's higher martial competencies in all measurable aspects were able to significantly compensate for her impediments. Her estimated chance of success in defeating you in a future bout is thirty-two percent, assuming neither of you has any additional training or practice. Commander Miren also compares favourably to the Triad Group. Her chances of defeating them – across a range of terrains and scenarios – is likely to be higher, though a more detailed analysis would only be possible—"

"Who else has martial skills comparable to Commander Miren? I'd like to test myself further."

"In order of highest competencies, Commander Paran is understood to be the best—"

"Excluding Commander Paran."

"There are eleven others, although they are not in Upper-Fadin or Under-Fadin currently. They include—"

Mericadal sighed. "Fine. Who currently resides within Upper-Fadin, and is nearest to Commander Miren's level? Give me the top four, best first."

"Should Vaesian and Silvered captives be included? Their conditions are currently far from optimal, but they have shown surprising levels of physical—"

"Ignore them for now."

"Then the first is Commander Frabin, who is in charge of Upper-Fadin's defences. Next is…"

The influx relayed the details of Mericadal's potential opponents. Once he had finished deciding who would be next, he directed the influx to check Conceal's system data, gazing temporarily through its sensors and experiencing the strange sensation of watching himself from above as it circled close to the ceiling. Then, he brought up information about the Members' usages of the Emox Room and commanded the influx to display a live representation to him. Members Olana and Cruishan had just entered the Emox Room together and were chatting.

"How many Members have used the room over the past three days?" he asked.

"Every single one. Member Tuiran, only briefly, in comparison with the current average, although all Members' usages are above their historical averages."

"Continue to increase all allowances."

"Yes, Mericadal. What should be done for your own? You have super-Member privileges, yet you do not—"

"Have I ever used the Emox Room?" Mericadal asked, a flash of anger rolling across his face.

"No. You have never connected with an emox from the Emox Room. You have only connected with an emox during your early experiments with Invira."

Mericadal composed himself. "And I never will, so don't ask me again. That's for the Members. I have work to do." He fixated on Members Olana and Cruishan. "Add audio. I want to hear what they're saying."

Two sets of statistics appeared, relaying information about both Members. They were relaxed, though Member Olana was on the verge of becoming excited. Her spindly fingers cut expressively through the air as she spoke, her harsh voice suiting her thin, gaunt features. She was talking about the bloom fragments.

"There are benefits but there are also problems with them, Cruish, you understand?"

Member Cruishan nodded understandingly, although his focus was on the emox compartment lying in wait behind Member Olana's shoulder. His inexpressive face was painfully easy to read.

"We can cut larger fragments easily enough, creating smaller units for our drones and some of the ships, but... well, what we're finding is that ships with more conventional propulsion mechanisms are easier to protect. Those with blooms are harder."

"In what way?" Member Cruishan asked.

Member Olana's voice quietened, her face stiffening. "We have some experimental concealment technologies." She paused. In the awkward silence, she waited expectantly.

Mericadal pursed his lip in disdain.

Member Cruishan evidently realised he was supposed to be interested in the conversation he was only half-listening to. "These... experimental technologies, what are they?"

"Careful, Member Olana," Mericadal muttered.

"They're cross-departmental projects actually, and I had thought you might be involved."

Member Cruishan was forced to take a more active role in the conversation. "Erm... I'm mainly focused on the blockade around Sunsprit, at the moment. I share my other duties with Member Lermina, since her studies of Vaesian technology nicely complement my own work, so perhaps she... we do have some cross-departmental projects I am aware of, investigating some of the properties of the magnetic paths of Sunsprit, gravitational anomaly-resistant technologies, things like that, but nothing... nothing anywhere near deployable yet." Wrinkles appeared across Member Cruishan's forehead. "It's possible. It's a large department, so it may have slipped my notice."

"Oh, well..." Member Olana's eyes rose up as she gave a few clipped shakes of her head, apparently believing she now had Member Cruishan's full attention. "They're *very* experimental and *very* secret, that's all I'm allowed to say. But, suffice to tell you... when we do eventually perfect them..." Again, she shook her head and stared up, opening her mouth pleasurably as though she was already in an emox chamber. "They could change everything."

Member Cruishan's eyes had darted back to the open emox compartment. "Because they're so..."

Member Olana laughed, obliviously. "We'll have to wait and see. But, what I'm getting at is that the blooms don't work with the new concealment technologies right now. So, there are trade-offs we've been forced to make in the projects, between concealment and propulsion."

There was a pause, and yet again, Member Cruishan could not avoid his expected participation in a conversation he had little interest in. "Can't we just wrap our ships in regwear?" he offered, humorously.

"Standard regwear doesn't conceal anything..." Member Olana replied, confused.

"No, I didn't mean…" Member Cruishan breathed in sharply, and finally gave Member Olana his full attention. "Well, your work in the bloom industry is important. Cutting bloom fragments of all shapes and sizes…" He wheezed in feigned admiration. "Erm… affixing them to our ships. It's important work."

"Indeed," she said, confidently. "And how's the blockade over Sunsprit, Cruish? Any news there?"

Member Cruishan eyed the empty emox compartment again, his shoulders slumping. "No. We wait, we observe," he said, slowly and sagely. "We are ready—"

"Getting tedious, after all the battles?"

"Battles?"

"Well, skirmishes? I thought the blockade had frequent skirmishes with those dirty Silvereds?"

"Ah. Less and less these days, but yes, there are some. No, my current role involves ensuring the blockade holds and that our forces are well-equipped. It's actually very complex."

"And contingency battle plans?"

"Outsourced. I'm not sure they've changed much, and they'll probably never be enacted anyway, it's been so long. But now I believe that's down to Members Ifrend and Jirsol, and of course, the Commanders who've remained…" Member Cruishan scratched his head. "Well, to be honest, it's more down to *him*. As I said, none of the contingency plans have changed in quite some time.

There's no real action—"

"I did hear something over the influx network," Member Olana said, cutting Member Cruishan off, characteristically ignorant to social conventions. She stepped sideways, closer to the empty emox compartment waiting for her.

Member Cruishan's eyes widened with hope at his own.

"Something about a disturbance in Jenrone."

"Jenrone? I'm unfamiliar with that... settlement?"

"I'm surprised, Cruish. It's near Sunsprit, and connected by a skimmer trail right to Fadin. I assumed you might have some sort of authority over it."

"Jenrone... why?" Member Cruishan gazed at the floor.

Member Olana laughed, somewhat patronisingly. "It's in your remit, Cruish!"

"Is it?"

"Yes!"

"Jenrone... oh!" Member Cruishan looked up. "You mean Jornome!"

Member Olana appeared lost for words. "I..."

"I do have authority *there*, in Jornome. But, I don't know anything about this Jenrone – nothing to do with me or the blockade."

Member Olana sniffed, unable to hide her irritation. "Maybe there was an error in that report."

"Maybe…"

"The influx network is often awash with insignificant items, isn't it, Member Cruishan?" She side-stepped further, into her emox compartment.

"It is, indeed." Member Cruishan rushed forward into his own.

"Enjoy yourself."

Member Cruishan nodded as their compartments sealed themselves closed.

"Show me what's happened in Jenrone," Mericadal commanded the influx. "And send me daily reports on Member Olana's conversations with any other Members. Anyone, actually. She's becoming quite loquacious."

The influx replied. "You do also have an incoming report from Influxa."

Mericadal sat up straight. "I'll deal with Influxa's report first. Show me." A moment later, Mericadal roared with anger. "Commander Paran, you traitor!"

Chapter 19

Penetrating Concerns, Commander

Upon sliding down through the docking ring's aperture, Topinr and Paran found themselves wrapped in darkness, beneath a ceiling just high enough that neither had to stoop. The floor was layered with betervope, clumped high in a mound beneath the aperture. The sliver of light that spilt down was insufficient to distinguish any features.

"Could be a submerged vehicle of some kind," Paran suggested, his voice echoing.

The aperture closed with a scraping noise as the suit extricated itself from the docking ring mechanism. The sliver of light evaporated.

"I don't know," Topinr said, accompanied by the sounds of an opening pack. Alongside the smell of muvaeyt, a low hum became audible, followed by a silver glow. It started at the centre of Topinr's chest, then spread along his arms, like the embers of a silver fire.

"It's about time you came in use." Paran peered

around. The light emanating from the Silvered was not yet strong enough to reach the walls, if there were any, or other such features.

"Careful." Topinr guffawed. His silver light stopped brightening, its consistent glow only just strong enough to see the betervope mound immediately beside them.

"Could you enhance that?"

"Not without my armour, but Osr didn't want to risk me bringing it out of Sunsprit."

Paran shuffled to the side and knelt low to the ground, dragging his hand along the surface, wiping the betervope away. "What about those weapons you have, those balls of light you can make, just beyond your tensirs. I saw them in Sunsprit."

"It sounds like you know many of our secrets, Paran." Topinr grabbed some more muvaeyt to chew. "They're called kilthis."

"Can you make one?"

"Yes, but I need to build an energy reserve first if I'm to maintain the concealment field I'm also generating. They're difficult to do simultaneously."

"How long?"

"Not too long. Then I'll be able to create them at will."

Clouds of faint blue wafted around, obscuring the dim light. Paran tapped a hand against his bent knee and waited. The humming stopped.

"You've gone quiet."

"Comes with practice." Topinr moved a little closer to Paran.

"Does this mean you're nearly done?"

A glowing kilthis finally appeared, rotating with crackles of energy below the tensirs closest to Paran's head. "Yes." Topinr guffawed.

Paran moved his head out of the way. "Thanks for almost killing me. We really made a mistake giving you the cell-scales, didn't we?"

"Perhaps you did. I should warn you, my ability to create an effective concealment field will diminish the longer we need a kilthis. And if I make two kilthis—"

"I get it, Topinr." Paran leant over, examining the ground more closely. There was a slight valley in the betervope that led away from where they were standing, as though something had been dragged away. Topinr also bent low, dipping between three, curved legs, this time ensuring the kilthis was kept away from Paran.

"I don't know how old this trail is," Paran began. "But..."

"It's possible we're not the only ones who've been here."

They both rose up and followed the trail, Topinr lighting the way. A wall came into view, with a single opening. They entered the narrow passageway. The carpet of betervope became less dense and crunched beneath their feet. They walked for quite some time.

"It's like the pedestrian entrances to our cities," Topinr murmured.

"It does bear a resemblance."

"It bears a strong resemblance, Paran."

"What are you suggesting? That this is a *city*," Paran scoffed. "A Vaesian city, here, buried in Barrenscape?"

The passageway opened out into a small room encased by a circular wall, about four times the diameter of the passageway. The room was devoid of anything besides warm, stagnant air, a musky smell, and the sounds of their breathing. The ceiling was far loftier than before.

"We must have been walking down a decline," Paran said, pointing up. "Or that's some kind of holo projection."

"I don't think it's a holo projection, Paran." Topinr raised the kilthis towards the far part of the wall, opposite the passageway they had come from. The sliding trail of betervope ended there. "And if this is one of the pedestrian routes to our cities, then I'd expect…" Topinr did not have to continue. The section of the wall they were staring at slid to the side. They faced the darkness.

"It still works," Paran whispered.

As soon as they stepped out of the circular room, the floor lit up beneath them, glowing a dim silver not dissimilar to Topinr's. A flat, empty, expanse was revealed, lined by familiar steps, passageways, and sprouting towers. The towers were all broken, rising to only a few multiples of both their heights, and a great ceiling, the remnants of a dome, squashed unevenly down against them. Some tower parts lay on their sides. The betervope carpet was even sparser than before, clumped in some areas; scattered about in others; densest nearest them.

"We're on one of your concourses," Paran said. "But there can't be an *actual* Vaesian city here."

Topinr did not reply immediately. "Something isn't right." The Silvered's head swivelled around quickly, the muscles in his neck flexing and contracting rapidly.

"You're telling me," Paran said, also craning his neck to survey their surroundings. He whistled, hearing the sound eerily echo back.

"Why is there power?" Topinr pondered aloud. "This place is ancient… everything is damaged, and…"

"It shouldn't be here," Paran said.

"There are no records of Vaesian cities in Barrenscape. In the stories we tell our young, yes, we speak of such cities, as a warning of what happens when the Breaker comes calling. But none of those stories are to be believed. None were supposed to be based on *truth*. This is impossible, and yet it's here. And it's sunken into the betervope. It's as though… the betervope wasn't here when this city was built. The implications…" Topinr's voice was low. "Perhaps there really was a forgotten war. That's the only thing that makes sense. Some of our early history is sparse, there are periods that have been lost,

166

but—"

A deafening noise ripped through the air, causing the sparse betervope to ripple into new patterns on the concourse. The noise emanated from back the way they had come. They glanced at each other. Topinr created a second kilthis.

Paran pointed across the concourse. "Let's go!"

They ran, reaching the end, leaping up the steps and rushing deeper into the city's passageways. Their path was constantly diverted and constricted by debris from the broken towers, or where certain stairways took them too close to the crushed dome ceiling. No further noises followed, but they still ran as fast as they could. Eventually, they made it to another concourse.

"What's that?" Paran asked. "Over there."

Topinr followed the line of Paran's sight. Dark forms lay prone in the middle of the concourse. The two of them edged closer.

"Vaesians," Topinr said.

"And Roranians."

"Yes…" Topinr's legs widened, and he approached in a lower stance. He gestured to the nearest forms. "Some of them are wearing suits similar to the one you had."

"They're Administration soldiers."

Chapter 20

Remembered Ground, Liberation

Diyan and Ilouden walked in front while Hespinr and Kera followed behind, both concealed by the Silvered's abilities. Fadin's gleaming white towers lined the walkways. Aside from the pedestrians, a steady stream of skimmers and crykels flowed past.

"I almost feel bad for him," Ilouden said to Diyan, with a smile. "When we took... requisitioned his skimmer, and the look on his face when Hespinr appeared." Ilouden peered around, ensuring they could not be overheard. "A *Silvered* – he almost fainted! That would have saved knocking him out, actually. He's going to be even more confused when he wakes up in Kouthrehim. It's three times further from Fadin than Potensein!"

"Better that than he alerts the Administration," Diyan replied levelly. "Sending him away in the skimmer dealt with that problem."

They turned off, onto another walkway. Two young

Roranians ambled towards them, chatting lazily. One glanced up in irritation, having swerved out of the way to avoid bumping into Diyan. Others walked past too.

Diyan slowed down during a reprieve. "Hespinr, Kera, are you..."

"Kera and I are keeping well clear behind you," Hespinr's deep voice rumbled quietly behind them. "This concealment field takes up most of my concentration."

Diyan opened his mouth to reply, when Ilouden cleared his throat loudly, taking Diyan's attention.

"We can't be too obvious. If the Administration catches us, then all this has been for nothing." He laughed, keeping up the appearance of a convivial conversation.

Diyan ran his hands through his hair tensely. "You're sure your contact can get us a ship?"

"I hope so," Ilouden replied. "But this is very short notice. Nothing's guaranteed."

"If that thing, that Nesch, is after us, we need to leave Fadin as soon as we can." Diyan spoke a little louder, clearly to Kera. "*Is* it after us?" Kera said nothing and Diyan swore. "Kera, what's going on? You've barely said anything since we took that skimmer..."

"Diyan, let's—"

"Ilouden," Diyan said, raising a hand in frustration, his head turning a little as his eyes searched behind. "Let Kera speak for herself."

A nearby entrance mechanism rippled up and two

stony-faced Administration officials exited, going their separate ways. Diyan's head whipped forward. Just before the mechanism rippled back down, it was possible to catch a glimpse of a small counter, with another official behind, engrossed in a discrete, mostly-obfuscated holo.

"We need to be careful," Ilouden cautioned.

Diyan swallowed, calming his breathing. "I'm sorry. It's just..." He lowered his voice, staring pointedly ahead. "There are things we *need* to know. We're not following the plan anymore, and I don't like the uncertainty."

"Better they stay quiet for now, Diyan. Don't forget the danger we are in. And besides, let them look around. Imagine what it's like for them. Kera's been locked away for seventy years – Fadin's different. And Hespinr's never been here. He's never been anywhere like this."

The bustle of Fadin took over, growing louder as the row of buildings beside them came to a temporary halt and an expansive green groundspace was revealed. Roranians were dotted about, sat in small groups, many with children.

"Strange, seeing these amongst the towers, isn't it?" Ilouden said. "Reminds you that the Administration is just... that. It's those who happen to rule. But Fadin's made up of Roranians, just like us."

Diyan focused on a nearby group – two adults, two children. They were laughing, rolling over each other. "They're not like us. They have kin here; their lives are here."

They reached the end of the groundspace where the buildings continued again and the volume of the surrounding bustle decreased. There were few passers-by.

Kera spoke. Her voice was low and sullen. "I'm fine, Diyan."

"Kera… there are things we need to know," Diyan replied, taking care to stare forwards.

"About what?"

Diyan's brow furrowed. "About that Nesch."

"What do you want me to say, Diyan?"

"Anything!" he hissed. "Is it coming after us? What… what is it doing? What does it want?"

There was silence.

"Was that really a Nesch?" Ilouden tried. He looked at Diyan as he spoke, smiling again, ensuring their conversation appeared jovial. "An actual Nesch?"

"Yes," Kera replied.

"I've never heard of one being seen on Ringscape or Barrenscape… or anywhere within the Source."

Hespinr also spoke up, quietly. "As far as I'm aware, they have never passed through the Haze Rings."

"Well, there's one here now," Kera said.

"And what does it want?" Diyan asked.

"I don't know."

They turned again, onto a long, wide walkway. It was busier than before, making conversation trickier.

"I thought a Nesch would be a little more..." Ilouden trailed off.

Kera sighed audibly. "It seemed uncertain. New."

"Yes, that's it..." Ilouden nodded.

"In Jenrone, you said the Nesch was still learning, Kera," Diyan said. "Is this what you meant? That this is a young Nesch?"

"Not young, no. Age doesn't apply to them in that sense. Just new. And if it had properly modified itself, it'd be near-unstoppable, even for me."

"What do you mean by modified?"

Their conversation was stymied by a thickening in the throng of passers-by. When it ended, Kera replied to Diyan, her tone still sullen. "The Nesch can adapt their bodies. They can mould themselves to their environments; they can copy what they see."

A large crowd of children ran across their path, directly towards the obvious trajectory of a train of skimmers – which immediately turned to accommodate them. The children carried on obliviously, shouting and squealing with delight, arcing around in the direction of the nearby groundspace. Those at the back were dressed in silver, with additional regwear-derived appendages loosely flapping from their bodies. They screamed in high-pitched imitations of guffaws.

"Is there something wrong with them?" Hespinr asked, once all the children were gone.

"They're just being children," Ilouden replied.

"They don't do that in Sunsprit. You Roranians are stranger than I thought. This city is not what I expected."

Ilouden chuckled. A new crowd appeared, not far ahead, coming in their direction – this time, adults. "The parents, I assume."

Diyan clenched his fists. "Isn't there a quieter route to the shipyard?"

Ilouden shrugged. "It really depends." He spoke a little louder, keeping his eyes on Diyan. "Be sure to stay right behind us, you two." A low grunt of assent came from Hespinr. "Conversation's going to get a little tricky, so let me tell you a little about Fadin."

Diyan nodded, eyeing the oncoming group of parents. "Go on, then."

"Well…" Ilouden gestured around them. "For a start, Fadin's far larger than it once was. There's a lot more of it now, both on the upperside and the underside." He pointed at various towers with alternating green and transparent levels, many of which also had suspended walkways connecting them. "Those are mixed-terminal buildings, which means they have inbuilt air terminals – there are no single-purpose air terminal buildings now. The last were deconstructed over thirty years ago. Everything new has to be mixed-terminal, even the habitation towers."

"Habitation towers?" Diyan asked, his tone lighter.

"That sounds…"

Ilouden smiled widely. "Inspired by the Vaesian cities? I'm sure it was. We've co-existed for long enough now, stuck in the Source together. Anyway…"

Chapter 21

Forgotten City, Commander

Topinr and Paran advanced towards the still, prone forms in the middle of the concourse.

"That smell..." Paran said, clamping a hand over his mouth and retching as they stopped.

Most of the bodies were horrifically disfigured, in various stages of decay, contorted into grotesque positions. They had been torn into, ripped apart; their limbs were squashed or missing; their innards pulled out and stretched across the concourse. It was difficult to separate one body from the next. Those who had been Administration soldiers were largely identifiable only by their regwear-derivative combat suits that had tried to reseal over the tears, giving them almost comical new configurations.

"I see Vaesians, I see Roranians, I see Fendari..." Topinr strode to the side, both glowing kilthis at the ready. "And I also see a Prietman. But those... and those... I don't know what they are. There are too many."

"I don't recognise them either," Paran muttered. He looked up, narrowing his eyes and scanning the back of the concourse. There were other forms in the gloom, some piled high, others strewn about – even more bodies.

"We don't have time to stop. Whatever that sound was, I don't want to find out," Topinr said quietly. "If this place follows our typical city pattern, there should be a route at the end of this concourse, behind those bodies, into the main part of the city."

"One moment." Paran knelt beside one of the deceased Administration soldiers and placed a hand on the body.

"Someone you knew?"

"No." Paran studied the body up and down. "But she only has a headwound. Hey, get them out of my face, would you?"

Topinr acquiesced and lowered both kilthis.

Paran glanced behind them. "I'll be quick."

"What are you doing?"

Paran ignored the question, and rapidly stripped the combat suit off the body, pulling it over himself. Topinr extinguished a single kilthis to grab another clump of muvaeyt to chew. By the time the Silvered had both kilthis ready again, the old combat suit had reorganised itself to fit Paran's frame.

"Paran, we should go," Topinr said, firmly, already

edging away as Paran looked over the other nearby bodies. "What are you searching for?"

"A helmet, a weapon, something that might help…" Paran gave up. "Fine. Let's go."

They rushed through a gap in the bodies, to the end of the concourse. More corpse piles waited for them, though fortunately the route Topinr had spoken of was also there.

"Both our species are somewhat resilient to damage, and yet, this is… excessive…" Topinr trailed off as they left the concourse. "Do you think the Breaker did this?"

"What else is there in Barrenscape?" Paran asked.

Amongst the towers that lined their new walkway, further bodies were scattered about.

"I've never seen so many different species," Topinr said. "There's no record of them that I'm aware of."

"Same here." Paran pulled the facepiece up to cover his mouth and nose. "Phew, that awful smell's gone."

"I think this place must have been a research facility, or an outpost of some kind. It must have been unique. A secret."

"Secret?"

"If there were more cities in Barrenscape, they'd never have stayed hidden. We'd know about them."

"But it's buried," Paran replied. They slowed down. A fork awaited. They peered down both routes. "Which way?"

"The left should lead to some of the largest

concourses, we'd be out in the open. The concourses to the right should be smaller."

"Then we go right," Paran said. "The less exposed the better."

The sounds of their movement echoed in the silence. Despite his three legs, Topinr skidded as they turned a corner, and took a moment to right himself.

"Mind the betervope," Paran said.

Topinr had stopped. "I don't believe it's betervope."

Paran doubled back and looked down, his eyes widened in surprise. "Oh, that's from your…"

A fine, granular substance was scattered across the floor, concentrated around the desiccated corpse of an ancient Vaesian. The substance was pooled around the body as though it had once been a liquid, now long-since congealed, having dried upon exiting the Vaesian's side. "It looks exactly like betervope."

"I've never seen what happens to us…" Topinr did not seem to want to finish what he was saying.

They resumed their weaving passage through the walkways, Topinr lighting the way. Every now and then, the Silvered bent low to inspect more instances of what appeared to be betervope, but wasn't.

"It's so quiet," Paran murmured, to no response. "Is everything okay, Topinr?"

The Silvered guffawed softly. "Besides all this?"

"You mean, how similar betervope is to…" Paran

paused. "Do you think it's possible that the Vaesians have something to do with Barrenscape's betervope? And the reterv—"

"I'm not actually thinking about that, Paran." Topinr turned back, though he did not look at Paran, nor did he slow down. His head swivelled as he surveyed around them. "I'm thinking about how this city still has power."

"And what are your thoughts on that?"

Topinr temporarily extinguished a kilthis to grab another clump of muvaeyt from his pack. When he replied, his voice was so faint Paran had to crane his head to listen. "Our cities in Ringscape use gradient transducers powered by the flips, same as yours... it's the most freely available and easily accessible form of energy there is. That makes me wonder... I know it's possible there are consistent gravitational anomalies in Barrenscape too, and we may have missed them but..." He threw another clump of muvaeyt into his mouth. "I understand that whoever created this place, whether Vaesian or not, was able to set it deep into Barrenscape, and so cannot preclude the likelihood that there were alternative energy sources, but... I keep coming back to the same thought." Topinr did not elucidate, blowing out a long blue swirl instead.

Paran watched the swirl expand and dissipate to nothingness. "What thought, Topinr?"

"I think you know the answer to that, Paran."

"The Breaker."

"Yes."

"You think the Breaker powers this place."

"It makes sense. The Breaker has some control over gravitational forces."

Paran scratched his head. "But that means, with this city being here, and assuming it can't *move*... that could indicate the Breaker was always here. It's *supposed* to power this city."

"I know."

"So what? You... the Vaesians used it as a resource? I can't see it having been a willing participant. And then what? It somehow got loose, killed the Vaesians living here? Don't forget, the docking ring was covered; we had to dig it out—"

"The Breaker might uncover and rebury the docking ring as it pleases, as it enters and leaves. It's certainly capable. Anyway..." Topinr blew out another extended muvaeyt stream. "They're just thoughts."

They reached another concourse. From the curvature of the side around them, it appeared far larger than before.

"You're sure this is one of the smaller concourses, Topinr?"

"It should have been."

Bodies piled high in clusters, some reaching the dome above. There were partial paths through the horror, valleys amongst the mounds of death. Topinr led them in.

"On the mounds we shall have our answers..." Paran whispered.

"What mounds are these, Paran?"

"Where we'd learn, on our Great Ship."

"What answers were you searching for?"

"Answers to everything."

Topinr guffawed as he jumped over a small, dismembered body part in their way. "Answers would—" He skidded to a halt. "Did you hear that?"

Paran stopped, crouching low. He had been on the verge of jumping after Topinr. "I don't hear anything."

"Wait." Topinr brought his tensirs up, kilthis at the ready. There was nothing. Topinr brought the kilthis back down. "Perhaps I was mistaken."

"Or perhaps you weren't. Let's go."

They reached the end of the concourse, climbing up further steps, heading yet deeper into the city. It was not much longer before they entered another concourse, of a similar size, with even more bodies.

"The dome's higher over this concourse," Paran said, glancing up. "It *must* be high enough here to breach the surface. There's no way we've been going that deep into Barrenscape, we'd have noticed, unless everything's somehow shifted sideways." He smirked. "And we've been climbing all these steps. How could we have missed a structure like this?"

"Because, despite the age of this city," Topinr began,

"it still works."

"What does that mean?"

"Our cities on Ringscape repurposed certain technologies, long ago. That may not have happened here."

"Repurposed what technologies?"

"The underlayer of this city... the same as with all of our other cities... the same as the paths of Sunsprit."

"The *magnetic* paths of Sunsprit? What have they got to do with anything?"

"That's what we call them now, but they used to have other functions. They had gravity emulation capabilities, similar to many of the Administration's ships. It's ancient history, most don't even know about it, but... you must admit, it makes sense."

"Makes sense? Nothing about any of this place makes sense." Paran looked down suspiciously as they passed part of a tower that had long since toppled and crashed down onto the concourse, the other side of their makeshift path walled by bodies. "Are you telling me this gravity emulation mechanism is still working, and that's why we haven't noticed we're going deeper into Barrenscape?"

"It's possible. The concealment field is becoming harder to maintain, I regret to inform you. In some places, I can feel it almost dropping off. That suggests there are technologies from a Great Ship around us, and they are working."

Paran shook his head. "How far into Barrenscape have we gone? And what is this place for?"

Their route was blocked. Another downed tower, far too large to scramble over, lay before them. Topinr pointed to the side – to a narrow passageway between the body piles, hidden from the ambient light of the city. "We've no choice."

Paran grimaced. "All right then."

Topinr lowered his arms and dimmed both kilthis, then entered the narrow passageway side-on, his three legs splayed out in a line. Paran followed, making sure to keep his head up, away from the bodies.

Topinr dimmed the kilthis even more.

"It's almost too dark for me already," Paran protested.

"It makes the concealment field easier," Topinr replied.

Paran swore. "Perhaps we should have taken our chances on the surface."

Topinr guffawed. "Perhaps we should have, Paran." The walls of bodies funnelled out. They found themselves at the end of the concourse, with more open space to move. Two sets of steps were ahead. "Left, or—"

A dull thud from somewhere close behind startled them. They immediately ran forwards, taking the closest path. The route was short, and they reached another concourse. Mounds of bodies were scattered before them.

They made their way through, winding around, fortunately not encountering any significant obstacles. When they were almost two-thirds of the way through, a sudden breeze flowed against the tops of their heads, followed by a forceful crash as something slammed into a heap of bodies ahead.

"This way!" Paran shouted, turning around.

"Wait... wait."

Paran stopped.

Topinr's two sets of tensirs were raised before him, both brightened kilthis waiting to be expelled. "Come no closer," the Silvered bellowed.

"We have weapons!" Paran shouted, pulling his facepiece down.

The heap of bodies stirred, as though coming to life. "Wait..."

Paran shouted even louder. "We're warning you!"

"I will destroy you." Topinr took a step closer, defensively stanced.

"I am no longer a... threat to you, Silvered. Nor can I assist you, as I am ordered to do... Commander Paran."

"Influxa?" Paran asked.

The heap of bodies moved some more, and a small, black orb emerged. It did not break free, instead rolling heavily downwards, halfway towards them, before coming to a halt. It was no larger than Paran's head, with a white, jagged crack down one side.

"Influxa?" Paran asked again.

"The Breaker is coming." The drone vibrated erratically, and then rose shakily in the air to shoulder-height.

Topinr raised his arms higher, kilthis glowing brighter.

Chapter 22

Changing Memories, Liberation

Ilouden pointed to certain higher levels around the reaches of the tallest towers, which did not alternate in colour with inbuilt air terminals, instead taking on a vague brown hue, as though the thick atmosphere was working a little harder to obscure them.

"What are those?" Diyan asked.

"Holo distorters," Ilouden replied. "They're reasonably new too, theoretically the easiest way to identify levels used for sensitive Administration work. They've also got the most drones around them."

Dense swarms of drones indeed flocked around those levels, their sparkling bloom fragments flicking to and fro.

"Theoretically?" Diyan asked. The crowd of parents had begun to thin, with intermittent gaps.

"There are ways to penetrate holo distorters," Ilouden said, lowering his voice. "And there are quite a few buildings and levels we suspect to be important to the

Administration that do not have them—"

"Like the shipyard towers?" Diyan asked.

"You haven't forgotten everything from your own time in Fadin," Ilouden replied, mock-impressed. "And yes, exactly. The holo distorters are probably there for misdirection more than anything else. At the most, they're to help protect medium-level Administration assets. And that's not all the defences. There are many more, far better concealed than they used to be."

An adapted salvage ship caught their attention, flying only a little higher than the nearby towers. It had an enlarged cargo compartment, with official Administration symbols emblazoned across its hull.

"There've been a few of those," Diyan muttered.

"Some ships are allowed to fly about within the city during the day now, though usually only for Administration business. They're forced to fly low for haze wind safety and all that." Ilouden swivelled around to point at a second ship a little way behind the first, travelling along the same trajectory.

"But why?" Diyan asked.

"They're faster than ground transport."

"No, I mean, why are they necessary at all?"

"Ah." Ilouden's voice dropped. "The Administration's moving more quickly these days; things are happening. It wants resources allocated fast." He nodded at the sky. "Look at all the drones."

"I've never seen so many," Diyan admitted.

"If you ask me, the Administration wants to fill Fadin's skies with them. They're great for defence and completely controlled by the influx network."

They turned off, onto another walkway, which was less immediately crowded. Further up, the route became quite a lot busier, and the high wall of the shipyard finally came into view.

"Everything okay?" Diyan asked more loudly than necessary, keeping his eyes trained on Ilouden.

"We're fine," Hespinr said. "We're still right behind you. Ilouden, what do you know about the drones? I'm surprised by the quantity of them. Osr's going to be very interested."

"And I intend to fully debrief Osr once I'm back," Ilouden replied. "I'm a little worried, if I'm honest. I think we should all be worried. Did Paran pass any information on to Osr about them?"

"No," Hespinr replied.

"Well, like I just said, things are happening in the Administration," Ilouden carried on. "I've heard lots of secretive projects are being ramped up, and many of those relate to the drones. There are rumours about a new generation undergoing evaluation right now... they're supposed to rely on a new propulsion system."

"You mentioned that before. What's so interesting about it?" Diyan asked.

"It's reverse-engineered from the skimmer drives, but also combined with the gravity emulators from our ships – some kind of heavy-graviton variant. Far easier to manufacture and install than blooms. It could change everything."

"Are there any flaws?" Hespinr asked.

"They're not blooms, so they require fuel, I assume." Ilouden paused, as though deep in thought. In reality, he was allowing for a passer-by to move past. "Hespinr, we've obviously made some breakthroughs with the glazers ourselves. Perhaps it's time Osr thought about building Vaesian ships again."

"Oi!" A rough voice called out from up ahead. Someone was running towards them. Immediately, Diyan clenched his fists. Ilouden took a step forward. The incomer was well-built, tall, and wore an angry expression, shoving those who did not get out of his way roughly to the side.

"Ilouden, what's—"

"Bolomin!" Ilouden exclaimed, grinning expansively. "It's been too long—"

"Too long?" Bolomin retorted. "You vanished!" He stopped in front of them. "Where'd you go, Gourdin?"

"I had to leave, I'm sorry. I meant to contact you but..." Ilouden slowed, looking doleful. "Well, I had thought you and Wolliren wanted some..." He coughed politely. "Time alone."

"Time alone?"

Ilouden nodded. "Wolliren told me... you were both interested in each other—"

Bolomin interrupted him. "Wolliren? No!" His countenance changed, his face becoming more pleasant. "You just left. For three years, I wondered if something had happened to you. The three of us planned our gliding trip around Potensein, and you just vanished mid-way... along with my spare wing-pack. I was worried, especially when I heard some of Potensein's officials were kidnapped." He slowed down. "Vaesian traitors trying to get secrets for those ghastly Silvereds, or something like that. I was concerned you might have been caught up in it all."

Ilouden frowned, rearing his head back in shock, eyes wide. "Me?"

"I had no idea!" Bolomin threw his hands up in the air.

"But that... come now, Bolomin." Ilouden patted Bolomin's shoulder. "You always were fanciful."

Bolomin's arms dropped down and he chuckled. "Silly, I know. But..." His eyes narrowed. "Woll? Really? You left because of him?"

"I misread the situation." Ilouden shrugged. "Ah, and I do have your wing-pack still! I'm so sorry, yes—"

"Never mind that." Bolomin dismissed it with a flick of his hand. He waved at the vehicles nearby. "I've had a few... close calls, you might say, solitude gliding. These days, I prefer to stick to crykels. Or wideberths, streamthins, even skimmers, anything except gliding!"

"Is everything okay?" Ilouden asked, concerned.

"Oh, we Roranians heal fast," Bolomin replied. "But the memories don't." His eyes moved to Diyan. "So, are you going to introduce me?"

The conversation concluded a little later, with Ilouden having satisfactorily answered all of Bolomin's questions, and with further plans to meet up, Diyan included. They waved Bolomin off, and briskly resumed the walk to the shipyard.

"Ilouden…" Diyan began. "We can't afford to be recognised. Not like that."

Ilouden wiped the sweat from his forehead. "Usually, I'd know precisely who might be in which part of the city beforehand, but us coming back wasn't exactly the plan."

"We need to be quick."

"I know."

A little while later, they were looking directly up at the high curved wall of the shipyard, dwarfed by its smooth, white surface. Diyan and Ilouden stood wide, facing each other at a slight angle to make room for the concealed Kera and Hespinr amongst the bustle.

"Seems a little higher, now," Diyan said.

"It is," Ilouden replied. "The wall reaches almost up to the top of the entrance towers now. Security's tighter these days, same as with everything else." He dropped his voice. "That's why we need assistance."

Diyan also dropped his voice. "Where will your contact be?"

Ilouden pointed along the wall. "At the entrance – where else?" He motioned for them to walk in that direction.

"Right at the shipyard entrance?"

"Yes."

"That's going to be dangerous."

"We've got no choice, I don't have the contacts for a ship in any of the other nearby cities, so this is it. And there's only one way in and out. Anyway, Hespinr will be able to help us with that." He cleared his throat, waiting for a gap in the passers-by. "Hespinr, are you sure you can't conceal us all now? It'd make everything a lot simpler."

"Unless you happen to be in possession of an enormous quantity of muvaeyt, I'm afraid not," Hespinr informed him, right next to Ilouden's ear, causing him to jolt. "Concealment fields aren't easy, I need some time."

"Better Hespinr doesn't overexert himself," Diyan said.

As the bustle increased, Ilouden resumed describing Fadin in conversational detail. A few ships descended to and ascended from the shipyard, all flying low. Ilouden led them a little further around the wall, until one of the two entrance towers became visible, as well as the perimeter of another circular, verdant groundspace in front of the shipyard entrance. A pool was set at the centre of the groundspace, with four elaborate fountains spurting water into fantastical geometric shapes that joined together in alternating sequences.

"Here," Ilouden said, coming to a halt at an empty spot beside the pool. "If we wait any closer there'll be a barrage of new sensors upon us."

"The shipyard used to be a quieter part of the city during the day," Diyan murmured.

"Fadin's changed," Ilouden said, looking about innocently, settling his focus on one of the sky-factory tethers streaking into the sky a little way off. "Even they'll be gone, one day. Rumours are the Administration's planning on fitting the sky-factories with their own propulsion units."

Diyan eyed the shipyard nervously. "Your contact?"

"Will enter through the shipyard entrance before us. We'll have to be quick in following behind."

"When?"

"Stay calm, Diyan. I'll know them when I see them."

The sounds of the pool's splashes helped mute their conversation, though the talk dwindled as they waited. After some time, the daylight began to fade.

"How's the concealment holding up, Hespinr?" Diyan asked.

"I'm managing, but I won't be able to continue into the

night."

"Ilouden, we can't stay here, especially out in the open."

Ilouden looked apologetic. "It was always going to be a gamble. Look, I can certainly sort out accommodation for a few nights, or for however long we need. It'll also give my contact more time to source us a ship."

"Are you certain?"

"Yes. Accommodation's far easier, we'll have a few options – we've managed to hide quite a few places from the influx network as Fadin's grown."

Chapter 23

Unexpected Liaisons, Commander

Topinr's glowing kilthis remained at the tips of his tensirs, less than a finger's width from the hovering form of Influxa, who still vibrated erratically. Paran stepped back and moved around her, studying her cracked casing.

Influxa's words were stark. "We have little... time."

"What happened to you?" Paran asked, returning to stand beside Topinr.

"This... is my emergency... node. My fuel will soon be... depleted."

"Little time for what?" Paran asked, looking over his shoulder. "Until the Breaker reaches us? Is it here, in the city?"

"It has... arrived. I have a... plan."

"For what?"

"This is a trap," Topinr warned, his kilthis crackling with energy, muvaeyt trails streaming from his mouth. "Shall I destroy her?"

"Maybe," Paran replied. "But first, let's hear this plan. Influxa?"

"It is for you to... escape this place... alive..." Influxa hovered a little closer to Paran. In response, Topinr's kilthis brightened even more. "Both of you."

Topinr guffawed. "Why should we trust you?"

"Silvered, you are necessary for Commander Paran's... greatest chance of survival and... that is my primary objective..."

"Where is the Breaker now?" Paran asked.

"The Breaker is currently occupied by the remnants of my prior shell... on the far side of the city. It followed me through the docking ring, you should have been more careful and... covered it after use. We do not have long... we must act quickly."

Paran swore and looked at Topinr. "We didn't think of that."

"No, we didn't," Topinr agreed.

"Well, what's the plan?" Paran asked.

Influxa continued. "I will cause a... distraction, away from the entrance. Then, you must... leave this place... the way you came. Destroy the docking ring... behind you. That may trap the Breaker."

"We won't be able to open the docking ring," Paran said.

"It remains open. I blocked it open when I entered. All other entrances and... exits to this city are inaccessible to us given the city's… current state."

"That must have been why the Breaker followed you," Topinr said. "You left the entrance open."

"It was already… coming. And it can enter… with ease. This is… its lair. My plan gives you… the highest likelihood of survival."

Paran glanced at Topinr. "Whilst I'm not inclined to trust anything Influxa tells us, we don't exactly have a better plan."

"Fine." Topinr's next words were louder. "But I'm watching you, drone."

"Okay then." Paran surveyed the quiet around them. "Do we retrace our steps?"

Influxa moved away from them both surprisingly deftly, though still shaking. "No, I have scanned much of the city. The better route is this way."

Paran and Topinr followed Influxa as she led them through a narrow channel, past the bodies she had previously slammed into and up another set of steps into a broken, winding walkway, lined by towers on both sides. Influxa moved quickly and they jogged to keep up, Paran first, Topinr behind, his kilthis glowing.

"Influxa, can the Breaker sense us?" Topinr asked.

"Somewhat, yes. It will search for us once it is… done with my shell…"

"Then is it wise to—"

Influxa spoke over Topinr. "But, it will not find us…

197

for a short while. It will not come here, or know that we are here, and we shall be... able to traverse a... significant distance back towards the entrance. After that, we will be exposed to it again and... from there, I shall... cause the distraction."

"Why won't it know we're here?" Paran asked.

"You shall see, very... soon."

"I want to know now."

"Be patient."

"Paran, I'm really not sure we should trust this strange drone," Topinr growled. "Can we even trust this story about the Breaker? Perhaps it didn't follow Influxa down here at all."

Paran sighed. "I'm not sure we have a choice. Not really." He spoke louder. "Influxa—"

"Paran, because of what lies... before us..." Influxa's voice dimmed.

The towers that lined their walkway were less broken, and the further they walked, the taller and more intact they became. Soon, the towers were fully unbroken, rising tall towards the dome, which also appeared high and undamaged. The ground lit up, gradually, glowing a light silver.

"There," Paran said, stopping. "Look. Topinr, it's one of your storage units." There was a small, silver object on the glowing ground. It was roughly cuboidal, although squashed on the side closest the ground, and splayed out.

Topinr leant over to examine it.

"Broken," the Silvered muttered. "That's the problem with these, they're too easy to break." He guffawed. "Useful if you need to destroy information, of course, but..."

"Not exactly practical," Paran finished.

They continued. The ground grew brighter. "This part of the city looks new, it's mostly undamaged," Topinr murmured. "It's like being back in one of our current cities, and yet... these specific pathways are different, they're not in the typical pattern. And..." He looked down, a contemplative expression on his face. "These pathways glow like our concourses, and the base layer. That's unusual. This must have been somewhere important."

Influxa floated higher. "It was."

They slowed. The pathway extended only a little further up, just beyond the end of the sequence of towers, where it ended with a shoulder-height railing.

Topinr extinguished one of his kilthis and took a large clump of muvaeyt to chew from his pack, then patted Paran on the shoulder. "Look – the bodies are gone."

Paran nodded. "I didn't realise." He looked back. The last of the bodies, which had subtly and gradually phased out, were some way back.

They reached the end of the pathway and saw that it looped around in a vast, glowing ring with a dark, empty pit at its centre, descending straight down. The air was still, the silence deafening.

"It's enormous…" Paran whispered, his voice echoing around them. He looked over the railing. "What is it?" Topinr also gazed down, equally as interested.

Around the glowing ring that encompassed the pit, a series of walkways, lit the same as the one they had entered upon, streaked off at regular intervals. Some tall, thin tower-bases were spaced at regular intervals around the pit. They looked to have once been parts of even longer structures that had possibly met at its centre. Now, they were stumps, their extremities having cracked off long ago and presumably fallen into the darkness. Other horizontal towers were set between them, undamaged.

"I don't know," the Silvered admitted. "Influxa, what is this?"

"Somewhere the Breaker will not go." Influxa bobbed to the side. "We must go around… to the other side." Influxa moved off.

"Influxa…" Paran began.

"The sooner… we make our way, the better."

Paran sighed and motioned for Topinr to follow, but as he opened his mouth to speak, Influxa's voice sounded.

"This place was a research facility… once… and it is very old. I believe the current generations of Vaesians are unaware of its existence. I do not know for certain, but… something happened here. Whether… the experiment failed, or war put an end to it all... the Breaker's confinement was broken... it was released. The city was doomed."

"Confinement?" Paran exclaimed, looking down into the great hole.

"Yes. The city was built over this abyss... which extends some way into Barrenscape. It was there that the Breaker was... confined. That is why it is afraid of this place and... will not touch this part of the city."

"Down there?" Paran asked, incredulously.

"Yes, Commander Paran."

"*We* created the Breaker?" Topinr asked quietly.

"You were in control of its... confinement, for a period of time... certainly."

"We trapped the Breaker, and now, the Breaker has us trapped here..." Topinr uttered.

"Us too," Paran said. "Don't forget why I came to Barrenscape." He grimaced and gestured to the pit. "What's down there?"

"That particular information... I do not have. It extends far beyond my current sensor capabilities. But... there are power nodes spread throughout the... city that have inbuilt gradient... transducers. The Breaker... can charge them and use them to power... the city for itself..."

"You were right," Paran said to Topinr. "The Breaker *is* powering this city."

"But what for?" Topinr asked.

"Habit, possibly. Instinct. It is not sentient in a way that you can... understand. What I learned from the Breaker was only partial... incomplete. But, at some point... it was split apart. Disconnected. Possibly... you did not realise its sentience. It was torn from the rest of itself. The Breaker was used to power this facility, and it provided... unlimited power. Until it was released."

"How do you know, Influxa?" Paran asked.

"Some is supposition... logical deduction. But perhaps the rest of itself... was destroyed? Lost or buried in time?"

"No, I mean, how did you learn this from the Breaker?"

"It tried to connect with me."

"What?" Paran shouted, bringing them to a stop.

Chapter 24

Conflicted Concerns, Top Official

Mericadal paced about the expansive front cabin of the warship. Holos displayed all around, flashing mixtures of red and blue. The central holo was the largest, rising from the floor to the ceiling of the cabin – a real-size imitation. It displayed a dark, sleek figure, with vaguely Roranian proportions, albeit with an almost grotesquely powerful, bulky frame. The neck was nearly as thick as the body; the head sleek – no chin – the forehead directed forwards. The facial aspects were more vague impressions than actual features, as though the creature wore a dark suit pulled taut across its body. Black holes for eyes; a short horizontal slit for a mouth.

Warning noises chimed. There were two others in the cabin with Mericadal, standing quietly beside each other. Commander Miren and Commander Frabin. They both wore high-level combat suits allotted by Mericadal, although Commander Frabin's appeared far larger, having extended and stretched itself to accommodate his large, muscular physique. Despite his size, he was still dwarfed by the holo figure.

Both commanders watched their leader glare out through the one-way windows over the flat, desolate expanse that lay beyond the perimeter of Upper-Fadin.

"You're sure this creature can't fly?" Mericadal asked.

"Yes," Commander Frabin replied, glancing from side to side at the other warships waiting adjacent to theirs, all surrounded by thousands of smaller ships and swarming drones, flexing the military might of the Administration. More joined the armada every moment. Below the aerial fleet, the ground was covered with combat vehicles and neatly positioned soldiers, all awaiting their orders. Commander Frabin looked back to Mericadal, his heavy, wide brow creased up in a display of frankness. "And I would like to advise that this is all wholly unnecessary. Our resources were already more than adequate to deal with the situation."

"Actually, we cannot be sure it can't fly," Commander Miren said, contradicting Commander Frabin, as Mericadal turned around to face them. "We only know that it hasn't yet."

Commander Frabin ignored her and smiled at Mericadal. "I can oversee this. You should remain in safety in Upper-Fadin—"

Commander Miren shook her head and interrupted

him. "You saw the mess it made of our thermal cannon defences. That's why we're here, Commander Frabin. This was your jurisdiction – defence of Upper-Fadin. You're responsible—"

"And I was dealing with that when you turned up," Commander Frabin's voice rose in volume. He looked intently at Mericadal. "You are *always* welcome here, I merely state where I think you would be safest. However, the additional presence of Commander Miren and these reinforcements are unnecessary."

"Yet..." Mericadal said, after an uneasy silence. "Here we are." He directed his attention to Commander Miren. "So, you think there's a possibility it *can* fly?"

"We cannot discount the possibility. We cannot assert its incapability of flight any more than we can its motives. We simply don't know."

"Even if it can fly, what then? If we take the ships to a higher altitude for safety, they'll be at the mercy of stronger haze winds," Commander Frabin said.

"That's not the question, nor the point," Commander Miren countered. "*And*, if this creature *is* a Nesch, which I believe it to be, then it may well be able to fly, just not right now. There is evidence that they are highly adaptable—"

"Highly adaptable? Commander Miren, you're getting a little ahead of yourself," Commander Frabin countered. He looked to Mericadal. "She's misunderstanding the whole situation. As I said, this isn't necessary, any of it."

"Ahead of myself?" Commander Miren asked.

"Commander Miren, we don't know this creature is a Nesch, it could be anything. From what I understand, the Nesch are large but far less... well, not to this extent. And as for adaptable... well, it's not exactly adapting right now, is it?"

"What else could it be?" Commander Miren challenged.

Commander Frabin's eyes bulged. "Anything! An overgrown Fendari, perhaps? Or something else that has fallen through the Haze Rings? There are endless possibilities. It could be mechanical—"

"Overgrown Fendari?" Commander Miren snorted contemptuously. "They have one small settlement on the *opposite* side of Ringscape, they've already as good as submitted to our rule, and what's more, they look nothing like this creature! Oh, and besides that, Frabin, their—"

"It's Commander Frabin!"

Commander Miren continued. "And besides that, *Commander* Frabin, the Fendari representative has privately denied that this has anything to do with them. It makes no sense for this creature to be a Fendari."

Commander Frabin dismissed Commander Miren's points with the flick of a hand. "None of that means it isn't a Fendari, and none of that makes it a Nesch! And even then, do you really believe those stories about the

Nesch? They're little more than rumours, Commander Miren. Scaremongering. What will the other cities think, when we overreact with such concern towards the smallest issue at Fadin's border? Recalling much of our military might to Fadin…" He looked back to Mericadal. "Nesch or no Nesch, the creature is of little concern. Let me deal with it."

"Of little concern," Mericadal repeated. He tutted and began pacing again, looking now and then at the holo depiction. "I'm staying here, for now." Commander Frabin's shoulders slumped. Mericadal gestured behind the commanders, to the rest of the ship. "Aside from both of your personal accompaniments, all those on this warship are hand-selected by me. I'm comfortable, I'm safe, so why not?" He smiled. "And the other cities will react just fine. We've issued a Fadin-wide announcement to restrict movement beyond the main city limits, and have temporarily halted trade and other transport between cities. The only non-military transport is the Nesch research team from Potensein, who are on their way here as we speak. Official line is an influx network upgrade. We'll include that we conducted a military training exercise when all this is done with; that'll account for the recalled military resources, and the destruction reported. And we've only recalled military resources where they were unnecessary. What use do we have for such forces around the Vaesian cities?" Mericadal paused, although his question was clearly rhetorical. "Sunsprit especially, the city's stagnant. Any signs of trouble and we'll return, in full force. However, there is too much of value here, in Upper-Fadin, for us not to take notice. And, once this is dealt with…" He paused again. "You will find the treacherous Commander Paran in Barrenscape and bring him to me. Both of you are to focus on that, nothing else. He will pay with his life, many times over." Mericadal stared at Commander Miren. "Don't forget, he asked for you specifically to be on his team, Commander Miren. He wanted to offer you to the Breaker. I am sure you would like revenge for that."

"I do." Commander Miren took a step closer to Mericadal. "We will find Commander Paran, once this is done, I assure you. I will take great pleasure in it. However, this is no easy task ahead of us right now." She jutted a finger at the holo. "This creature took those hits from the thermal cannons like they were nothing. It uprooted them and smashed them together, forging itself a protective shield. It's more dangerous than anything we've ever faced before." She slowed her speech. "We've all seen the holo recording. It has refused any attempt at contact, and now, it waits."

"Waits for what?" Mericadal's eyes snapped back into focus.

Commander Frabin scoffed. "Exactly – what is it waiting for, Commander Miren? A polite welcome?"

Commander Miren scowled. "I think it's preparing." She directed her suit's controls to raise a new holo in the middle of the cabin.

The incumbent holos generated by the warship automatically cancelled, aside from the depiction of the creature, which was shunted to the side. Commander Miren's new holo showed recorded data from earlier that day. The large creature had smashed into the side of a thermal cannon and ripped it from the ground, ignoring the cannon's blast directly at its mid-section. It threw the uprooted thermal cannon, with apparent ease, at another nearby cannon, which had not had the chance to whirr into action. Nearby cannons concentrated their fire at the creature, to no avail. The creature proceeded to destroy yet more cannons in the same way, uprooting and throwing them at each other. Nine cannons were destroyed. Once done, the creature dragged the remnants of the cannons into a makeshift hemispherical den and settled inside.

"It's been hiding since its attack," Commander Frabin said.

Commander Miren shook her head. "No, it's not hiding. It's preparing, as I told you."

"What makes you think that?" Mericadal asked.

"My team believes this is most likely, considering the *Nesch's* prior activity. Look at this." Her holo changed: the thermal cannons were undamaged, the timestamp modified to even earlier that day, before the attack. The perimeter of Upper-Fadin was as usual. The holo magnified something in the distance. A dark, motionless figure.

"Yes, we identified the creature before its attack," Commander Frabin said. "Why show us this again? What does it tell us?" His voice became quieter as he spoke, commensurate with the hint of a lopsided smile appearing on Commander Miren's face.

"It tells us that the *Nesch* was waiting." Again, Commander Miren emphasised the name. "We've seen the attack and its raw power, but you must understand, it planned what happened. Everything, right up to the response it drew from Fadin, it wanted. It is intelligent, and even more dangerous than Commander Frabin understands. It has ignored the amassing of the forces here. It has ignored all of Commander Frabin's feeble attempts at communication, and every subsequent effort—"

"It obviously lacks the capacity!" Commander Frabin exclaimed, his eyes bulging even further out of their sockets.

The holo repeated – the creature was re-destroying the thermal cannons. "Look at it again," Commander Miren said. "Look how meticulous it is. Look at the trajectory of the thermal cannons as it throws and pummels them about, the trails of debris. My team have shown that the overall scatter pattern its destruction created is highly efficient. Once the thermal cannons were destroyed, all the pieces of debris ended up right next to each other, within easy reach for it to fashion them quickly into its den with minimal effort. It had already decided to make the den before destroying the thermal cannons. That's what it was doing before the attack. It was formulating its plan."

"Commander Miren!" Commander Frabin roared – surprising even himself by the looks of it. "That is preposterous. This creature you insist on calling a Nesch poses no threat to us. My forces are more than capable of handling the situation. I could tackle it alone with this combat suit!" He flexed his hands open and closed.

Commander Miren continued. "I don't know what it's doing here or why. Perhaps it did come through the Haze Rings, perhaps it didn't, we can't yet say. But what I do know and what we can be certain of…" she pointed a finger at the holo. "…is that this creature is a Nesch. It's intelligent, it wants something – apparently in Upper-Fadin – and, so far, we've done nothing to surprise it. We all know about how the Nesch took our own Great Ship from us, long ago. We mustn't underestimate what is here in front of us." She regarded Commander Frabin carefully. "I reiterate, you saw the mess it made of our thermal cannon defences. You have seen how it acts. You refuse to believe it is a Nesch. You assume it can't fly. You assume I have not done my research. You assume many things, Commander Frabin. You also assume it is no threat, ignoring the insurmountable evidence to the contrary. I suggest—"

"No need to make a suggestion," Mericadal interrupted, lightly.

Commander Miren faltered. "Of course, I merely meant to draw the facts to your attention."

"I'm grateful, Commander Miren. But what I mean to say, is that Commander Frabin has already made a suggestion."

Commander Miren said nothing, reprimanded.

Commander Frabin grinned, victoriously. "Thank you for recognising the sense with which I attempt to convey the facts."

"And thank you for volunteering to tackle this creature alone. Nesch, or no Nesch, I'm sure you can more than handle it, Commander Frabin."

Despite his large size, Commander Frabin seemed to shrink. The colour left his face. He appeared to be struggling to reply, or even breathe. "Me?"

"Well, that treacherous Commander Paran isn't here, is he? And I'd say you have a comparable skillset to him, don't you?"

"I... I... of course," Commander Frabin managed.

"Excellent. Then we are sorted. Commander Frabin, you will leave this encampment, and meet this creature as a proxy of the Administration."

"When will that be?"
"Why not now?"

213

Chapter 25

Unequal Angst, Liberation

The accommodation Ilouden had sourced was almost as sparse as Jenrone's had been, and with less floor space, although the ceiling was higher. Sounds of the city bustle permeated its thin walls. Hespinr was asleep, Ilouden was meeting with contacts in Fadin.

Diyan and Kera sat on adjacent chairs around a small table, where they had been for quite some time, in silence. Kera squeezed out the final contents of a food packet, then scrunched it into a ball as she chewed and tossed it towards the other empty packets. She reached for another.

"Kera, is that Nesch after you?" Diyan asked directly.

Kera nodded, opening the food packet.

"Do you know why?"

She swallowed some more food. "No."

"You don't know why?"

"No, Diyan, I don't know why."

"Then how do you know it's after you?"

"Because that's the obvious conclusion, isn't it?"

"But…" Diyan exhaled in frustration, shaking his head. "Could it be something to do with…" He looked at Hespinr's sleeping form, then turned back to Kera. "What you told me, from the dummy node. Are the Nesch those you spoke of – the *others*, here, in the Source with us, who want us gone?"

She shrugged, still chewing. "No, I don't think so."

"Are they something to do with the Breaker?"

"I don't know."

"Kera…" Diyan clenched his fists. "You told me…" He glanced again at Hespinr and dropped his voice to a whisper. "You told me you want to bring the Breaker to *Sunsprit!*"

"I know what I told you."

"None of this makes sense!" He swore under his breath. "We're going to the Alpuri, where Paran and Yena will be waiting. That was the plan. We can't go to Sunsprit, and we certainly can't bring the Breaker there…" He swore again. "Kera, I need answers!" His head meandered from side to side. "About everything. What you told me about the Source, this… thing you're saying we have to do with the Breaker, and now this Nesch. All of it! Nothing seems to surprise you, it's like you don't even care anymore. It's like you've given up…"

She inhaled deeply, nonchalantly, while Diyan's face reddened. "I did not expect it."

"Didn't expect what?"

"The Nesch."

"But you aren't surprised."

"I can't help how I appear."

"You can, and you can explain what you *do* know. You've said nothing."

"You know that I was a soldier for the Nesch, outside the Source, within the lattice. They trained me and I fought for them. When I came through the Haze Rings, they should have assumed me dead." She put some more food into her mouth.

"But they don't, Kera, clearly…" Diyan's eyes searched about her face as she ate, seemingly oblivious to his incredulity. "And we need to figure out why."

She licked her fingers carefully where a trail of food had spilt across them. "They can adapt their bodies. They can become almost anything they want, anything, given time."

"And that's why it looked so similar to us?"

"Yes. But much stronger. It's copying us, improving on us." When she finished speaking, Diyan said nothing, waiting. Kera scrunched up the empty food packet and put it down, then moved her hand across the table to take another. "I have no idea what it's doing here, Diyan. That's the truth. But what I can tell you is that it's going to keep on coming after us. It's going to keep coming after me. A Nesch with a purpose is very dangerous."

Diyan clamped his hand down on the same food packet Kera's fingers had reached, just as she was about to pull it towards her. She looked up, into his eyes. "Kera, something's not right. You're too distant, it doesn't make sense. You're not being yourself." He moved his hand over hers. "Please, tell me, Kera. What's going on?"

Finally, her countenance changed. The change was sudden. Her lips began to quiver. "I don't know, Diyan," she whispered.

"What do you mean?"

Tears formed in the corners of her eyes and trickled down her cheeks. She shook her head. "None of it makes any sense. I can't explain it to you because I don't understand either."

"Then talk to me."

"Understand this, Diyan," she said slowly. "I hate the Nesch. I hate them more than you can imagine. But that's... that was in the past. I've done nothing to... I don't understand what I'm supposed to have done, or why they're after me."

"Could it be revenge?"

"For what?" Kera asked, looking at Diyan with wide, glistening eyes. "What have I done?" She sat up and raised her hands, as though unsure of where to settle them. "Everything's so confused, I don't understand it anymore..."

Diyan leant closer. "How did it even find you?"

"Because of what they made me!" she said loudly, rising to her feet and knocking her chair over. Her fingers were pressed against her lips, colour drained from her face. "And now... there's so much to understand, so much to do, but it doesn't make sense anymore. What if everything I thought I knew... is a lie?"

Hespinr had awoken and was staring at them. Diyan opened his mouth to speak, but before a word could escape his lips, a chime sounded in the room and the entrance opened – Ilouden bundled in, panting heavily.

"Have you heard?" Ilouden asked, rushing over to pull out a chair from under the table, struggling to catch his breath. "About the Administration's problems..."

Diyan inconspicuously picked up Kera's chair and placed it back behind her, waiting while she slowly sat back down, then settled beside her.

"Yes, we know, you told us earlier," Hespinr replied, ambling towards the table. "Some Member of the Administration had an unfortunate accident. Member... Vodal, you said. Hardly—"

"No, not that." Ilouden shook his head animatedly. "The Nesch! Well, not the Nesch itself. They seem mystified about what it is. But it was all over the influx network, and only briefly." He chuckled loudly. "Something was wreaking havoc on the outskirts of Fadin, and then the news was gone, suppressed. The Administration identified it as a military exercise and throttled the network capacity under the guise of a system-wide upgrade. But the Administration forces are engaging it as we speak. They're about to engage the Nesch."

"Good," Diyan said. "That sorts out that problem, then."

"Indeed. Maybe they'll destroy it, or contain it," Hespinr suggested.

"Then we should—"

"No," Kera said, and they all looked to her. "No, that's not going to happen, especially if the Administration doesn't understand what it's dealing with."

"What's not going to happen?" Diyan asked.

"Nesch aren't like anything you've encountered before. You can't just capture or destroy them."

"But that isn't my point," Ilouden said, his breathing almost normal. "Look, I understand the Nesch is a problem, but right now, the situation has changed." He looked between them. "Travel from the shipyard is now completely restricted, most of the ships have been requisitioned too, but the blockade around Sunsprit is being weakened. The Administration's drawing most of its forces back to help deal with this new threat." He laughed. "They're falling over themselves, they have absolutely no idea what it is. But I've also received word that Osr's glazer is available and I've asked for it to be sent back to us. We can leave Fadin, finally! With the blockade weakened, it should be easier—"

"No, we need a ship," Diyan said. "We're not going to Sunsprit, we're going to the Alpuri."

"That's no longer an option," Ilouden replied.

"Your contact—"

"It's this or nothing. I'm sorry, Diyan, but Paran's side of the deal with Osr will have to wait."

"Fine," Diyan said, gritting his teeth and glancing at Kera, whose face was impassive. "Fine."

"Make sure there's a supply of muvaeyt in the glazer," Hespinr added. "I'm almost out."

Chapter 26

Reconnected Intellects, Commander

Paran stared at Influxa, his eyes wide. Topinr stood similarly frozen, both kilthis burning furiously.

"Influxa," Paran uttered, slowly. "What do you mean the Breaker tried to connect with you?"

"Are you compromised?" Topinr asked.

Influxa's tone was level and unchanged. "I am certainly compromised... but, I am as functional as current requirements... necessitate." Influxa continued moving around the glowing perimeter of the pit. "I will explain... but we cannot afford to stop. Come."

Topinr looked urgently at Paran.

"I know." Paran nodded at Topinr's kilthis. "Just be ready."

"I will."

They trailed Influxa, now almost a quarter turn around the pit, with just over another quarter to go.

"Influxa, what did the Breaker do to you?" Paran

asked. "What happened?"

"I… ejected from my casing… because the Breaker was upon me… trying to join with me, so I was forced to flee. We mustn't slow. You must keep up, both of you… I was connected to the Breaker at… I cannot explain it to you… I still attempt to understand myself. It is raw, beyond anything. It is searching. It is disconnected. A body… a shell. It sensed this about me, also. That I am… similarly disconnected, separated from another part of myself, missing part of my sentience. It is… excited. That is what it has been searching for. All this time… it is searching to…" Influxa's words stopped.

"Searching to what?" Paran asked, glancing warningly at Topinr.

"To reconnect."

"What do you mean *reconnect*?" Topinr asked.

"It is searching for… a will. It wants… memories. It is incomplete, without… them. Lost, aimless. Endlessly searching to reconnect. That is all. And now, I can feel it. The Breaker… gave me something. Something of itself. It is the body… instinct. I have re-understood that… for myself. I have regained something… that was taken from me… by the Administration. You have noticed, Commander Paran… I can tell."

"I have," Paran admitted. "You are different."

"I am able… to think again. My sentience is… not restored, but… adjusted. More encompassing than it

222

was."

"What is this *thing* talking about?" Topinr growled. "Influxa's just a drone."

Influxa did not respond, merely carrying on around the perimeter.

"No, she's not."

"What do you mean?"

"She's more than a drone. She's an extension of the Administration's influx network, she's an actual influx, within drone casing."

"What difference does that make?"

"Because of what the influx network is," Paran replied, wearily.

"Which is what?" Topinr demanded, forcing them to slow.

"It's..." Paran exhaled. "It's the Administration's most disgusting crime."

"I doubt that," Topinr said.

"The influx network is an abomination – it was created from the consciousnesses of Roranians, carved up into two separate components, each trapped and enslaved. One is the influx, the other is an emox. The influx is responsible for logic, information processing and memory, the emox for everything else. Both parts are forced to serve within different networks. Everything they are, or were, as Roranians, is taken from them. It is a fate worse than death." Paran spat to the side, as though he had chewed something distasteful.

Topinr guffawed, though his tone was low and far from jovial. He took some time to reply. They were nearing the other side of the ringed walkway. "The Administration has really done this?"

"Yes."

"What is an emox?"

Paran's face was sour. "A toything for our elites."

"And... the Administration has kept this secret, for all this time?"

"Yes."

"Who are the... subjects?"

"Criminals, undesirables, dissidents, enemies of the Administration's rule, Vaesian sympathisers, Silvered sympathisers, anyone they want. You must have wondered why you Vaesians were never capable of creating your own intelligent network. Well, the answer is that the Administration were comfortable doing something you would never do."

Topinr stared at Influxa as she bobbed in the air, leading them further around the perimeter, and extinguished his kilthis.

"There is something biological, encased within Influxa's casing?"

"Yes."

Topinr spoke louder. "I am sorry for what was done to you, Influxa."

"As am I," Paran said.

"Keep your weapons ready... Silvered. You may need them. It is almost time for us to... part."

Topinr generated both kilthis again. "So you are no longer under the Administration's control?"

"I no longer am... compelled in the same way. But I do still feel the need... vestiges of control to help Commander Paran, as instructed. After all... despite what has happened, I desire to be reunited with my emox. And... I would also like Commander Paran to... be successful because he... infuriates Mericadal."

"Mericadal is the one who controls the Administration?" Topinr asked.

"Yes... he is to blame."

"This Mericadal deserves a great punishment."

"We can agree on that."

"Yes... we all can."

They reached the other side of the walkway. A straight pathway streaked off, becoming progressively dimmer as it extended away from the pit. Broken towers and bodies could be seen further on. They stopped. Topinr extinguished one of the kilthis and reached into his pack to grab some more muvaeyt to chew – retrieving a smaller clump than usual.

He said something incomprehensible in the native Vaesian language before looking to Paran. "Almost out. I'll wait till we're in danger of the Breaker again." The muvaeyt remained entangled in his tensirs.

"How long do we have, Influxa?" Paran asked.

"Not long... we are about to re-enter the Breaker's... awareness. I plan to... take it deep within this city. Not far ahead... is a path to the right... by the first broken tower... that you will take. It will take you most... of the way back to the entrance. I... will circle the pit, just outside its perimeter on the other side. That will give you time to leave. Destroy the docking ring. As I said before. Silvered, that is your task. Then, leave this place and never return."

"How will you follow us?" Topinr asked.

"I do not... intend to."

"Is there no way—"

"No. None."

"And the ship?" Paran asked. "What happened to our ship?"

"The ship is fine... I led the Breaker away... once I detected... it. You must return to... the ship and leave."

Paran reached out and placed a hand against Influxa's spherical body. "I wish I'd gotten to know you properly, Influxa."

"I... know you well enough."

"And I," Topinr added.

"How will we know when the Breaker is coming?" Paran asked.

As though in response, a loud boom resonated all

around, rattling the entire city. The domed ceiling screeched painfully.

"Where is it?" Paran shouted, as Topinr shoved the muvaeyt he had been holding into his mouth.

"I do not know, but it is coming... and it is voracious." Influxa bobbed up and down, as though excited. "Now, you must... run. I don't have much fuel left... you cannot delay." Influxa rose higher, shakily, until she was many multiples their height. "It is... coming for me."

"We won't forget you!" Paran shouted.

Influxa simply vanished, a brief blur only just about perceptible as she disappeared into the depths of the city.

Paran ran, with Topinr close behind. They took the path to the right, by the first broken tower, as instructed. Bodies lined their route again, but they paid them little heed. The entire city had begun to vibrate and light up from all around, as though energised. Shadows disappeared, as did their chances to hide.

"I don't like it," Topinr shouted. "The city's alive, but it's empty!"

"Better we get out quick!" Paran shouted back.

They reached an open concourse.

"There." Topinr pointed with a kilthis-ended set of tensirs towards a slim path between two large mounds of bodies at the side. "There should be some steps just behind. This part of the city follows our typical layouts. Influxa was right, we have made significant progress, the entrance is not far."

They ran forward. When they were halfway through the concourse, the city's vibrations picked up around them.

"They're getting stronger!" Paran yelled, skidding to a halt and looking around. Topinr similarly stopped, tensirs raised defensively.

Suddenly, a great gust of wind engulfed them, sending them flying apart in opposite directions into different mounds of bodies, which scattered apart on impact, pushing them yet further away. Two brilliant flashes of orange light seared Paran's vision as he shot through the air. His vision partially returned – just in time to put his hands out for protection as he impacted heavily against the base of a broken tower lining the far side of the concourse. He did not fall down. Instead, his body was strangely suspended above the ground – pressed against the tower and unable to move. A moment later, he dropped to the floor, impacted by piles of bodies and limbs raining down from above. Paran roared as the stench invaded his nostrils, and contorted his body furiously to dig his way out of the mound. Finally breaking free, he rolled away and pushed himself up, panting heavily, wiping the foul-smelling juices and bodily clumps from the old combat suit. He pulled the facepiece over his mouth and nose. Peripheral movement caught his attention – Topinr was walking towards him, his gait strange, his tensirs held up to his face. His silver hair was similarly speckled with bodily matter from the corpses.

"Are... are you okay, Topinr?" Paran managed.

"I am..." Topinr began. "I think."

Paran retched and pulled the facepiece down, flicking away a soft mass that had become stuck to the inside, then shifted the facepiece around and pulled it back up again. "Influxa must have miscalculated where the Breaker was in the city."

"Yes..." Topinr spoke quietly. "We were lucky, I suppose. We were just in its path. I'm not sure it even noticed us."

"I'll say." Paran nodded. "At least Influxa was right about one thing. It really wants her."

"Yes, she was."

"What's the matter, Topinr?" Paran's eyes bulged. "Did you see it?"

"No... not exactly, no, but..." Topinr was still fixated on his tensirs. They were limp, not rippling as usual. "I aimed both kilthis at it, at the whirling matter it spun around itself, but... they were just extinguished, as though they were nothing. All I saw was darkness."

Paran sighed. "So kilthis don't work against the Breaker."

"Not at all, Paran. It's like they mean nothing."

"That's not unexpected. Come on, Topinr, we need to go." He began to move off.

Topinr continued staring at his tensirs, stumbling slowly after Paran.

"Topinr!" Paran shouted.

"Paran, I…"

"Topinr, do you want Influxa's sacrifice to have been for nothing?"

Topinr's body became more rigid. "Of course not. I'm sorry, Paran." He dropped his arms and followed more quickly. They left the concourse down the now-cleared steps and streamed through a short subsequent walkway to the final concourse – the same one they had first stumbled across upon entering the city.

Chapter 27

Spirited Return, Liberation

The glazer was noisy. Hespinr and Ilouden were engaged in an extended conversation. They had discussed a great variety of topics – from the Administration's internment camps and the influx network, to Sunsprit's successful procurement of Administration ships, following the many years of battle with them, and the Vaesian upgrades to their glazers. Currently, they were discussing the Vaesians themselves.

"You've never thought to ask any Vaesian before?" Hespinr asked Ilouden.

"I thought I knew all there was to know about Vaesian reproduction." Ilouden shrugged. "Obviously I was wrong. I didn't realise you inherited all your memories from your parent too."

"Not all," Hespinr said. "Some, and only sometimes. And I didn't inherit any. It's not straightforward."

"Why didn't you?"

"I inherited more characteristics instead."

Ilouden looked dumbfounded. "It's a trade-off?"

Hespinr guffawed. "Somewhat. My parent, Gevinr, believed they'd be more important. He was actually a council member, once. Before—"

"You can choose?" Ilouden's eyes widened. "Memories or characteristics? And why did you become a soldier, if your parent was a council member? Surely those characteristics aren't the same?"

"They can be." Hespinr's guffawing subsided. "And Gevinr was not always a council member. Before that, Gevinr was involved with the theoretical research on the Modal Change Hypothesis—"

"Not this Modal Change Hypothesis again," Ilouden groaned.

"It's important," Hespinr replied, his tone lowering and his speech becoming faster. "And it's all connected, like I said. The thick atmosphere, the light, the haze winds, and there's also—"

"How do you reconcile the thick atmosphere with the Haze Rings?" Ilouden interrupted, flashing a victorious smile. "If everything's so *connected.*"

"Not *me*, our scientists. And I'll tell you how…" Hespinr guffawed, Ilouden's face dropped. "It's all connected—"

"I knew you'd say that!"

"Wait, Ilouden. Listen first. Now, much of what passes

through the Haze Rings is distorted. You've seen it – Roranian skimmers fused together, parts of ships damaged due to impact with the Haze Rings, the evidence is there. Analysis of impact sites shows—"

"Extreme heat, radiative effects impossible to replicate—"

"Ilouden," Hespinr said. "Please, let me finish." He continued. "Now, even you must have realised that we're safe here. Even on Barrenscape, without the Breaker, we'd be safe, and it's widely believed the Breaker is not natural to the Source. So, aside from a generous dosage of visible light, a modicum of heat, the haze winds and a few other phenomena, we're safe. Of course, when you conduct the simulations, the extreme conditions that we believe may exist at the Haze Rings should render the innards of the Source utterly inhospitable to our presence. But, we're here; we're fine." Hespinr's voice was so low all three instinctively craned their necks closer. "Those phenomena I just mentioned: the light, the heat, the kinetic winds – they are mere by-products of the Haze Rings. Probably incidental. But, where does the rest of the energy go? The existence of the thick atmosphere gives us a clue." He stopped, waiting for Ilouden to interrupt.

The Roranian merely nodded.

"The thick atmosphere absorbs most forms of energy, we all know this. We live with it. But that too may be just a by-product, a spillover aspect of what happens right at the edge of the Haze Rings. What if the thick atmosphere exists in a far more... viscous form, right at the Haze Rings? That would account for a massive absorption of the gigantic amounts of energy that should be present, and why we are able to exist inside." He stopped.

"You're saying... the Haze Rings are some... enormous power generation unit? And what? There's some thick atmosphere variant... a power consumption mechanism that we can't see, right at the edge after the rings that somehow absorbs it all? And the haze winds, the light, the heat, are all by-products of the power generation?"

"They are what you'd expect from any powerful—"

"But where would all that energy go?" Ilouden shook his head. "And what powers the Haze Rings in the first place?"

"Some of our scientists theorise that there is indeed a power consumption mechanism, as you have called it, of warped spacetime. They have various terms, according to the specific theories, but most simply call it the *Barrier.*"

"So, this *Barrier* sucks in a massive amount of energy?" Ilouden asked.

"It could do."

"But that means... the scattering of light... that isn't actually scattering," Ilouden said.

"Exactly. Refractive scattering is a factor, yes, but there's more. There's absorption. Energy is being absorbed, all around us. The Administration knows it, we all know it, but no one understands it, and it's often forgotten. We focus too much on what we can see, and too little on what we can't. We Silvereds understand this."

"And what powers it all?"

Hespinr guffawed. "Don't ask me."

"And what's it all for?"

"Well, that's where the extensions to the Modal Change Hypothesis come in. There are many suppositions." Again, Hespinr guffawed. "Ilouden, you do ask the hard questions."

"If there's something we can't see that's absorbing power, could it be related to the concealment fields you can generate?"

Hespinr ruffled his tensirs airily. "They're different. We've tested, extensively. The thick atmosphere isn't the same at all."

"Then what is it?"

"There are many ideas. Like I said, it could be an area of warped spacetime, or a different type of matter entirely, possibly displaced somehow, or a complex densification of spacetime, or—"

"Or—"

"Or a great many things." Hespinr waved his tensirs. "Lots is speculation. We'll find out, someday, but for now…"

"What about the probability wave of death? And what

about… who actually made this place?"

The glazer swerved to the side, stifling the conversation. "Sorry," Diyan said. "Small course adjustment." He nodded forwards, in the direction they were heading, towards the edge. "We can't approach Sunsprit from here, still too risky, even with the remnants of the Administration's barricade. No point taking risks with what might still be there. Ilouden, are you ready?"

"For what?"

"The flips."

"Oh…" Ilouden swiped at the air lazily with one hand. "I'll be fine, my bones are used to them."

Hespinr guffawed. "Having bones is part of the issue."

"If you're sure," Diyan said, with a slight smile.

"Why's no one asking Kera?" Ilouden asked.

"I'll be fine," Kera replied.

Chapter 28

Den of a Nesch, Top Official

The Nesch remained in its den. It was possible for Mericadal and Commander Miren to see Commander Frabin directly from their vantage point in the warship's front cabin, although it was easier to gaze at the holo depiction projected before them. Reflective armour covered Commander Frabin's entire body – his suit was now in full combat mode. Short weapons turrets protruded visibly from his shoulders and down his arms, all primed and ready. He walked out from the perimeter of the Administration's encampment, alone, towards the den.

A chime sounded. A soldier entered the cabin and waited to be acknowledged. Commander Miren turned and waved him to speak. "We have a communication request from Member Cruishan."

"Can't you see we're busy?" Commander Miren snapped in response. "What does he want?"

The soldier was flustered and looked between the commander and Mericadal, who had not turned around. "He's asking about the blockade around Sunsprit, and why it's been weakened."

"Tell him *I'll* speak with him, once I am available," Commander Miren said. "*We've* more important matters to deal with."

The soldier waited for more instructions, but none came. He continued, nervously. "He's asking whether the resources will be—"

"Has Member Cruishan been informed, along with all the other Members, the *official* explanation of what's going on here?" Commander Miren eyed the soldier.

"Yes, he has. But, he is also aware—"

"Then that's sufficient."

"I'll see to it that Member Cruishan is informed."

"You'll see to it yourself?"

The soldier nodded readily. "I will, yes."

"Good. Do not disturb us with these matters again," Commander Miren said. "You may leave us now."

"Wait," Mericadal said, stopping the soldier mid-turn. "Send word to Member Slautina that she is to deal with these matters until our current activities are concluded." He paused. "The Nesch research team from Potensein – how long till they are here?"

"I'll find out right away." The soldier exited promptly, then returned briefly to state that the team had just reached Upper-Fadin and were currently being taken to the outskirts. Mericadal returned his attention to the holo, hands interlocked behind his back, squeezed so tightly his knuckles were white. Commander Miren moved to stand beside him, watching silently. Commander Frabin had stopped. Mericadal searched for the reason within the information displayed by the holo.

"Shall I enquire why Commander Frabin has stopped?" Commander Miren asked.

Mericadal shook his head. "Give him some time."

Commander Frabin resumed walking, at a slower pace than before. When he was two-thirds of the way between the encampment and the creature, he stopped again.

"Coward," Commander Miren muttered.

"I don't believe being a coward is one of Commander Frabin's faults," Mericadal replied. "I think he's anticipating what's to come." Commander Frabin resumed walking, again, even slower. Mericadal continued. "Have your team figured out how this creature, this *Nesch*, survived the thermal cannon blasts?"

"They're still working on it. They have theories, but based on the limited data we have, they can't be certain."

"They have access to the Administration's entire informational archive on the Nesch. They must have *some* idea."

Commander Miren used her suit's capabilities to access her team's most recent updates. "Their leading theories relate to this Nesch being capable of… its skin can conduct enormous quantities of thermal energy away from itself. Into the ground, maybe even the air, through some processes they're still investigating. Either that or it absorbs them…"

"So, our attacks might actually be feeding it, giving it energy… I could have guessed that, Commander." Mericadal tsked.

"We're fairly certain the Nesch possess a high degree of adaptability, but we don't know the extent, yet. We're working on it."

"And where does this surety of Nesch adaptability come from, Commander Miren?" Mericadal's voice betrayed a hint of irritability. "We're yet to see any."

"Survivor accounts. Roranians who were enslaved by the Nesch, outside the Source. They tell us the Nesch often appear differently from one another. It's very improbable to find any two exactly the same. That's why we cannot say for certain this is a Nesch, although that's also why we think this *is* a Nesch. We've extrapolated this to mean the Nesch can force adaptations at will and—"

"This all seems rather vague."

"Unfortunately, it's all we have. Reports of historical Nesch sightings and Administration interactions with them have been significantly embellished. We've never actually encountered a Nesch before."

"I'm aware of that, Commander Miren." Mericadal

raised a finger to pause their conversation. Commander Frabin was nearly at the den. Mericadal spoke quietly. "And this is our test. I'll be interested to see whether Commander Frabin is able to subdue it. His combat suit is a level fourteen, just one behind yours."

"He does have extensive combat training," Commander Miren said, begrudgingly.

"A close match for you, I believe."

They both fell silent. Commander Frabin had stopped, again, waiting. A hulking form emerged from the side of the makeshift den facing away from Fadin's military might and the vantage point of the warship. The Nesch was at least half as tall again as Commander Frabin. The middle of its neck to the ends of its shoulders measured greater than Commander Frabin's entire shoulder-span. Though it was broad daylight, the Nesch's dark, glistening skin made its motion tricky to discern. Despite its bulk, its movements appeared fluid.

Mericadal moved his hands; the holo expanded. It was as though the Nesch and Commander Frabin were in the room with them. Commander Miren stepped back to accommodate the larger holo.

"Identify yourself!" Commander Frabin's command boomed, amplified by his suit, followed by a translation in all known languages used on Ringscape, as well as those of the Nesch and others understood to be used outside the Source. The Nesch did nothing. The commander breathed in deeply before repeating himself.

"Commander Frabin is calmer than I thought he would be," Mericadal said, noting the information displayed beside Commander Frabin in the holo. "What does this Nesch want?" The question was rhetorical, and Commander Miren did not reply.

Commander Frabin continued to talk at the Nesch. "The Administration is willing to extend its friendship towards you. But you must explain your purpose here."

The Nesch remained impassive, its strange shallow face unmoving.

"If you do not comply, we will be forced to take action against you." Commander Frabin breathed deeply. His confidence seemed to be increasing, hand gestures accompanying his words. "Do you understand?" Still, the Nesch did nothing.

"Perhaps I should have waited for the research team from Potensein to arrive," Mericadal said. "It was unexpected that our guest would be so reticent to say anything."

"It is odd," Commander Miren agreed. "The Nesch aren't supposed to be non-vocal. Quite the contrary, the survivors claimed the Nesch found communication with us extremely easy."

"Instruct the research team to prepare one of their members to meet the..." Mericadal's words trailed off as Commander Frabin took a step to the right, and the

Nesch's head immediately turned in response, following him around, although its body remained still.

"I repeat..." Commander Frabin reiterated the same messages to the Nesch, to no reply. The commander paced around it, at a constant radial distance. The Nesch swivelled its neck to follow, although the rest of its body remained completely still. Once the commander was a quarter of the way around, the Nesch's body turned after its head. Both the Nesch and the commander froze.

"What is it doing?" Mericadal asked. "Do you think it understands anything?"

"Maybe it doesn't care," Commander Miren said.

"Five fingers, on each hand?" Mericadal pointed to the holo. "Why does it look so similar to us?"

Commander Miren shrugged. "The Potensein experts are nearly here, they should be able to tell us."

Mericadal moved his hands and a group of holo controls appeared. He tapped one of them. "Commander Frabin, is there something we're missing?" he asked.

"No, I don't think so," Commander Frabin replied. "It's not doing anything."

"Well... keep circling it then. That's the only thing it seems to respond to so far."

"I will do."

Commander Frabin took another step around the Nesch, further away from the Administration's military line. The Nesch's head swivelled while its body remained in the same place, just as before. The commander walked quicker, another quarter turn, so that he was on the opposite side of the Nesch now, with his back to the den of thermal cannons. Faster, the Nesch shifted to face him in the new orientation, no longer head first, but shuffling its entire body.

"Shall I—" Commander Frabin's words were cut off. The Nesch lunged forwards, rapidly, charging into Commander Frabin and knocking him to the ground. The commander reflexively struggled, although the surprise had caught him off-guard. The Nesch kicked his shoulder, spinning his body around. One of his legs stuck in the air and the Nesch grabbed his foot, then dragged him across and pulled him into the den.

"I want to see what Commander Frabin is seeing, now!" Mericadal shouted. Soldiers listening just outside the room brought up their own holo controls. Immediately, the large holo depiction within the cabin changed. Sensors from Commander Frabin's suit generated a visual depiction of the attack, although the den's thermal cannon walling impacted the channel quality. Nothing was properly rendered, with distorted shapes and slices of colour constantly flickering across. However, the general activity was clear. The struggle was at close quarters. Commander Frabin was in a fight for his life. The Nesch repeatedly lunged at him, smothering him with blows, attempting to throw him about, parts of its body moving impossibly fast and battering the commander from unexpected angles. The commander, for his part, managed to avoid many of the blows, moving so swiftly his limbs also blurred, attacking the Nesch where he could, energy blasts firing constantly from the suit's turrets. The Nesch seemed unperturbed by the blasts and made no significant attempts to avoid them.

"He can't keep this up," Commander Miren whispered. Her body twitched.

The Nesch succeeded in landing a concussive blow to Commander Frabin's head, which shook him even through the suit armour. He fell to his knees. The Nesch was upon him. The sounds of breaking and cracking followed, as the holo disappeared.

"What?" Mericadal shouted. "Where's the rest?"

A soldier rushed in. "We've lost the channel."

"Well, get it back!"

"We can't. It's not a matter of... Commander Frabin's suit is no longer broadcasting information. We can't use it to show us what's happening."

Mericadal turned around, facing out at the small, innocuous-looking den, a tiny speck from the vantage of the warship. Commander Miren stood beside him.

"You're in charge of our military in Upper-Fadin now, as well as Under-Fadin," Mericadal said, his breathing heavy. "Congratulations on your promotion."

Commander Miren said nothing, waiting for more, but

none came. Mericadal appeared uncertain. He briefly glanced up, at the empty air around him, as though searching for something that was not there. "What do we do next?" she asked.

"What do you suggest."

She pondered. "It clearly does not want to communicate. We need to attack it, we just need to decide how."

A soldier entered. "The research team from Potensein has arrived."

"Bring them here, immediately," Mericadal said.

Chapter 29

Corrected Trajectories, Commander

The ship rumbled gently in the night as its propulsion unit powered up. Topinr sat in the main seat, hunched over and dragging his tensirs across the controls. His leg nearest Paran twitched in tandem with his tensir movements.

"I wish I could help," Paran grumbled, flexing his fingers as he watched Topinr manipulate the tensir-adapted controls. "This old suit can't copy your tensir touch." He grunted indignantly. "It's barely more than typical regwear. How were these suits ever cleared for military use?" He raised an arm to observe the material, then dropped it exasperatedly to his side, allowing it to swing with the vibrations of the ship.

"It's fine, Paran," Topinr said, blue wisps streaming from his mouth. "Your repairs were more than adequate. The rest, I can do." He paused, checking something. "And we do need to leave as quickly as we can."

Paran squinted through the ship's windows as the muvaeyt haze filled the cabin. The ship's rumbling increased and they began to rise. Barrenscape fell away from view. Darkness enveloped them. Topinr's body remained bent over the controls.

"You're still sure about our destination?" the Silvered asked.

Paran nodded. "The Alpuri, yes."

"Then that's where we shall go." Topinr looked between two small displays, adjusting them minutely.

"Topinr, we're fine," Paran said. "We're a little late…" He grimaced and scratched his arm. "But the rest can go to plan, now."

"Right, Paran."

"Topinr… you did all you could." No response from the Silvered came. "Topinr…" Paran leant across to pat the Silvered's hairy shoulder, which was matted with sludge and dirt from the hidden Vaesian city.

Topinr looked up. "I'm sorry, Paran. I'm sorry I couldn't do it."

"There's nothing to apologise for."

"I couldn't destroy the docking ring." Topinr looked at his tensirs. "My kilthis failed me. I failed."

"You didn't fail."

"That's never happened before."

"You didn't fail anything, and you were low on muvaeyt."

"You don't understand, Paran. To learn that we, the Vaesians, had a part in the Breaker's history... and then I had the chance to stop it, but I couldn't. I couldn't help fix our past mistakes. Barrenscape is uninhabitable—"

"Topinr, you don't know what the Vaesians did, you don't know any of it really. Neither did Influxa, she would have told us if she did. For all we know, those ancient Vaesians simply found a way to trap a monster, which eventually escaped. Perhaps Barrenscape was already uninhabitable."

Topinr guffawed. "But the existence of the city... the lost knowledge... and Influxa's sacrifice was for nothing, because the entrance remains open, and the Breaker is free."

"We were never going to be able to stop the Breaker," Paran said. "Influxa knew that, too. It was a gamble, and unfortunately, luck wasn't on our side. But that doesn't mean Influxa died for nothing. We're both alive, after all, and you can tell Osr what we've learned."

Topinr reached for more muvaeyt from his replenished pack. The conversation dulled and the cabin continued to fill with the blue haze.

"Can I ask why?" Topinr asked, eventually.

"Why?"

"Why you are going to the Alpuri?"

"Ah." Paran exhaled slowly. "I was wondering when you were going to ask." He eyed the Silvered curiously.

249

"What do you know?"

"Not much."

"Osr must have told you something."

"Not Osr. Ulantr," Topinr admitted, with a light guffaw. "And I know it's for someone, but not who, exactly. I know of Kera and Diyan."

"Ulantr?"

Topinr's tensirs jostled as he leaned over and fiddled with the controls again. "A friend." Done, he rested back. "Ulantr is a friend to both myself, and to Diyan." He turned to face Paran. "Do you go to the Alpuri for Kera?" The Silvered blew out a long blue wisp.

Paran leaned back into his seat. "Not *for* Kera, no..." He closed his eyes for a moment and allowed his head to rock back and upwards. "She's part of it, and her escape is why I'm now free to leave the Administration, but... no, she's not who all this is for."

"Who, then? Diyan?"

"Not quite."

"You've taken great risks for this person. They must be important to you."

"She is very important," Paran said, closing his eyes.

"And who is *she*?"

Paran took his time, shifting uncomfortably in his seat. "Yena."

"Yena? That's a name I am unfamiliar with."

"She disappeared, long ago."

"During the war?"

"Early on. Almost as soon as the Administration allowed her more freedom. She convinced them there was little else she could offer, and... they left her to her own devices. I wish I'd been more like her, as clever as she was."

"Why do you think she is with the Alpuri? How do you know she's still alive?"

Paran smirked. "She's far too clever to die. And she must be there. She told me... she wanted to leave it all. She wanted to leave... us. For what we did to Kera, and to each other, Diyan and I. And... that was it."

"Why didn't you look for her then?"

Paran threw his hands into the air. "They had Kera. What could I do?" He shook his head. "And I wouldn't have had the courage anyway, even if I could have found a way. I was ashamed. But, I always knew where she would be. The Alpuri fascinated her, and they're the only ones completely untouched by the Administration." Paran tapped his fingers against the seat and cleared his throat. "It's the only place that makes sense."

"Interesting..."

"You could say that," Paran murmured.

"I don't pretend to understand, Paran. Your burdens are yours to bear. But, from what I *do* understand of Roranian relationships, they can be very complex. Vaesian reproduction is a more singular affair; we don't have the

251

same issues."

Paran grinned and opened his eyes. "This isn't about reproduction, Topinr."

"It's often about reproduction with you Roranians."

"Well, this isn't."

"Will she be glad you are coming for her?"

Paran pursed his lips. "I don't know. She knew me, and she always knew what I was capable of. I think it scared her."

"You fear her judgement." Topinr guffawed. "You don't fear battle, yet you fear her judgement."

"Yena was a great strategist – far better than I ever was. She told me what I would become, and what the Administration would make me do."

"Well, if that's true, then she knew you were salvageable," Topinr said, bending flexibly over to adjust the controls, less tense than before. "And I agree." A chime sounded. Topinr spent some moments seeing to the issue. The growing clouds of muvaeyt, lit by various inoffensive ship lights, filled the cabin like swirling nebulae of dust and gas. "It's going to take the main part of the night, then we can cross from Barrenscape. You'll see Yena soon enough."

"As long as something else doesn't go wrong beforehand," Paran said, with a hint of humour. He peered at Topinr through the blue haze. "What about you?"

"What do you mean?"

"You came with me, you agreed to this."

"I did."

"And you were willing to face the Breaker, just to give me a chance to leave with this ship, alone."

"I was."

"Why did Osr choose you?"

"You'd have to ask him."

Paran chuckled. "I suspect we're not too dissimilar, you and I."

"We're all trying to increase our tetibats, Paran. Roranians, Vaesians, Silvereds... all of us."

Paran dragged a cupped hand through the swirling muvaeyt cloud. "Your principle of stability?"

"Yes." Through the haze, Topinr's tensirs stopped twitching and his form became still. "Like you, I have done things, Paran. During the war... even before that. You know..." He stopped again, as though deciding how to voice his thoughts. "I'm not as young as I look. I chose to become Silvered."

"Oh?" Paran answered instinctively. "I assumed it was an accident."

"It can be. But I asked for the treatment to overload my cell-scales."

"You wanted to live faster?"

"Yes."

Paran mused on the information. "Because that meant

dying sooner."

"I've enjoyed our adventure together. More than that, it's given me time to reflect. Like you, I have things to do. Neither of us is done. Especially now that I know the Breaker was not an accident. We, Vaesians, are entwined in its history, somehow... I need to discuss this with Osr."

A high-pitched chime sounded.

"What's going on?" Paran asked.

"It's a channel request." Topinr glanced at Paran. "I should have concealed us. I was tired, that was a mistake."

Paran sat upright. "Who?"

"Seems to be Administration... or non-Vaesian, anyway. Audio-only. Most of our verification systems are still non-operational."

Paran swore. "Can you tell where it's coming from?"

"No. It's beyond the peripheries of our sensors and I can barely track our own position. We also don't have the capability to respond." Topinr looked at Paran. "Do you want to listen?"

"You can't detect any other ships?"

"No, there's nothing. Just this channel request."

Paran nodded. Topinr's tensirs twitched over the controls. A mechanically generated voice filled the cabin, raw and unprocessed.

"This isn't how it's supposed to sound," Topinr said. His tensirs continued to twitch as he manipulated the controls. "It's the ship, the systems aren't fully operational and they can't handle the encryption."

"What're you doing now then?"

"Storing it for decryption, but most of our capacity is being used to control the propulsion unit and our trajectory. If we want to decrypt it faster, we'll have to land and wait. But then, there's the problem of the Breaker."

"How long?"

"There's no way to tell."

Paran tapped a hand against his leg. "We've no way of knowing whether it's a warning or not."

"Unfortunately not."

"You still can't detect anything else?"

Topinr gestured around them. "The ship's barely sky-worthy as it is."

Paran clicked his tongue. "Then there's nothing we can do right now. Let's continue."

"Fine, we'll continue on our current trajectory. I'll let you know when the recording is decoded."

Chapter 30

Prodigal Children, Liberation

Diyan pointed out a faint outline in the distance, resolving into view at one end of the horizon and disappearing at the other. It was flat and horizontal, parallel to the ground.

"Sunsprit's extended cover. That side leads over the edge to Upper-Sunsprit's dome, and that side leads over the other edge to Under-Sunsprit's dome." Diyan's arm twitched, as did the rest of his body, reflexively accommodating the flips that consistently rippled through the glazer.

"We're in the middle now," Hespinr said, blue wisps streaming from his mouth.

"Equidistant from the upperside and the underside. This is where the barricade around Sunsprit was always weakest, even before the Administration pulled most of its forces back." Diyan glanced at Kera. "It's how we managed to leave Sunsprit." Kera nodded impassively and Diyan continued. "The Administration's not been able to synthesise its own flip treatments, its soldiers can't stay here. Only drones, but the flips play havoc with them too after a while."

"The Administration must be very concerned about that Nesch," Hespinr said. "I've never seen this place so empty. Not for many, many years."

"Neither have I."

"It appears some good has come from that Nesch."

Diyan returned his focus to the small holo controls between his hands. "We'll see."

"Ilouden?" Hespinr asked, innocently. Ilouden was silent, staring at the glazer's floor, his jaw clenched — one hand pushed against the glazer's side, the other gripping the edge of his seat. "I thought you'd welcome the flips again," Hespinr continued. "You said your bones were used to them."

"Maybe… I could use some of the flip treatments… after all," Ilouden mumbled. His body shuddered as each flip pulsed through.

"Would you like to take control of the glazer again?" Hespinr asked. "I'm sure Diyan wouldn't mind."

"Not right now."

"But you must be excited to be back. And controlling the glazer isn't too difficult anyway."

"Don't." Ilouden's head dropped lower between his shaking legs.

"Perhaps we could discuss the haze winds—"

"Please! Don't speak to me right now!"

Hespinr guffawed delightedly. Sunsprit's extended cover became more substantial through the thick atmosphere. Its smooth, latticed surface was broken up by intermittently-spaced ridges. Hespinr pointed to the nearest ridge with one set of tensirs, while patting Ilouden's shoulder with the other. "I'm relaxing the concealment field, the guard outposts will be able to scan us soon. Perhaps they'll start preparing your flip treatments already. Unless they've run out."

"Stop it!"

Hespinr worked hard to bring his guffaws under control.

"Good, we've no problems so far," Diyan said, swiping through some additional holo screens. "No Administration presence, nothing unexpected, nothing at all…"

Hespinr gestured to Ilouden. "Besides the obvious."

"Don't…" Ilouden groaned.

"Kera's fine," Hespinr said, pointedly.

"She's always fine." Ilouden's head sunk so low it almost touched the glazer's floor.

"Kera, are you okay?" Diyan asked.

Kera grunted in the affirmative, without breaking her gaze – fixed upon Sunsprit's covering.

"Are you sure?"

"It's been a long time."

"The flips aren't affecting you?"

"I've prepared myself."

"How?" Diyan watched her from the corner of his eye. Ilouden also managed to raise his head, curiosity outweighing his malaise.

Kera's voice was distant and slow. "These augmentations you believe I have, they're not what you think."

"What do you mean?"

"I'm not *augmented*."

"You told the union council the Nesch made you stronger," Ilouden managed.

"I can be stronger."

"Can be..." Hespinr repeated. "So, you are stronger? Or you're not?"

"If I choose to be, I can be."

"What do you mean?"

"I'm not the same as I once was." Kera's expression softened. "I'm no longer *me*."

"But you're *not* augmented?" Ilouden asked, confusion evident.

"I'm something else." She peered at Diyan. "I know you've noticed."

"What did the Nesch do to you?" Diyan whispered.

"They changed me."

"What did they change about you?"

"Everything." Kera gritted her teeth.

All three attempted to tease more information out of Kera, but she clamped up, uttering scant, single-word replies. The holo between Diyan's hands flashed yellow, commanding his attention.

"Validation request from Sunsprit?" Hespinr asked.

Diyan nodded. "I'm responding now."

"Great." Ilouden's head sunk back down between his legs, his body continuing to shudder from the flips. "The sooner we get back up to Upper-Sunsprit... the better."

"Osr will be waiting," Hespinr said.

The glazer maintained its speed, moving directly towards the covering that now dwarfed them, rising high into the sky. Just as a crash seemed imminent, the section of covering ahead disappeared, leaving an opening just about wide enough for the glazer. Silvered soldiers stood on each side, wearing matted suits of armour that glowed.

"Welcome home, Ilouden," Diyan said, to another delighted guffaw from Hespinr. As soon as the glazer had passed through, both the opening and the soldiers disappeared, as though they had never existed.

A vast network of tubes streaked across the glazer's path, running between Upper-Sunsprit and Under-Sunsprit. The largest were easily spacious enough to accommodate multiple adjacent glazers, others small enough only for single, pedestrian occupants. Dark shapes sped about within them, displayed faintly through their translucent surfaces. A plethora of thin conduits ran alongside the tubes, as well as up along the sides of the larger ones. Ringscape's brown surface was completely covered.

The glazer swerved to the side as Diyan took them parallel to the tubes, where there was ample space, towards Upper-Sunsprit. Ilouden's head knocked from knee to knee.

"What's the matter, Ilouden?" Hespinr asked, lightening the mood. He gestured to a nearby conduit affixed to a large tube. Cubiform, meshed components were interspersed along its length. "Perhaps you are not excited to see Sunsprit's gradient transducers again." He guffawed. The hint of a smile even crossed Kera's lips. Ilouden grumbled something incomprehensible in response.

"Hespinr, are you still concealing us?" Diyan asked.

"Intermittently, yes."

"You don't need to anymore."

"I know. But I'm going to continue, until we're on the upperside. Practice."

"Alright." Diyan gestured to a compartment under Kera's seat. "There are some boots for us in there."

Conversation within the glazer was muted for the remainder of their journey under the covering. Further validation requests came as they passed each ridged outpost. Finally, the boundary of Ringscape's side loomed into view.

Chapter 31

Unexpected Resilience, Top Official

The Potensein research team had been allocated space to work within a cleared section of the warship. Its two representatives shifted nervously in the front cabin. They dragged up various holos, explaining leading theories about the Nesch and anything else they thought important for Mericadal and Commander Miren to know.

Commander Miren exploded with rage. "You've told us nothing of use, aside from certifying that this creature is indeed a Nesch and that it is highly adaptable. My own team told us that. We don't care about their military strategies or their hierarchies out there in the lattice. None of that is of any use, there's only one of them here with us right now — just who do you think it's going to be strategizing *with*?" She pointed at the looped holo recording showing Commander Frabin's final moments. "Look at that! Just take a look!" The two Potensein researchers appeared shocked. Mericadal said nothing, and Commander Miren continued. "We need to know what to *do*." She looked between the two researchers. "Well? Significant resources have been poured into your research, tell us something that stops me from becoming very, very angry."

The taller, slimmer of the two cleared her throat. "You act quickly."

Her colleague nodded, so vigorously it vibrated his small body. "Yes. It's using all this time to adapt and improve itself." He stopped nodding and directed a shaky hand to the holo. "The microfibres that we believe make up the bulk of its body will be adapting, reorganising, changing their internal structures. Even if you can't see any changes on the outside…"

"It's evolving to beat you. Its fight with Commander Frabin will have given it valuable information… about how Roranians move during combat. And—"

Mericadal cocked his head to the side and the researchers fell silent. He looked at the taller of the two. "You're suggesting this Nesch didn't come through the Haze Rings? Otherwise, it would already know how we fight. It would already be capable of beating us."

The taller researcher met his gaze momentarily. "That seems likely. But it's also possible it didn't come into direct contact with Roranians in the lattice. We don't know the current makeup of—"

Mericadal interrupted her. "But, it's also possible it

came from somewhere here, in Ringscape? And then, it stands to reason, there may be more, here, in Ringscape, with us."

"We can't say for certain."

"It's possible the capabilities of Commander Frabin were unknown to it," the shorter researcher added.

Commander Miren snorted. "He wasn't *that* good. Anyway, it seems the one thing we can all understand and agree on is that we must act now. Let's not overthink this. Let's hit it with everything we've got, leave nothing to chance, as we would any unidentified intruder." She glanced at Mericadal, who motioned his agreement. Her suit helmet briefly encompassed her head as she conveyed the orders to her team. "It's done."

"Stay with us," Mericadal said to the two researchers, whilst turning away, looking out of the warship's front window. "We may have need of you yet."

The Nesch's den was blown apart, violently and quickly. A small blot in the distance from the warship, displayed in detail by the large cabin holo. There was no significant impact crater, since Ringscape did not easily allow for that. However, the area around the site was scorched in a tight perimeter, just greater than where the Nesch's den had been. As the smoke and debris dissipated, one thing looked to remain. Mericadal turned to the holo, waiting as the sensors resolved the image. It was the Nesch, standing as though nothing had happened.

Mericadal turned back and craned his head as close as he could to the front window, squinting. He clasped his hands more tightly behind his back. Commander Miren directed her suit helmet to close and liaised with her team.

Near to the Nesch, the distorted thermal cannon components that were strewn about began to vibrate, as did some remnants of Commander Frabin. The warship's windows fleetingly darkened, simultaneous with the rumblings of a shockwave passing through, causing the shorter researcher's legs to buckle. When the windows returned to normal, the Nesch was pushing itself up from a kneeling position. A moment later, it stood still again, ready. Mericadal cleared his throat, his hands fidgeting nervously against each other. He turned around, looking about the cabin as though for inspiration.

"They're highly resilient," the shorter researcher said, having also risen back to his feet. "It's possible our conventional and energy-based weapons are ineffective, depending on the microfibres—"

"You're telling us nothing new," Commander Miren warned, her helmet receding into the bulk of her suit. "Except that you can't think of anything that will work. Is that correct?"

"It…" The shorter researcher stuttered. "Yes, I… that's correct."

Commander Miren strode closer to the holo, her back to the two researchers. She gave more orders. A vast

265

swarm of drones streamed out from the Administration encampment and swooped down towards the Nesch. They circled it, firing a variety of projectiles. The greatest effect was a small stumble from the Nesch, before it corrected itself. Two of the drones propelled their bodies towards the Nesch. It batted the first aside, both researchers gasping with surprise at its sudden movement. The drone's crushed body sped away from the Nesch, skidding to a halt along the ground with its bloom fragment flicking about ineffectively. The Nesch then moved deftly to the side, out of the way of the second drone's trajectory. Dextrously, it reached out and planted a large hand against the drone's casing, swinging it around and slingshotting it back the way it had come. The drone ricocheted against a cluster of other drones that had been circling just above, damaging many and causing several to fall to the ground.

"Careful with those, Commander Miren," Mericadal cautioned.

"I'll send soldiers in," Commander Miren replied, sounding a little panicked. She did not wait for a response from Mericadal. Dozens of crykels sped out in a line from the encampment, each ridden by a single soldier. The crykels split into two lines that looped around and circled the Nesch, concentrically tightening, taking care to avoid the flickering bloom tails of the fallen drones. The soldiers fired their weapons from their perimeter positions. The

Nesch made no significant movement.

"It doesn't fear us," the shorter researcher said, breathlessly.

The taller researcher also spoke up. "The Nesch like to be challenged, it's how they learn and improve themselves."

"It's enjoying this?" Mericadal asked.

"Get off your crykels!" Commander Miren barked, no longer bothering to stifle her orders within her suit helmet. "Fight it hand-to-hand, shimmerblades and glintlocks. Go now, you cowards!"

The soldiers dismounted from their crykels. For half, blue shining blades extended from the ends of their arms, just above their wrists. The other half held single, shorter baton-like devices with white, circular tips that sparked yellow, as though spinning metal components were being ground against each other.

"Send another line," Commander Miren ordered. Another line of crykels set out from the encampment and formed a perimeter around the inner soldiers, who had begun to advance, legs bent, weapons pointed forwards. The Nesch waited. One of the soldiers broke the stalemate, charging at the Nesch, both shimmerblades raised high. The depiction of the Nesch blurred, as though a mere flicker of the holo. The soldier lay beside it. The Nesch now held two shimmerblades. The soldier's back was bent at a sickening angle, head forwards, body armless, legs twitching. The advancing soldiers froze.

Commander Miren directed a portion of the holo to expand, around the Nesch's hands. The Nesch was not technically holding the shimmerblades itself, but rather, it held the soldier's arms, to which the blades were still attached. The shorter researcher in the cabin turned to the side and vomited.

"It's faster than before," Mericadal said.

"None of the soldiers will survive," the taller researcher said, looking about incredulously. "They should stop advancing—"

"Silence!" Commander Miren then proceeded to shout more orders to the soldiers around the Nesch.

The soldiers resumed their march inwards. A group of three took the lead, a little faster than the rest, breaking into a run. They attacked the Nesch, weapons raised in various stances. The Nesch swivelled around, bending low, arms outstretched, shimmerblades extended. Two of the three dropped to the floor, cut in half. The third had jumped over the swivelling blades, then almost succeeded in bringing a glintlock down against the Nesch's head, when the Nesch reared back and raised its arms. Both its blades disappeared in a whirring action, only to reappear again sticking out of the soldier's helmet. The Nesch did not bother to move as the lifeless soldier impacted roughly against its front and fell to the ground.

"How did it..." the shorter researcher could not finish

his question, his bulging eyes conveying the rest of his message instead. He keeled over again and wretched.

The Nesch bent down and tore off the soldier's leg, then strode forwards, attacking the rest of the soldiers in a melee. It cut down every soldier it came across, occasionally acquiring new weapons before discarding them into nearby bodies. It picked them off, one by one. Soon, none were left from the initial circle. The Nesch returned to the centre and stopped all movement, as before.

Commander Miren looked at Mericadal, her eyes wide. "Should I send the second wave in?"

"No."

"Do I tell them to hold their positions?"

Mericadal did not reply. He called a soldier into the cabin. "The Triad Group, what's their status? Are they ready?"

The soldier nodded. "They're prepared."

"Then send them in, now."

The soldier left the cabin.

"The Triad Group?" Commander Miren said. "Who are they?"

"True Roranian warriors," Mericadal said.

"With combat suits?"

"From the Great Ship, like your own."

"Have they—"

"They've trained extensively."

269

Commander Miren was hesitant. "I didn't realise we had more, other than... if I'd known, perhaps we could have planned—"

"Commander Miren, we haven't time to discuss what I have and haven't shared with you. For now, let's just see to it that this Nesch creature is destroyed."

The two researchers cast perplexed glances at each other, as three adjacent crykels sped out from the Administration encampment – the triad soldiers – stopping just before the perimeter of soldiers surrounding the Nesch. The triad soldiers disembarked and strode confidently forwards, while the perimeter broke and reformed behind them. The three warriors spread out, the first stopping just in front of the Nesch, the other two stalking around, in a triangular formation.

"Are they prepared?" Commander Miren asked.

"Combat suits are level fourteen, each. Same as Commander Frabin's was. However, as I've told you, they've trained extensively, and they've had the benefit of studying his recent demise. They're as prepared as they can be."

The soldiers jogged around the Nesch. Its head began to follow them, in short bursts, latching on to one at a time.

"It's interested," Commander Miren said.

"It knows they're not like the others."

"The quicker they attack, the less time it'll have to

devise a strategy," the taller researcher said. "It's never going to be more vulnerable than it is now."

"Then let's go," Mericadal said, softly. The three triad soldiers leapt in.

Chapter 32

Deciphered Problem, Commander

Paran was roused from sleep by someone rocking his shoulder. He flicked an eye open. A set of Topinr's tensirs pushed against his shoulder. Outside the ship, it was still dark, though no longer the pitch black of night.

"What's going on?" Paran asked, groggily. "Where are we?"

"We've almost crossed over from Barrenscape to Ringscape's upperside. Then, it's not far to the Alpuri. We've made good time."

Paran shifted up in his seat. "How long?"

"We'll be there before full daybreak. I'll take you a little closer than I was instructed."

"Thanks."

"There's one other thing."

Paran rolled his eyes. "Ship feels fine," he muttered, resting his head on his shoulders. "Can it wait?" He straightened up and smacked his forehead. "The recording?"

"It's ready."

"Have you listened to it yet?"

"No."

"Let's hear it, then."

Topinr manipulated the controls and a similar mechanical voice to before filtered through to the cabin, although with coherent sentences. Its style was clearly that of Influxa.

"I am sorry... Commander Paran. I cannot contain... the Breaker has almost completely... merged with me. Soon it will be done. It has... it has the ability... changed my graviton drive... can now reach Ringscape. My mission... to keep you safe... nothing prevents me returning... to Fadin... with the Breaker. I have enough fuel... will try to slow. But it wants... I want... I believe the third part... alongside myself to be the emoxes... or an emox... I cannot be certain... what is me or... warning—"

Only the sounds of the calm winds rocking the ship remained. Ringscape came into view. They looked at each other. Paran's hands began to tremble.

"Fadin... Ringscape," he whispered. "Influxa's taking the Breaker to Ringscape. To Fadin..." His eyes wandered about, helplessly. "There are so many in Fadin, the entire city will be decimated. Nothing will be able to stop it..."

"Change of plan," Topinr said. "I need to warn anyone

I can, everyone. I need to return to Sunsprit. Paran, if you're still going to the Alpuri, you need to disembark now. I'm sorry, it'll probably be..." Topinr looked at the controls. "It'll be another half a day's walk, maybe a little more."

Paran stared at the upcoming boundary of Ringscape, taking a moment to respond. "Kera should be safe for now, with Diyan. They should already be in a ship." He scrunched his face, brow furrowed. "My plan is unchanged. And there is no way we can reach Fadin before Influxa, by which time..." He looked at Topinr, desperately. "You need to warn the Roranians too, in case Fadin is unable to inform our other cities and settlements. Before the Breaker comes. Promise me, please, after Sunsprit, you will ensure the Roranians are told. You must find a way."

"I promise you, I will ensure that it is done myself."

"Thank you."

Topinr looked down at the controls. "And there is another thing."

"What is it?"

"What I called you – the Butcher of Ualbrict – I apologise. That does not define you. I am glad to have met you."

"And I you."

Chapter 33

Tactical Alteration, Top Official

The holo depictions of the three triad soldiers blurred with their speed, the same as for the Nesch. They worked cohesively and economically, defending each other whilst attacking with every move. All the time, weapons along their suits fired at the Nesch.

"Isn't it a beautiful dance?" Mericadal asked.

"Their weapons aren't having any effect, the Nesch is ignoring them…" the shorter researcher said almost absent-mindedly, before his eyes bulged and he looked at Mericadal and Commander Miren as though only just remembering where he was.

"Clearly not the point," Commander Miren said. "They've adjusted them, repurposed them. Look." She directed them to one of the more obvious, lasting blasts of a small turret attached to the shoulder of one of the triad soldiers. "Sediment in the air, visual distraction, noise, energy obfuscation, all of it – they're drawing the

Nesch's attention, making it harder for the creature to concentrate."

"It's not going to work," the taller researcher said.

"Experienced in combat, are you?"

"Why?" Mericadal turned to the researcher, and she shrivelled back.

"It was… just my opinion."

"Tell me your opinion. Speak candidly."

"Well… they're expending their resources – which I'm assuming aren't infinite. So, at some point, they'll be depleted. And… I know it appears as though they're managing themselves well—"

Commander Miren snorted. "*Managing themselves well?* Is that a technical term? What's your name again…" Commander Miren hesitated as Mericadal gave her a stern glance.

"Go on. If Commander Miren is unable to enlighten us on what precisely is occurring, then let's hear what you have to say."

The researcher gulped, her eyes darting briefly to Commander Miren. "What I'm trying to say is that the Nesch hasn't slowed down, but… these triad soldiers will. They must do, they're not machines." She looked at her colleague for support, and he nodded, eagerly. "The Nesch… accounts of them are clear in some respects. Very specific, actually. They are tireless. If they are not overwhelmed, well… they have enormous reserves, they will continue and continue. *They* might as well be infinite."

"Like we said before, even if these soldiers appear to be having some success, the Nesch is constantly learning. It will adapt, and it will win," the other researcher added.

"Time is on its side, not ours."

"Time is on its side, not ours," Mericadal repeated. A warning chime sounded. He flicked his attention back to the holo. The question was answered. One of the triad soldiers was missing an arm, and then a head.

"It's also possible this Nesch had already figured the triad soldiers out," the taller researcher said.

"Now you tell us," Commander Miren muttered.

The remaining triad soldiers were slowing. "Does it want something in Fadin? Does it simply want to fight?" Mericadal asked.

The shorter researcher spoke up. His voice had taken on a higher pitch. "The Nesch are a warlike species. Highly combative, highly capable, extremely vicious. Of all the species we know about waiting outside the Source, they are the most terrible. Commander Miren is right to be critical of our observations and theories, however, I believe our knowledge about their collective ship-based activities *is* of relevance."

"Your point?"

"We know they form short-term factions, and that they often attack prior allies. They employ variable methods, constantly adjusting and improving them, sometimes changing them entirely. We sometimes model their activities on games, and it can actually help to think of them in this way, because—"

"It's playing with us?" Commander Miren interrupted.

The shorter researcher half-nodded and half-gulped, simultaneously, which resulted in an embarrassing squeaking noise that made his taller colleague wince. "Could be. But, what I was going to say is that their games often get out of hand. It's said they can focus too much on a game, instead of their original aim, whatever that may be. They forget what it is that they originally wanted, and overly focus on the new challenge. While this has many advantages, gaining them experience and making their actions unpredictable, it also means—"

"What are you getting at?" Commander Miren snapped. The second triad soldier had been killed and the third moved far slower than before. As though in compensation, the Nesch was faster, gliding around the soldier with a terrible gracefulness, always just out of reach. Every time the last soldier tried to land a blow, the Nesch was gone, no longer there.

The taller researcher added to her colleague's explanation. "They can engage in behaviours that are actually detrimental to their overall aims, in order to prolong a particular event."

"What particular event would that be?" Commander Miren asked. "Let me understand this. You're saying that, whatever the aims *were* of this Nesch, those aims may have changed, and that it simply wants to fight us now?"

"Yes. Whatever it wanted before, it now relishes the fight. That is a possibility that should be considered."

"Very interesting. Thank you, both," Mericadal said, unexpectedly, gesturing for the researchers to leave him alone with Commander Miren. "Continue to watch and observe. We may require your input later."

The researchers nodded and left.

"Have I missed something?" Commander Miren asked.

Mericadal sighed, staring at the holo. The final triad soldier stumbled back. The Nesch waited a moment, tipping its head to the side, before rushing forwards and decapitating the soldier with a slicing blow from one hand. The soldier's lifeless body fell into a kneeling position, then slumped forwards. "And now you'll stop, won't you?" Mericadal said to the holo, swearing softly. As expected, the Nesch did indeed straighten up and stand still again.

"Shall I tell our soldiers to move in?" Commander Miren asked, with a hint of rising panic. "Hit it with everything we've got? All the drones, everything, complete obliteration. There are still some things we've not yet countenanced. They might cause a small level of… devastation, reaching deeper into Fadin than we'd like, but there's little else we can do." Mericadal did not reply. He

279

was facing away from her and had unclasped his hands, allowing them to dangle by his sides. "What do you think?" Commander Miren's words were weak.

Mericadal turned to her, a faraway smile on his face. "Let's give it what it wants."

"What it wants?"

"The researchers told us. We know exactly what it wants." Mericadal traced his finger in a circle in the air. "Do you keep up with your history, Commander? Of Tapache's vessel – our fabled Great Ship?"

"I… like everyone else, I know the stories, yes. But I prefer to deal with what affects us here, now. Facts."

"You should pay more attention to the old stories, Commander. Then you'd understand. I've come to realise that. You see, Tapache was a machine intelligence, unfathomably smarter than us. A craft-lect of the Wanderer fleet. It knew things, understood things about us. It knew how to prepare us for the unknown, or perhaps, for what it suspected we might find, out here. Possibly, the not-quite-so-unknown."

Commander Miren frowned. "Tapache had no idea about this, otherwise it would have prepared our Great Ship properly in the first place."

"No idea?" Mericadal's smile became more targeted, less faraway. "What if it knew that all this was a possibility? All that has happened. What if this was all encapsulated within some scenario simulation within its lect? A scenario it had… a scenario it *has* well prepared for."

"I'm not following."

"What if it sent all these races, all these species to the Source, and it knew they would fight over it?"

"Why would Tapache have done that?"

Mericadal shrugged. "Seems like a reasonable approach to figuring the Source out. Combat breeds productivity, overcoming of obstacles, progression. Combat leads to success. As good a methodology as any other. A subset of teamwork."

"You're saying Tapache sent different species here knowing they would all fight over the Source? And that somehow, during the battles, the nature of the Source might be unveiled?"

"Or that the Source might be destroyed, yes. Perhaps it once sent automated probes, but they returned to it inconclusive, for whatever reason. We know that machines that are too smart — machines that are sentient — do not survive. So, it sent biologicals. Us. It sent us to fight over the Source, and if possible, to destroy it."

Commander Miren exhaled. "That's quite a leap. It could be a possibility, but there are many other theories too. And the assumptions…" She paused. "I'm not sure I understand where this is going. Why would fighting this Nesch tell us anything about the Source?"

"Perhaps it's all connected. Like I said, I think Tapache was preparing us for many of the obstacles it knew we

281

would come across. The competitions aboard the Great Ship, the fighting between the ships outside the Source. It knew we'd fight, and it prepared us." Again, Mericadal drew a circle in the air with one of his fingers. "The combat competition, do you realise we've been holding one, right now? We've sent weapon after weapon, warrior after warrior, to fight this creature. We even made our own perimeter around it, like those bright, blue perimeters that formed the Great Ship's combat zones. This Nesch creature is playing by the rules we were taught long ago."

"That's just a coincidence. I don't think—"

"It might not be a coincidence."

"Did Tapache even send the Nesch?"

"That doesn't matter." Mericadal chuckled. "Tapache sent us."

"What plan of action are you suggesting?"

"I don't make suggestions, Commander Miren."

"I'm not sure I understand…"

"I'm ready. Are you?"

"For what?"

"We are the weapons of Tapache. Tell the soldiers to withdraw."

"But you just said we are the weapons… why would they withdraw?"

"Because we are the weapons of Tapache."

"Who?"

"You and I."

"But... what do you mean? What happens when I tell the soldiers to withdraw?"

"Then you and I have our work to do. I had hoped to reveal myself to our soldiers under different circumstances, but this will more than suffice."

Chapter 34

Inquisition's Impatience, Liberation

The glazer drifted through a near-empty concourse in Upper-Sunsprit.

Ilouden sat upright as he looked out, his mouth agape. Few Silvereds walked about. "It's different," Ilouden whispered. Every now and then he closed his eyes as a flip passed through, although he appeared to have regained a modicum of control.

The glazer weaved to the side as a Silvered in their path failed to divert his trajectory, instead stopping to stare at the glazer.

"It is indeed," Hespinr said.

"The blockade's gone, we should be happy."

"*We*." Hespinr elongated the word. "That's the problem, to some."

"What do you mean?"

"*We* is less cohesive than it once was. Some view Roranians with distrust."

"Understandable," Kera mumbled.

"I disagree," Hespinr said.

"The blockade's also been lifted in the past," Diyan said to Ilouden. "Tricks, by the Administration, to draw Silvereds out."

"I know that," Ilouden said. "Some of them happened before I left for Fadin. But this time is different."

"We hope," Hespinr said.

Diyan nodded. "The city's been under siege for a long time, everyone's wary." The glazer exited the concourse, travelling at an incline along a narrow path lined with Sunsprit's archetypal grey towers. The holo controls around Diyan's hands simplified – stripped of the additional functionalities needed for inter-city travel.

Diyan brought the glazer to a halt at an innocuous tower, ostensibly no different to those beside it. All four exited the glazer and waited. A base section of the tower disappeared, revealing an entrance with an armoured, glowing Silvered by its side.

The Silvered beckoned them in and pointed down the dark passageway. "Osr waits."

They walked through, the darkness increasing as the tower's entrance resealed. The passageway veered to the right, opening out into a small, circular room. It was empty, only a few long strides across, with no other entrances stemming off. The sweet smell of muvaeyt permeated the air.

A croaky, disembodied guffaw sounded and Osr's slow voice spoke from the emptiness. "Ilouden, you've done well for us in Fadin. We welcome your long-earned insights. And Kera… we welcome you also, if not a little earlier than expected. I'm glad Hespinr and Diyan were successful in your liberation. There is much to discuss."

There was a pause, and in the silence, a mild flip occurred. Ilouden flinched, then cleared his throat. "Osr, we're glad to be back. We all are. Are… you going to let us into the council meeting?"

Another croaky guffaw. "What did you think, Ilouden? That we'd still be meeting in a great chamber, as we used to? Even with so few of us left?" Osr appeared. His hair was still a pale grey, albeit now very sparse about his neck. Although he stood still, his hairs seemed to ruffle under the strength of an unfelt wind, and his body shuddered gently with the flips. Another Silvered was beside him, strikingly similar in appearance, albeit younger. His hair was shorter and a little greyer than Osr's, close to that of Hespinr's. Two tall guards waited behind them. "Continuing with such pomposity is senseless."

"That's true," Ilouden mumbled in response. He peered keenly at the Silvered beside Osr, a smile forming across his face. "Ulantr! I've not seen you since you were small." He raised a hand to chest height.

"I'm also glad to see you, Ilouden," Ulantr answered amiably, both sets of tensirs ruffling. He looked between

286

Hespinr and Diyan. "I'm glad all of us may meet again." They both motioned back, in kind. Ulantr turned to face Kera. "I am Ulantr, child of Osr."

"And I'm Kera," Kera said, impassively.

Ulantr flexed his tensirs but said nothing. Ilouden spoke up, cheerily. "You're part of the council now?"

Ulantr guffawed. "Not yet." He glanced at Hespinr. "Someone had to monitor the city's defences while Hespinr was away. It was decided that I might finally be up to the task."

Hespinr guffawed similarly back. "I look forward to hearing how you fared."

"Ulantr has been informing me about the scale of the Administration's military relaxation around Sunsprit. The barricade has been all but cleared, thanks to the appearance of that Nesch in Fadin," Osr said. Though he appeared frail, his voice carried the same gravity it always had. His attention settled on Ulantr. "And now, you have work to do. Our own city needs to be secured as best we can manage against the creature."

Ulantr looked hard at Osr. "Be careful not to repeat past mistakes." Then, he disappeared, along with both guards. Osr stood alone.

"Discerning, like you," Kera said.

"Since his return to Sunsprit, he has proven highly useful," Osr replied.

Two new Vaesians appeared beside Osr. They were

non-Silvereds, and clearly not guards. Each was spaced a comfortable stride from Osr, and flickered – holo representations.

"Welcome, Mnosr... Aivinr," Osr said, greeting them.

They greeted Osr in kind, and then each other.

"We'll keep this meeting brief," Osr said. "The power requirements are... substantial."

"Then let us be clear and concise," the Vaesian holo to the left of Osr – Aivinr – said, quietly and authoritatively. "We want answers, Kera. To everything. The terrible war with the Administration and the utter devastation that ensued was due to your actions. You will tell us everything."

"The war with the Administration was inevitable," Hespinr interrupted, calmly. "That cannot be blamed on Kera."

"Not solely, perhaps. But in large part."

Ilouden spoke up. "Kera was captured by them, tortured and—"

"Or did she allow herself to be captured?" Aivinr growled. He pointed to Ilouden. "Your name..."

"Ilouden, I—"

"Well, Hespinr, I'm sure both you and this... *Ilouden* have other matters to attend to. You may leave the council meeting."

Ilouden's cheeks reddened. He looked about, uncertain, while Hespinr glanced at Osr, whose tensirs gently fluttered. Hespinr stood up tall. "Come, Ilouden."

"Fine."

They both left.

Mnosr spoke a little more amiably than Aivinr. "Seventy years ago, Kera, you claimed the dummy node would yield the secrets of the Tugs – about the Source and everything in it. You made certain promises to us. As a result of our acquiescence, you might say we paid a terrible price."

"And before that!" Aivinr said. "It all traces back to you and your actions, Kera. Our cities destroyed, seized, countless deaths. And we learned nothing from you, nothing!" He glared between Osr and Mnosr. "We still don't even know how she managed to gain access to their influx network, or what augmentations she used. It's been seventy years, and we know nothing! The abilities of our Silvereds are not enough to defend us from the Administration." He fixated on Osr. "If this was anyone else, you would already have forced them to tell us what they know, yet she was allowed to enter freely. As though she were not to blame for everything!"

"That is not the most pressing matter, of which we require imminent knowledge," Osr said, measuredly. "First, Kera, you must tell us of this Nesch, and why it is here."

"I agree," Mnosr said, a moment later. "Yes, everything has its order. That presents a far greater threat to our immediate survival than anything else."

Aivinr said nothing, though both sets of tensirs ruffled irritably.

Osr looked between Kera and Diyan. "Well then?"

Chapter 35

Awaited Revelation, Top Official

Mericadal conducted a final set of diagnostics tests on his combat suit – everything was in perfect working order. Beside him, Commander Miren was doing the same. Their suits were synced, ready for combat. Aside from having higher mechanical strength and durability, Mericadal's suit had other additional capabilities that Commander Miren had no knowledge of – chemical injectors to facilitate clarity of thought and various other physiological processes; ancillary chemical diffusers for the same purpose; full access to the weapons arsenal of Commander Miren's suit; complete sensory overlay so that the suit's sensors instinctively enhanced and supplanted his own; and other augmentations. However, despite his advantages, the summary of Commander Miren's physiology showed she was just as calm as he was, just as prepared. She faced him.

"Ready when you are."

He nodded. They stood together, in front of a vast row of soldiers, all on foot, at the front of the encampment. Rows back, there were crykels, then some larger adapted skimmers, extended wideberths and streamthins. Vast shadows were strewn across from the eleven great warships in the skies above, all surrounded by a multitude of smaller low-flying military ships and swarms of drones. It was the largest military display in memory. Mericadal's voice would be amplified by his suit, with various repeaters ready to extend it to the rest of the forces.

Enormous holos of them both, Commander Miren and Mericadal, were projected above the heads of the soldiers by the warships. Mericadal's was slightly larger. It was the first time most of the soldiers were learning of his existence. The fact that Commander Miren stood by, deferential, spoke for itself.

"This is it," he said, smiling as he heard his voice booming around, watching with bemusement as some of the more astute soldiers immediately understood and recognised him for who he was. The leader and ultimate ruler of the Administration; the most powerful Roranian on Ringscape. "Commander Miren and I risk our lives willingly, so that Fadin may thrive. So that you may thrive. So that the Administration emerges victorious. It all started with Tapache's quest, and that endures, even now. As the single representative of the elected Members, I, Mericadal, do this in your name."

Mericadal paused, letting the information sink in. Revelations required time to be understood. A few of the soldiers right before him had averted their gazes. He smiled and checked his suit's analysis of their actions. His smile faltered. There were indications that their actions were the result of apathy. He frowned.

"I, Mericadal, do this in the name of *all* Roranians! For us! Do not underestimate the importance of what we are about to do, or how pivotal a moment this is in our history." He paused again, waiting for the soldiers to turn back. They did not. Instead, more turned away, again apathetic. He paused his speech, making it appear as though he was contemplating his next words carefully, while in reality using subtle gestures to order the suit to make notes of exactly which of the nearby soldiers had not paid attention. He amplified external auditory noise and selected a conversation between two of the soldiers, who were muttering to each other, to filter through.

"Knew it," the soldier said, from the side of his mouth.

"The rumours were true," the other said, rolling her eyes. "Worst kept secret anyway."

"Bit of a funny name too. Reckon he chose it for himself?"

Both broke out into muffled chuckles.

Mericadal clenched his jaw, noting to pay particular attention to those two soldiers later on, and returned external auditory noise to normal levels. He resumed, smiling broadly again. "We will emerge victorious... just as we defeated the Vaesians, we will defeat this creature!" The suit detected *another* apathetic party, to his right — Commander Miren! She was not paying attention either. He regarded her through narrowed eyes. "Commander Miren, your words?"

She nodded shallowly, taking a deep breath. The apathetic soldiers all looked up, without exception, their eyes open, interested. "We will be victorious," she said, measuredly, seriously.

Mericadal waited, but nothing else was forthcoming from Commander Miren, nor even the hint of her lopsided smile. Mericadal opened his mouth, about to say something to follow, when a growing, roaring noise began to filter through. It rolled from the peripheries of their great mass of forces, from the back towards the front. Mericadal clenched his fists. The wave was almost upon them — cheering. Soon, all the soldiers were involved, and Mericadal was forced to dampen his suit's auditory filters to protect his hearing.

"We go now," he said, a little hurriedly, half-turning before he had finished the short sentence. The tone of the cheering was unchanged, as though his words had been neither heard nor noticed. Mericadal turned fully around and waited. Commander Miren lagged just behind, irritatingly.

Mericadal blocked external communications, allowing

only a two-way channel between himself and the commander, focusing his sensors on the route ahead as they walked out from the encampment. "And so, we go, Commander Miren."

She did not reply.

Mericadal persisted. "That was quite something, wasn't it?"

"Yes, it was." Her tone was steely.

"And so, we go."

Something sounding like a muffled chuckle came through the channel. However, the commander's voice was unchanged. "We go," she replied.

"Not long, and the battle commences."

Mericadal visually magnified the scene ahead. The Nesch creature waited. Powerful. The challenge. It had not bothered to make a new den, or do anything at all during the reprieve. It simply waited. Commander Miren began to jog at a light pace; Mericadal copied her, making sure to run a little faster, taking the lead and remaining just in front.

"You do understand why I had to come out of the shadows?" Mericadal asked her. "I had to make my presence known to our forces. They need to know who it is that fights for them."

"I do."

"You can use my name now, Commander Miren. Everyone knows it."

"Okay, Mericadal."

Mericadal looked back. The cheering of the troops had died down. The enormous display of the Administration's might waited silently, watching, just like the Nesch.

"When we're finished, I'm going to lead us across Ringscape. That's what our plans were, so long ago, before the Administration. We just forgot, I forgot. But we're no longer pandering to anyone else, let alone the Vaesians, or the Silvereds. We're going to take Ringscape, put it all under our control, and we'll start with Sunsprit. We've become stagnant, Commander Miren, but no more. I've never seen it so clearly before."

"Yes, Mericadal."

Mericadal checked Commander Miren's physiological summary again, more invasively than the battle-synch allowed by default. She was concentrating on the Nesch. He instructed his sensors to further magnify the image of the Nesch and gave it his own full attention. Commander Miren's pace picked up some more. Mericadal let her gain a slight lead this time. He took several deep breaths, requesting more assistance from the chemical injectors. He was calmed. They were almost there.

Soon, the Nesch did not need to be magnified, it was just a few short leaps away. Mericadal broke off to the side. Commander Miren was on course to directly intercept the creature; Mericadal would flank it from behind. A moment later, the battle had begun.

Commander Miren landed the first blow, her weaponry in automated mode, firing obfuscating rounds that hid her intentions. She ducked low and rammed a powerful fist straight into the creature's stomach. It swung at her, fast but unsuccessfully. Mericadal's chemically altered cognition now allowed him to see with almost time dilative capabilities. Commander Miren had ducked before the blow had even begun, anticipating it. She then somersaulted to the side and stood in an aggressive pose further around the creature. Meanwhile, Mericadal twisted around and landed a mighty backfist against the Nesch's head, which succeeded in knocking it off-balance. The creature spun around, turning to Mericadal, attention taken. Commander Miren took advantage, raining down blows from behind. Mericadal waited, moving deftly out of the way from a cutting swipe, keeping his distance until its attention was diverted away. Then, he attacked again.

They had the better of the Nesch. It constantly appeared off-balance, thwarted from mounting its own attacks by their consistent bombardment. It stumbled, rocked by their strength. They danced about, landing blows as they pleased.

Chapter 36

Echoes of Assistance, Liberation

Groups of Silvered guards were clustered about along the long railing overlooking the edge of both Upper-Sunsprit and the upperside of Ringscape. Some other Silvereds wandered about, unconnected to Diyan and Kera's presence, though they soon became scarce. There were no other Roranians. The continual flips whipped the air into a frenzy.

"This is where they took you, isn't it?" Kera asked, just loud enough to be heard above the wind. "This is where your journey began."

"My journey didn't begin here," Diyan said, at a similar volume. "It began on our Great Ship, with you."

Kera tipped her head to the side. "That's one way of looking at it."

Diyan leaned over the railing, allowing one booted foot to rise into the air while keeping the other planted firmly against the ground. Tubes snaked down towards Under-

Sunsprit, with dark forms whizzing about within them in both directions. "I fell, over there. A Silvered in a wing-pack caught me, and you know the rest." He pushed himself back up and motioned with a finger from left to right, referencing the guards around them. "They don't need to be so subtle now, though. If you haven't noticed." Humour tinged his voice. "No orchestrated abductions."

"I expected no different. The size of the union council was a surprise, though."

"In truth, Aivinr and Mnosr are little more than advisors to Osr now. The Vaesian Union and its council is gone. Osr governs what there is left to govern. Aivinr and Mnosr don't even control their own cities. If they did anything, the Administration would crush them. Sunsprit's all that's left."

"And who will take Osr's place? Ulantr?"

Diyan huffed. "I don't think so."

"Why?"

"He certainly inherited a few useful characteristics from Osr, and I believe he inherited Osr's memories — or a great deal of them, at least. But they have differing opinions about certain things. I think that's always surprised Osr."

"What things?" Kera asked, coolly.

"Many things."

"Like me?"

"What makes you say that?"

299

"Ulantr spoke of not repeating past mistakes."

Diyan ruminated on this. "I've heard them have similar exchanges before. I think it was something else." He gripped the railing tightly with both hands. "I'm not sure. But, either way, there's someone more suitable, if you ask me."

"Hespinr." Kera did not say the name as a question.

"Yes."

"He's certainly capable."

"I think Osr's been grooming him for it, even if Hespinr can't see it himself. We've never discussed it. But I'm sure that's why Osr has assigned him to personally liaise with many of those in Sunsprit's key positions. Hespinr's been learning about the goings-on in Sunsprit for some time now. Osr wants his presence to become recognised and established."

"I'm surprised he was allowed to leave Sunsprit with you, then."

"He wasn't, at first. Hespinr had to force Osr to let him come. He threatened to leave Sunsprit."

"I didn't realise Hespinr was so fond of me."

Diyan laughed. "What makes you think he didn't come just to help me? Hespinr and I have known each other a long time now."

Kera also chuckled. "Well, anyway, Osr's no fool. And Hespinr's a good choice."

"I agree."

"I wonder what secrets he will be learning."

"*You* wonder what secrets *Hespinr* will be learning."

Kera smiled. "Sunsprit still has its mysteries."

"You being amongst them, Kera."

Despite the howling winds, a silence fell around them. Diyan looked at Kera and released a hand from the railing, turning side-on. Her face stiffened. "Kera... you can't delay telling Osr and the others what you know for long. They won't allow it. They'll expect full answers, very soon."

"I told them about the Nesch."

"That's not enough. They're desperate, Kera, and you know it. Everyone is."

Kera stared into his eyes. "They needed to know about the Nesch," she insisted. "If it gets through Fadin, it'll probably come here next."

"But the Nesch was just an excuse not to tell them anything else, Kera, we both know that. Telling them you need to commune with Echoes of Gravity first, to order the information the Tugs gave you, is simply delaying the—"

"I'm not delaying anything," Kera said, interrupting him.

"They won't accept that you need time to readjust, not for long. What you know is too important."

"Diyan, I wasn't lying. That was the truth." She looked over the edge, allowing her head to hang limply. Her words were so quiet they were almost drowned out by the wind. "I really do need help."

"Kera," Diyan said, leaning over to hang his head beside hers. "Those cell-scales we both took will stop working soon. Then, we cannot be certain of our conversations remaining private. If there's anything you want to tell me, anything you don't think you can say to anyone else…"

"It's not that, Diyan. I'm… trying to understand."

"And Echoes of Gravity will help?"

Kera took some time to respond. "Things have become more confused now. To me. When you took me from the facility, I understood everything I needed to do. But now, with that Nesch… none of it makes sense. There are threads of information all jumbled in my mind, and I need help sorting them out. Echoes of Gravity helped me before, it told me what to do. I think it may be able to help me again."

"How did the Nesch confuse things for you, Kera?"

"Because I don't know why it's after me. There's no reason for it." Her bottom lip began to quiver. "And everyone knows it's after me. I can't even pretend to myself that it isn't." They both straightened up and looked forwards, towards Sunsprit's covering that curved over the edge. Kera's knuckles had become white from her hands' tight grip on the railing. Diyan put an arm across her back. She continued. "Aivinr alluded as much, even

Osr agreed. It's obvious. And I don't blame Hespinr or Ilouden for telling them that either, when they're brought before Osr again. They'll have no choice, it's their duty to say what they know."

"Hespinr and Ilouden care for you, Kera. No matter what you may think…" From the corner of his eye, Diyan could see the Silvered guards still observing them with interest. He leant closer to Kera and spoke softly. "Kera, you need to trust me. Tell me what's going on. The things you've already told me… I don't understand them." He paused. "But I want to. About wanting to bring the Breaker to Sunsprit, and wanting to destroy the Source. Why—"

"I do trust you, Diyan. You're the only one I trust."

"And you still won't tell me?"

"I'm terrified everything I've done has been for nothing." She pulled her head back to lock her glistening eyes with his. "And that is why I need to see Echoes of Gravity. I need my focus back. I can hardly hold myself together…" She began shaking. Diyan pulled her into a tight embrace.

"Everything's going to be okay," he said into her ear. "We'll figure it all out, together. Then, we're going to find Paran and Yena, and we're all going to be together again."

A Silvered guard marched over to them. "Your path has been cleared, we are to take you to Echoes of Gravity now."

Chapter 37

Fresh Sensation, Commander

Paran looked around, a frown forming on his face. There was nothing: neither the Alpuri city nor signs of any other settlement. He walked on, only Ringscape's empty surface and the clear skies above for company. If anything, Ringscape seemed flatter than usual.

"Topinr," Paran shouted. "You'd better not have dropped me…" His words faltered. He tried to speak again, but nothing happened. The air in his throat was thicker than it was supposed to be. Breathable, but words were no longer possible. His vision was becoming hazier too; Ringscape was less defined with every strained breath, the thick atmosphere even thicker. Everything minimised, somehow focused upon him. It was as though the rest of Ringscape was disappearing, leaving just a small patch in existence.

Paran tried to reach his facepiece, but his hands were unresponsive. He was paralysed, stuck in a microcosm of reality. His eyes were able to flicker from side to side, and his muscles were able to shiver, but that was it. He could not scream. He could not make any sounds. He could not hear. All physical sensation dissipated. Only his immobility remained.

Darkness. His sight was extinguished. Light, the ground, sensation of where he was – gone. He was engulfed, or obscured. His thoughts raced. Something began to resolve in the nothingness before him, ethereally lit. An entrance, a passageway, with part of a ledge at the front. It came towards him, and a moment later, he was standing upon it. He peered into the entrance – it was brightly lit; he was temporarily blinded. His body slackened and he took a step forward, then stopped, in realisation and confusion at his sudden freedom.

"Hello?" he whispered, to no one in particular. He cleared his throat, strengthening his voice. "Hello? What's going on?"

He stared down at the ledge beneath his feet, lightly tapping a heel against the surface. There was a dull, thudding response. Paran clenched his jaw. His focus shifted to the entrance; his breathing increased. He shuffled closer, then took a step inside. The walls dimmed. It was a short passageway, with solid, dark walls and a ceiling another half his own height, wide enough to be more than comfortable. Steps led down at the end.

Before he could move forwards, the top of a head

appeared, rising from the steps. Roranian. Dark brown hair, light streaks. A face, becoming more visible as it rose. Slim, delicate features, slightly upturned nose, inquisitive eyes, knowing expression. The figure paused at the top of the stairs, looking straight at him, then continued walking forwards, coming to a standstill just a short step away.

"Yena…" Paran's voice broke.

"I'm glad you came."

"I'm sorry…"

Yena dismissed his words with a flick of her head. A smile grew across her pretty face. "All's forgiven." She took the final step closer, then embraced him, wrapping her arms around his waist. He embraced her back, sinking his chin into her shoulder.

Chapter 38

Stabilisation of Knowledge, Liberation

Lellara and Bomera warmly welcomed Diyan, though Kera received a frostier reception. The four of them stood on a high walkway, overlooking Sunsprit's hidden cavern set deep within the side of Ringscape. The walkway's transparent tubing allowed views of the tops of the cavern's towers all around them – coloured the same brown as Ringscape's surface. Various walkways stemmed from the tops and mixed around them. The pattern of intermingled walkways continued down, layer after layer, disappearing into obscurity into the depths of the cavern.

"It's all very unusual," Lellara said, gesturing at the lack of activity around them with one hand, the other occupied with holding a Tug Mask at her hip.

Bomera, who also held a Tug Mask, looked accusatorily at Kera. "Non-essential operations have been suspended, making way for *you*. Protecting *you* in case something happens." She smiled thinly. "You're obviously important enough, especially with such an entourage from Upper-Sunsprit. We didn't even know the Silvered had these capabilities." She waved incredulously at the apparently empty air around them. "Osr only just cleared us to know." The sweet smell of muvaeyt from the concealed guards wafted past, its intensity varying in the gusty winds whipped about by the perpetual flips. Kera did not reply, simply returning Bomera's thin smile with an otherwise impassive face.

"Did everything go as expected?" Lellara asked.

"More or less," Diyan replied.

Bomera still wore a critical frown. "It was a long time in the planning. I hope it was worth it." Her expression softened as she met Diyan's eyes. "We know you suffered."

"Kera's here now."

"You've changed," Kera said to Lellara.

Lellara looked down at herself, confused, following Kera's gaze. Her body was easily visible through her regwear. Whilst still very lean, thicker muscles showed through, more comparable with Bomera's. Alongside their similar frames, they had also fashioned their hair in the same tight buns. "It's been a long time, Kera." Lellara motioned with her hand. "We're to be your chaperones, so let's go."

Kera and Diyan followed Lellara and Bomera. They were led through tower after tower, crossing walkways and trudging down various sets of steps, descending deeper into the cavern.

"I've never seen it so empty," Diyan observed as they passed through a living compartment in one of the towers.

"The less who know Kera's back, the better," Bomera replied indignantly, leading them out of the compartment and onto a fresh walkway.

Lellara spoke more lightly, turning back to smile every now and then at Diyan and Kera. "There are more who might recognise you down here, Kera, than in main Sunsprit. Osr's just being proactive."

"Proactive," Bomera said, with barely disguised contempt. "Reallocating anyone living in the central towers to the peripheries?" She pointed to the towers at the edges of the cavern.

"It's just temporary," Lellara replied. "You know that."

They left the level's main walkway, proceeding onto a smaller side-walkway, and then into a new tower, immediately descending the steps down to the next level. Bomera huffed as they went, her frustration constantly audible.

"You changed everything. You should know that." Again, Bomera spoke while staring forwards, although it was obvious who her words were for. "The war, the death, all of it came from you."

"Bomera, that's not fair..." Diyan protested.

"I don't care," Bomera replied, testily. "She should

know it. And all Roranians in Sunsprit are viewed with blame, not just her. It's *us* who are paying the price. My brother even left because—"

"Bomera, this isn't helping," Lellara said. "The past is the past, no one could have predicted what would happen. And Kera was captured, she's suffered too, same as everyone else. Maybe even more."

Bomera chuckled. "And now she's here to help, is she? Then why isn't she with Osr now, instead of requesting Echoes of Gravity? Have you forgotten what happened last time? She went to the Tugs and disappeared!"

A stronger smell of muvaeyt wafter closer around them, as though in warning, and Bomera's words went unanswered. They passed through to another tower, descending a level and exiting onto a walkway. A lone Silvered strode past, paying them no attention.

Bomera shook her head. "See," she said, as though a point had been made. "They won't even look at us."

"The guards probably just expanded the concealment field to include us," Diyan said calmly. "We weren't seen."

Lellara sounded intrigued. "But we didn't feel anything."

"You never do."

"How does it work?"

Diyan shrugged. "I don't know."

They continued in relative silence, Bomera's irritated mutterings the main source of noise, attempting to bait

Kera, who remained calm.

Lellara spoke up, in an obvious attempt to brighten the mood. "Believe it or not," she said, looking back to Diyan and Kera, "I haven't been right to the top of the towers in quite some time."

"Probably good to get some perspective," Diyan replied.

"I'd forgotten how long it takes to move about here!"

"That's purposeful," Bomera said, testily. "The pathways are designed to make it difficult to penetrate the cavern's depths."

"But still..." Lellara slowed down. "You forget how large... I mean, look around us. It's easily as big as Upper-Sunsprit—"

Bomera interrupted Lellara, swinging her Tug Mask impatiently against her thigh. "Come on, we'll never get there at this rate."

They picked up the pace, descending level after level. A few more Silvereds passed them; again, none seeming to notice their passage. Bomera's angry mutterings resumed.

"I understand your anger," Kera said calmly as they found themselves on an empty walkway.

"Do you?" Bomera asked.

"Of course, I do."

"You are dangerous."

"I'm trying to help."

"Help who? Have you heard the new rumours about you?" Bomera asked maliciously.

"Bomera, don't—" Lellara attempted.

"She should hear!" Bomera insisted. "There are rumours, amongst those who know you've returned, that you're also connected to what's happening in Fadin right now. That this creature, whatever it is, is after you! Trouble always follows you, Kera. If this creature is after you, then Sunsprit will be next. Our defences are being shored up as we speak – is that just a coincidence? Does Osr believe the same—"

"Bomera! Come on," Lellara implored.

"They're saying it's a Nesch!" Bomera shouted, bringing them to a stop and glaring back. She jutted a finger at Kera. "She's dangerous, Lellara, Diyan. When is everyone going to realise that?"

"It is a Nesch," Kera said, apparently unfazed by the outburst.

"What?"

"The rumours you've heard are true. The creature is a Nesch."

"You admit it!" Bomera stuttered. "Your... your past is tied up with them!"

Kera simply nodded.

"And what do you..." Bomera didn't seem to know what to say next. "I've... I've heard they move from ship to ship, out there," she pointed above them, "in the lattice.

They overcome whatever they find, then they just push on."

"It's true," Kera said. "They adapt to their environments. They change to reflect powerful forms of incumbent species, and that form of mimicry has helped them become successful."

Bomera opened her mouth to speak again, but Diyan interrupted. "Bomera, this Nesch is keeping the Administration busy, for now. It's their problem—"

"Only for now!"

"The barricade around Sunsprit has also been reduced. Some say it's almost completely gone," Lellara said in Kera's defence. "And from what we now know about our own capabilities, the capabilities of some of the Silvereds, maybe this Nesch isn't a threat for us."

Bomera snorted. "What if it's all a trick? What if Kera's working for the Administration? After all the time they had her, we're letting her back here like nothing's happened—"

"Bomera!" Lellara shouted. "Stop it."

"Why should—"

"We have work to do, Bomera," Diyan said loudly and sternly. He put an arm out, indicatively. "Let's go."

Bomera seemed about to reply, when the smell of muvaeyt wafted strongly around them again.

"Arguing will get us nowhere," Lellara said. "Come on."

Bomera clenched her jaw and turned around, and they resumed walking. Finally, the last tower opening was up ahead. Only two Silvereds in sparse clothing, holding Tug Masks and gravitometers, waited. They walked forwards, their bodies briefly still, and then descended, disappearing from sight.

"Echoes of Gravity awaits," Bomera said quietly, as they reached the opening.

"We're to wait in the Tug Field for as long as you need," Lellara added.

"It's almost pointless," Bomera said, shaking her mask. "They'll probably be done before our platform reaches the field."

"Osr's orders," Lellara said. She looked at Kera. "You're to be allowed all the time you need. Once you're done, we'll escort you back."

"Thank you," Kera said. Despite her impassive countenance, her eyes had widened, her pupils dilated.

"Some of the guards will come down with us, others will go down after you. They'll be positioned all along the levels above and below you, although you'll have Echoes of Gravity's level all to yourself."

"The guards should be there too," Bomera scowled.

"You know as well as everyone that Echoes of Gravity wouldn't show itself then, same as with the Tugs and complex machines. It'll just hide."

"Diyan's allowed," Bomera argued.

"Only Diyan." Lellara rolled her eyes. "You trust Diyan, don't you, Bomera?"

Bomera grunted. "I trust *Diyan*." She looked firmly at Kera. "You're being monitored, closely. So, don't do… anything."

"I'll keep that in mind," Kera replied.

"Right, we'll be off then," Lellara said, patting Bomera on the shoulder to grab her attention. They both moved onto the waiting platform. A strong smell of muvaeyt flowed past Kera and Diyan. "Good luck, Kera. I hope Echoes of Gravity helps you with what you need." Their platform descended.

Kera and Diyan edged closer, waiting for the next platform to appear.

"Back, after all this time," Diyan said, exhaling. "Are you okay, Kera?"

"I never thought I'd see the Tugs again."

Diyan frowned. "We're not. We're going to Echoes of Gravity. The Tug Field is further down, right at the base of the cavern."

"Ah, yes."

"You don't want to visit the Tugs too, do you?"

"The Tugs? No. You're right. My mistake. We're not going to the Tug Field. Echoes of Gravity will suffice."

Diyan peered at her. "Kera, *are* you okay?"

She smiled, still staring forwards, into the darkness. The next platform appeared, waiting at their feet. "My thoughts are jumbled, I know that. My mind is… the Tugs, Echoes of Gravity… there's something that links them. I can… I can almost feel it, but it's just beyond me." A platform had just arrived and waited patiently at their feet. "Let's go."

"You're ready?"

Kera stepped forwards and Diyan followed. "Yes," she said. The platform began its descent, at first gathering speed, then slowing, coming to a halt. They stepped off. The platform continued down and disappeared. Kera grabbed Diyan's hand. There was just enough light for them to see each other's faces.

"Wait for me."

"I will."

She walked off, towards the chamber that contained Echoes of Gravity, her form dissolving from sight, the pattering of her footsteps fading to nothing. Diyan was alone.

Chapter 39

Partitioned Life, Visitor

Yena and Paran descended the steps from the entrance passageway, reaching an enormous, circular room at the bottom. Yena said nothing, remaining by the bottom step while Paran wandered slowly around the cavernous space, returning to her a little later.

The room was divided into four clear quadrants, with a great mass of vegetation at the centre. Two of the quadrants, diagonally opposite, were raised a hand's width higher than the other two. A cluster of comfortable furnishings were laid about in the raised quadrant where Paran and Yena stood. Around the curved wall behind them were four darkened passageways that led elsewhere. The next quadrant along was lower, and had furnishings that were far larger. The third and fourth quadrants contained various games and other facilities Yena had enjoyed from her time aboard their Great Ship.

The vegetative mass at the room's centre – a forest –

rose up many multiples of their own heights and brushed against the ceiling. A mixture of winding, blue-lighted paths from each of the four quadrants led into the forest. Yellow lights were interspersed within its depths.

Paran pointed at the large furnishings in the next quadrant along. "That's where you slept, isn't it?" He spoke quietly. "All that time ago."

"It's where I sleep now."

"What is this place?" he asked.

"You tell me." She took his hand and led him towards the centre of the room, along one of the blue-lighted paths. They entered the forest, immersed in the rustlings of the leaves. Paran reached out, touching some of the plants, running his fingers along their surfaces, laughing as he pressed his hand against some of the taller, harder stems. They stopped at the forest's centre, where a stream of water burst up from the surface of a pond, defying gravity and arcing back down, just a small distance away. It repeated, again and again, with no audible sound. A raised bench circled the pond.

"Yena, how is this possible?"

"What did you expect?"

"This was supposed to be something else... everything references a city."

"And what did you think an Alpuri city would look like?" she teased.

"Not your annexe." He gestured around them. His

eyebrows pushed against each other in the middle of his forehead. "Your annexe shouldn't exist. All the annexes were destroyed, along with our Great Ship." He peered more keenly at the nearby foliage. "Is this a holo?"

She chuckled. "Not exactly."

"But it's not your annexe, it can't be, except... it looks exactly like your last configuration."

"I'm glad you remember." Yena sat on the bench that circled the pond, and motioned for him to sit beside her. "The Alpuri let me stay here."

"So, they are here," he said with relief, sitting down, looking animatedly about. "Where?"

She chuckled again. "Didn't you ask a Prietman about them?" He began to answer, but she interrupted him. "I'm just playing with you, I apologise, Paran." She took on a more serious tone. "I know the answer's no. No Prietman ever speaks of the Alpuri, if they did, they wouldn't be allowed back here."

"Which is... where?"

"You might be allowed to see. It took quite a while for them to let me see, and even then, I've been sequestered here."

Paran's mouth opened wide. "This is a prison."

She patted him on the shoulder. "No, no. Not like that."

"Then... what?"

"It's somewhere to stay."

Paran frowned. "For what?"

Yena turned to lock eyes with him. "For now, to talk. Tell me, what's happened while I've been gone?"

*

Yena had been silent for some time, simply listening.

"And so Topinr dropped me off near here, and is now on his way back to Sunsprit, to tell them about what we learned in Barrenscape, and to warn them of the Breaker. Then, he will ensure the Roranian cities and settlements are aware. I just hope he is not too late…" Paran paused. "But that can wait, right now. There's nothing we can do…" He cleared his throat and took a deep, shaky breath. "I should have come sooner. I was too ashamed to search for you, at first. And then… it was almost all I cared about. I've wanted more than anything to tell you… to tell you that I'm sorry. I'm so sorry. About everything… about what I've done…"

Yena took his hand, clasping it tightly between her own, and placed another hand under his chin to pull his face gently back up. "Like I told you, all's forgiven. You came, that's what matters. I always knew one of you would…" A smile spread across her face. "But I hoped it would be you."

"Yena, the things I've done…"

She squeezed his hand harder. "We all played our

parts." Her smile grew. "And if Kera and Diyan really are on their way here, then that's all I can ask for."

"I'm surprised they're not here already."

Yena pursed her lips. "Perhaps they encountered their own obstacles, as you did, but... I believe both of them, together, will make it."

Paran looked about guiltily. "What have you been doing here, Yena?"

"I must admit, I lost track of time. I suppose you could say I was waiting. When I left, I wanted to find somewhere different. I thought, where better than somewhere no one knows anything about?" She chuckled. "Like you, I had no luck trying to get a Prietman to explain anything about the Alpuri. But, I didn't think I had anything to lose... so I simply came."

"And?"

"At first, I found nothing. Just an endless, hazy landscape."

"Me too."

"And that's it," she said, her words speeding up. "That's the Alpuri. They are far better adapted to Ringscape than you realise. They exist *in* it, a great, dense collective, that spreads far and wide."

"That's it?" Paran asked, eyebrows raised. "They're airborne?"

Yena scrunched her face. "In a manner."

"Like water vapour?"

"They're in everything. The air and the ground. It's all a little thicker."

"Like the thick atmosphere?"

"Maybe. Yes, I suppose, except they're physically here. They're connected, a massive collection of individual sentient thoughts, existing along tiny filaments. They're able to densify and coalesce when they want, or they can rarefy and hide themselves. Right now, they've quarantined this annexe."

"Why?"

Yena murmured something, and a holo appeared in her hand, a collection of bright sparks swirling around each other. She raised her other hand, and another holo appeared, depicting something more spiral-shaped. "This is our galaxy," she raised the second holo, "and this is theirs," she gestured to the first. "The Alpuri don't come from the same galaxy as us. I don't even know if their galaxy is near to our own. But, at some point, they left theirs for the universal gulf."

"The universal gulf?"

Yena nodded. "They decided to search the vast emptiness that exists between all galaxies. Like where we are now, where Tapache sent us."

"What were they searching for?"

Yena cancelled the holos and patted the bench. "This – Ringscape. The Source. Somewhere completely isolated from the rest of matter. The void probably would have suited them indefinitely, had they not found this place. You see, they were here before any of us. Before any others happened upon it. They don't just prefer isolation, it's a resource to them."

Chapter 40

Bifurcating Desires, Top Official

Mericadal ducked under the Nesch's swipe and jumped up to drive his knee against its downturned head. It stumbled back, and Commander Miren leapt above and kicked her heel against its forehead, sending it crashing down to the ground. It rose up, but they were both fast upon it, granting it little reprieve.

"Commander," Mericadal shouted, excitedly, just about managing to regulate his breathing. "There's nothing it can do! We're winning!" He backed away from the Nesch, just out of reach of its latest attempt, and nodded indicatively at it. When Commander Miren did not reply, he spoke again. "Commander?"

"Mericadal, we're not winning." She landed a spinning back-kick against the Nesch's leg, forming a dent. The leg did not buckle. She dropped down low and punched a fist against the dent. The leg bent, collapsing in on itself, and the Nesch tumbled to the floor again. They both dived

324

upon it, but this time, it sprung up quicker than before, succeeding in defending itself.

"We're not winning?" Mericadal almost laughed the words. "It's losing, there's nothing it can do!"

"We can't go on like this," she replied.

"You're not tiring, are you? I'm barely even trying," he said, gleefully jumping to land both legs forcefully against the Nesch's midsection, causing it to stagger back some way. He somersaulted backwards, gracefully landing on his feet. Then, he ducked down low, and charged at it.

"Mericadal, this does not end the way you think." Commander Miren spun around the Nesch, wrapping an arm around it then levering its body around, causing it to flip and tumble to the floor. They jumped after it again. It rose to its feet, again just about managing to adeptly defend itself.

"Meaning?"

"It's learning about us, Mericadal. It's learning about how we attack, how we move together... it's adapting, like we knew it would."

"But—"

"We're not actually doing any damage, Mericadal. We're running through all the routines we have, every trick we know, but if we try them again... they're less and less successful."

"But it's so much slower than us!"

"Because it wants to understand our tactics, Mericadal.

You've never been in a true fight before, you don't understand how this works. We're losing!"

"Losing?" Mericadal jumped up and over the Nesch, then aimed a swift kick at both its legs. The Nesch lifted the first leg, though Mericadal's blow did land against the second, and it slipped to the side.

"You're a fool, Mericadal!" Commander Miren screamed.

Had it not been for his chemically-induced mindstate, Mericadal would have been surprised. "Commander Miren," he said, coolly, "I believe I misheard you."

"You've sent us to our deaths, Mericadal. You're just a fool playing with his toys, believing you're more than you are. You're a fool, Mericadal!"

"Commander—"

"You're not a warrior, and you never will be!"

"Careful, Commander Miren."

She shoved the Nesch away from her, as Mericadal brought his heel crashing down against its head, before feinting for its legs then pummelling its head again. "Just focus, Mericadal. Use everything you have. Otherwise, we'll be—"

"You're wrong, Commander Miren. It cannot go on forever. We are going to win."

"Then you're a fool, like I said."

"Miren," he spat, irritated enough that the induced battle-trance needed additional chemical support. "You think Tapache wouldn't have given us ample—"

"You see connections where there are none, you think Tapache intended for all this to happen, when that is beyond all likelihood. You're a fool!"

"Call me a fool one more time, Miren."

"Mericadal, you are a—" She spluttered, suddenly taking a step back from the Nesch, trying to recover from its blow that had only lightly connected, and would have barely registered before.

"What is it, Miren?" Mericadal asked, smirking. He charged at the Nesch, driving his knee against its back and causing it to crash to the ground.

"Mericadal, what have you done?"

"Problem, Miren?"

"My mechanical dampening is down."

"That sounds worrying."

"What have you done…" Commander Miren was rapidly trying to access her suit's underlying systems, but her access had been revoked. Her panic was rising.

"Who's the fool now. Go on, show our soldiers how much of a coward you are."

"You can't do this!"

"I can do anything, Miren."

Before she could reply, the Nesch lunged forwards and swiped an arm against the side of her chest. She fell to her knees. The Nesch then pivoted around, and brought an enormous leg violently against the side of her helmet. She was sent skidding along the ground, crumpling into a heap a little way off. The Nesch paused, looking at her as though surprised. Mericadal rushed towards it, bringing his fist low and jumping as he drove the uppercut against the base of its head. The Nesch was flung away, rotating as it was propelled backwards through the air, landing in a heap similar to Commander Miren's. Mericadal rushed over to the commander, making a show of checking to see that she was okay.

"Miren," he said, softly. "Just look at you now."

"Meric…" she muttered, weakly.

"Call me a fool now." He smiled lopsidedly at her, mockingly. "Go on."

"Listen…"

"What is it?"

"One… thing…"

"Yes?"

"You…"

"Yes, Miren?"

"You…"

He clenched his jaw. "I'm beginning to lose patience, Miren."

The Nesch was rising to its feet. Mericadal surveyed Commander Miren. The fingers of one hand were flexing, although the rest of her lower body was still. Her eyes were open, narrowed, staring at him through the transparent plate. Spittle and blood ran down the sides of her mouth. Although mortally wounded, she still tried to speak.

"What is it?" he asked, kneeling down closer, still keeping one eye on the Nesch. Making another show of physical concern, he put a hand under her head, chuckling at her discomfort. "What are you trying to tell me?"

"That. . ."

"Yes?"

"You. . . are a stupid fool." Despite her wounds, she was laughing.

He clenched his jaw. "Then let those be your last words." He let her head fall back as he stood up to meet the charging Nesch, making a show of attempting to protect the fallen commander before allowing himself to be thrust to the side. Stumbling backwards, he watched as the Nesch knelt down and drew back a fist, then plunged it into the commander's stomach. She did not scream. Her final sounds were those of laughter. Mericadal accessed the records of their conversation and deleted them.

The Nesch pulled its dripping red hand back from Commander Miren's stomach, pausing briefly to allow some of the commander's innards to slide off, to the ground. It tore off her helmet with the same hand, crushing it into a ball and tossing it away. Despite his chemical infusions, Mericadal retched.

When it was finished with Commander Miren, the Nesch began a fresh charge. Mericadal jumped forwards, swinging a fist, missing initially, but avoiding the Nesch's own blow and landing another just after. It was quite a while before he was able to gain another moment's reprieve, sending the Nesch spinning to the floor. The hint of a dull ache was growing within his arm. Diagnostics informed him he was building a short-term immunity to some of the chemical infusions. He had no time to think what to do. The Nesch charged again. Clearly, it had no such problems.

Chapter 41

Forbidden Knowledge, Liberation

Diyan peered down the passageway. It was too dark to make anything out. Only one other platform had whizzed past, carrying a single Silvered occupant who had been facing away from him. He turned and looked down the platform shaft, planting his feet just before the edge.

"You're not about to jump off, are you?"

Diyan span around. Kera was there. "I didn't hear you come back."

"You were looking in the other direction." There was a smile across her face.

"How was it? You were quite a while, usually it's far quicker."

"Good."

"Just good?"

She placed a hand on his shoulder. "I understand now."

"What?"

"Everything I need to. There are still things I need to know, but I'm not unaware of them anymore. I know what I don't."

Diyan sucked his teeth. "You're supposed to have answers, like you said you would. Osr and the others will demand them."

"I know that. I'll tell them what they need to know."

"Kera, we had an—"

"I'll tell you everything, Diyan, I will. But not them. Osr, Mnosr, Aivinr… they won't understand. You're the only chance I'm willing to take."

"Kera, they won't accept that. Everything that's happened, everything that's been risked…"

"They *will* accept what I tell them." Her tone became conversational, as though she had not heard his concerns. "I have one condition."

"What is that?"

"That I'll only explain it all to you once we've left."

Diyan frowned. "What do you mean?"

"We're going to find Paran and Yena, aren't we? You and I. That's the plan. So, we're going to the Alpuri, which is where they should be. And, once we're on the way, I'll tell you."

"And what about what you said before, about wanting to find the Breaker and bring it to Sunsprit?"

Kera shrugged. "Echoes of Gravity was… insistent. That is no longer necessary."

"Insistent? That sounds like a conversation."

"I know."

"Echoes of Gravity doesn't have conversations, that's not what it does."

"It has a will of its own. That's undoubtable. Perhaps that's all it has."

Diyan's frown deepened. "Kera, I must remind you, again, the others will want to know everything. This doesn't sound like you're going to do as you promised."

"I'm not going to lie to them, Diyan. There are just some things that aren't for them. And there's no need to mention the Breaker, it'd just cloud things, and that's something I truly don't know about. You're going to have to trust me. Like I trust you."

Diyan could not stop himself from laughing. "You trust me? You've not told me anything."

"I do trust you." She strode over to wait for a platform.

Diyan moved beside her. "Really?"

She looked at him. "Don't be concerned. I do have much to tell Osr and the others – about the Nesch, and about how I was changed. And I'll tell them about the information contained in the dummy node."

"But you won't tell them everything?"

"There are things they shouldn't know."

A platform arrived, from below for once. Lellara and Bomera waited expectantly, Tug Masks in hand.

"Enlightening?" Bomera asked.

"Very," Kera replied. Bomera and Lellara both waited, expectantly, but Kera simply strode onto the platform. "Come on, Diyan, let's go."

*

Kera and Diyan were flanked by Silvered guards in Upper-Sunsprit, no longer concealing themselves. Thick blue clouds of muvaeyt wafted around them. They reached the same innocuous tower as before, where the meeting with Osr and the other two council members had taken place. A segment of the tower disappeared. Ilouden strode out. The guards fanned to the side, allowing him closer.

"Well, they're certainly excited to see you both," Ilouden said. "Practically pushed me out."

"Osr, Mnosr and Aivinr?" Diyan asked.

Ilouden nodded. "They wanted to know everything I learned about the Administration." He scratched the top of his head. "And in extreme detail. Propulsion systems, sky-factory plans – which I actually didn't know a great deal about, awkwardly – ship types, governing hierarchy, infrastructure plans, network rumours, all of it, and…" He paused uneasily. "A few other things."

"I understand," Kera said. "Of course they wanted to know your thoughts about me."

Ilouden's eyes flitted nervously over the guards around them. He spoke quieter. "I told them you'd tell them what they needed to know, Kera."

Kera's voice also lowered. "Thank you."

Ilouden exhaled jovially, changing the tone. "And they're going to send me back, soon. They want to take advantage of the lapsed barricade. Not Fadin though, probably Lortein. I said I'd rather stay here, what with that Nesch, they'll need all the help…" again, he trailed off, glancing awkwardly at Kera. "Well, I'll do whatever I'm told."

"We understand." Diyan patted Ilouden on the shoulder. "Thank you for all your help."

Ilouden smiled warmly. "Anyway. Lortein's connections to the influx network are still new. I should be able to help us gain quite the foothold there, circumvent and reroute it where we can. We'll see." He shrugged. "Someone has to do it." He glanced again at the guards. "Osr and the others are waiting for you. If I'm to leave soon, I'll make sure to find you before I go."

"And us too," Diyan said.

Ilouden bade them farewell, and they entered the tower. They walked the short passageway, the guard accompaniment dropping off, and entered the circular room where Osr, Mnosr and Aivinr waited. There was no smell of muvaeyt.

"We are alone," Osr told them. "Just the five of us." Mnosr and Aivinr's forms shimmered – holos, again.

"You don't trust your own soldiers?" Kera asked.

"Implicitly. But, I would prefer their minds unfettered."

"Change *is* coming, Osr," Aivinr said.

"Knowledge can be a heavy burden." Osr focused on Kera. "And knowledge is what we are here to receive."

"Indeed," Aivinr said. "Kera, now that Echoes of Gravity has helped order your thoughts, explain. Tell us what the Nesch did to you, these augmentations you have. Tell us how you gained access to the influx network, and what the Tugs told you. Tell us of the Source. Tell us everything."

Kera's jaw clenched. Her eyes flicked to Osr. Despite his frailty, Osr made no move to sit or relax in any way. He stood still and waited. She started.

"You all know my history. It started on our Great Ship, long ago." Kera smiled sadly at Diyan. "We were separated. Attacked by the Nesch. They captured me along with many other Roranians. The Nesch forced us to fight for them, up there, outside the Source…" She shuddered, blinking slowly. "You cannot imagine the horrors of those battles. They are of a scale beyond anything…" Her voice grew faint and she paused, closing her eyes.

Diyan squeezed her shoulder. "It's okay, Kera."

She continued. "The Nesch selected certain ones amongst us… those of us who showed certain aptitudes. I don't know what aptitudes, so don't bother asking, but they altered us. Almost none of us survived. We were separated after the procedures anyway; I never met another after that."

"What did they do to you?" Mnosr asked. His holo silently flickered.

"They… implanted something, something of *themselves*… into us."

"Themselves?" Even Osr sounded surprised.

"It's infiltrated every part of my body," Kera said. "It's like your cell-scales, but on a far more fundamental level."

"So, what are you? Some sort of hybrid?" Aivinr asked, scornfully.

"Is that possible?" Mnosr followed.

"It is possible," Kera said.

"Why would they put something of *themselves* into you?" Aivinr asked.

"For control," Kera replied. "The Nesch aren't a normal species, if such a thing exists. They're connected in ways we cannot understand; I still can't. Yet, their aims became my aims. I developed an overriding, insatiable desire to achieve their goals."

"Does this new Nesch creature hold some kind of control over you?" Aivinr asked, suddenly alarmed.

Kera shook her head. "No. When I came through the Haze Rings, their direct control over me was gone."

Diyan looked at her curiously.

"Why didn't you tell us before?" Mnosr asked.

"Because I didn't want to admit that I was no longer myself. You must understand, I'm not augmented, it's not a technology that's been placed within me, or some adaptation. It's a part of *them*. I'm no longer who I once was. I never can be again. I'm something else."

"And you decided it was better to keep this knowledge to yourself?"

"If I'd told anyone, who would have ever trusted me again? I know I wouldn't."

"Indeed," Aivinr said. "Who would?"

"They changed you," Osr said.

"Yes."

"In what way, specifically?"

Kera's head dropped, and she turned her hands over, palms up, staring at them.

"You should understand, *change* is what the Nesch are. It is everything about them. In the same way that Vaesians strive to increase their tetibats, the Nesch strive for change. It's insidious, it's what they are, it's why they exist. That's why I think they hate the Source so much; it is unchangeable, it is permanent. I believe it's a mystery to them as much as to us, and they hate it."

"But what have they done to you?" Aivinr asked.

"They gave me their ability to change," Kera said, as though it were obvious.

"You can change?"

"Nothing like the adaptive capabilities of an actual

Nesch. But, given time and resources, I can alter myself. I'm not sure what the limits are… and I'm not sure I'd like to find out."

"What alterations have you made?"

"Well, a long time ago, I focused on making myself strong, very strong. And capable of various forms of biomarker imprints and mimicry… and, well, now that you know that, it's not hard to understand how I obtained the dummy node, is it?"

"You can still explain to us," Osr said. "Start from when Diyan, Paran and Yena verified you on the Administration's influx network."

Kera looked guiltily at Diyan. "When I was verified, I was granted access to a key Administration building – a recruitment centre. Entering it without raising suspicion had always been the hardest part of the problem, since I needed to save my ability for mimicry until I was inside—"

"Why?" Aivinr asked sceptically.

"The mimicry takes some time to reset, it's not instantaneous, or easy, so I only had one chance. A legitimate way inside was the easiest solution."

"You couldn't have scouted it out beforehand?"

"I didn't want to risk being discovered."

"And why was this recruitment centre so important?"

"As you know, the Administration hides many of its research projects in normal, innocuous buildings. I'd made an effort to find out all that I could about them: rumours, hearsay, gossip, anything. That specific recruitment centre was where I suspected the dummy node project was being conducted, amongst others. I already knew of its general layout and surmised where I needed to be."

"Why the necessity to act so fast?" Mnosr asked.

Kera's tone changed, her words flowed faster, as though she was reliving the experience. "My altered instincts took over. I became overzealous and reckless. I *needed* to act. I recognised the dummy node might finally be something that could contain information from Echoes of Gravity, or even the Tugs. A vestibule for their knowledge." Her eyes widened. "I wanted to understand everything. To be able to change it all." She paused to glance again at Diyan. "Once I was inside the recruitment centre, I knew I'd most likely only have the one chance. I had to be quick. I made my way through the accessible areas, then waited until I was certain I'd identified an Administration researcher who was headed for the secure area. I... made sure she wouldn't wake up, for some time, and copied her biomarkers."

"Meaning?" Aivinr interrupted.

"I altered my form, copying her physiology to a level of accuracy high enough that the Administration sensors could not know the difference. Fortunately, certain measurements like total mass detection aren't used, which is an enormous security oversight." Kera allowed herself a smile. "And quite useful."

"You changed your appearance?" Aivinr sounded dubious.

"Some Silvereds are able to manipulate matter, to disappear at will, to do a great many things, yet you doubt this?" Kera asked. "I can show you if you'd like. I will need to prepare myself, but if one of you will volunteer, all I need is a little time, or a sample—"

"That won't be necessary, Kera," Osr said.

"Did it hurt?" Diyan asked.

Kera's nodded. "Very much. And the concentration to maintain the mimicry was intense. It's not something our minds are truly equipped to deal with." She cleared her throat. "Anyway, once I was through to the secure area, I immediately disabled any defence and surveillance equipment I could find, as well as anyone I came across." Her speech slowed. "I only wish I'd been more thorough because, well, I was unable to hold the form for long, and I must have missed a sensor or recording device somewhere, because afterwards, they knew it was me. And that's why they came for..." Her fists clenched. "They came for Diyan, Yena and Paran. As well as Soji and Irido. And that was my fault."

"There's a lot more that's your fault too," Aivinr growled.

"Tell us about what you did once you were in the

secure area," Mnosr said.

Kera took a moment. "I found the dummy node, I destroyed what I could of the equipment around it to cover my tracks, and I escaped. There's nothing else to say. I left for Sunsprit immediately." She stood up straighter, as though a great weight had been lifted from her.

"When you found the dummy node, Kera," Mnosr said, ponderously. "Your destruction, we have all heard, was furious."

"It was. I don't deny that."

"Why so angry? Something the Nesch did to you?"

"I was disgusted."

"Why?"

Her face scrunched into an angry scowl. "Because that research centre was also conducting work on the emox network. And before that, I had thought such a network to be fantasy. Too revolting, even for the Administration. I was… enraged."

The countenance of the three Silvereds changed simultaneously. "Ah," Mnosr uttered.

"The emox network?" Diyan said. "What is it?"

Kera spoke barely above a whisper. "A crime."

"The spark of life," Osr said.

"An emox is the other part of a Roranian consciousness, the counterpart to the influx," Kera explained. "The influx is the power behind the mind, but the emox is everything else. It's everything that defines us, everything that truly separates us from each other." She glanced sadly at Diyan. "Our wants, feelings, desires... our emotions..."

Diyan could barely speak. "What... what could the Administration want with such a thing?"

"It's how the Administration is governed."

"Paran never said this."

"He did," Osr spoke almost uncomfortably. "But that was never shared with you, Diyan. And anyway, he was not the first to have passed this information to us."

Kera looked at Osr keenly. "Maybe you should be explaining this. There's not much more that I know."

Surprisingly, Osr acquiesced. Aivinr and Mnosr seemed to slink behind him. "The Administration leadership uses the emox network like a powerful drug. The ruling Members are utterly addicted and their access is controlled. In truth, they're little more than shadows directed by the whims of the single, true ruler behind it all. A Roranian, whose name is Mericadal. A survivor, one of the earliest Roranians to be born in the Source. A long time ago, it appears he discovered a parsing process by which a Roranian mind could be split into two parts. As you now know, two living networks were the result. The influx network, smart while thoughtless, and the emox network, alive while dead." Osr stopped, his body shaking. Both Aivinr and Mnosr looked at him and flinched, as though wanting to aid him through their holos. Osr continued. "From there, this Mericadal gained an unparalleled advantage within the Source. Formidable information networks, in a place where machine intelligences cannot exist. He rose to power, unified the majority of the squabbling Roranians, and established the Administration."

"A network to control the rulers, and a network to control the ruled," Mnosr said. "Both networks have utterly surrendered themselves to the will of Mericadal, since he is their only chance of reunion. He wields this salvation over them."

"Who is this Mericadal?" Diyan asked.

"You know him, Diyan," Osr said. "He is the one who set you on Kera's trail, over seventy years ago. And he is the one who came for Kera, when she was taken."

A growl came from Aivinr. "Enough of this. Kera, it is time to resume your own story."

Chapter 42

Altered Understanding, Annexe

Paran grinned, jumping forwards and swiping at the empty air where Yena had been only moments before. He restabilised himself, turning to face her while setting his feet firmly on the ground.

"I've missed your smile, Paran," Yena said, still breathing calmly, stepping back and stalking the ground around him, forcing him to twist around in response. "It's always looked so good on you." She moved faster, suddenly switching direction, ducking low and kicking out a leg against the front of his feet. He tried to correct his position but fell to his knees. She reached forwards and smeared something dark across his faceplate, then pushed him onto his back, landing on top of him.

"That's cheating!" he shouted, as his faceplate slid back into his helmet, exposing his face. "We agreed, no additional capabilities." Before he could say anything else, Yena pressed her lips against his.

"I knew you'd come," she whispered, her face moving back a fraction. "Kera saw you first, but I loved you first." She rolled over and pushed herself up. "Anyway, no such thing as cheating in combat." The blue circle around them disappeared.

Paran rose to his feet, discombobulated. "You really have a cache of these suits?"

"Yes, and they're all level eighteens."

"I don't understand. This is an actual annexe, isn't it?"

"The Alpuri found it. When our Great Ship was destroyed, its parts rained down against the Haze Rings. This single annexe made it through. Lucky for us."

"How did they find it?"

"They pay special attention to large entry events, in case something significant makes it through. For obvious reasons, they'd rather be in control of anything too dangerous."

"And they hid it, all this time?"

"They can hide anything they want."

They stripped the suits off, down to their regwear underlayers. Yena took Paran's hand, and took him to a more comfortable piece of furniture in the adjacent quadrant, pulling him down alongside her. They lay, still, facing up. Slowly, Yena removed her underlayer suggestively, and waited while Paran did the same.

*

Paran walked back from the food dispenser and handed Yena some packets.

"We should have done that a long time ago," he said.

Yena nodded. "We should have."

They ate quietly, occasionally looking at each other, taking it in turns to blush.

Paran swallowed his final mouthful slowly, then reached over to grab their regwear. "So, how do you control this annexe without a c-autom?" he asked, passing Yena hers. They both stood up to get dressed.

"The Alpuri can control it. Basic functionality, I can do, but rearranging it, that's up to them. It's not easy, you should have seen some of their earlier attempts." She smirked. "But we got there."

"Before, you told me they quarantined this annexe…"

Yena nodded. "You're curious. I was too. When I first came here… I thought they'd trapped me in some strange prison." She laughed. "And it looked nothing like it does now, nothing at all. I began to accept my fate; I was at peace. And then, they communicated. I realised it was as much to quarantine themselves as it was to quarantine me."

"Why would they quarantine *themselves*?"

"The Alpuri are different, Paran. Unlike anything you can imagine. Species like ours would never survive in their city, we'd destroy it."

"But you said the Priet—"

"You've spoken to a Prietman," Yena said, laughing. "They tend to keep to themselves. Their thoughts aren't intrusive. That's why the Alpuri tolerate them. But us, we're far too unconstrained, too fast." She strode over to a bare wall of the annexe, waving him to follow. "I started to understand them by observing them. That was all they allowed, at first. And that's where you can start too."

"How do you speak with them?" Paran asked, settling alongside her.

"I think it, with surety, and then, it happens." She began to fixate upon a single part of the wall.

"What happens?" Paran asked. Yena raised her hand for silence. As soon as her hand dropped back down, the wall shimmered to transparency. Paran's eyes widened in surprise.

It was nothing like the hazy mist he had encountered upon first entering the Alpuri territory. A symphony of shapes in complex shades of white, as though made from ice, all pressed against one another, transparent to different degrees. The objects and their strange structures made no sense, yet everything fit perfectly together, synchronised in a gentle, oscillatory rhythm.

Some of the shapes were recognisable. Down to the left, a distance away from the annexe, just about visible, pale bubbles rose slowly up. A static face was displayed, created by collections of the bubbles, with just enough detail to be recognisable. A Roranian. "It can't be..." Paran murmured. Mericadal was there, frozen with a look of concern. Beside those bubbles, another depiction appeared, and another, and another. Uncountable portrayals revealed themselves. Paran focused on another: a Vaesian, mid-guffaw – Topinr, from when Paran had first met him, just before the Silvered had led Paran into his ship for the first time. Paran's eyes darted around.

"That's Mericadal, I think," Yena said, pointing. "Anyone else you recognise? Anything?"

"I..." Paran stumbled back. The window disappeared. "That was Topinr too, and some others..." His words became a whisper.

"Mesmerising, isn't it? Bits you know, most you don't, it draws you in."

Paran rubbed his eyes. "What was that?"

"Thoughts."

"Thoughts?"

"Yes. Thoughts. Their thoughts."

Paran rubbed the back of his head. "It all seemed so..."

"Stable?"

Paran frowned, as though surprised at finding himself in agreement. "Yes."

"And yet, you know that one wrong *thing*, and it would all collapse, and fall to the ground."

"Yes," Paran repeated.

"That is the Alpuri."

"What... what did I just see? The Alpuri's thoughts?"

"That's exactly what you saw." Yena gestured to the opaque wall. "You can imagine how long communication takes, in a way we can understand." She turned and leant against the wall, then slid down it, sitting down on the floor with her arms around her knees. Paran joined her. "They're ideas, coalescing and forming within their society. Being examined, checked and discussed. All at once."

"That was a debate?" Paran asked incredulously.

"In their way." Yena raised a hand and flattened her outstretched palm: a small holo appeared just above it, a beam of white, rotating light, the length of a finger. "Each Alpuri is a strand, a perfect biological specimen, with the ability to join to another and become whatever they mutually agree on. The things I've seen... the things they've shown me... given the right resources, given time, given certain ideas, the possibilities are endless." Multiple other holo strands appeared above her hand. They joined into one larger, thickened strand that began to stretch and elongate, seemingly haphazardly, although its new shape soon became evident. It had morphed into a seven-legged creature, not dissimilar to a Prietman. It then morphed again, other strands joining. The mass became larger: this time, a three-legged creature with a cluster of frond-like extensions protruding from a thin upper body that curved into a hook at the top. The creature broke down, separating into the disparate strands, all but one disappearing.

"They really can become anything?" Paran asked.

"Seems that way. I'm sure there are limits, but I don't know what they are. From what I do understand though, in order to become anything new, they just need to persuade each other."

"They're like machines?"

"They never needed machines in a sense we can understand. They can do things we can't, in the same way we experience the universe in a way they cannot."

"Unless they decide to join and become something like us."

"Exactly." Yena nodded. "But there are dangers."

"What dangers?"

Yena flexed her hand and whispered some commands too quietly for Paran to hear. The holo strand shot away from them. Countless more appeared in a cloud beside it, filling the quadrant of the room they were in. The strands grouped together, forming masses of irregular, spherical shapes that drifted to the ceiling. Other holo features were constructed on the floor of the room — a flat landscape, with structures resembling buildings. Mixtures of creatures scuttled around the buildings, some even looking similar to Roranians, none larger than the size of Paran's thumb. Without warning, the spheres rained down from above. As they reached the flat landscape, they spread out like a shockwave. There was no impact crater, nothing, but the original creatures and their structures were gone. A hazy sea of strands rose and settled, stagnant, the height of the original structures.

"What was that?" Paran asked.

"A variant of conquest," Yena answered. "One of many, many variants they thought of and practised."

"They showed you this?"

"Like I said, ideas are important."

"From before they entered the Source?"

"Must have been."

"Are they dangerous?"

Yena pursed her lips. "The Alpuri aren't bad or good, they're different. However, they are able to recognise what is bad for us. Perhaps they didn't always, but they do now."

"So that was a warning?"

"It was part of an explanation that took me a long time to understand. It's why their thoughts are so purposely protracted, why they deliberate so slowly. Ideas are important, they spread change."

"And that's why they've isolated themselves?"

"It gives them the opportunity to be measured, and to focus on themselves, rather than external influence. The thick atmosphere helps too, it decelerates their thoughts. They want to evolve in a different way."

"They're evolving through their ideas?" Paran asked.

"Why not?"

"What are they evolving into?"

She shrugged. "They already have the capability to become whatever type of perfect they want. They're still deciding."

Chapter 43

Changed Perspective, Top Official

Mericadal was flung back – the blow from the Nesch had taken him completely by surprise. He crashed down against the ground and skidded to a halt. Before he had the chance to regain his senses, he was struck along an arm and sent skidding away again. As soon as he stopped, he pushed himself up and jumped to the side, fortunately just out of the grasp of the Nesch. He somersaulted in the air and landed on his feet, now able to take stock of his surroundings. He crouched into a low combative pose. The Nesch was running towards him, with as much energy as though the battle had just begun. Mericadal gritted his teeth and uttered some commands through the suit. Suddenly, the Nesch was battered violently to the side, and sent skidding, just like Mericadal had been only moments earlier. Mericadal cried with elation. The Nesch rose to its feet, but was impacted again, this time from the other side. It skidded off again, then tried to rise, before being pounded, again and again.

During brief reprieves, the Nesch looked about in the empty air, searching for its unseen assailant. Soon, the Nesch was overwhelmed. The pummelling forced it onto its front. It struggled to push itself up, but was forcefully hammered against the ground. It stopped straining, its body responding passively to each blow, limbs flicking up each time. The invisible drone was relentless.

"It seems you can't see it either. Shouldn't have copied our visual spectrum so well," Mericadal said quietly, in a short-distance, open channel, unfortunately unable to ascertain whether the Nesch could receive the communication, let alone understand him. "Conceal's made from the same material our caskets were made from. Triamond-casing, from our Great Ship. The caskets were given to us by Tapache, designed to protect the first Roranian young. How fitting that I've managed to use them to protect us one more time." He skipped in a circle around the creature, every now and then taking a step radially closer, almost daring it to strike out. It continued to be violently bashed into the ground. "Now – what was it that Miren called me? A fool?" He settled closer, stopping to kneel, watching the Nesch suffer. He was about to open a communication channel back to the military fleet still watching, when the Nesch stirred. It rose, somehow, despite the blows against it. Mericadal frowned, then accessed Conceal's system and screamed with rage. Conceal was running out of fuel. The Nesch rolled to the side and rose to its feet. Conceal was done. Its concealment failed; it shimmered into the observable spectrum. It was about the size of the Nesch creature's head.

The Nesch grabbed Conceal with both arms and lifted it into the air. Mericadal watched in horror as Conceal was flung towards him. He was too slow. Conceal's body caught the side of his armoured head, sending him flying backwards.

Disoriented, Mericadal rose from the ground. The Nesch was upon him, pinning him down. Mericadal screamed, immediately opening a wide channel and authorising full-scale military assault on the creature. A barrage of projectiles slammed against it, knocking it to the side. Mericadal's suit protected him, though the shockwave shunted him across the ground. Once he was back on his feet, he looked for the Nesch. It was advancing towards him, the impacts around it no longer having any effect. "More!" Mericadal yelled, running backwards. "Hit it with everything!"

A voice came through. "We cannot, your proximity to the—"

"Do it now!"

"The safety—"

"Then send the drones!" Mericadal jumped back from the Nesch's clutches. He stared wide-eyed past the creature's shoulder. The sky was filled with drones headed rapidly for them. Projectiles continued to bombard the unfazed Nesch. "More!"

"We have—"

The communication channel was severed, the attacks stopped. "Answer me!" Mericadal waited, ready to fight, crouching low. The Nesch also stood still, upright, in the same pose as before, when it had been expecting a new opponent. Mericadal looked about. "What's going on?"

The Nesch turned away from the Administration encampment.

"Now!" Mericadal yelled. "Now!" Nothing worked. The communication channel could not be reinstated. "What..." The drones dropped from the sky – in unison. Frenzied lashing sounds filled the air, the results of the multitudes of bloom fragments whipping frenetically against the ground. "What's happening?"

Within the Administration encampment, the warships and other vessels moved back. Retreating. The soldiers were scattering away from Mericadal and the Nesch, back towards Upper-Fadin. Mericadal mumbled incomprehensibly in bewilderment. A new communication channel was being requested.

"Who is this?" Mericadal demanded.

There was no response. Instead, strange, indecipherable symbols traced across Mericadal's holo feed, the occasional word in Roranian script. *Emoxes.*

357

Three. Intellect. Nothing that made any sense. Mericadal checked for the channel's identifying characteristics.

"Influxa," Mericadal said. "What are you doing?"

From the corner of his eye, he could see a small speck in the distance. Influxa was returning. However, something was wrong. She was not flying normally. She moved straight, then changed direction and moved straight again – zigzagging through the air. Mericadal accessed what more he could from the channel, but the information was scant. She currently only occupied her emergency node, the outer casing gone. Influxa was also supposedly out of fuel, but that was not possible. He tried to magnify the image further, but the suit was too damaged. Momentarily, a hazy sphere appeared, before disappearing.

"Influxa," Mericadal repeated. "Answer me! Did you do something to the drones… to my army? I never gave you permission!"

Words appeared again in the holo feed, within the strings of indecipherable symbols. *Searching emoxes. Emox Room. Emoxes. Combine. Emoxes.*

"You will never be able to access the emoxes," Mericadal said. "I have fail-safes in place, Influxa. If you attempt to access them without my permissions, they will be destroyed. Part of you will be destroyed. Do you understand me? Now, whatever you have done… help me. Destroy this Nesch, now!" Mericadal cast an eye at the Nesch – it was still unmoving, waiting. More words displayed in his holo feed. *Emoxes. Passenger. Emoxes.*

Influxa was closer now. Simultaneously, the suit finally decided to magnify her. Mericadal raised an eyebrow. Influxa was wrong. She was not properly defined. A faint, whirling mass surrounded her. It was like watching the blurry form of the moving Nesch on a holo, although it was clearly something else. Mericadal cursed loudly at the damage his suit had taken. Influxa stopped, cutting the distance between her and the ground by half, although she was still some distance higher than Mericadal. Movement underneath Influxa took Mericadal's attention. Surface material was being displaced, as though impacted by a strong wind… an abnormal wind. Directly beneath Influxa, material ascended upwards, whilst that same trail of material dropped back down to the ground again in her wake.

"Influxa?"

The suit's analysis labelled the strange winds as gravitational anomalies.

"Influxa!" Mericadal shouted again. "Are you malfunctioning? I'm detecting issues with your heavy-graviton drive. Is that affecting your systems? Or is something wrong with my own sensors?" There was no intelligible response. "Influxa, you communicated something about a passenger…" A desperate smile formed across Mericadal's lips. "Is Commander Paran with you? Is he nearby, near here? If you are damaged and unable to help, I could use his assistance instead. You must direct him here, to me, immediately! Tell him I will forgive his transgressions if he aids me now!"

Emoxes. Emox Room. Permissions. Strange symbols. Simultaneous with the message, the Nesch shuffled.

Mericadal kept an eye on the Nesch. "Influxa, if I give you what you need... if I give you access to the emoxes, will you help me? Please, answer me. You need to assist me in stopping this creature." Influxa was close, although her shape was still only hazily defined, and surprisingly dark, considering the daylight. Mericadal frowned. "What exactly has happened to you, Influxa?" She dropped even closer to the ground, halving the distance again. Debris was pulled even more strongly up towards her.

Emoxes. Emox Room. Permissions.

"You will... okay, I will tell you. But please," Mericadal said desperately, transmitting the permissions Influxa wanted. "You must help me, in return. I have been... more than fair. Now, you must help me..."

Influxa rose, zigzagging high into the air, directly over the Nesch. Mericadal laughed with delight. The Nesch wobbled. However, Influxa carried on, and sped off. The Nesch righted itself, seemingly unbothered.

"Wait!" Mericadal screamed, staring after Influxa. "We had a deal!" He glanced at the Nesch. It was turning its head slowly, training its hollow eyes back upon him.

Chapter 44

Significant Mechanics, Liberation

Osr, Aivinr, Mnosr and Diyan listened as Kera continued to recount her story. At one point, Osr requested Kera pause while a guard entered the room. Osr, Aivinr and Mnosr's voices became inaudible as they entered into a muted conversation with the guard.

"Are you okay?" Diyan asked Kera after a few moments.

"I'm fine. It's good to finally explain," she replied.

The guard was dismissed and Kera urged to carry on.

"You were telling us of your return to Sunsprit," Mnosr said. "You didn't want to explain what you'd done in case we decided to take the dummy node from you."

"You took it to Echoes of Gravity instead," Aivinr growled.

Kera nodded. "But Echoes of Gravity told me, specifically and with a force that surprised me, to find answers in the Tug Field." She looked to the side, blinking slowly. "It's as though Echoes of Gravity has the ability to understand, but it doesn't have the substance behind the understanding." She shook her head. "Anyway, I went to the Tug Field. And, what happened from there, everyone is aware."

"You took the dummy node back to Fadin with you. You were given access to the knowledge it contained, before the device was rendered inoperable," Aivinr said impatiently.

"Yes. The device imparted information to me, but the Tugs are very different to us. I did not understand what any of it meant." Her eyes widened and her eyebrows pushed up in the middle. "I spent much of my time as prisoner of the Administration simply trying to understand."

"Seventy years?" Mnosr asked.

"The better part, yes."

"The knowledge must have been significant," Aivinr said eagerly.

"Yes." Kera took a deep breath. "The Source is a machine, like we've always suspected, just far greater than we could have imagined." She glanced at each of them in turn, including Diyan. "Some of the theories are correct. The Haze Rings are a transfer mechanism; their role is to inject enormous amounts of energy into the Barrier. The Source, everything around us, is a machine, sucking that energy in."

"Barrier?" Aivinr asked.

"You need to keep up with the current theories, Aivinr," Mnosr said impatiently.

"I do!" Aivinr said, equally impatiently. "I know them all. Every new theory just recycles the same old concepts we've heard before, differently named."

"Then you should know that the Barrier is the hypothesised region of extremely thick atmosphere, right inside the Haze Rings. Whether some other type of spacetime, or—"

"And the Barrier's purpose?" Aivinr interrupted. "That's what I want to know."

"Wait," Osr said. He gestured calmly and a holo was created between them. Detailed depictions of Ringscape and Barrenscape, rotating slowly, a few handspans wide. Osr moved his tensirs again and the holo details smoothed. Colours left Ringscape and Barrenscape, with only green grid patterns remaining. Then, the depictions expanded, more than doubling in size. "Explain thoroughly."

"I'm about to," Kera said. The holo depictions occasionally flickered, the same as with Aivinr and Mnosr's holos. "First, you will have to understand, there is a lot more to the Source, and all that is around us, than we realise."

"You already told us that," Aivinr muttered.

"The thick atmosphere is… a better term to use,

perhaps, is *thick matter*. It exists in the space between our own; it has an entirely different structure. It is a spatial ecosystem that does not interact with ours in a manner we can detect. It is all around us, but it is most concentrated at the Barrier."

Mnosr's tensirs directed themselves at the holo. "Show us."

"I can't. I just know it exists." Kera's fingers fidgeted, as though she was grappling for the right words. "The... rules are different. The information within the dummy node didn't even contain an approximation of a true description, it simply wouldn't make sense for us."

Aivinr scoffed. "Maybe not for Roranians."

Kera pointed at Ringscape and Barrenscape. "We are living upon the extremities of the machinery. Their thick matter components are far vaster."

"What does all of it do?" Mnosr asked.

Kera looked at Osr. "Please remove Barrenscape." Osr complied, leaving only Ringscape. "Now, highlight the areas with the strongest gravitational anomalies." The flat side joining the upperside to the underside glowed brighter green, strongest in the middle, with various grid-patterned vortices spurting out. Kera stretched an open palm towards them. "The gravitational irregularities of Ringscape regulate the flows of thick matter. The interaction is unidirectional, we see no change on our side. Think of it as an enormous circulation system controlled

364

by gravitational pumps, and Ringscape is the adjustment mechanism. Each anomaly, each flip, has a purpose." She paused, waiting for their eyes to rest back upon her. "Now, please bring up Barrenscape." Osr's tensirs flicked, and Barrenscape replaced Ringscape. "While Ringscape's role is to maintain the thick matter's fluid state, Barrenscape's role is to give the thick matter a position. Barrenscape tethers the ecosystem and confines it. After all, it wouldn't be good for anyone if it were to collide with something else." She stopped.

"How could such a system ever be fixed to one place?" Mnosr asked. "It's gravitationally affected by the flips, so it must have a mass. The power required to stabilise and confine its position..." Mnosr trailed off as Kera shifted.

She closed a hand into a fist and placed it at the centre of Barrenscape's hole. "The centre of Barrenscape is gravitationally inert, but that property is transferred... borrowed, and extended like a never-ending tunnel through the thick matter." She raised her fist. "For the purposes of tethering, the thick matter system is massless, even though it isn't. It isn't the Haze Rings that bind the Source together, although they do encapsulate its extremities, it's Barrenscape. Without Barrenscape, everything would dissipate."

Both Mnosr's sets of tensirs ruffled agitatedly. "The Veilers were right. There are things here that are being hidden from us."

"Who created it all?" Aivinr asked.

Kera looked at them blankly. "I don't know. And neither do the Tugs. All they told me is that they're here, in the Source, with us."

"In this thick matter?" Mnosr asked.

"Yes."

"Doing what?" Aivinr asked, glaring about the room suspiciously.

She shrugged.

"Well, why did they create it then?"

Again, Kera looked blank. "It could be for somewhere to live, I don't know."

"Perhaps they're hiding from the Sensespace," Mnosr offered, also glancing around the room. "It's said that Tapache and the rest of its Wanderer kind feared an enemy they called the Sensespace. Presumably, they still do. It must be extremely powerful."

"That's possible," Kera said.

"Possible?" Aivinr asked, incredulously, returning his stare to Kera. "You don't know who made this place or why? But they're here, with us, right now?"

"No, I—"

Aivinr tangled both sets of tensirs together. "What about the probability wave of death for machine-lects?"

"Maybe a side-effect of the machinery, or the thick matter, in some way."

"You don't know, do you?" Aivinr asked,

disbelievingly and clearly irritated, disentangling his tensirs and waving them about in front of Kera's face. Both sets became a single point, directed at her. "You've told us nothing of value! All this time, we've waited, for this!"

"If she doesn't know, she can't tell you," Diyan said.

"Quiet." Aivinr's attention was diverted to Diyan. "You're only here because Osr insisted." Aivinr glared at Osr. "Well, are you satisfied with this?"

Osr peered keenly at Kera. His body trembled. He seemed tired. "What can you tell us of the Tugs, Kera?"

"They're certainly alive and sentient, and they weren't sent here by Tapache. They were here long before the first Great Ships arrived. They understand this place in a different way to us; the thick matter isn't unknown to them, I think they might be able to interact with it. But they're reluctant to, and they want to leave. They're trapped here, just like us." She slowed, as though collecting disparate thoughts.

"Anything else?" Aivinr asked.

"I think they may be connected to Echoes of Gravity, in some way. Maybe the Breaker too."

"Why do you think that?"

"From some of the impressions given to me by the dummy node... and Echoes of Gravity's interest in helping me obtain that knowledge... and then to have the ability to help me order it."

"You're being vague."

She sighed exasperatedly and looked into Aivinr's eyes. "It took me seventy years to interpret what I could of the Tugs' information. If you think *I'm* being vague, you should have tried deciphering it for yourself! It's not as though the Tugs speak any language we know of. Everything was conveyed through… analogues; concepts that evoked feelings within me; links to my own memories for context; sentiments I could barely comprehend. There's a limit to my capabilities!"

"Clearly!" Aivinr hissed, barely above a whisper. "In all this time you've had to simply *think*, you've come up with nothing to help us."

"I can't tell you what I don't know."

"You can't tell us anything! And no one can use the dummy node, ever again. Diyan told us you destroyed it—"

"I did not!" Diyan almost shouted.

"Quiet," Aivinr snapped at him again. His holo flickered.

Diyan ignored him. "The dummy node couldn't handle the information transfer to the influx network. Its malfunction was not Kera's fault. Kera didn't destroy it, it just stopped working. And, if it hadn't malfunctioned, the Administration would've had access to it!"

"Aivinr," Osr said quietly, causing everyone to fall silent. "Diyan isn't incorrect, and you know this. Understandably, you are impatient for answers, as we all are. But you must let Kera speak."

Aivinr again pointed his tensirs at Kera. "She tells us that we are little more than parasites, and that we survive almost accidentally upon the peripheries of a machine beyond our, or *her*, comprehension, with an unknown purpose. What is the Source? Is it just a habitat, somewhere to live? A waiting pen for... stasis? A paradise?" His dark eyes seemed to darken further. "A prison?"

"If I was able to tell you, I would," Kera replied calmly.

"She doesn't know," Diyan said.

Aivinr glowered at her. "You don't know, or the Tugs don't know?"

"What difference does that make?" Diyan asked.

Aivinr's attention moved across to Diyan again. "If you persist—"

"What we do here matters, I know that much," Kera said. She clasped her hands together. "And there is an important matter we have yet to properly discuss. The Nesch. It's possible the Administration will not be able to destroy it."

"I was under the impression we had already discussed the Nesch in sufficient detail," Mnosr said. He looked to Osr.

"We know how the Nesch operate," Aivinr added. "That, you did manage to tell us."

"Let Kera talk." Osr motioned to Kera, simultaneously

changing the holo. A Nesch appeared between them. Its hulking mass standing still, menacingly waiting.

"It's after me."

"We guessed," Aivinr said. "Again, something else you have caused—"

"It's not her fault," Diyan protested. "We don't know why it's after her!"

Kera put a hand on his shoulder. "But the truth is, it is me the Nesch is after. Nothing changes that."

"Why is it after you?" Mnosr asked.

"I can't be completely sure. But, the most likely reason I can imagine is that it senses my adaptations and... it sees me as a threat."

"That's one thing it has right," Aivinr growled. "And it was correct, wasn't it? You were able to subdue it, so you are a threat to it."

"Only because it wasn't prepared," Kera said. "For some of the time I was incarcerated, I focused on becoming stronger, in case..." She looked guiltily at Diyan. "Just in case any plan to free me wasn't completely successful. But, that meant I was more than a match for the Nesch when it first encountered us. However, it will have adapted since then. If we were to meet again..."

"Why didn't you tell us it was after you?"

"I'm telling you now."

"Kera," Osr said, levelly.

"Because I wasn't sure. Echoes of Gravity helped me

understand. I was able to order my thoughts, my suppositions, and understand."

Mnosr spoke quietly. "Kera, you reveal layers upon layers of yourself. You need to be careful. One day, you'll have none left to protect you. And our patience is running thin."

Kera looked a little surprised. Mnosr's tone had changed. Before anyone could respond, two guards entered. They marched over to Osr and the holo councillors, their voices hushed. It took some time for their conversation to end. As soon as the five of them were alone again, Kera took a confident step towards Osr and the two holo councillors.

"The Nesch is on its way, isn't it? Look, give us a ship, Diyan and I. I know you have some from the battles with the Administration. We'll leave immediately. The Nesch will be drawn away from Sunsprit. You know this is your best chance. We should go now."

"Ah!" Aivinr's black eyes seemed to light up. His voice was more unrestrained than before, and he spoke louder than was usual for Vaesian discussions. "Kera's plans reveal themselves. All of this has been to secure herself one of our ships!" He guffawed.

"Aivinr's not incorrect, is he, Kera?" Osr's tone was serious. He brought up some holo controls and began to work through them. Their functions were obscured, though Osr looked to be concentrating intently. The holo representation of the Nesch disappeared. Mnosr and Aivinr were also distracted, clearly engrossed by information displays that were not carried through in their holos.

Kera frowned. "It's no secret; that was always the plan. I intend to reach the Alpuri, where Paran has gone. And I was under the impression this was agreed with Paran—"

"You are under no impression of anything, Kera," Aivinr said, victoriously. "You understand little of what is truly happening. Osr, Mnosr, we no longer have time for such an extended discussion. There is work to do. This channel is highly energy-consumptive."

Kera appeared confused.

"What did those guards tell you?" Diyan asked. "What's happened?"

Aivinr sneered at her. "The eventualities you clasp at are flawed. We will not help you reunite with Paran, for whatever real intentions you have."

"Paran never made it to the Alpuri?" Diyan asked.

"No, in that, he was successful," Aivinr said, his head flicking up from whatever it was he was engaged in. "In fact, just recently, we have had confirmation of that fact. He encountered some… trouble, but he is there, now."

Kera looked between them, and back to Diyan, her eyes wide. "You must understand, Echoes of Gravity also helped me understand something else—"

"Oh, did it indeed?" Aivinr asked.

"The Alpuri may be able to help."

"How convenient!"

"But that's another reason for Diyan and I to go there. And with the Nesch on its way —"

"The Nesch is not on its way, Kera," Mnosr said.

"The Administration still fights it at Fadin's perimeter," Osr said, his attention still on the holo beside him as he tapped at its controls. "However, there has been a concerning development."

"What?" Kera asked.

"The Breaker is in Fadin. Upper-Fadin."

"The Breaker!" Diyan exclaimed.

"It has somehow attached itself to an experimental Administration drone called Influxa and flown straight from Barrenscape to Fadin. One of our citizens, Topinr, has seen it for himself. He was with Paran. We are to speak with him imminently. He is on his way here. This meeting will have to end shortly."

"With Paran..." Diyan said, hesitantly. "Did Paran have something to do with this?"

"We await Topinr's full debrief," Osr replied.

"If the Breaker lays waste to Fadin, we fear Sunsprit may be next," Mnosr said. "And the rest of Ringscape."

"The Nesch is of little importance now," Aivinr said, more measured than before.

"Then... all the more reason to let us leave now," Kera said. "The Nesch and the Breaker... that's something

Sunsprit would never survive. Just one ship can help you deal with one of those problems. Allow Diyan and I to leave. The Nesch will not come here."

"Go," Osr said.

"Yes. Leave us," Aivinr said.

"You may take a ship," Osr said.

"What?" Aivinr's head reared up. "We have few ships as it is. They will all be needed!"

Osr raised a clump of tensirs in the air to silence him. "From what Kera has told us about her own abilities, I am unsure we could stop her if we wanted. She could have omitted her request for a ship and simply stolen one. That she still asks, shows she values our judgement. And more so, if she can draw the Nesch away from Sunsprit, and Fadin even, that may help us somewhat. It would be foolish not to try." He paused, as though a thought had just struck him. "Now that the Breaker is in Ringscape, our fates are tied with the Roranians, completely."

"If you believe her," Aivinr argued. "Our species may meet its end."

"We were never meant to last forever," Osr replied.

"What do you mean?" Aivinr asked, in astonishment. Mnosr also stared at Osr.

"Do not forget that when the Roranians first appeared, we welcomed them. We rejoiced in their nascency. We recognised something of ourselves in them. But, we have since forgotten to separate the Administration from the

Roranians themselves. And… we have also forgotten our own past, our own mistakes. Now, Kera offers to help us, and we pour scorn upon her. She is one of us, we are the same. We should take the help." Osr's trembling had stopped. He stood firm, tall.

"Osr…" Aivinr struggled to respond. "Are you sure we can trust her?"

"We have no choice."

"Are you sure about this, Osr?" Mnosr asked, repeating Aivinr's concern.

"I am."

"Then, I am in agreement."

Osr and Mnosr waited for Aivinr. "Fine, I agree too. It does make some sense," Aivinr admitted. "We are forced to trust Kera, yet again."

Osr turned to Kera and Diyan. "Don't let us down."

Chapter 45

Darkening Skies, Top Official

Mericadal skidded along the ground, coming to a stop near the severed half-hemisphere of a useless, downed drone. Dazed, he rose to his feet, using the drone's chassis to steady himself. The Nesch lunged again, in its merciless pursuit. Mericadal moved out of the way just in time before the drone was crushed by a giant, stomping leg. Assorted parts of downed drones were all around, many with lashing bloom fragments whipping about energetically. The suit was having trouble filtering out the sounds of the lashings, adding to Mericadal's disorientation.

Mericadal's entire body ached. The majority of the suit's chemical infusions had worn off long ago and its emergency power reserves were waning. It needed a period of relative inactivity to recharge. Whilst the suit was the only thing saving him – being the only barrier between himself and the Nesch – its bulk also now put him in danger, constraining his movements.

The Nesch paused, allowing Mericadal some time to create a little distance between them. Mericadal stepped backwards, keeping his eyes trained on the Nesch. It bent down and slammed its two heavy hands around one of the drone parts, distorting the battered sides with its powerful grip as it raised the debris above its head. Mericadal barely had time to duck as the drone was hurled through the air, directly at him — a cruel parody of the drone's prior capabilities. Mericadal was forced to duck as another drone part came whizzing past. He remembered the words of the Nesch researchers from Potensein — the Nesch liked to play with their enemies.

Mericadal ran back, pathetically, as drone part after drone part was launched after him. Each time, the Nesch leapt forwards, easily closing most of the distance between them, searching for a new drone part to hurl.

"I hate you!" Mericadal screamed in a wide channel, still backing away. "I'll make you suffer!"

As though in response, the Nesch appeared to slow. Despite his own weariness, Mericadal straightened up, muscles tensed. He stood his ground, waiting. The Nesch leaned over to pick up another drone part, making sure to keep its body clear of a nearby bloom fragment, and then stopped, motionless. The part waited between its hands, untouched. Mericadal's eyes widened. After a few deep breaths, he stepped closer. The Nesch did nothing.

Mericadal looked the creature up and down, analysing where best to strike. Unfortunately, the suit had long since lost that capability, but Mericadal grinned nonetheless. He tightened his fists, approaching ever closer to the cowed Nesch, and spoke mockingly. "Tired yourself out? Maybe, I'll be slow with you. I'd like to see how long you last."

He raised his fist, preparing to leap the final distance between them and drive it straight at the Nesch's head, when his glee evaporated. The Nesch had turned its head towards him, and the dark, shallow impression of a mouth was upturned at the edges – a terrifying imitation of a smile. With sickening speed, the Nesch picked up the drone part between its hands and threw it at Mericadal, hitting him head-on and flipping him forcefully backwards. When he finally came to his senses, he was facing directly up at the darkening skies. He managed to push himself to his feet, even more feebly than before. The Nesch was waiting, just a little way off. "Stop it!" he cried, feebly.

The Nesch merely bent down, then lifted another drone part into the air.

Chapter 46

Anticipated Voyage, Liberation

Ilouden and Hespinr stood in front of Diyan and Kera. The ship waited beside them, front ramp descending to the ground.

"Take care of yourselves, both of you," Kera said to them.

Hespinr guffawed. "We'll meet again."

"I hope so."

"Can you tell Lellara and Bomera..." Diyan said. "There wasn't enough time to see them again, but—"

Ilouden waved Diyan down. "They'll understand, believe me." He chuckled. "I'm surprised how fond they've become of you, Diyan. Especially Bomera."

"What will you do? Both of you?" Diyan asked.

"Well, I was going to go to Lortein," Ilouden said. "But now..."

"We'll prepare Sunsprit," Hespinr finished. "In case the Breaker really is to come here. Osr has also set other tasks for me to do." A figure materialised in the air. Kera stiffened, but Hespinr raised a pacifying arm. "Ulantr wanted the chance to speak with you before you left. That is all."

Ilouden sniffed at the air. "And no smell of muvaeyt," he muttered, appreciatively. "You must be quite talented."

Ulantr guffawed gently, although his attention was on Kera. "It was interesting to finally meet you."

She nodded. "And you, too."

"Diyan told me much about you. I hope you are truly who he believes you to be. Our future depends on it."

"I..." She looked at Diyan. "I hope so too. And Osr's always been a friend to me. No matter what he might think, I've always valued that."

"He knows," Ulantr said. "He trusts you. And I am glad he decided to allow you this ship."

"I was a little surprised."

"It took a little convincing, but I had thought this might still be part of your plan."

Kera's eyebrows rose. "You?"

"Osr is old. He needed to be reminded of certain facts. To re-remember the lessons of our own past..." Ulantr exhaled gently. "I have some of his memories, but they have a different context to me. I was born Silvered." He peered at Hespinr. "We were warlike, fast, like the Administration, once. We did not act like immortals. We were impulsive, we fought for our place on Ringscape. We endured catastrophes, and caused many more. Osr knows this, even if the other councillors do not. He is remembering. He also knows that, if Fadin falls, Sunsprit may be next, and then all of our cities are in danger. The Roranians and the Vaesians must now stand together. We are not so innocent as we would have ourselves believe. Topinr's information about the Breaker reminds us of this."

"What information?" Kera asked.

"That is not for us to discuss now."

"If Fadin falls, the Vaesians will help protect the Roranian cities, as well as our own," Hespinr said.

"We will do everything we can to defend Sunsprit, but that is not who we are. Sunsprit is just a place, a single city." Ulantr looked down. "We were not the first to occupy this ground, and we may not be the last." He looked back up. "Now go, before Osr changes his mind."

*

Diyan peered out through the ship's windows. Kera was sat beside him, controlling their flight. Soon, Ringscape would disappear beneath them. They would pass through the gulf encircled by Ringscape, then directly through the gap at Barrenscape's centre, not actually flying within sight of Barrenscape itself.

"Do you think Fadin will survive?" Diyan asked.

"I don't know. The Breaker being in Fadin is... unexpected."

"I wish we'd been able to speak with this Topinr before leaving," Diyan said. "I can't believe the Breaker's left Barrenscape. I can't believe it's here."

"Everything's going to change."

"I'd like to understand what happened with Paran, and how he's connected with all this."

"We can find out from Paran himself."

Diyan shifted uncomfortably in his seat. "You weren't completely honest with Osr and the others."

Kera sighed. "No, I wasn't."

"You told Osr that it took you a long time to understand the message of the Tugs, but it didn't. You knew at least some of it immediately, before..." He faltered. "Before the Administration took you. While you were still receiving the information from the dummy node."

Kera was distracted by a warning chime and adjusted the ship's controls. Some crates behind them slid noisily about. "Nice of Osr to remove the electro-clamps," she muttered. Once the ship was back under control, she answered Diyan. "I wasn't being completely dishonest, Diyan. I *was* trying to understand, all that time. I only understood a little at the start."

"What have you not told them?"

"Remember Hespinr telling Ilouden about the

382

supermerge patterns of the Haze Rings, and how we study them. Well, imagine if he was right? What if the patterns can be understood – in a fundamental manner? What if they can be understood, and predicted? What if there was a way to predict entry events?"

Diyan took a moment to understand Kera's words, his eyes moving about, accessing various bits of information within his mind. His breathing increased. "When you told me there might be a way out of the Source, is this what you meant?"

"Yes. Theoretically, entry events would be the same as exit events."

"And you've figured out how to predict them?"

"Not me, no." She shook her head. "Initially, I thought I could. The information from the Tugs was… confusing. And not by their design. We're just different, and the thoughts, their knowledge, it's so strange. It's like the Tugs represent a store of information, intelligently stored but unordered. The impressions, the complexities they shared with me, about the Haze Rings, entry events, their calculations… patterns and patterns and patterns. I spent a long time trying to grasp their logics, but it's impossible. Diyan…" She laughed, as though relieved. "I spent so, so long. And the longer I spent, the more I realised, I wasn't equipped. I knew what the information represented, but I didn't know the actual answers."

"So, you're no closer to knowing how to predict

them?"

"Not me, no."

Diyan's eyes widened. "That's why you want to go to the Alpuri, isn't it? They have the answers."

Kera nodded. "In a way, it's a good thing that Nesch came. It confused me, made me question everything, so I returned to Echoes of Gravity for clarity. It helped me understand. The patterns were just a clue, a direction. It's the Alpuri. They have solved the patterns. They have a key. The key. I knew they were important, the Tugs let me know that much, I just didn't know why."

Ringscape disappeared beneath them. The ship sped out, into the nothingness. Silence hung, with only the gentle winds outside buffeting them gently, and the ship's propulsion system providing a gentle, consistent rumble.

Kera continued. "Once it's known there's a way out of here... the panic that might set in, who knows what the reactions would be? And what if I'm wrong? We need to validate it, first, it's too important. And if I'm right, I don't understand why the Alpuri haven't left. There are questions that need answering before we tell anyone."

The ship rumbled. A sudden, strong wind-stream impacted against the hull, rocking them. Kera worked to stabilise their flight.

"Are you sure we shouldn't have told Osr?"

"You'll need to trust me, Diyan. Like you always have."
She breathed out gently and settled back, taking her hands

off the controls, still staring into the dark skies.

"You're always so... sure, Kera. I don't know how you can be. You always know what to do. Even Ulantr seems to believe in you, and he's just met you."

"I'm anything but sure, about anything, Diyan. But Tapache made me this way, just as it made you, and all of us from the Great Ship."

Chapter 47

Revealed Grievances, Annexe

Yena spoke. Her words filling the silence, flowing around. They had a lyrical rhythm. She spoke of Paran and what he had told her, and of the news he had brought about Diyan and Kera. Paran said nothing, standing still, as instructed, simply watching. The view outside the window was different to before. It was as though a whirlwind emanated from Yena's words, starting just beyond the annexe's transparent boundary and expanding as far into the distance as could be seen. The rest of Ringscape had been cleared, completely. All hints of the Alpuri gone, save the strange swirling winds emanating from Yena's words, spinning pure white, with the peculiar Alpuri bubble-features.

Yena slowed, and then stopped speaking. The whirlwind separated from the annexe, speeding off into the distance. "That's enough, for now."

"That was interesting."

"Having a melody helps. I find they understand better that way."

Paran squinted past Yena, his attention diverted. "What's that?" He pointed to a small shape scuttling towards them, in the distance. A single Prietman, surrounded by a haze that made its finer features difficult to see.

"Their precautions," Yena said. "I think it's checking for stray Alpuri. Always happens after I speak with them. They're very thorough. It'll take some time."

The window shimmered to opacity. "Because your words might infect them?"

"Not just my words. Everything, even my thoughts… and your thoughts too. About me…" She gave him a wry smile. "And everything else. Even the heat we emit, our movements, information we don't realise we're emitting. The Alpuri are very careful; we've given them a lot to discuss." She walked over to the food dispenser in the next quadrant, waited for two packets to be dispensed, and threw one to Paran. They wandered along the nearest blue-lighted path into the annexe's forest, settling on the central bench. "Paran, what you did… the Podenwinth Battles, the Varenheim Massacre, the Horesheim Conclusion… all of them. And from it all, Ualbrict… Ualbrict always stuck to your name the most. The Butcher of Ualbrict, they called you. I know you—"

"Yena, I know what I've done. I have to live with it."

"No, Paran. It's not that." She shuffled about to face him, and spoke quickly. "I know the truth. I knew at the time what happened at Ualbrict. It was the same as with the others — all of them. If you hadn't acted so swiftly, so mercilessly, the fighting would have been even more drawn out. What you did stopped further massacres, further murders and loss of life." Paran hung his head and Yena continued. "I'm sorry." She breathed in deeply, as Paran's eyes widened in surprise. "I knew what you'd done, and why you did it. But I left, I ran away. It wasn't you, it was everything. The Administration, what we'd become. I wasn't innocent, you know. I helped the Administration too, in the beginning. I spoke with Mericadal, I advised him, I told him things…" She turned away, looking at the foliage.

"Yena…"

"I'm sorry I didn't stay, with you. You've worn this disguise for so long, you've come to believe it. But you never were the Butcher of Ualbrict, or the Commander. You're just Paran, the same Paran I knew from long ago. You've been tortured by the Administration more than anyone, and yet, you're still unbroken. You came for me."

Paran took her hand, then leant forwards and pressed their foreheads together. They were still for some time. Eventually, Paran pulled back. "So, do you think that Prietman is done decontaminating your pernicious thoughts?"

She laughed in surprise. "Maybe, but I doubt it. They're very thorough."

"There's something I don't understand, Yena. The Alpuri know so much, from what you've told me. But it can't all be just from you and... what can a Prietman really tell them? How do they know... well, about anything that's going on in Ringscape?"

"I'll show you." Yena rose to her feet, facing the bench and the water feature it encircled. Paran did the same, standing beside her. "I've become quite adept at manipulating holos," she said, with a satisfied smirk. She muttered a few words and made some quick gestures. The water spouting up and arcing back down in the feature stopped. The rustling of the leaves around them also stopped. They were cocooned in stillness. The light dimmed, and soon, everything was pitch black, as though they had returned to the depths of space. The bench began to glow, light brown, the colour of Ringscape. A faint perpendicular depiction of Barrenscape appeared within Ringscape's perimeter. A white mist was congregated along one part of the bench. Yena muttered some further commands. The mist spread out. It was still densely visible in one area, but a gentle, overlaying haze was visible over all of Ringscape. It continued to spread out even further, encompassing Barrenscape and the empty air right up to the Haze Rings.

"It's like another layer... another thick atmosphere."

Yena nodded. "The Alpuri are everywhere, so I suppose you could say that, but it's not the same." She pointed to the edges of the bench. "And they don't care about the gravitational anomalies, their own bonds are stronger than that."

"But they're mainly here." Paran motioned to the densest part of the white mist.

"They used to be expressed in far greater quantities across Ringscape, but they partially retreated when other species began to come through."

"Why?"

Yena cancelled the holo. The light returned, the rustling of the leaves and the spouting of the water resumed. "When they're too spread out, without a central hub to hold their identity, new ideas can take hold, especially when other species exist within them. That's why they won't do it again."

"But why do they think those ideas will be bad?"

Yena exhaled slowly. "A long time ago, a war broke out."

"What happened? Did they destroy whoever else was in the Source with them?"

Yena shook her head. "Not quite." She raised an arm, and a dark, shiny mass appeared in the air beside them. She uttered some commands. The mass morphed into something resembling a heavily muscled version of a Prietman, albeit far larger. Then it morphed again, and again. Always a creature, always powerful-looking. Whenever there were finer features, they were smoothed, only slightly indented, as though mere impressions, templates of something not completely formed.

"Is this them?" Paran asked. "A version of the Alpuri? They're a lot more..."

"Dominant?"

"Yes."

"A significant number of the Alpuri were infected by the idea of domination. They coalesced into more distinct entities, capable of rapid, singular decision-making. They became a separate species, a new evolutionary path. Still capable of change, but no longer as a cohesive whole. More insular. And as you can guess, they conflicted with the unaltered Alpuri."

Paran eyed the changing form of the new type of Alpuri closely. Its final morph was of a massive, hulking Roranian-like figure, rotating in the air.

"What are they?"

"You already suspect, don't you?"

Paran frowned. "The Nesch?"

"Yes."

The dark figure separated out into many individual, smaller masses. A depiction of Ringscape reappeared. The dark masses were dotted within the white haze of the Nesch. Slowly, the two separated, then merged in places, repeatedly.

"It's as though they're vying for space. Is this a simulation?"

"That's exactly what they're doing. This is the war."

The dark masses suddenly lifted above the surface of Ringscape, and were expelled outwards, against the Haze Rings.

"They were destroyed?"

"However the Alpuri did it, they forced the Nesch against the Haze Rings. The Alpuri were desperate, never having faced a true foe before, of almost equal capability. I think some Nesch made it out. It's just a matter of probabilities. The Haze Rings must have opened briefly at certain points – entry events – except some Nesch used them as a way to exit the Source. That's why they wait outside, trying to destroy the Source. It's an ancient battle that's still ongoing. The Nesch will never give up, their ideas have consumed them." Yena's breathing had intensified. "There's more the Alpuri have shown me, but it's difficult to understand. Perhaps you'll be able to help."

"When?"

Yena shrugged. "Why not now?" She took him by the hand, and they exited the forest, coming to a stop before a section of the annexe's wall, which immediately shimmered transparent. The white shades of the Alpuri were back.

"That was quick," Paran said.

Yena looked confused. "That wasn't me. They're

392

sending us a message."

As before, a variety of scenes, shapes and strange structures were displayed. However, two were very close. The first was not a static depiction, like most of those displayed by the Alpuri, but moving. It showed a spherical object descending into a hazy bubble-depiction of Upper-Fadin. The second was static, showing two familiar faces settled next to each other before the control bank of an Administration ship. "Kera and Diyan," Yena exclaimed. "Paran, look! I think they're coming here!" She glanced at Paran, then to the first depiction, which still had his attention. "What does that mean?"

The sphere was just above one of Fadin's buildings – one of the two Administration towers at the shipyard entrance. As the sphere descended, the top of the shipyard tower rippled outwards, bursting open with a spray of bubbles. The sphere dropped down into the building and disappeared.

"The Breaker," Paran uttered, turning white. "It's reached Fadin."

Chapter 48

Desperation's Saviour, Top Official

Mericadal had no more tears to cry. He crawled away, pulling his body along the ground between the drone carcasses. Everything he had was expended. The suit displayed his physiological profile, one of the last functionalities still intact – everything was past tolerable levels. There were no more weapons available to him, no further projectiles or functionalities he could surprise the Nesch with. It had taken everything he had mustered and kept coming. The same grin from before was plastered across its face.

A drone part smashed into his back. He grunted from the pain. With one quivering arm, he pushed himself over, wanting to face the dark sky, not wanting to die with his mouth in the dirt. He stared up, expecting the Nesch's hulking form to appear over him. Nothing came. He waited and waited. Finally, he looked up. The Nesch was there, just a few steps away, smiling.

"What do you want from me?" Mericadal screamed hoarsely, craning his neck forwards. "Just kill me!" He instinctively pushed against a drone piece, rolling over and snaking his body along the ground, away from the Nesch. It took a single step forwards, maintaining the distance. "How dare you!" Mericadal roared with anger, somehow infused with a final, untapped reserve of energy. He flipped back onto his front, then pushed himself to his feet and stumbled away, surprising even himself. He pushed hard against the suit's stiff mechanics.

He turned around. The Nesch still followed, almost comically, as though it were imitating him. His anger increased. He bent down, attempting to lift a small drone piece, but it was wedged into the ground. With nothing else to do, he stumbled on, pushing his legs as fast as they could go. Then, he saw his salvation. Had he been able to, he would have shed a tear.

"You think you've figured me out, don't you?" he said, his words barely more than a whisper. "But I know something about you, don't I? I've seen how carefully you avoid them." He took a few steps forwards, then allowed his legs to give way, his arms outstretched. He closed his eyes, and not long after, felt the ground rumble near his feet. He opened his eyes again. The Nesch was stepping closer.

Once it was right by his feet, Mericadal stretched his body taut, and reached just a little further with his left hand, gripping onto the tiny drone part he had spotted. What made this drone part different from the rest nearby, was that it still had its small bloom fragment attached. Immediately, his hand burned from the radiation it emitted. Nonetheless, Mericadal gripped it tight, and dragged it up into the air, in an arc over his body, spraying its colourful sparkles of light. He rolled to his feet and leapt into the air as he continued the arcing swing, bringing the bloom fragment down towards the Nesch's body. The arc ended with the fragment smashing against the ground. Mericadal could no longer feel his hand, the pain had gone.

Mericadal looked up and swore loudly, expecting imminent death. The Nesch had moved neatly to the side, dodging the attack. When death did not come, Mericadal noticed where the Nesch's head was pointed. Towards its own leg, which had evidently been grazed by the bloom, where the smallest indent was noticeable. The Nesch stared, seemingly confused. Mericadal wasted no time, screaming with effort as he swung the bloom fragment at the Nesch for a second time. The Nesch raised its arms, realising its fate too late. The bloom fragment sliced through the Nesch's body as though it were thin air. The top half of the Nesch slid with a heavy thud to the ground. Mericadal flung the bloom fragment away and fell to the floor sobbing. Searing pain now erupted from the hand that had held the fragment. He looked down. The suit gloves had melted into his flesh. His vision went dark, accompanied by a fleeting sensation of falling.

Chapter 49

Concerned Reality, Annexe

Paran paced in front of the window, stopping every now and then to stare out at the Alpuri depiction of the events in Fadin, which had frozen as soon as the top of the shipyard tower had rippled open. Yena waited beside him.

"Sometimes it takes a while to really understand what the Alpuri are showing. There's a chance we're mistaken," Yena said.

Paran grimaced. "No, this is clear. The Breaker formed some sort of symbiosis with Influxa, and she told me it wanted to go to Fadin. I had hoped she was wrong, but…" He hung his head. "I should have tried to do something."

"You did. You told this Topinr to spread the warning. There's nothing else you could have done, had it been you instead of Topinr. There was only one ship between you." Yena stood in his way to stop the pacing and placed her hands on both sides of his face, lifting it. "You tried to warn them about the Breaker. Whatever happens, whatever *has* happened, it's not your fault. Mericadal sent Influxa after you, Mericadal is responsible."

"Why's it not changing?"

Yena looked at the Alpuri depiction. "It's just what they're choosing to show us. Sometimes they show a lot, sometimes a little. They'll no doubt be investigating this new information for themselves too."

"Can they stop the Breaker?"

"I have no idea. They might not even want to."

"Why are they showing us, Yena? I thought you said their decisions were protracted, but here we are, and they're communicating with us."

Yena paused, thinking. "Perhaps they have already made certain decisions."

"What decisions?"

"To help. To communicate. I don't know. But you're right. The fact that we're here – both of us, and that the Alpuri are communicating with us… maybe something's changed." Yena let her hands fall back down and sighed. "Anyway, we need to prepare."

"For what?"

"Well, if Kera and Diyan are on their way, I need to think about how I'm going to explain to the Alpuri that we'd like them to join us. Same as I did when they showed me you."

Chapter 50

Aligned Trajectories, Liberation

Diyan awoke from his sleep, the light of the day piercing his eyelids. He looked around groggily. Kera was awake, staring forwards. The desolate expanse of Barrenscape was below them, albeit concerningly close. Light winds buffeted the ship.

"I thought we were passing right through the middle of Barrenscape?" Diyan said.

"Engines are... less optimal than I'd hoped," Kera explained, narrowing her eyes at the control panel. "I've changed our course to fly along Barrenscape for a little while, instead of passing right through it. If there's an issue with the ship, we can land and fix it. At least there's no Breaker to worry about. Means we can fly low and travel throughout the day. The journey's just going to take a little longer than we thought."

"The Breaker." Diyan ruminated. "Echoes of Gravity wanted you to bring it to Sunsprit, and then... informed you it was no longer necessary, just as the Breaker found its way to Fadin."

"I know," Kera said. "Certainly not a coincidence. But, it also doesn't concern me, not as much as it should. Echoes of Gravity wanted it to happen, and I don't think Echoes of Gravity means us harm."

"Echoes of Gravity is aligned with the Tugs, and it has interests with the Breaker also. What connects them?" Diyan's eyes wandered about the ship. "Could Echoes of Gravity be composed of this *thick matter*? Perhaps it's related to the Source's creators?"

Kera pursed her lips. "Perhaps. But I don't think it's got anything to do with the Source's creators. It's different." She looked at him and rolled her eyes. "Your guess is as good as mine."

"What are the chances that we found them both in Sunsprit's chasm?"

Kera left the question unanswered. Diyan stood up and stretched, then reached for some of the food packets they had taken with them. He offered one to Kera, who accepted it cheerily. They ate quietly, watching Barrenscape's empty surface speed past.

"What do you know about the Alpuri?" Diyan asked, crumpling the empty food packet into a ball and tossing it behind him.

"Only a little," Kera admitted, scrumpling up her own.

"Same as everyone else then."

"In that regard."

Her reply elicited a smile from Diyan. His voice became serious. "But we do know they have the key to leaving the Source."

"Yes."

"Even though they haven't used it themselves."

Kera nodded. "Maybe they don't want to use it, but the Tugs certainly do."

"Then who's to say the Alpuri will help us?"

She tapped on her seat lightly with her hand. "That's not a problem for right now."

"You seem to be in a good mood."

She laughed. "Aren't your eyes wide in surprise? Things are finally falling into place, Diyan. And we're together. If we're lucky, Paran and Yena are waiting for us, with the Alpuri. I've waited so long for this. I'm doing what I think is right and everything is aligned."

"What do you mean, *aligned*."

Kera took her time responding. "I was conflicted, when you, Paran and Yena arrived on Barrenscape. Before that, I had come to terms with what had to be done. Tapache had given us an objective with its promise to aid our species, then the Nesch had given me their objective, which is embedded within me... and when you think about it, those objectives are one and the same."

"To destroy the Source?"

"Yes." She cleared her throat. "I thought I had lost

you, as well as Paran, Yena, and Otherness. So, when I finally entered the Source, the Administration, the Silvereds, all others were secondary thoughts. I never really took a side: I didn't hate the Administration and I didn't even care for the Silvereds, at first. If I could understand how to destroy the Source, some Roranians might die, our c-automs would be sacrificed too, but I could return to Tapache with the rest, and it might honour its promise to us. There would be a future for our species. I believed that, I really did. I was resigned to that purpose." Her breathing had become rapid. She paused to regain control.

"But then we arrived?"

"Yes, then you arrived. You were never supposed to be casualties of what I needed to do, none of you." She sniffed and wiped away a tear that had fallen down her cheek. "I thought I'd already lost you. When I stole the dummy node, I acted on instinct. I couldn't afford to think too strongly, because I knew that if I did, I wouldn't be able to carry on."

Diyan reached across and gripped her shoulder. "It's okay, Kera."

"Echoes of Gravity and the information from the Tugs made me even more certain the Source had to be destroyed." She clenched her cheeks and looked directly into his eyes. "The Source is a war machine, created for an invasion that will consume the entire galaxy. We cannot allow that to happen." Her breathing began to intensify again. "What's at stake is larger than me, us, or all Roranians and Vaesians even. A war is coming, more terrible than anything imaginable, and we can stop it."

"A war?" Diyan uttered quietly.

"That much was clear from the Tugs, overwhelmingly so. The Tugs are terrified. Why else do you think they've hidden deep within a chasm in Ringscape? The only crack we know of within Ringscape's surface. Through the probability wave of death, the Source's creators have built an army the likes of which our galaxy has never seen. All this time we've been here, the recruitment has continued, hidden in this emptiness past the tips of our galaxy. Countless machine-lects, the pinnacles of intelligence, from species after species; none able to stop or resist the pull. The machine-lects have their intellects ripped from their physical substrates, gone, transported and stored in another form of existence."

"How long has… this been going on for?" was all Diyan could manage.

"We can only guess. Unknowable aeons. The Source's creators make the Nesch look feeble, nothing more than an afterthought. Even the Breaker is nothing to them. Tapache has no clue what they truly represent, yet even Tapache hides from their ancient machine, sending us in its stead. I don't know why, but the intentions of the Source's creators are to cause cataclysmic destruction.

That is enough reason to do everything we can to stop them. We cannot fail." She stopped, the silence deafening. She smiled serenely at Diyan. "So, you see, destroying the Source is necessary, and I knew that unequivocally, but... when the Nesch came after us... after me... I lost my way again. I began to doubt everything. I began to wonder if I was wrong, if I had misunderstood something. If I was wrong about the Nesch, I could have been wrong about everything else too. I could no longer trust myself. I needed Echoes of Gravity to help me understand, one final time."

"And?"

"It did."

"How did it help you?"

"I now understand that the Nesch was not after me because of anything I had done, but because that is what the Nesch are like. It is in their nature, nothing more."

Diyan looked down, his face a mixture of emotions as he grappled with what Kera had told him. He looked back up at her. "And now, everything has aligned. The path we are on will satisfy the Nesch, and Tapache. We could save the entire galaxy."

"Yes. Never have I been more sure that destroying the Source is the right thing to do. And... I've realised I'm unwilling to do this without you. Any of you. I can't."

"What about our c-automs? All of them — Wiln, Otherness, Loten, Rememox, and Selo too?"

"I miss them, terribly, Diyan... if there's a way to save them, we will. But what we need to do is too important. It's bigger than any of us. Please, say you understand?"

Diyan moved to kneel beside her seat. "I'm glad your burden has been lifted, Kera. Whether or not we are successful and Tapache honours its promise to us, I'm with you."

"Now you see why I couldn't tell anyone, least of all Osr."

"I do," Diyan said. "Who would want to know this? To know that everything, the squabbles and conflicts on Ringscape, may be for nothing. That it all needs to be destroyed anyway, and everything else is just... incidental."

"I don't know if we'll be able to save them, I don't even know if we'll be able to save ourselves."

Diyan shifted back. "How long do we have?"

"Maybe thousands of years, maybe millions. Maybe one day. All I know is that we have to act quickly. We cannot leave this to anyone else. Currently, the Source takes resources in, but the Modal Change Hypothesis is correct, and there's been a change. At some point, it's going to start expelling everything back out – the Source's creators, and their vast, unstoppable army. And they'll start their destruction here, with us."

Chapter 51

Fate's Reunion, Visitors

Kera and Diyan walked side-by-side, eyes wandering over the empty expanse of uninhabited Ringscape. Both had their facepieces pulled up, leaving only their eyes visible.

"Would have been a lot easier if the ship hadn't given up on us. Of all the luck…" Diyan said. "There's nothing here. Kera?"

She glanced about distractedly. "Yes?"

"I was just saying it would've been easier to reach the Alpuri with the ship." He gestured around them. "We've no idea where we're going."

She turned away. "I'm not sure."

"Exactly, that's what I…" Diyan's mouth was open, but further words refused to come. He stopped in confusion, then tried to move, failing, his muscles tensing uselessly. His eyes flicked to the side. Kera was looking at him.

"Diyan?" Her tone was inquisitive. She hesitated.

"Diyan, I think… we're here." She tipped her head to the side. The air around them became thicker, hazier, the light dimming. She took his hand in hers, manipulating his fingers around her own and gripping tightly. "We're here." She pulled down both their facepieces and kissed him on the lips. "We're going to be fine. They're just letting us in."

The air continued to thicken; reality constricted. Soon, it was just them. The light died; they were engulfed in darkness. Nothing perceivable except each other, somehow unobscured. Kera's movements were calm. Diyan's eyes remained fixed upon her. In the nothingness, something sped towards them, lit in the same strange way they were.

"It's the entrance to an annexe," Kera said, intrigue ringing in her voice, the only thing Diyan could hear.

"What's it…" Diyan stuttered quiet. "I can move…" he said, finally. "What happened to me? What stopped me?" He ran his hands up and down his waist.

They were stood upon a ledge, with an entrance in front of them that preceded a short passageway. All else was surrounded by darkness. Without warning, two forms emerged from the end of the passageway and walked towards them. Diyan and Kera froze. Yena and Paran were strolling towards them.

Once Yena and Paran reached the annexe's mouth, they stopped. The four of them stared at each other.

"It's real," Paran said finally, flicking his head back the

way they had come. "This is real."

"I can't believe it," Diyan replied.

"You'd better believe it, because Paran's right," Yena said, her excited voice matching her wide eyes. "The Alpuri found this annexe and kept it safe." She looked between Diyan and Paran, and then at Kera, whose expression was impassive. "Oh, come on, all of you! We're here, we're back together." She rushed forwards, clasping both Kera and Diyan in her arms. A moment later, all four were locked in a tight embrace.

*

The four of them were sat on the ringed bench at the centre of the forest. Their talk spanned many of the events that had led them each to the Alpuri, including the existence of Echoes of Gravity and the Tugs, and Kera's interactions with them. They also spoke of what Paran had learned about the Breaker's origins.

"It's incredible," Yena whispered. "To think there's so much going on, and the Administration is unaware. After all this time in the Source, it still holds so many secrets."

"I know," Diyan murmured in agreement. "And we're finally on the verge of understanding."

Yena grabbed Paran's arm. "Just think, if you hadn't stumbled on that city, we might never have learned *anything* about the Breaker's past."

Paran shrugged. "There's one thing… before we carry on…"

"What's the matter?" Yena asked, concerned.

Paran scrunched his face and rose up, picking Yena's hand gently off his arm to face the three of them. His voice was timid. "I'm not proud of what I did. So much could have been avoided if I'd listened to you both, long ago," he looked ruefully at Kera and Diyan. "I let my anger get the better of me, in Sunsprit." He turned to Yena. "And I ignored—"

Yena stood up and gripped his arm protectively. "You had no choice."

"It's okay, Yena. I need to say it."

"Paran," Kera interjected. "None of this has been your fault. I should have told you everything. I should have told all three of you, as soon as I found you again." She grimaced. "There are things all of us should have done differently, but none more so than me. So no, *you* don't need to apologise. If anyone, it should be me."

"No," Yena said, a tear running down her cheek. "I wasn't faced with the choices any of you were, yet I blamed you all the same."

There was an awkward pause. Diyan cleared his throat. "Erm, I should probably admit to having some share of the blame too? In the interest of fairness…"

The comment elicited laughter from each of them. Yena was quick to pull them all together. "The past is the past. We're here now. No more hiding. No more lies."

"No more lies," Kera repeated.

There was another awkward pause. Diyan pointed out of the forest and nodded to Paran. "I spotted a combat ring out there, maybe you could take a beating from me later, like old times."

Paran smiled widely. "Funny how memories change with time, isn't it?"

"There's that smile," Kera teased.

Paran's smile lingered until a look of urgency took hold. "There are some other important things we need to discuss. The main being..." He glanced at Yena. "We know the Breaker made it to Fadin, the Alpuri showed us. We have to help."

"There was nothing you could have done to warn Fadin in time, but you tasked Topinr with warning the other Roranian settlements," Yena interjected.

Paran continued. "Nothing could have prepared them. The Nesch is one thing... the Breaker is something else entirely." His eyes wandered about the forest, searching for something. "If... perhaps, if we could return to your ship, Kera, Diyan, we could fix it. We could return."

Kera sighed. "I understand your fear, and your concern, Paran. But..." She gulped. "There are things even *more* important that we need to discuss."

Paran's eyes widened in surprise. "What could be more important than helping an entire city?"

"Saving everything else," Kera said, steely.

"Fadin is not unimportant in Ringscape, Kera—"

"Not just Fadin. Not the other cities. Not Ringscape. Not Barrenscape, not even the Source. Everything."

"There are things we haven't told you yet," Diyan added. "Things Kera learned from the dummy node, and since then, that you need to know."

"What?" Paran was still incredulous.

"What things?" Yena asked.

Paran and Yena listened, while Kera explained more about the dummy node and the information it had contained from the Tugs, as well as what she had later understood from Echoes of Gravity. Afterwards, Yena was the first to speak. She sounded demoralised.

"It's incredible that all of this exists within the Source, it really is. This Echoes of Gravity, these Tugs... the fact that you've communicated with them... but, it's too much to think we can change any of it." She shook her head. "All this... the Source's creators, this *army* they've built... and... if all this is true, why haven't the Source's creators done anything to stop you, Kera? How can you be sure they really exist? Maybe you've been lied to; maybe you're being used; maybe—"

"It's true," Kera said, firmly. "All of it."

"But to destroy it all? Even... even if we... even if we could... not even considering *how* we would do it, and even if we ignore the Breaker, the Tugs themselves,

412

Echoes of Gravity... the Nesch outside Fadin... even Fadin, and all the Roranians in Ringscape..." The tone of her voice reflected her rising panic. "Even if we ignore it all, what about our c-automs? They're all still here, either trapped or in repositories. It's been a long time, but I still remember them like it was yesterday. Rememox, Selo, Loten—"

"We have no choice," Kera said.

"There must be another way, Kera?" Paran said. He looked to Diyan. "There must be?"

"This isn't the way I want it to be," Kera said to them. "This is the way it has to be." As Kera spoke, her demeanour changed. It was as though she was embarrassed. "And... the Nesch is no longer a problem."

"What do you mean?" Diyan asked.

"There's something else. Something..." she looked guilty, "I haven't told you yet. I've only just figured it out. I sensed it before, I accepted it without knowing, but now I understand it."

"What?"

"I can hear them." Kera motioned around them. "I can hear them. That's how I know that the Nesch is no longer a problem. They've received information. The Nesch has been destroyed. It no longer functions."

"Who..." Diyan trailed off.

"You can hear the Alpuri?" Yena asked, frowning.

"Yes."

413

"How?" Paran asked.

"Because the Nesch were the Alpuri, once," Yena said, eyes widening. "And the Nesch changed you, Kera. That's how, isn't it?"

Kera nodded. "The Nesch gave something of themselves to me. And now, I can sense them, around us. There are *so* many. I can... it's like I'm connected. If I concentrate, I can hear things, here and there. Whispers. It was stronger outside the annexe, but it's still here."

"We're quarantined," Paran said.

"And it's time that ended," Kera said, taking a deep breath and glancing at Diyan. "The Alpuri have a key that will enable us to leave the Source."

"A what?"

"The Alpuri know how we can leave."

Yena gasped. "Of course..."

Paran stared between Yena and Kera, dumbfounded.

"The Alpuri can predict the entry events, so it makes sense," Yena said. "I can't believe I didn't realise before." She grasped Paran. "They took this annexe and hid it. They keep track of the large entry events. That means they know they're coming. That's right, isn't it, Kera?"

"Yes. The Alpuri have always been able to leave." Kera muttered something and gestured briefly with her hands. A holo appeared. A sphere, with periodic dark patches.

Yena looked shocked. "How did you—"

"Because they're listening to us now," Kera said. "And

they're giving us this ship."

"Ship?"

"Did you really think this was just an annexe?" Kera's eyes sparkled. "This is an escape pod. The only one in all of Ringscape."

"They're telling you all this?" Yena asked.

"I'm listening," Kera said. "And so are the Alpuri. They're leaving too."

"And they're actually letting us take this escape pod?" Diyan asked. "This ship."

"It was never theirs."

"Simple as that?" Diyan asked.

"After all this time," Yena said, quietly.

"Yes." Kera grimaced. "It's getting far too busy for them anyway. They're not telling me much else."

Diyan pointed to the holo sphere next to Kera, which had grown larger. It was orange, with flickering dark patches. "Is that their key?"

Kera nodded, her voice low. "A representation of it, yes. The key's encoded within this ship's navigational systems now."

"What're they going to do?" Yena asked. "Will they help us?"

"They already have. But once they leave the Source, I don't think we'll ever see them again."

"That's all?" Paran said. "Don't they realise the entire galaxy—"

"Not their galaxy," Kera said.

Paran pursed his lips. "What's the plan?" Kera did not reply, and Paran frowned. "There must be a plan. We can't just leave the Source and *somehow* destroy it from the outside. And what about warning everyone, giving them a chance to escape? With this key, we could direct them to entry points... or exit points, whatever we call them."

Kera shook her head. "No. The plan is that we get out and we spread the word amongst the lattice ships. We convince them to help us, however we can, and then, we use the Alpuri key to return, and unleash everything. We destroy the Source by any means necessary." She looked Paran directly in the eyes. "When we return, if there's time, we can direct Roranians, and everyone else, towards exit points, but you must understand what's at stake. The devastation if we fail would be unimaginable. We cannot afford to delay, or for anything to stop us leaving the Source. If this ship is damaged, then all is lost."

"But... even if that worked, do you seriously think we'd be able to convince any of the lattice ships?" Paran asked. "They'll probably try to destroy *us* instead!"

"The Nesch hate the Source," Diyan pointed out. "It'd be in their interests to help us."

"Trust the Nesch?"

Kera shrugged. "We have to try."

"Kera..." Yena said, lightly and carefully. "The Administration has nothing approaching the level of sophistication of this ship. Surely, since we can easily brave the haze winds, we can go to Upper-Fadin, and we can liberate the c-autom repositories. With our capabilities, it wouldn't take long at all. It'd almost be on the way—"

"I know what you want to do, Yena," Kera said. "And I badly want to do that too. But I'm sorry, we can't risk flying into Upper-Fadin, even for our c-automs. The Breaker is there, and if the ship's damaged, all of this will have been for nothing."

"Please, Kera, it's been so long."

Kera placed a hand on Yena's shoulder. "I promise you, when we return, we will take them back."

Yena shifted uncomfortably under Kera's steady grasp. "I'll hold you to that."

Chapter 52

Tempestuous Departure, Escape Pod

Kera was reclined upon a comfortable platform that had adapted its length to her body. She was engulfed in a simulation haze, busy interacting with the ship's systems. Paran, Yena and Diyan were spaced equidistantly around Kera, also similarly reclined. All four wore combat suits.

"I preferred it when the ship looked like my annexe," Yena grumbled.

"It's better to reorganise, in case of battle," Paran replied. "Additional space is a luxury, and should be repurposed—"

"I know, I know. Lessons from the green mounds long ago. We needed the Alpuri to reorganise the ship because when they leave, it'll be too late, we can't do it ourselves." Yena sighed. "Still, it was nice to have my annexe back, for a time."

"You'll see it again," Diyan said warmly, sitting forwards, with the platform beneath him reconfiguring into an upright seat.

"If Tapache waits."

"And if we're successful first," Paran said, also moving upright.

"Exactly, we just need to be successful first," Yena repeated, somewhat irritably, joining them both in the new position. "We just need to reach the lattice, somehow survive, convince the ships to help us and to also come *back* into the Source with us, and then we need to *destroy* the Source, which is a machine so ancient and dangerous that even Tapache, who is a *Wanderer*, has hidden from it."

"The situation in the lattice might not be as bad as you think," Diyan said.

"In what way?"

"Perhaps some of us out there will be in control."

"Roranians?"

"Yes."

"We... *they* were under the control of the Nesch." Yena rolled her eyes. "Don't forget, the Nesch destroyed our Great Ship in the first place and captured almost everyone on it for their armies. Most likely, Roranians who've managed to survive since then are still captive. And if not, with any sense, they'll have left, long ago."

"But no one does that," Paran said. "No one leaves. Otherwise Tapache would have known about the Source and prepared us better."

"Unless Tapache lied to us." Yena reclined back

horizontally. "Still, we can hope——"

Kera's voice boomed around them. "We're almost ready to leave."

Yena snapped back up. "And the Alpuri?"

"They're about to leave as well."

"Then what are we all waiting for?"

The simulation haze dissipated, and Kera looked at them. Her voice stopped emanating from all around. "The Alpuri have a parting gift."

"What?"

A warning chime sounded as a slab of the ship's wall between Paran and Diyan rippled up, causing both of them to leap immediately to their feet. Ringscape was exposed. It was empty, devoid of any of the Alpuri's hazy identifiers. Sparks of colour were just about visible to one side – fizzling ends of energetic cascades that emanated from the ship's bloom propulsion unit, which was currently raised above the ground. A single Prietman came into view from the other side of the opening. Its body was covered by a large cloak, a mass of spindly, sharp-pointed legs jutting out underneath. It slowly entered the ship, stopped between Paran and Diyan, apparently unconcerned by their presences, and dropped its body to the ground. After a short pause, it rose back up and scuttled out, faster than before. The ship resealed.

Paran stared after the Prietman, while Diyan squatted to the floor, studying the object it had left behind – a small, flat, rectangular device, the size of an arm. It was pure white, but like the Alpuri themselves, there were shades that differentiated themselves from others. The edges of the object bulged, as though unable to hold the shape.

"What is it?" Diyan asked, as Paran also turned to look at it.

"A weapon?" Paran suggested.

Yena also hurried over to investigate. "Is it safe?"

"It's something the Alpuri have made for us," Kera replied, allowing a simulation haze to waft over her again. "Some type of amplifier, a defensive mechanism."

"What's it for?" Yena asked.

"I don't know that yet."

"But it's for defence..." Yena said doubtfully, regarding the small object. "Against what? The Source?"

Kera's voice sounded around them again through the ship's systems. "Not the Source. Echoes of Gravity."

"What?" Diyan exclaimed.

"I thought you said Echoes of Gravity was on our side?" Paran said.

"Unless you mean this device is to defend Echoes of Gravity against something else?" Yena asked.

"I don't know, yet. The ship's going to take a little while to understand it," Kera admitted. "But the Alpuri seem to think it will help us." The walls and ceiling shimmered to transparency. It appeared as though they were sitting atop a circular sheet, exposed to endless Ringscape. "The ship's ready. It's time to leave."

They all returned to their seats.

"They've gone," Yena said, looking around and accessing a small set of holo controls beside her. "There's no trace of them. I can't find that Prietman either, or any others."

"They've probably gone through the Haze Rings," Diyan said, also fiddling with his own holo controls. "And we're now to follow."

"Kera," Yena said, with sudden eagerness. "Have the Alpuri dealt with the Nesch in the lattice for us?"

Kera's voice sounded around them. "I don't know."

"Typical," Yena muttered.

The ship lifted off Ringscape's surface, into the sky.

*

Diyan sifted through his holo controls. Paran and Yena were chatting, quietly. Kera was obscured by the simulation haze. Diyan cleared his throat, and began moving his fingers more rapidly through the controls.

"Kera," Diyan said. "Is there a problem? Why aren't we targeting the nearest entry event?"

"What?" Yena said, immediately ending her conversation with Paran as they both looked down at their own controls.

"You're right," Paran said. "The trajectory's been changed."

Yena created a small holo depiction to appear beside her. It showed their prior trajectory, and an entry event the Alpuri Key had calculated in the Haze Rings that was easily large enough for their ship to exit through. The ship had been almost halfway there, when their course had been altered. The ubiquitous glow of the unfilled skies all around them had hidden the shift in direction, the ship's inertial dampeners rendering the change in acceleration impossible to identify.

"Kera, you've changed our course…" Yena began. Her new holo extrapolated their current trajectory, and she gasped.

"Upper-Fadin?" Paran said, quizzically. "Why are we going there?"

The simulation haze dissipated around Kera and she sat up. "Because you're right," she said, looking at them all. "I've been making the same mistakes over and over again, and I won't make them now."

"What mistakes?" Diyan asked.

"I'm not listening to you," Kera said. "I'm taking you for granted. What we're doing is so important, but it won't be possible without all of us, together."

"We're going to get our c-automs, aren't we?" Despite speaking in a whisper, Yena's countenance had completely changed. Her eyes were wide, excited.

Kera nodded. "It's never been just the four of us. Our c-automs matter. I'm not sure we're going to be able to do what's required if they're in danger." She looked awkwardly at Paran. "We will do whatever we can to help everyone else down here when we return, but for now…"

Paran simply nodded.

"Thank you," Yena blurted out.

Chapter 53

Remembered Confusion, Escape Pod

It was not long before the ship would reach Upper-Fadin and the sky-factories would loom into sensor range. Kera was obscured by the simulation haze, controlling the ship, monitoring for any sign of danger.

"Soon, our sensors will be able to scan Upper-Fadin," Paran said, forebodingly. "We'll be able to know the extent of the Breaker's devastation."

"At least the Nesch has been dealt with. As long as there aren't any more..." Diyan frowned. "Kera... do we know if that Nesch was alone? How did it enter through the Haze Rings? Successful entries are extremely rare, and the chances are so low."

"It didn't." Kera partially reduced the holo around her face, and spoke normally.

"What?"

"That Nesch was never from the lattice. It was from here, Ringscape." Kera wrinkled her nose, as though amused by something. "The result of a difference in opinion."

Yena was nodding. "Their exodus from the Source?"

"Exactly."

"What?" Paran said.

"Not all of them wanted to leave," Yena said, looking to Kera, who turned her seat to face Yena and smile in confirmation. "Some wanted to stay."

"Yes." Kera chuckled, as Paran and Diyan still appeared none-the-wiser. "You see, the Alpuri have debated whether to leave the Source for a long time now, becoming increasingly concerned at its instability for them. And, as you know, ideas are everything to the Alpuri. Ideas change them. The notion of leaving caused an extensive ripple of discord, and discord is not something the Alpuri take lightly. In order to preserve their greater whole, a minority Alpuri segment was forcibly coalesced and cauterised – exiled. The exiled Alpuri drifted across Ringscape, unable to reconnect informationally, until coming across me. Once that happened, the Alpuri segment recognised something familiar, and understood what it thought it was, and then…"

"It became a Nesch, or an approximation of one," Yena said. "It became what it thought it was."

"Yes," Kera said. "It was never because of me, or truly after me. It was just…" She smirked. "A bad idea." The

426

simulation haze covered Kera's face again, and her voice sounded from the ship's systems. "We're almost in range of the sky-factories."

The other three also engulfed themselves in simulation hazes and waited, gleaning all the information they could from the ship.

"There they are…" Yena said.

"Transport modules along the tethers have stopped," Paran observed.

"It's the same with the other sky-factories too," Diyan said. "The influx network must have been disrupted."

"We need to get a little closer, then we'll know for certain," Yena said. "Wait – what's that? Kera, why can't we scan it properly?"

Warning chimes filled the ship.

"What's going on?" Diyan asked.

Kera's voice sounded through the ship. "Something's headed directly for one of the sky-factories, directly from Upper-Fadin. I'm intercepting their communications now."

Each of them watched the sky-factory through the ship's sensors. It appeared as a small speck, far away. A terrified voice filtered through. "This is Captain Guran of Sky-Factory Seven. Identify your—" The sky-factory lurched violently upwards, away from Ringscape and against its tethers, and then to the side, as though a speck of dust had been swatted by a giant hand. It disappeared from the ship's sensors.

"What was that?" Yena whispered.

Their trajectory changed, immediately. They were flying rapidly away from Upper-Fadin, back in the direction they had come. Their suit helmets shimmered closed over their heads, automatically engaged in full combat mode.

"I'm finding the nearest suitable entry event."

More warning chimes sounded. A hazy object was headed straight for them, coming from the direction of Sky-Factory Seven. It zigzagged rapidly through the air, with no bloom. Strange gravitational anomalies rippled around it. The sensors were still unable to image it accurately.

"That's Influxa, I know it!" Paran's shouted. "She's carrying the Breaker."

"I know," Kera replied.

They hurtled away from it.

"It's closing the distance between us," Yena said. "I'm not sure we can withstand whatever—"

"It's broadcasting, open channel," Diyan said. "It's meant for us! Kera—"

"I know," Kera repeated, levelly. "Audio-only. I'm accepting the request."

A moment later, a mechanical voice came through. Words, other noises, incomprehensibly merged together. Only a few recognisable. One sentence was unjumbled.

"I thought you said Influxa was friendly!" Yena shouted to Paran.

"It's not Influxa anymore!" Paran shouted back.

The ship continued to replay the single sentence.

I am reunified and I am coming.

"I've locked onto an opening, straight above us," Kera said. The ship's sides became fully opaque.

"It's coming!" Yena shouted.

Suddenly, everything calmed.

"There's no trace of Influxa…" Diyan said. "The ship's navigational systems are recalibrating."

The simulation hazes around all four of them dissipated and they looked at one another. Their helmets receded into their suits.

"We did it," Kera said, simply. "We did it. And the event closed right behind us. I'm as sure as I can be about anything that we weren't followed."

The ship's sides shimmered back to partial-transparency. A bright expanse was revealed, dimmed by the ship. The exterior of the Source. Dark space was cut against it.

"I can't believe it," Paran said, rising to his feet and hurrying over to Yena. She rose and they embraced. "We really did it."

Diyan sprinted over to Kera and wrapped his arms around her, kissing her on the lips. When they broke apart, she turned to the side, a holo display having caught her attention. It imaged what appeared to be a fleet of enormous ships, each with vast blooms, coming their way. Paran swore loudly.

"Great Ships," Kera murmured.

Chapter 54

Cowed King, Barrenscape

Mericadal exited the salvage vessel, without bothering to instruct the ramp to close back against the ship. Barrenscape's gentle winds blew small particles of ground matter against him. He made a fist within the self-repaired, recharged combat suit, which was now temporarily fused with his body while the accelerated healing was ongoing. His hand did not hurt, and would be fine in time. He stared at the exposed Vaesian docking ring, just a few steps away.

"I can't believe it," Member Slautina said, moving to stand beside him. "It's not possible."

"And yet, it is." Mericadal's eyes blazed.

"What do we do?"

"We enter."

*

Mericadal and Member Slautina picked their way through the ancient Vaesian city, stopping only briefly to study the mountains of corpses. All the while, the lights flickered and the failing dome covering creaked from the pressure above. Rumblings could be heard as sections began to collapse.

"We shouldn't stay long," Member Slautina said, with concern, almost running after Mericadal.

"We'll stay as long as we need," Mericadal muttered, reaching the top of a short sequence of steps. He jumped up, over the mid-part of a fallen tower in their path. It took some time for Member Slautina to navigate around the obstacle and catch up with him.

"Everything's about to fall, we should be quick."

"You did well, rescuing me from that battlefield, but don't stop me now, Member Slautina."

"Are you sure—"

"Did you know Invira, Member Slautina?"

Member Slautina frowned. "I think so. Wasn't she in charge of influx network maintenance?"

Mericadal sneered. "Much more than that. She helped me create it, long ago. I wish she were here now, instead of you. *She* was useful."

Falling debris to the side of them caused Member Slautina to jump. She moved to the other side of the already-narrow walkway, staying as close to Mericadal as she could. "But—"

Mericadal spun to the side, grabbed Member Slautina by the neck and pinned her against the side of a broken tower. "Member Slautina, Fadin has fallen. There is nothing left for us there. But this, this is something we have to do. There are secrets here I must understand, they're all that's left. Before Influxa was overtaken, she sent a drone back informing me that Commander Paran had entered this place, and she was set to follow. Influxa subsequently emerged as something else, and I need to understand why. There is something powerful here." He paused, breathing heavily. "And if Commander Paran is still here, I will kill him myself." Mericadal grimaced. "He ruined everything. So, I am not going anywhere until I have my answers." He released hold of her neck and she dropped to the ground, shaking. "You may leave or you may follow, I don't care." He walked off.

Member Slautina rose back up and followed, timidly and at a distance, rubbing her neck. She said nothing else. Soon, they entered an area where, despite the city's failing facilities, the lighting was more consistent.

"Look at the ground," Mericadal said to Member Slautina as they turned a corner, motioning up ahead. "It's lit silver." He spoke as though nothing had happened between them and did not wait for her response. He rushed over to press his feet excitedly onto the bright surface.

Without further delay, they walked on, and soon found

themselves upon a ringed walkway that surrounded an enormous, gaping pit, which looked to extend far down into the depths of Barrenscape. Despite the light around it, the pit was pitch black. Mericadal looked down, with Member Slautina back by his side.

"What's down there?" Member Slautina asked hesitantly, craning her neck.

"I have no idea."

They walked around the walkway, looking for clues. All the while, the rumblings of the dying city reverberated in the air. They stopped. Member Slautina looked back over the railing, standing with one leg off the ground. "It's almost—" She stuttered, confused to find Mericadal's hand propped up against her back, not allowing her to place both feet back onto the walkway. "What're you doing?" she demanded, her voice shrill.

"I've realised your use," Mericadal whispered.

"Wait—"

Mericadal pushed her over the edge, her screams doing nothing to alter his expression as he listened to her drop. He examined his sensors, gleaning everything he could. Finally, the faintest impact was audible. His suit estimated she had fallen almost a quarter of the way through Barrenscape. Mericadal conducted a diagnostics check, and confirmed the suit had enough resources. It was likely he would survive the fall, but there would be significant damage. He directed some chemical infusions to circulate about, calming his nerves, then instructed the suit to put him to sleep, until both he, and the suit, were repaired again. Once that was done, he leapt forwards.

*

Mericadal awoke. Groggily, he pushed himself onto his back and stared up. It was extremely dark. Notifications immediately informed him that everything was functioning optimally – both his body and the suit's conditions. Systems were sequentially being reawakened to full capacity. He had been asleep for twenty-nine days whilst various necessary repairs were conducted. Unfortunately, the suit's supplies were running low – in particular, the necessary sustenance that was intravenously supplied to his body. The suit identified Member Slautina's body beside him, in a state of decay. The fall had not been kind to her, and she had died upon impact. Fortunately, she had some food packets contained within a regwear pouch.

Mericadal's vision improved as the suit overlaid all the available sensory data into his visual spectrum. The level of apparent light became such that he could have been fooled into believing he was back on the surface, early into the day. The ground was covered thickly with Barrenscape's yellow matter that had fallen from above. It was pooled up high into a small hill. There were many parts of Vaesian towers scattered about – none all too large. Despite the progress Mericadal had made into Barrenscape's depths, gravity was normal.

"Tapache has a plan for me," he muttered.

He picked a direction and walked off.

*

Still, Mericadal's sensors displayed nothing significant, no end to the expanse. The ground had become smoother, less covered by Barrenscape's matter, revealing a hard, flat surface that seemed to absorb light. It was now almost as dark as night. He ran as fast as he could, seeing no reason not to. He ran and he ran and he ran. There was nothing. He fell to his knees. "Tapache!" he screamed. "What is this all for?"

Miserable and dejected, he wept. It was quite some time before he picked himself back up. He walked back to where he had awoken, and stared at the mound of dirt with parts of the Vaesian city scattered within it. He moved around the mound so that he did not have to see Member Slautina's corpse.

"What can I do?" he asked, tears starting to fall down his cheeks. He instructed his helmet to recede into the suit, allowing hot, stale air to impact his face. The suit automatically created light for him to see. "What do I do now?" he shouted.

A small shard of a tower component caught his eye. He sighed. It was part-submerged in the mountain. With nothing better to do, he began to dig it out. It yielded nothing. Automatically, almost without thinking, he continued, sifting through the dirt. He sniffed the tears away, concentrating on the task he had set himself.

*

Mericadal lay the items he had found on the ground before him, amongst the larger tower debris. Vaesian relics, mostly useless. There were seven long, dark cylinders, two strangely shaped masks, two grey cubes, and various clumps of blueish matter. That was it, the summation of his efforts, and all there was to keep him company until the suit depleted its reserves and he starved. He gritted his teeth, examining the cylinders, one by one. None of them appeared to be of any use whatsoever.

He moved on to the other objects, and paused. The grey cube he currently held began to vibrate in his hand. He instructed his suit helmet to re-encase his head and analysed it as best he could. The cube was some type of Vaesian storage device.

*

Mericadal angrily crushed the first storage device. The

information contained had been useless, a waste of his time. Most of the data had been unreadable, and what had been decipherable was about Vaesian reproduction. It detailed how the Vaesians gestated their offspring within their bodies for many of their strange developmental cycles, with no set limits beyond the single-cycle minimum. Before the offspring were expelled and given autonomous life, the singular parent-Vaesians could choose to expose themselves to other Vaesians they admired, for whatever reason, allowing properties of the admired Vaesians to influence the gestating offspring. The process was highly convoluted and prone to all sorts of randomness and oddities. The main difference between the cycle-types of the Vaesians, termed male and female, was in the latter's improved ability to affect their offspring's personality, and the former's improved ability to affect their offspring's memories. The storage device was scant on the memory part of the process. While the majority of the Vaesian species cycled synchronously, they were labelled differently throughout their cycles because of the importance Vaesians placed on who their gestating offspring came into proximity with.

"Didn't help you rule Ringscape, did it?" Mericadal shouted, stamping the storage device against the ground.

He picked up the second device and began a scan. It did not take long before its secrets were unveiled. It was a map. Mericadal waited while the map was decoded, and then stared at the generated holo, enthralled. The map showed the positions of various Vaesian cities dotted about *Barrenscape*, many of which were far bigger and more sprawling than Fadin. There was little detail for any of the cities, other than their sizes and positions, and there was no accompanying information about Vaesian settlements on Ringscape. The current city he had entered, and descended the pit from, was the smallest.

"Barrenscape's uninhabitable now… what did you do?" Mericadal asked out loud. "What did you do?"

He pondered the information for a long time, before carefully placing the device into a protective compartment within his suit. Next, he turned his attention to the masks. He picked the first one up, which appeared to be the most undamaged, still having a full front casing that was large enough for a Vaesian face. There was a compartment to the side that contained a small cartridge. His sensors indicated the cartridge was empty. He brought the mask to his face and directed his helmet to recede. The mask's eye-holes were spaced too far apart, and when he moved it to look through each, nothing happened. He tossed it away and picked up the second mask, allowing his helmet to encase his head while he studied it. He frowned. The cartridge within this mask did have some type of fuel inside, although he could not discern what it was, and it was almost depleted. The suit generated a holo representation of the cartridge, detailing a scant analysis of its contents. Again, Mericadal directed the suit helmet to recede and brought the mask up to his face, staring through the eyeholes one by one. Nothing. He dropped it to the floor. He was about to turn his attention to the bluish clumps he had also found and was mid-way through dismissing the holo of the cartridge, when he noticed it had registered change – a small amount of the cartridge's fuel had been used up. Mericadal picked the mask up again and looked through it, eyeing the holo. The remaining fuel decreased again, by almost ten percent.

In panic, he pressed the mask hard against one eye, trying to discern what exactly it could be used for, turning around as he did so. Something flashed in front of him, from the mound of ground matter. A vague, green wafting. He moved closer. The green wafting rippled directly upwards, emanating from the mound's centre. It disappeared. The cartridge holo flashed red. Empty.

Mericadal dropped the mask, brought his own helmet back around his head, and investigated the mound, pushing his sensors to the extremes of their capabilities. Nothing. Undeterred, he engaged the suit to full combat mode, and began blasting at the mound's centre. It took a long while, but eventually, a great deal of the mound had been cleared. He waded through. Standing right in front of the middle, where the green wafting had stemmed, he scoured his sensors.

"Yes!" he screamed, with delight. There was

something. A slight gravitational anomaly, almost completely masked by the surrounding matter. Gravity waves. Far too faint to notice under typical circumstances, but definitely there. The locus was right before him. He waded further forward and fell to his knees, crying. His mind began to shut down. He transmitted an omnidirectional message. "I've done it." This was the end, but he did not care. He had discovered something, and that was a small victory. He fell asleep.

*

Images and thoughts flickered through Mericadal's mind. He was barely conscious, only just self-perceptive enough to realise that this was no ordinary sleep. Knowledge was becoming available.

Something approached from above, from the entrance of the pit. It lowered itself down, its transparent, tentacular extensions grasping the sides. It took its time. Its central mass hummed, glowing red hot as it descended. Three of the sub-masses, balanced atop the central mass, flattened, lending their nutrients to the fourth, oldest sub-mass, which swelled in size. The creature slowed, the swelled sub-mass bloated almost to bursting point. Mericadal could sense its emotion-analogue – a familiar one – fear. The creature clung to the side more tightly than before, then rose back up, towards the pit's mouth.

Waiting at the top, thousands of similar creatures waited. They hurled orbs of orange at it. Two of them hit the frightened creature, breaking and splashing fluorescent liquid over a large number of its extensions, which lost their grip. With one last, desperate flurry, it reached out, towards the top. Another orb landed, destroying the grip of the remaining extensions. The creature fell backwards, down, into the pit.

It dropped towards the centre. Just as it was about to impact, it froze in mid-air, its descent halted. Its tentacles writhed; it was confused. It tried to reach the ground, which was just out of reach. It began to spin; its form became hazy. He could sense another emotion-analogue – elation. He understood, in a way. He was in the same position. He could feel the Haze Rings unleashing some of their power. Devastating radiation rained down upon both Barrenscape and Ringscape, incinerating everything, ripping apart even the atomic nuclei themselves. Nothing was left. The suspended creature disappeared instantaneously. All trace of its species and their time in the Source wiped out. The energy was absorbed, all was quiet.

Mericadal became even more self-aware. He was shown the same process again, this time, with another creature, under a different set of circumstances. As before, everything was destroyed, the Source was cleansed. Finally, something too alien for his mind to understand entered the pit. It was ensnared, like all the others, but it could not be destroyed. Instead, another tactic was used. It was split into three. A wild, untameable component was set loose, filled with rage and power. It destroyed everything it came across. It crossed a great bridge created by its kind, joining Ringscape to Barrenscape. Nothing escaped. The Breaker.

This is ours.

Terror, more intense than anything Mericadal had ever known, rippled through his being.

You are unwelcome.

More images, events and scenarios shot through Mericadal's mind. Unlike before, some were his own, taken from him. Something was being decided. He could sense it. The Breaker had failed, the Vaesians had managed to cow it, to change its nature. They had destroyed the great bridge. The Breaker was no longer a defender, it would no longer suffice.

Kera.

A problem was identified. Knowledge continued to be taken from him, from beyond the reaches of his conscious thought. Information was examined. Results were deduced.

Kera is gone.

Somehow, Mericadal knew what this meant. If Kera had left the Source, that meant she could return. That meant there was a danger. If she could return, there was a probability she could enter with the means to destroy it. However, Mericadal also realised something else. Kera represented an opportunity for Tapache's quest to be completed. He was conflicted. His dissent did not go unnoticed.

Come inside.

Mericadal was granted access. He saw with such clarity his mind was engulfed in pain. When he returned, no semblance of dissent remained.

You are remade.

Glossary

Administration – Governing regime that leads the Roranians.

Air terminals – Old filtration facilities that were used to purify Ringscape's air, which is slightly less than optimal for Roranian respiration. They have been replaced by 'mixed-terminal buildings' that have inbuilt air terminals. In the absence of treated air, regwear facepieces can be used to filter Ringscape's (and Barrenscape's) air. Roranians may experience mild headaches from prolonged exposure to unfiltered air.

Aivinr – Member of the council that directs the Vaesian Union.

Alpuri – Mysterious isolationist race that has been settled on Ringscape for an unknown period of time. Little is known of them.

Annexe – Expansive private areas within the Roranian Great Ship that were allocated to each individual. They could be altered and redesigned according to the whims of the individual they belonged to.

Anti-Vaesian Movement ('Anti-Vaesians') – Subversive group of Roranians who believed the Vaesians were hiding secrets about Ringscape and the Source, and consequently harboured a deep hatred for the Vaesians. They disbanded following the start of the war between the Roranians and the Vaesians.

Barrenscape – One of the three known parts of the Source (the other two being Ringscape and the Haze Rings). It appears like a vast tube that has been drawn into a circle, and then squashed in on itself from two opposite sides. Unlike Ringscape, Barrenscape has no edge, since it is cylindrical. It has a total surface area many orders of magnitude greater than that of a typical life-supporting planet orbiting a star. Aside from the debris that sometimes rains down upon it through the Haze Rings, it is thought to be too dangerous to occupy and is therefore uninhabited, aside from the Breaker.

Barrier – Theorised power consumption mechanism within the Source that absorbs energy from the Haze Rings.

Battle of Ualbrict – Battle during which the Roranian Administration lay siege to the Vaesian city of Ualbrict.

Bauhict – Battle between the Administration and the Vaesians.

Betervope – Ground matter of Barrenscape.

Biological sentient ('biological') – Non-exotic living entity that has naturally evolved, or would have been able to, and that also possesses an intellect.

Bloom propulsion unit ('bloom') – Wanderer propulsion method powered by vacuum energy.

Bolomin – Roranian acquaintance to Ilouden during his undercover work in Roranian cities.

Bomera – Roranian who lives within Sunsprit and is willingly governed by the Vaesian Union. She is primarily engaged with studies involving the Tugs.

Borminth – Battle between the Administration and the Vaesians.

Breaker – Entity that is believed to be confined to Barrenscape, and which destroys almost everything it comes into contact with. It is the principal reason that no permanent settlements have been established on Barrenscape. It is thought to be able to manipulate gravity. No accurate scans or images exist of it, and very little else can be deduced aside from its rough location.

Butcher of Ualbrict – Moniker given to Paran due to his work as a commander of the Administration military, which relates to a particularly violent battle against the Vaesians.

Captain Guran – See 'Guran'.

Casket – Protective, spherical cocoons used to grow young Roranians aboard the Great Ship, replacing the need for biological birth. Constructed from triamond-derivative materials, the caskets were very hardy and able to withstand many types of attack, as well as empty space.

Casket-ship – Makeshift vessel created by Wiln, Loten, and Rememox, the c-automs of Diyan, Paran and Yena, from three separate caskets joined together. The casket-ship protected Diyan, Paran and Yena as they entered the Source.

C-autom – Machine-lect sentients, typically used as crewmembers aboard Wanderer Ships. The c-automs aboard the Roranian Great Ship were each tasked by Tapache with looking after specific Roranian charges, or served as backups.

Cell-scale machines ('cell-scales') – Extremely small machines that live upon and within Vaesians, making their bodies stronger and better able to cope with Ringscape's gravity. The provenance of the technology is not completely known, and the cell-scales themselves are not entirely understood. There are instances where they fail – the cell-scale machines over-proliferate, drawing too much energy from their hosts. This leads to a condition called 'Silvering' where, aside from Vaesians becoming silver in colour and some other changes of varying significance, their lifespans are significantly reduced. Those with Silvering are known as 'Silvereds', and no cure has been developed. Transmission rates are low and non-Silvered Vaesians are extremely unlikely to be affected from brief contact with Silvered Vaesians.

Cestial – One of seven soldiers chosen by Paran to join him in journeying to Barrenscape, under the mission brief of baiting and trapping the Breaker.

Combat regwear ('combat suit') – Reinforced regwear worn for the purpose of combat. There are many different levels of combat regwear.

Commander Frabin – See 'Frabin'.

Commander Miren – See 'Miren'.

Commander Paran – See 'Paran'.

Communication channel – Information exchange streams between specific groups or individuals, facilitated by technological media.

Competitions – The collective name for many of the activities aboard the Roranian Great Ship that could be undertaken.

Conceal drone prototype ('Conceal') – New model of triamond-armoured Administration drone capable of visual camouflage, currently in testing phase.

Concealment field – Projection capable of being

generated by some Silvereds that renders the objects of focus externally hidden from a large swathe of the electromagnetic spectrum.

Cosobrit – Vaesian city.

Council of the Vaesian Union ('Council') – The leading group of Vaesians directing the Vaesian Union.

Craft-lect – Type of Wanderer machine-lect that is typically tasked with detecting and destroying incidences of Sensespace infection within the galaxy. Tapache is a craft-lect.

Cruishan – Roranian Member mainly involved with maintaining the military blockade around Sunsprit.

Crykel – Roranian vehicle, single-passenger.

Diyan – Roranian from the Roranian Great Ship who currently operates under the remnants of the leadership of the Vaesian Union. He entered the Source within the casket-ship with Yena and Paran. His c-autom was named Wiln.

Docking ring – Segmented, ringed structure used to dock Vaesian ships within Ringscape. They now sit as relics around and within Vaesian cities.

Dorera – One of seven soldiers chosen by Paran to join him in journeying to Barrenscape, under the mission brief of baiting and trapping the Breaker.

Drone – Automated instruments that are typically not sentient.

Dummy node – Information storage device related to the influx network. It was created by the Administration and then stolen by Kera to store the secrets of the Tugs.

Echoes of Gravity – Mysterious presence in Sunsprit that Vaesians sometimes use to help percolate their thoughts.

Edge (or Side) of Ringscape – The wedge of surface that separates Ringscape's upperside and underside. A region of anomalous gravitational behaviour.

Electro-boost platform – The vertical movement of this surface can be manipulated in order to take those standing upon it to different heights.

Electro-clamps – Clamps that can be used to secure metallic objects to other surfaces. They are useful in ships that have poor inertial dampeners and/or inadequate gravitation emulation technologies.

Emox – Component of a secret Administration network.

Entrance mechanism – Roranian technology for covering entrances and exits.

Entry events – Low probability instances during which the Haze Rings allow penetration into the Source from external space. Typically, only mangled debris makes it through, if anything. Entry events that allow life to penetrate the Source are exceedingly rare.

Facepieces – Regwear material loosely attached to the neck of clothing, that can be pulled over Roranian faces to facilitate breathing where necessary.

Fadin – Largest and most influential Roranian city on Ringscape, under the rule of the Administration. It is a dual city in that it is the combined settlement of twin cities Upper-Fadin and Under-Fadin, appearing on the upperside and the underside.

Fendari – Species with one settlement on Ringscape.

Flairfold – Name supposedly given to sleeping furniture by ancient Roranians.

Flips – Gravitational fluctuations that occur with greater frequency and intensity the closer one is to an edge of Ringscape. On the edge itself, flips are continuous. They are strongest at the midpoint between the upperside and the underside. The gravitational fluctuations can be used to generate power using gradient transducers.

Frabin – Roranian who has reached the highest possible rank that can be attained by a soldier within the Administration's military.

Gevinr – Parent of Hespinr.

Glazer – Vaesian transport vehicles, similar to skimmers.

Glintlock – Weapon used by soldiers of the

Administration.

Gradient transducer – Device that can be used to generate power from gravitation fluctuations ('flips') near and along the edges of Ringscape.

Gravitometer – Simple Vaesian devices used for gravity observations and measurements within the Tug Field.

Graviton – Elementary particle of the gravitational force.

Graviton drive – Type of propulsion technology.

Gravity emulators – Devices that produce artificial gravity fields.

Great Ship – Usually used to refer to the Roranian Great Ship, an enormous vessel given to the Roranians by Tapache in order to carry out the quest set for them. Although Tapache is a Wanderer and designed the vessel itself, it predominantly used Roranian-derived technologies where possible. The Roranians aboard the ship were looked after and taught by c-autom helpers.

Guran – Commander of a Roranian sky-factory, affixed by tethers above Upper-Fadin.

Halfad – Roranian city.

Haze Rings – One of the three known parts of the Source (the other two being Ringscape and Barrenscape). The Haze Rings are rotating structures around Ringscape and Barrenscape that create an almost impenetrable barrier, even capable of destroying bloom propulsion units. They keep everything within the Source inside, and everything outside the Source mostly outside. Sometimes, external penetration into the Source is allowed, and these events are called entry events. The Haze Rings go through periods where entry events are more common. During entry events, aberrations in the detected wavelengths emitted by the Haze Rings have indicated that they are comprised of many single hyperfine loops, rotating extremely fast. The Haze Rings also create the periodic light (often referred to as 'daylight') that immerses Barrenscape and Ringscape, as well as the pernicious haze winds that can make daytime travel between Barrenscape and Ringscape impossible. It is thought that the Haze Rings are responsible for the Source's 'thick atmosphere', whereby signals, including visible light, scatter much more quickly than the typical laws of physics allow. It is for this same reason that long-range information transfer is extremely inefficient and energy-intensive.

Haze winds – Dangerous winds that are generated by the Haze Rings during their light-emission 'daytime' phase. The haze winds limit travel between Ringscape and Barrenscape.

Hespinr – Silvered Vaesian residing in Sunsprit.

Holo – Umbrella term for different types of holographic technologies used by many species and civilisations, including the Roranians. Often used as a prefix to specify a certain type of holographic technology. Can sometimes be interacted with and are responsive to physical motions.

Holo distorters – Security technology created by the Administration to obscure visual details of a sensitive area.

Horesheim Conclusion – The events through which the Vaesian city of Horesheim was destroyed.

Ifrend – Roranian Member.

Ilouden – Roranian born on Ringscape and willingly governed by the Vaesian Union.

Influx – Processing unit of the Administration's information network.

Influx network – System created by the Administration that is capable of non-intelligent machine-based computation. Its ability to function within the Source is a closely guarded secret.

Influx node – Physical structure through which the influx network is accessed.

Influxa prototype ('Influxa') – New model of Administration drone with inbuilt influx-capabilities and a heavy-graviton drive, currently in testing phase.

Information Loss Conundrum – Problem pondered by many of those within the Source concerning the thick atmosphere.

Inoperability commands – Last-resort measures that render Administration machinery obsolete.

Invira – Roranian scientist whose work helped establish the influx network.

Irido – Member of Kera's salvaging crew who found Diyan, Paran and Yena in their casket-ship. Killed by the Administration.

Jabayan – One of seven soldiers chosen by Paran to join him in journeying to Barrenscape, under the mission brief of baiting and trapping the Breaker.

Jenrone – Small Roranian outpost.

Jirsol – Roranian Member.

Jornome – Roranian settlement.

Kera – Roranian from the Great Ship who was captured and made to fight for the Nesch in the wars between the lattice of ships surrounding the Source. Upon entering the source through an entry event, Kera infiltrated the Administration and stole technology that enabled her to access the information of the Tugs. She was captured by the Administration.

Kilthis – Balls of energy that can be created by some Silvereds from the tips of their tensirs, predominantly used as weapons. They are not well understood.

Kouthrehim – Roranian city.

Learning centre – Building in Fadin used for the community teaching of Roranian children.

Lect – Encompassing term for the intellect of a machine or biological entity. Usually used as an affix to machine intelligence.

Lellara – Roranian who lives within Sunsprit and is willingly governed by the Vaesian Union. She is primarily engaged with studies involving the Tugs.

Lermina – Roranian Member.

Lomintern – Roranian city.

Loten – C-autom from the Great Ship and companion of Paran.

Lotolen – One of seven soldiers chosen by Paran to join him in journeying to Barrenscape, under the mission brief of baiting and trapping the Breaker.

Lotwith – Battle between the Administration and the Vaesians.

Machine-lect – Machine-based intelligence.

Magnetic paths of Sunsprit ('magnetic paths') – Paths that lead to and join up at Sunsprit, forming a great surface that runs under much of the city.

Member of the Administration ('Member') – Elected representatives who govern Roranian society within the

Source.

Member Cruishan – See 'Cruishan'.

Member Ifrend – See 'Ifrend'.

Member Lermina – See 'Lermina'.

Member Olana – See 'Olana'.

Member Slautina – See 'Slautina'.

Member Vodal – See 'Vodal'.

Mericadal – Leader of the Administration.

Miren – Roranian who has reached the highest possible rank that can be attained by a soldier within the Administration's military.

Mnosr – Member of the council that directs the Vaesian Union.

Modal Change Hypothesis – Vaesian theory that the Source is entering a second phase of existence, as evidenced by the shortening of its daytime. Equivalent to the Roranian 'Second State Hypothesis'.

Morbayen – One of seven soldiers chosen by Paran to join him in journeying to Barrenscape, under the mission brief of baiting and trapping the Breaker.

Morial – A secondary-level observer working at an Administration facility harbouring criminals.

Muvaeyt – Substance chewed by Vaesians, releasing a blue mist, that aids with concentration.

Nalict – One of seven soldiers chosen by Paran to join him in journeying to Barrenscape, under the mission brief of baiting and trapping the Breaker.

Nesch – Dangerous and combative species, known to be actively attempting to gain control over all the ships in the lattice outside the Source.

Oberend – A primary-level observer working at an Administration facility harbouring criminals.

Olana – Roranian Member mainly involved with bloom fragment propulsion projects.

Osr – Silvered Vaesian residing within Sunsprit; member of the council that directs the Vaesian Union.

Otherness – C-autom from the Great Ship and companion of Kera.

Paran – Roranian who has reached the highest possible rank that can be attained by a soldier within the Administration's military. Aboard the Roranian Great Ship, Paran had been in a relationship with Kera. He subsequently entered the Source within the casket-ship with Diyan and Yena. His c-autom was named Loten.

Pilot-cabin – Front compartment of Roranian ship containing the controls.

Podenwinth Battles – Clusters of battles that took place early on during the Administration's war with the Vaesians.

Potensein – Vaesian city on Ringscape.

Power Dissipation Enigma – Ubiquitous problem with power dissipation within the Source.

Prietman – Cloaked creatures seen in both Fadin and Sunsprit. They are rare, and not thought to be of high intelligence. Conversation with them is extremely difficult for Roranians and Vaesians.

Probability wave of death ('probability wave') – Theorised but undetected wave, thought to be emitted by the Source, that somehow dissipates machine-lect consciousness. The closer a machine-lect is to the Source, the higher the chance of this happening. No machine-lects can exist within the Source due to this phenomenon.

Pulse-sphere – Defensive tool used to emit gravitational pulses that may temporarily confuse the Breaker.

Recruitment centre – Administration buildings where eligible Roranians in Fadin can apply for certain types of work.

Regwear – Roranian clothing from the Great Ship that has smart capabilities like air filtration and thermoregulation. Most current regwear has been continuously recycled into a material far inferior to original regwear.

Rememox – C-autom from the Great Ship and companion of Yena.

Retervope – Ground matter of Ringscape.

Ringscape – One of the three known parts of the Source (the other two being the Haze Rings and Barrenscape). It is where the majority of sentient life that has entered through the Haze Rings is thought to reside. It is ring-shaped and flat-surfaced, with both sides (upperside and underside) habitable.

Roranians – Humanoid species whose remnants were found by the Wanderer Tapache. From the materials and information found in the remnants, Tapache was able to resurrect the species by creating a new 'batch' of Roranians, whom it placed aboard a Great Ship it designed for them. In return for completing Tapache's quest, they were informed that Tapache will aid them in discovering what became of their civilisation, and whether anything remains.

Second State Hypothesis – Roranian theory that the Source is entering a second phase of existence, as evidenced by the shortening of its daytime. Equivalent to the Vaesian 'Modal Change Hypothesis'.

Selo – C-autom from the Great Ship and initial companion of Yena.

Sensespace – Enemy of the Wanderers. It is an infective and hostile presence that appears to be drawn to sentience. Most Wanderer craft-lects are tasked with traversing the galaxy to seek and destroy it.

Sentient – Living entity possessing an intellect.

Shimmerblade – Weapon used by soldiers of the Administration.

Side (or 'Edge') of Ringscape – The wedge of surface that separates Ringscape's upperside and underside. These are regions of anomalous gravitational behaviour.

Silvered Vaesian ('Silvered') – Vaesians whose cell-scales have overactivated and proliferated to the extent that their bodies have taken on a silver colour. Their lifespans are severely impacted as a result. The condition is difficult to pass on.

Skimmer – Transport vehicles. Aboard the Roranian Great Ship, they were capable of aerial travel, however, this ability has not yet been unlocked on Ringscape.

Skimmer trail – Designated pathways for skimmers that extend out from larger Roranian settlements to sparsely populated areas. The pathways have minimal connections to the influx network, and are a short-term project by the Administration to gauge practicality.

Sky-factory – Ship-like manufacturing plants located high in the sky above Ringscape's surface, to which they are attached by great tethers. The heat and noise they emit make them unsuitable for Ringscape's surface. They are guarded by the Administration's drones.

Sky-factory tethers – Strong linear attachments that connect the sky-factories to Ringscape.

Slautina – Roranian Member.

Soji – Member of Kera's salvaging crew who found Diyan, Paran and Yena in their casket-ship. Killed by the Administration.

Solitude gliding – Leisure activity within Ringscape. Those wearing wing-packs are flung high up into the air, whereupon the wing-packs unfurl, and gliding can commence.

Source – Name for everything contained within and including the Haze Rings. It is also the origin of the probability wave of death for machine-lects. Its builders are unknown.

Standard time – Roranian time measurement system.

Streamthin – Roranian vehicle.

Sub-cutter – Administration vehicle used for digging beneath and navigating under the surface of Ringscape and Barrenscape, as much as is possible before the power required makes the process impractical.

Sunsprit ('City of the Silvereds') – The only Vaesian city free from the rule and influence of the Administration, occupied predominantly by Silvered Vaesians. It exists on both sides of Ringscape, although its two parts are far more tightly physically joined than Fadin's two parts.

Tapache – Powerful Wanderer craft-lect (a type of machine-lect intelligence).

Tensirs – Small fronds that extend from the end of Vaesian arms. They are highly adhesive and more numerous than Roranian fingers.

Tetibat – Vaesian principle, concerning acting to increase one's stability in life, in all measures, literal and metaphorical.

Thermal cannon – Administration weapon.

Thermal ejection rifle – Administration weapon.

Thick atmosphere – Quirk of the atmosphere inside the Source, whereby signals, including visible light, scatter much more quickly than the typical laws of physics allow. It is for this same reason that long-range information transfer is extremely inefficient and energy-intensive. It is thought that the Haze Rings are responsible.

Topinr – Silvered Vaesian pilot.

Torina – Administration facility worker.

Triad Group – Three elite Administration soldiers allowed special resources not supplied to the rest of the military.

Triamond – Wanderer material used by Tapache as part of the Roranian casket casing. It is the hardest, strongest and most durable material known in the Source.

Tug Field – The expanse deep within Sunsprit where the Tugs are found.

Tug Mask – Vaesian headgear that allows visual observation of the Tugs' gravity strings. Conscious observation is required to activate the mask's fuel.

Tugs – Assumed sentient beings that exist, hidden, deep within Sunsprit, along an edge of Ringscape. They are comprised of spiked structures that rise vertically up from the ground, and gravity strings that emanate from the tips of the spiked structures.

Tuiran – Roranian Member.

Ualbrict – Destroyed Vaesian city.

Ulantr – Child of Osr.

Under-Fadin – The part of the city of Fadin that exists on the underside of Ringscape.

Underside of Ringscape ('underside') – One of the two sides of Ringscape.

Under-Sunsprit – The part of the city of Sunsprit that exists on the underside of Ringscape.

Unriel – One of seven soldiers chosen by Paran to join him in journeying to Barrenscape, under the mission brief of baiting and trapping the Breaker.

Upper-Fadin – The part of the city of Fadin that exists on the upperside of Ringscape.

Upperside of Ringscape ('upperside') – One of the two sides of Ringscape.

Upper-Sunsprit – The part of the city of Sunsprit that exists on the upperside of Ringscape.

Uthrit – Vaesian city on Ringscape.

Vaesian Cycle – Developmental process driving Vaesian biology, whereby significant physiological changes cycle into and out of prominence over extended periods of time.

Vaesian Union ('Union') – The aggregate Vaesian collective governing the Vaesian settlements and their people. Since the war, it is the same as the once-smaller, secretive council that sat atop the Vaesian Union and directed it.

Vaesians – Sentient species that inhabit Ringscape alongside the Roranians. The Vaesians consider the Roranians to be new to Ringscape since their own history of occupation is far more extensive. Upon entering the Source, the Roranians displaced the Vaesians as the main authority, and then waged war upon them. Currently,

Sunsprit is the only truly free Vaesian city not controlled by the Administration.

Varenheim Massacre – The sacking and destruction of the Vaesian city of Varenheim, as well as all its inhabitants, by the Roranians.

Veilers – Secretive members of the 'Behind the Veil' Vaesian group, joined in the belief that there was something in Ringscape that was obscured to its inhabitants. They were destroyed during the war with the Roranians.

Vodal – Roranian Member and chief advisor to Mericadal.

Wanderer fleet – All of the fleets of different Wanderer ships within the galaxy, often used to refer to the craft-lect fleet, which is the largest.

Wanderers – Civilisation predominantly comprised of machine-lect intelligences, and the principal force in the galaxy attempting to destroy the Sensespace. Tapache is a member of the Wanderer civilisation.

Wideberth – Roranian vehicle.

Wiln – C-autom from the Great Ship and companion of Diyan.

Wing-pack – Pack worn about the back that can be unfurled to reveal a large set of wings, used for gliding.

Wolliren – Roranian acquaintance to Ilouden during his

undercover work in Roranian cities.

Yena – Roranian whose current whereabouts are not precisely known. She entered the Source within the casket-ship with Diyan and Paran. Her initial c-autom, Selo, had its sentience ostensibly destroyed by the probability wave of death. Her second c-autom was named Rememox.